THRONE OF WHEYLIA

THRICE BORN

By *Summer Hanford*

Martin Sisters Publishing

THRONE OF WHEYLIA
Martin Sisters Publishing Company

Publishing History
First edition published in 2014
Second edition published in 2016

Published by
Martin Sisters Publishing Company
Kentucky, USA

Martin Sisters Publishing Company
ISBN: 978-1-62553-089-9

Science Fiction/Fantasy/Young Adult
Printed in the United States of America

Visit our website at www. martinsisterspublishing.com

DEDICATION

To my husband, Jeff Girard. Thank you for being the most wonderful man in the world and for helping me follow my dreams.

THRICE BORN SERIES
MARTIN SISTERS PUBLISHING COMPANY

Gift of the Aluien
Hawks of Sorga
Throne of Wheylia
The Plains of Tybrunn
Shores of K'Orge (2017)

COMPANION SHORT STORIES
BY SUMMER HANFORD

The Forging of Cadwel
Hawk Trials for Mirimel
The Fall of Larkesong
The Sword of Three

ACKNOWLEDGEMENT

My gratitude, as always, to Martin Sisters Publishing for their continued confidence and support, and to Simply Marcella, the Baltimore Woods Nature Center and Sycamore Hill Gardens for allowing me to participate in their events.

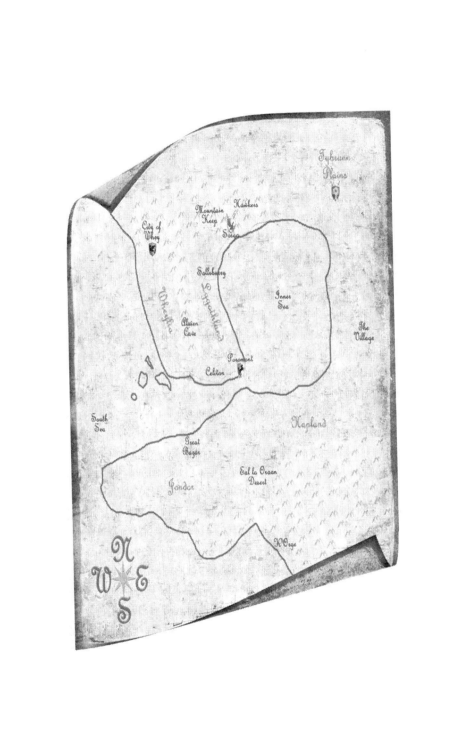

Chapter 1

Ari twisted to the side, avoiding the sword aimed at his face. In the stands surrounding them, the tourney crowd cheered at the near miss. Ari would have been disturbed by their glee at his brush with death, but he and Sir Cadwel had already been sparring for a quarter hour. The crowd had long since gotten over any fear of them hurting each other. They were both too good, too in control, to make that sort of mistake.

Or for either of them to win.

Ari's blade snaked out in a blow Sir Cadwel easily parried. The thrust wasn't meant to land, only to keep Sir Cadwel at bay while Ari regained his stance. There were no points for hitting someone in the face, but Ari knew Sir Cadwel's attack hadn't been in search of one of the three hits he needed to win. It was a ploy to throw Ari off balance.

The people filling the tourney stands were on their feet, their cheers nearly deafening. The knight's lips curled into a grin under his drooping gray mustache, making Ari nervous. So far, he'd countered every trick Sir Cadwel had thrown at him, but Ari knew there were more. Though his hair was silver and his face creased by age, Sir Cadwel was the greatest knight to ever live.

What Ari didn't know was who the people wanted to win the exhibition match he and his mentor fought. The undulating sea of blue and white Sorga flags surrounding them made it impossible to tell if they were rooting for Ari, Sir Cadwel, or both. Ari was sure the people liked him. When he'd won the fall tourney earlier that day, they were jubilant. Ari felt they wanted him to keep winning tourneys so that, when Sir Cadwel stepped down as king's champion someday, Ari could take his place. It would give the land continuity. The people would feel safe, knowing the lords of Sorga would always be there to protect them and their king.

Ari realized he was letting his mind wander and brought his focus back to the fight. If there was anyone in Lggothland who could beat him, it was Sir Cadwel, the man who'd trained him. The man who'd plucked Ari from obscurity and made him a lord and heir to the dukedom of Sorga. Of course, Sir Cadwel could beat anyone.

Then Ari saw it. A flaw. A slight overextension from Sir Cadwel. A mistake most wouldn't have noticed and even fewer would have the speed and skill to take advantage of. Ari lashed his blade under Sir Cadwel's slightly too elevated guard.

Even as his sword sped toward Sir Cadwel's breastplate, even as the noise of the crowd swelled, Ari realized his mistake. He longed to pull back, but he was already committed. Sir Cadwel pivoted as Ari struck, forcing him to lunge too far forward, too far out of balance, in order to land the hit.

Ari's mind cried out that it was a trick, but his training was too strong. Sir Cadwel had taught him to battle first and duel second. In a battle, Ari would have landed a killing blow, gutting his opponent. There on the tourney field, with dulled weapons and Ari reining in his magically enhanced strength, the blow amounted to only one thing, a point.

As Ari's blade landed, the dull clank signaling the first point of the bout, the crowd roared. Their joy at the hit sounded almost murderous to Ari, where he and Sir Cadwel sparred on the hard packed earth between the stands. The tourney master raised his arm, signaling a point. Ari tried to wrench his sword back, to regain his stance before Sir Cadwel could strike. Ari's entire right side was undefended.

In an incredibly fast series of attacks, before even Ari's Aluien-enhanced speed could help him recover from overreaching, Sir Cadwel struck. Three blows, raining down hard in an unfathomable blur. Three points.

There was a moment of stunned silence.

"Three hits for Sir Cadwel," the tourney master called, his voice higher than usual, colored by surprise. "Sir Cadwel is victorious."

The crowd erupted once more, waving flags, yelling, cheering and tossing flowers. A row of young women had worked themselves to the front of one of the stands and they leaned over the railing, waving handkerchiefs and calling. Ari realized he was staring and looked away, hoping no one had caught him gawking at how close they were to impropriety.

He lowered his sword, giving Sir Cadwel a rueful smile. Trust the old knight to be cunning enough to use Ari's own speed and training against him. Ari would have to think on the weakness Sir Cadwel had just exposed. Ari was so fast now, his fighting reflexes so well honed, he hadn't had enough time to think about what he was doing. If he'd been the slightest bit slower, he would have been able to keep himself from committing to the trap. From the gleam in Sir Cadwel's eyes and his wolfish grin, the knight guessed Ari's train of thought.

Ari stabbed the blunted practice sword into the ground before him. Castle pages ran up to relieve the two men of their gauntlets and weapons. Ari bowed to Sir Cadwel amid the crowd's raucous cheers. Sir Cadwel bowed back, still grinning, then turned to lead the way toward the royal box.

They crossed to stand in front of Ennentine, Sir Cadwel's oldest friend and the king of Lggothland. As they bowed to the king, Ari ran a hand along the three new dents in his breastplate. He shifted, wincing. He could already feel the bruises spreading along his side. Sir Cadwel hadn't held back much. The knight always maintained that the pain of failure helped Ari to learn faster.

King Ennentine rose from his gilded tourney throne, coming to the railing of the royal box to look down at them, a broad smile on his face. To his left stood Parrella, his queen. Ari always looked on her with a tinge of awe. Younger than Sir Cadwel and her husband by over a decade, the queen was a tall elegant woman with flowing golden hair, streaked with glimmering silver strands. In repose, her face was austere and beautiful enough to be imposing, but her face was almost never still. Usually, as now, it wore a smile, taking her from unfathomable to human with its warmth.

Beside the queen stood her son Parrentine, Crown Prince of Lggothland, and his bride, Princess Siara of Wheylia. The two held hands. Ari was glad for this evidence, along with all else he'd seen during this visit to the capital, that their relationship was finally one of cordiality, even caring. It seemed to Ari that Parrentine had at last given up mourning his lost

12

fiancée and surrendered to Siara's love for him. It was a love Ari knew would heal Parrentine's heart as well as seal the peaceful relationship between Lggothland and their Wheylian neighbors. The royal family inclined their heads in response to Ari's and Sir Cadwel's bows.

King Ennentine raised a hand, stilling the crowd. "It brings great joy to me and to all the land to see our champion, Sir Cadwel, Lord of Sorga and Protector of the Northlands, is still the paramount knight in the realm."

The crowd cheered again, but quickly silenced to see what more their king would say.

"It gives us equal pleasure to know his chosen heir and protégé, Lord Aridian of Sorga, is nearly as skilled. I doubt not that soon Lord Aridian's skill will come to equal that of our champion. Then, we shall not be able to have such entertainment any longer, for surely a bout between the two would last many hours into the night."

The crowd seemed to find the prospect amusing, or at least to feel they owed it to their king to appear to. Ari didn't as much, because he knew it was probably true. Back in Sorga, he and Sir Cadwel generally put a limit on how long they would spar, to avoid that situation. Ari should have known, though, that the old knight was holding back a few tricks for an occasion such as this, when half the kingdom was watching.

Ari wished Lady Ispiria had been there to see them fight. Now that the fall tourney was over, he and Sir Cadwel would be returning to Sorga. Ari had determined, before they left, that should he come home the tourney winner, he would ask Ispiria to marry him. He suppressed a shudder at the thought, unsure if it was one of anticipation or fear.

He came back to reality as Sir Cadwel bowed. Hastily, Ari followed suit. He hoped no one noticed he hadn't paid attention to the rest of King Ennentine's speech. Ari and Sir Cadwel left the tourney field to the sound of cheering, retreating to their pavilion to remove their armor.

Divested of his metal shell, Ari made his way into the castle, aware that he definitely needed a bath before the evening's feast. Ushering away a helpful servant once the tub was full, Ari closed the door of the bathing room. He removed his worn doublet, carefully transferring the small white stone he kept in a hidden pocket to his finer clothes. As he tucked it away, he wondered again if it was really necessary to keep it on his person. Aside from that spring, when the keep of Sorga and the nearby village of the Hawkers were attacked, no one had tried to take the stone. It didn't even do anything, being part of a lost set. Still, he'd promised he would guard it. Shrugging at the incomprehensibility of some vows, Ari continued his ablutions.

Once he was presentable, he took himself to the small walled garden off of the royal wing. He didn't have anything else to do before dinner, or anyone to talk with. Sir Cadwel was meeting with the king, and Ari's best friend and valet, Peine, had stayed behind in Sorga. Natan, chief steward of Sorga, had suffered a brush with mortality that spring. Since then, he was taking extra pains to train Peine to take his place. Sir Cadwel hadn't wanted to interrupt that training for the short trip south.

Ari was fond of the small garden. It was lovely in the fall, the only time of year other than winter he'd seen it. Small ornamental trees blazed red and orange, reminding him of Ispiria's hair. The air smelled of earth and pinesap, which helped him forget that he was in a large city crowded with people. Standing in the center of the garden where four paths converged at a pleasantly gurgling fountain, Ari raised his face, closing his eyes. The autumn sun turned the insides of his lids orange and warmed his skin.

"Whatever are you doing?" Princess Siara's slightly acerbic tone cut into Ari's daydreaming.

He turned to her, blinking sunspots out of his eyes to take in her pale perfection. In the bright afternoon light, her white skin seemed even more radiant than usual, emphasized by her glossy black hair. As she almost always did, she wore a dark blue gown, both in homage to the colors of the royal crest of Lggothland and to underscore her striking blue eyes. Ari wondered fleetingly if she would still wear blue were the king's crest devoid of it.

"My lady," Ari said, bowing. In spite of the fact that Siara almost always seemed a bit cross, Ari liked her. After their travels together the year before, she was one of his closest friends.

"It's your highness," she corrected, but she looked preoccupied and Ari could tell her heart wasn't in the reprimand. "It seems you'll win every tourney from now on, so long as Sir Cadwel doesn't enter."

"I'd be boastful if I agree." He grinned, admitting to himself that it did indeed seem likely. The competition that met him that fall hadn't caused him much concern.

She looked back at the two ladies in waiting who trailed her down the path, gesturing them away, although they were already keeping such a discreet distance that Ari hadn't even noticed them until that movement. They curtsied, retreating until they could hardly be seen among the shrubs and trees.

"It seems, then, you'll be king's champion come spring." Siara's voice was low.

Ari raised his eyebrows in surprise. "Why do you say that?" he asked, his heartbeat accelerating at the idea. His feelings about the position of king's champion were confusing. Along with the rest of the kingdom, he didn't want Sir Cadwel to step down. On the other hand, becoming king's champion was the sum of Ari's hopes and dreams and none could vie to fill the position until Sir Cadwel relinquished it or the king took the title from him.

"Parrentine told me," she said.

Siara had a habit of standing quite close to him when she spoke confidences. Ari supposed it was so he could hear her, but he always found it a little disconcerting, the way she looked up at him through her dark lashes, leaning toward him when she talked.

"He said Sir Cadwel told the king he's only waiting until your seventeenth year, when you're old enough to become a knight and take his place," she continued.

"I didn't realize Sir Cadwel was so eager to step down." Ari was torn between being hurt that Siara knew more about Sir Cadwel's plans than he did and pride in how certain everyone seemed that he would prove to be the best warrior and win the position of champion to the king.

"I think, perhaps, the rumors from Wheylia are what spur him." She leaned even closer. "It could be he doesn't relish the idea of undertaking such tasks as may soon lie before the champion of the king."

"What tasks? What rumors?" Ari wished Peine was with him. Peine always found out all of the gossip and passed anything important on.

"Oh, Ari." She shook her head, frowning up at him. "Don't you pay attention to anything but wielding a sword?"

He racked his brain for an intelligent answer.

"Never mind," Siara said. "I've come to tell you of them myself, to set straight truth and lies. It's easier this way, as I'll have nothing to confute."

Ari hated it when she used words he didn't know, but he wasn't going to give her the satisfaction of asking her what confute meant.

"It's true my grandfather is dead, and my aunt," she said.

Ari stared at her. "Dead?" he repeated before he recalled Sir Cadwel received a message to that effect several months ago.

"Yes, and under suspicious circumstances, but that's not to be generally known."

"I'm sorry, Siara."

She shrugged. "I've never met either of them, although I had taken up corresponding with my late aunt."

She looked away, the sorrow on her face denying her harsh words. Siara was always like that. She acted like she was angry all the time and didn't care about things, but really she did. He thought it was because her family had stuck her in a convent when she was little, to be raised by strangers, and she'd never really had anyone to love her.

"Is there anything I can do to help?" he asked.

"Not yet." She looked back up at him. "Why the matter concerns you, Ari, is because now only my two older cousins are left as heirs to the throne of Wheylia." She paused, her face almost fearful.

Ari tried to keep his confusion from showing. He knew Siara was next in line for the throne after her two cousins, but Siara could never be High Priestess of Wheylia. She had to stay in Lggothland and be Parrentine's queen. Even if she wanted to, she couldn't change that. Their worldly vows aside, Siara was bound to Prince Parrentine by ancient and powerful magic.

17

"My grandmother is very hale and my older cousin is to marry soon," she continued. "In all likelihood, she'll have a strong daughter by next winter, summer at the latest, and I'll no longer have to worry about the Wheylian throne."

"But you are worried." He softened his tone. Even if he didn't understand why she was upset, he didn't like to see her like this. "Why? They can't ask you to take your grandmother's throne. You can't leave Parrentine, and he's the only heir to the Lggothian throne. He can't abdicate."

"It isn't me I'm worried for." She bit her lower lip. "You're right, I can't ever take my grandmother's throne, even had I any desire to. A daughter of mine could, though. If both of my older cousins die without any heirs, my first born daughter would be the next in line for the throne in Wheylia." She wrapped her arms around her abdomen, hugging herself.

"And you're worried because if someone killed your aunt and grandfather, they may try to kill your cousins and then your daughter? Maybe you'll never even have a daughter." He winced. That hadn't come out the way he meant it.

"It's not only that." She glanced over her shoulder at her ladies, who peered through the fall leaves at them. "My grandmother's already made it clear to me," she whispered. "The heir to the throne will be raised in Wheylia. The Wheylian people will not have a princess of Lggothland, ignorant of their culture, sent to govern them. They would view it as tantamount to annexation. If it comes down to a daughter I bear being the next High Priestess of Wheylia, she will go to Wheylia when she is born and she will stay there, among them."

"You mean, they'll take your baby?" Ari asked, stunned. "Can they do that? Is that what you want me to stop if I'm king's champion?"

18

"No." Her lips trembled and he realized she was trying not to cry. "It's not something that can be stopped. There would be war. The Wheys would come to take her. No, I'll have to give her up." She looked down at the ground, drawing in a deep breath before raising her gaze to his. "I'm warning you it might happen because if it does, the king's champion will need to take her. If you become king's champion, you'll have to come get my baby and take her away from me."

Siara burst into tears. Ari put his arms around her before he could think better of it. Her ladies hurried forward. He shook his head and they stopped, looking uncertain. He supposed it was inappropriate of him to hold her. She was the future queen of Lggothland and Parrentine's wife, but she was crying. He didn't care what gossip comforting her started.

"Don't cry." Ari stroked her hair. He'd never seen her this upset before. She was even more upset than the time she'd admitted to him that she was afraid she was a witch, or when they'd found Parrentine nearly dead in the mountains. Usually, Siara staved off fear and sorrow with the fire of her temper, but this time, she was crying. Standing there, his arms around her, he was reminded of how petite she was, almost fragile in her sorrow.

"Don't worry," he said. "It won't happen. I'm sure your aunt's and grandfather's deaths were accidents. Your cousins will be well. They'll marry and have babies and there will be plenty of princesses of Wheylia to sit on the throne. No one will take your daughter away."

She leaned back, wiping her eyes.

He let his arms fall.

"Their deaths weren't accidents, Ari." She glared up at him. "I know you've never really believed me about it, but I am a Princess of Whey and I do have powers. I know they were murdered, and I know what is coming. As sure as you are standing here now, come spring, you'll take my baby away." With an almost feral snarl, she whirled away in a swirl of blue fabric.

Watching her storm down the path, Ari didn't know if he should be upset, annoyed or amused. Somehow, Siara always found a way to end up angry with him. He shrugged. She was right, he didn't really believe in her powers of premonition. Although, now that he thought about it, he was hard pressed to recall an occasion when she'd been wrong.

He shrugged again, easing the tension in his shoulders. It was almost time for the feast. He shouldn't have come wandering in the garden. Now he'd have to spend an evening sitting across from Siara while she was cross with him.

He turned, strolling down the path opposite the one she'd taken. It wasn't until he was back inside the castle's torch-lit corridors, almost to the great hall, that a new thought struck him. If Siara was so sure she'd have a baby by spring, didn't that mean she was already with child?

Chapter 2

The rest of the evening settled into a familiar blur for Ari. He'd won the fall tourney the year before and he was comfortably familiar with the social obligations accompanying victory. There was a long dinner with foods he found a trifle too exotic, women in whom he had no interest tried to gain his attention and King Ennentine and Prince Parrentine made speeches. Also as usual, Queen Parrella was radiant and lovely. Her nieces and nephew, who were visiting for the tournament, offered a welcome addition to the head of the table, but Ari still had to sit across from Siara.

Siara wasn't as angry as he expected, though. She contented herself with a single glare when she arrived, clearly indicating he wasn't to speak of their earlier conversation. He shot a look back that he hoped said he wasn't that much of an idiot, and concentrated on his food while she ignored him.

Ari looked down at a plate of suspiciously tentacle-like seafood. It wasn't that he hated being in the capital and being at royal feasts. It was rather that he liked it better at home in Sorga, where he knew everyone and Ispiria sat by his side.

He suppressed a sigh. He pushed the fish tentacles around on his plate, doing his best not to appear to be moping. It was exciting to be in the tourney. He loved testing himself against the knights of the kingdom, a fraternity he hoped to become a member of the following spring. It was just that the world never seemed right when Ispiria wasn't there.

He missed her red curls. He missed her open honest demeanor. Her smile. The way she laughed at the things he said like they were really funny. The way she looked at him.

"Ari." Sir Cadwel's voice broke into his thoughts. "Her majesty asked you a question."

Ari turned to the queen where she sat at the head of the table, beside her husband. She had a kind expression on her face.

"Your pardon, your majesty. I didn't mean not to hear you."

"I believe, Lord Aridian, you've already managed to answer my question," Queen Parrella said.

Beside her, Prince Parrentine chuckled. "I think you've guessed it, Mother. Such distraction could only be caused by love. Lord Aridian must have found an object of adoration in Sorga."

"The lad is quite smitten with my grand-niece," Sir Cadwel said.

"Her name is Ispiria," Ari told the queen.

"Have you come to an understanding with her yet?" Queen Parrella's warm smile held no mocking.

"She turned sixteen this fall, your majesty, while we were away. I haven't had the chance to ask her to marry me yet."

22

Ari could feel his face heat as he said it. He felt like those last few words came out unnaturally loud. Ask her to marry me. They almost echoed in the suddenly hushed dining hall, sounding slightly insane to him.

He loved Ispiria. He wanted to marry her and spend the rest of his life with her and make her lady of Sorga. Somehow, though, the idea of walking up to her and saying that, and then of having a wedding ceremony, seemed oddly terrifying.

Siara rolled her eyes, glancing at Parrentine. The prince seemed disinclined to mock Ari's discomfort, but his sympathetic look was nearly as bad.

"But surely this is the very same young lady you took an interest in when you first arrived in Sorga last year?" Queen Parrella glanced at her husband.

Ari nodded. He had the vague recollection of declaring his love for Ispiria to the king the previous winter.

"By now, your Lady Ispiria must be fully aware of how you feel about her and return your sentiment?" The queen's tone made the words a question.

"Yes."

Queen Parrella looked at him expectantly.

Ari had no idea what more she wanted him to say. "Your majesty," he added, in case her honorific was what she was waiting for.

"True, they've already proven their attachment has a certain steadfastness, but we haven't yet had the honor of meeting her." Siara leveled thoughtful eyes on Ari. "Is this Lady Ispiria worthy of the next Lord of Sorga and Protector of the Northlands?"

Though her tone was casual, Ari had spent enough time with Siara to realize she was quite serious about the question. He bristled, frowning.

"My grandniece, on my late wife's side, is a beautiful, spirited girl," Sir Cadwel said. "There is no finer maiden in Sorga. She and Ari are quite fond of each other."

Siara nodded, indicating her acceptance of the knight's words, but Ari could see the slight dent of thoughtfulness marring her brow. He knew that look. Siara wouldn't be happy until she learned all there was to know about Ispiria.

Ari didn't care. Nothing anyone could say or do would change the fact that he loved Ispiria and she loved him. It didn't matter what anyone thought, except Sir Cadwel, and Sir Cadwel was happy for them. Ari didn't even care that Ispiria's guardian, her great grandmother, hated him. He would overcome that. Besides, he was hoping his recent win, taking the fall tourney title for the second year in a row, would prove to Ispiria's great grandmother that he was worthy.

"I'm sure, knowing young Aridian's resolute nature and in view of your approval, Cadwel, theirs will be a happy union," King Ennentine said.

To Ari's relief that closed the topic. The conversation moved to Ari's and Sir Cadwel's travel plans. As always, the knight intended to leave the next morning, as the tourney was over. In spite of the fact that Ennentine was Sir Cadwel's oldest friend, Ari's mentor preferred to dwell in their northern home, keeping himself apart from the pomp and society of the capital. It was an inclination Ari had no desire to dispute.

The next morning, after a showy sendoff on the castle steps, Ari and Sir Cadwel rode triumphantly through the streets of Poromont, heading from the city. Ari found he didn't feel as insignificant as the first time he rode in with Sir Cadwel, over a year ago, nor as uncertain as when they'd left on their quest to save Prince Parrentine after Ari won his first fall tourney. This time, with another tourney win to prove him and nothing dire threatening the kingdom, he could allow himself to enjoy the accolade of the people. Not too much, of course, because knights weren't prideful.

The only thing hampering his joy was that he was still a page, not a real knight. In his finery, he could have been mistaken for a knight, if the loose reins of the packhorse didn't trail from his saddle. He had nothing against the packhorse. Rather, he was fond of the faithful old beast, but having to lead it was a constant reminder that he was still Sir Cadwel's page, not his comrade. That rather spoiled the image of grandeur Ari was creating for himself in his head.

It wasn't that Ari cared much how he looked. Being Sir Cadwel's page was a great honor and not something he wished to hide. He had a vision of himself riding into Sorga, though. The whole of the castle would be assembled on the steps, including Ispiria and her great grandmother. Everyone would applaud in welcome as he returned triumphant. Ispiria would run down the steps and into his arms, kissing him right in front of everyone, propriety thrown aside. Her great grandmother, seeing him so exultant and them so in love, would smile in benediction.

The old packhorse just didn't fit well into that image. Maybe when they got back, they could leave him outside the gate for a little while. Not long, of course, for he'd be eager to return home.

Ari kept his head high, smiling at the people as he and Sir Cadwel rode between whitewashed buildings, red tiled roofs bright in the morning sun. Throngs lined the streets to cheer them. Along with Ari's rise from the obscurity of being an orphan adopted by an innkeeper, the people's love for him had grown. Now, Ari had twice proven himself by winning the king's tourney. He was Sir Cadwel's protégé and heir to the

Dukedom of Sorga and the Protectorate of the Northlands. Ari was one of their own risen to greatness, a source of pride.

Looking down from his saddle, he saw young boys chasing after them, waving wooden swords. It dawned on him that some of those boys would grow up playing at being him, the way he used to play at being Sir Cadwel.

Ari was glad his horse, Stew, was secretly of an intelligent and magical race, because that thought so disconcerted him that he forgot to pay any attention to where he was going. The ride north out of Poromont became a blur of tossed flowers and well wishes. It wasn't until he and Sir Cadwel crested the lengthy hill leading up from the capital, Stew drawing alongside Sir Cadwel's mount, Goldwin, that Ari's thoughts worked their way back into any logical order.

Sir Cadwel halted, angling Goldwin so they could gaze down at the gleaming white buildings of Poromont. Stew turned too and Ari took in the sweeping green hill, cut through by the greatest road in the kingdom, the King's Way, tracing the path back. Ari looked over the red roofs of the city, the high white walls of the castle at the center. Beyond, the white docks of Poromont reached into the sparkling blue sea. Tall ships bobbed in the harbor, their many colored sails nearly as dazzling as the sun glinting off the rippling ocean.

Sir Cadwel's face was a mask, but Ari knew his mentor well enough to see the dark sorrow in his eyes. "Is all well, sir?"

"She's a tribute to peace, that city," the knight said, not looking at Ari. "Poromont prospering. The land and the people prospering. It's what we fought for, all those years ago."

"Yes, sir," Ari said, unsure at Sir Cadwel's mood.

"Then, I didn't dare hope it would last."

"It lasted because of you, sir."

Everyone knew Sir Cadwel was the king's law. In the twenty-odd years since the great war, any who dared disturb the peace faced swift and merciless retribution from Sir Cadwel. Ari knew it was merciless because he'd read accounts of it. Sometimes, he worried he wouldn't be able to maintain what Sir Cadwel and King Ennentine had built. There was a ruthlessness in Sir Cadwel, a harsh side to him, that Ari felt he could never mimic. In truth, he wasn't sure he wanted to.

Sir Cadwel gave the capital another long look before turning Goldwin away, his countenance strangely resolute. Stew followed without prompting. Ari frowned as they trailed Sir Cadwel and Goldwin into the forest, following the King's Way.

Why was Sir Cadwel's mood so dark? Was the knight falling back into his old depression, the enduring guilt of allowing his family's murder once again rising up to smother him? Ari could think of nothing new threatening knight or realm. There were Siara's premonitions about Ari taking her baby, but Ari didn't think Sir Cadwel knew about them and, regardless, the knight scoffed at that sort of thing. Was Sir Cadwel having second thoughts about Ari's ability to win the position of king's champion, or worse, his ability to perform the role?

Worry gnawed at Ari as they continued on toward the crossroads. North, up the King's Way, led home to Sorga, as did the eastern route, which only traveled east until it met the coastline and was forced to turn north. West lay Wheylia and the nunnery where Siara had been brought up. They'd traveled that road the previous fall, first to search for Prince Parrentine and later to seek out the magical race of Aluiens, hoping they could cure Parrentine's twice-doomed fiancée, Clorra.

When they reached it, Sir Cadwel halted before the dilapidated inn that stood at the crossroads. A young

27

stablehand looked up hopefully from the porch. Ari fidgeted, nervous at the scowl on Sir Cadwel's face and wondering why they'd stopped. He considered pointing out that the way home lay north, but experience told him that Sir Cadwel didn't take kindly to having the obvious stated.

The old knight slid from his saddle. "I won't be long," he said over his shoulder to Ari. He headed into the inn.

Shifting in his saddle, Ari looked about the clearing again. He toyed with the idea of following Sir Cadwel, but the knight reappeared. He handed a few coins to the stablehand on the porch. The young man clutched them tightly, gaping up at Sir Cadwel in awe.

"Take good care of him and there's another silver when we return," the knight said. He glanced at Ari. "We're leaving the packhorse here."

The stablehand scurried forward, looking up at Ari with still awestruck eyes while he waited for the reins. Ari untied them from the back of his saddle and handed them over. By the time he finished, Sir Cadwel was mounted. With a flick of the reins, the knight turned Goldwin left, to the west and Wheylia.

"West?" Ari asked, urging Stew to ride up alongside Goldwin.

"It's a comfort to know you've learned your compass points."

"We aren't going home, then? Why did we leave the packhorse? All our armor's on it."

He wondered if Sir Cadwel had thought to tell anyone they wouldn't be headed straight back. He certainly hadn't told Ari. Ispiria would be waiting for him. He could picture her on the wall each afternoon, straining for a glimpse of them, before turning away in disappointment. Not to mention, Chief

Steward Natan hated it when Sir Cadwel went gallivanting, as Natan put it, instead of returning to manage his dukedom.

"We're going to the Aluiens," Sir Cadwel said. "The packhorse would slow us down."

Surprise and worry filled Ari in equal measures, supplanting any concern he had for his armor. "Is something amiss? Is that why you were talking about peace? You know they won't want to help us."

The Aluiens, the magical race who had inadvertently endowed Ari with hidden powers, did not concern themselves with human affairs. Their leader, the Khan Dar, believed they must forever hide from the eyes of mankind or they would end up first as oracles, then as stewards, and finally, by his estimation, feared and hated enemies. Yet, the Aluiens could not truly sever their ties to the human race, for humans were how they perpetuated themselves. All but the Elders, the very oldest Aluiens, were once human.

Aluiens traveled the lands in disguise, seeking out those who were in some way exemplary and marking them. When a marked man died, the Aluien would return and, in that final moment, offer eternal life as an alternative to the darkness of death. Thus, the Aluiens augmented their ranks with only the best mankind had to offer. Sir Cadwel, Ari knew, was one of those humans found worthy enough. The knight was marked.

"We're not asking for help," Sir Cadwel said. "We're going because it's time."

Ari didn't ask time for what. He was terribly afraid he already knew. Sir Cadwel was seeking out the Lady, the ancient Aluien who'd marked him, because the time had come for the knight to die.

Ari worried at Sir Cadwel's words for the rest of the day. He tried out different interpretations. He replayed the way the knight had looked down at Poromont, as if seeing it for the last time. By evening, Ari had worked himself into a terrible state of distress.

"But, why?" he finally blurted after they'd settled around their campfire. He knew Sir Cadwel didn't like to be questioned, or to have conversations thick with sentiment, but it was impossible not to ask.

The knight regarded Ari across the fire. He didn't look angry, as Ari had feared he would. Eventually, Sir Cadwel shook his head, the corners of his mouth actually turning up in a rueful smile. "Pride."

"Pride?" Ari repeated, more confused.

Sir Cadwel's face returned to its usual frown. "Pride, and fear." He let out a sigh. He held up a hand, palm down. "Do you see this?"

Ari stared at Sir Cadwel's hand. It was thick, the joints showing evidence of hard use over the years, and scarred. It was also, to Ari's shock, shaking.

"It's a wasting sickness. My grandfather suffered from it, as have others in my line." Sir Cadwel lowered his hand, his gaze on the flickering flames between them. "It starts like this, with small tremors, easily ignored, but it grows. It worsens. By the end, my grandfather had to be strapped to a chair when we wanted to feed him, even his head, for he couldn't hold it still enough for someone to put food in his mouth. It's a slow way to die."

The hot sounds of the fire filled the silence between them. Ari didn't know what to say. He didn't even know what to think. Sir Cadwel was the most powerful warrior in Lggothland. Maybe in the world, for all Ari knew. His strength and skill were the stuff of legends. He couldn't be ill. He definitely couldn't be dying. "Maybe the Aluiens can cure you."

Sir Cadwel shook his head. "I spoke with the Lady about it, once. She has no cure. She told me everyone must face mortality."

"But, how long do you have? You don't have to . . ." He swallowed, his words halted by the pain on the knight's face. Ari realized that, betrayed by the body that had always served him to perfection, Sir Cadwel had finally found an enemy he couldn't conquer. "Isn't there time still?"

Sir Cadwel couldn't leave him for the Aluiens yet. Ari wouldn't even be seventeen until the following summer. He wasn't ready to be Lord of Sorga. He'd only been with Sir Cadwel for a year.

Looking across the fire at the knight's grim visage, guilt surged through Ari. How could he protest Sir Cadwel's choice to enter into the immortal ranks of the Aluiens, taking up a hidden life of observation and study, instead of going back to Sorga to battle this illness? Ari should be grateful his mentor was marked and wouldn't really be gone forever. He would be hidden away in the Aluiens' cave, from which they watched and recorded the knowledge and trials of man.

"I could wait, letting the disease worsen, but the Lady doesn't know if becoming an Aluien will restore what is lost," Sir Cadwel said. "They chose me, marked me to become one of them, for my martial skills and knowledge. I'll be a poor repository of those skills if I let the illness take me. What must be done is best done now. If I wait too long, it could be I'll end up in a state that warrants a refusal of immortality."

"But, I don't want to be duke yet." Ari stopped, forcing himself to swallow, aware he sounded like a selfish child.

"Don't worry on that score." Sir Cadwel's cunning look chased away much of the sorrow from his face. "I have a plan."

Chapter 3

Ari had to content himself with that as they followed the road west toward Wheylia. Sir Cadwel, never verbose, seemed to see no reason to expound as they traveled. Before they reached the mountains, the knight turned them onto a slightly less traveled road heading north, up the eastern side of the range separating Lggothland from neighboring Wheylian.

Ari briefly considered protesting on the grounds that he was supposed to keep people away from the home of the Aluiens. He'd even sworn an oath to do so. Of course, the Aluiens had deliberately left Sir Cadwel in possession of the knowledge of where they dwelled, so they probably didn't mean for Ari to defend them from the knight's approach. Ari sighed, knowing that as much as he balked at the knight's plan, interfering would be an act of unjustified selfishness. That was assuming he could stop Sir Cadwel, which he probably couldn't.

The knight rarely spoke during the long hours they traveled, nearly as morose as on their first journey together. Ari sorely missed their usual travel companions, Peine and the Aluien bard Larkesong. The endless silence of their days left Ari too much time with his own thoughts.

Mostly, when he wasn't worrying about what Sir Cadwel planned to do, he worried about Ispiria. If only Sir Cadwel had let him know they wouldn't go straight back, Ari could have sent her a note. She'd be anxious. She'd be waiting for them.

And what of Peine and Natan? It occurred to Ari that the knight had been devious when he hadn't allowed Peine to accompany them. It wasn't for the sake of Peine's training. It was so that Ari and Sir Cadwel would be allowed into the cave of the Aluiens. Though they hid from other mortal eyes, the Aluiens had a special link to Ari, allowing him to be one of the few who knew of their existence. Peine knew a small amount about them too, but that was a secret Ari guarded from them.

Finally, as an overly cool fall evening found them at the base of the path leading to the Aluiens' cave, Ari mustered up a tone he worked to make sound neither accusatory nor petulant, and said, "It's almost the day we were due back in Sorga. I hope no one will be worried about us."

"I left Natan a note."

Ari let out a sigh of relief.

"Set up camp," Sir Cadwel said, dismounting.

"We aren't going up?"

"It's late." Sir Cadwel eyed the foot of the path.

The trail up was barely visible on the boulder-strewn slope. Ari was sure, were they not among those few permitted to see it, they wouldn't even be able to pick it out.

Shrugging, he dismounted and untied Sir Cadwel's small tent. He wondered if the knight was having second thoughts.

To become an Aluien, one needed first to die. Sir Cadwel wasn't the sort to meet death with ease. Ari shivered at the thought.

He set up Sir Cadwel's tent before portioning out the hard bread, sharp cheese and dry fruit that were their evening fare. Sir Cadwel built a fire, taking up his customary position between it and his tent. Ari sat opposite him, on his bedroll. Already touched by the Aluiens' magic, though not actually one of them, Ari didn't feel the cold or heat as strongly as a normal man. He didn't bother with a tent for himself, even on so brisk a late autumn evening.

"You could have told me we weren't going straight back," he finally said, blurting out his annoyance. He braced himself for a reprimand, for Sir Cadwel didn't take well to being criticized, but the knight regarded him calmly.

"You would have had questions. I wanted your concentration on the tourney."

"It's just . . ." Ari stopped, fumbling with his words. "I'm worried Ispiria will be upset." He hoped he didn't sound as wretched to Sir Cadwel as he did to himself. It wasn't only Ispiria's feelings weighing on him, but his own misery at being away from her.

"She'll have to accustom herself to long absences. As will you. It's the life of the king's champion."

Ari looked down. Sir Cadwel was right. The knight spent at least as much time away from Sorga as in it. Ari had worked hard not to think about that aspect of being king's champion. He'd always dreamed of achieving the honor, long before he met Ispiria. In his daydreams, he never considered what the drawbacks might be.

It didn't matter. He squared his shoulders. Being king's champion was more than accolade. It was sacrifice, and perseverance. Sir Cadwel had taught him that. Ari had twice proved himself the most able for the task, and he wouldn't shirk from what was both a privilege and a duty. Not even if it made him, or Ispiria, sad.

Ari just hoped Ispiria's great grandmother would never be right. Her notion that association with the lords of Sorga only led to misery for the women they loved was troubling because, candidly, it seemed true. He wouldn't let it stay true, though. Ari never wanted Ispiria to pay a price for his choices, as Sir Cadwel's wife had. Thoroughly depressed by that line of thought, Ari stared into the flames. He jabbed at the charring wood with a stick.

"I've seen happier looking men at their own hangings." The melodic voice came from behind him.

Ari swiveled around to see the Aluien bard Larkesong descending the secret mountain path. "Larke," Ari cried, jumping to his feet.

Divested of his customary garish travel garb, Larke wore the long white tunic and loose trousers of an Aluien. He was also not bothering to hide the moonlike glow that suffused his people. The blue-white nebulousness leached his hair of its blond color and his eyes of their bright blue. As always when confronted with Orlenia, the mystical source of the Aluiens' glow, Ari felt a covetous pang. It had flowed through his veins once.

Larke stopped at the base of the trail, regarding them warmly. In spite of the bard's friendly expression, Ari was struck by the knowledge that, no matter how personable Larke always appeared, he was actually a magical being who was twice as old as he looked and commanded considerable power.

36

"Ari, lad." Larke nodded in greeting. He cocked his head to the side, his gaze shifting to Sir Cadwel. "What brings two of my favorite mortals so near our lair? Trouble in the lands?"

Larke looked slightly hopeful and Ari realized the bard's punishment, imposed that spring, chafed him. Having too often broken his people's rules of secrecy, Larke had been ordered to stay within the Aluien caves for as long as it took the sun to set a thousand times.

"Is the Lady in the deep sleep?" Ari asked, ignoring Larke's question. The Lady, knowing to what extent seclusion would torment the bard, had argued a way to mitigate his sentence. She was granted the chance to take some of his punishment from him, but only if she entered into the deep sleep, the near-death state that helped prolong the seemingly endless life of the oldest Aluiens. If the Lady was asleep, she couldn't turn Sir Cadwel into an Aluien. Ari tried to squash the happiness that rose up in him at the thought.

"The realm fares well," Sir Cadwel said, rising from his spot on the other side of the fire. Concern deepened the lines on his face. "Is the lad correct? Does the Lady sleep?"

"Not yet. You know she mistrusts it."

"But, your punishment." Ari made a sweeping gesture meant to indicate that Larke was outside the cave.

"This?" Larke grinned. "Why, this is nothing. The front steps. Hardly counts. It's not as if I'm headed off into the lands, participating in battles, composing great ballads." Larke sighed, his smile fading. "No, not me. I stay in the caves, striving diligently to capture the purity of music in works the world will never be allowed to hear. Besides, someone had to come see what you two want," he added, shaking off his melancholy. "No one else volunteered. A few may even have suggested if we ignored you, you'd go away."

37

"We wouldn't have." Sir Cadwel's tone was harsh enough to take the smile back off Larke's face. "It's time."

"Time?" Larke looked to Ari, then back at Sir Cadwel. "For?"

"For me to become one of you," Sir Cadwel said.

"An Aluien?" Larke stared at the knight. Sir Cadwel nodded. "My dear fellow, you do recall that to become one of us, you need to leave your mortal life behind, and I don't just mean figuratively. You have to die, old friend. End it all. Say goodbye to knighthood, to being king's champion, to your home in Sorga. All of it."

"I don't see why." Sir Cadwel hooked his thumbs on his belt. His jaw clenched at a belligerent angle.

"Why? So you can pass beyond life. Your body must be drained of its life's blood and infused with Orlenia. We don't glow for the fun of it, you know. The power of the Orlenia is what sustains us."

Sir Cadwel made an impatient slashing gesture. "I know that. I don't see why I can't go back to Sorga."

Ari felt a surge of hope. Was that Sir Cadwel's plan? To become an Aluien, but not abandon Ari and Sorga? But, the knight had seemed so sad when they left Poromont. Did that mean Sir Cadwel meant to go through with becoming an Aluien whether they agreed to his terms or not?

"Because those are the rules, old friend. We don't, some of us, stay in these caves for the fun of it either. When the Khan Dar created the first of us, the first human turned Aluien, he soon realized the trouble it would bring to allow us to stay linked to our mortal lives. We're chosen as repositories of knowledge, great minds dedicated to the pursuit of it. We're forbidden from shaping the course of history. You know that. A newly made Aluien isn't allowed out of the caves for three generations, to give them time to immerse themselves in their new lives, away from the temptations of the old."

"They let you out sooner than that," Sir Cadwel said, scowling.

"Aye." Larke grinned. "I talked them into it. I recommend against using me as your argument, though. I daresay my constant blunders have only hardened their resolve."

"And if I become one of you and then return to Sorga? Who would stop me?"

Larke pressed his lips together in a thin line. Ari looked between the knight and the bard. Larke's face was worried, Sir Cadwel's quarrelsome.

"They'll order you confined, as they have me."

"I'll disobey."

"Then they'll strip the Orlenia from you, leaving you empty and powerless."

"How bad can that be?" Sir Cadwel shrugged, but the movement was stiff with tension. "You traverse the edge of expulsion often."

"The two times it was deemed necessary, those cast out died by their own will, rather than live without Orlenia."

Sir Cadwel glanced at Ari. Ari shook his head. His memories of the short time he'd dwelled among the Aluien were taken from him in an attempt to hide their existence, but he could guess at what it would be like to have the Orlenia stripped from you. Even after Ari's brief exposure, and without having a memory of ever possessing it, he missed the Orlenia. Sometimes, if he let his mind dwell too long on it, he found he started to crave it, longing to have it returned.

"I'm not some weak-minded sod to be shaken by the loss of a little power," Sir Cadwel said harshly, turning back to Larke.

"You don't know, Cadwel." The bard's voice was soft. "You won't know, until you've touched it. It is beauty, warmth, strength. It flows through you like the finest summer wine and brightens the world like a cloudless day." The bard held up his hand, fingers spread wide.

Ari couldn't take his gaze from the luminous glow.

"Addle-minded popinjay," Sir Cadwel muttered. "I don't mean to stay in Sorga and govern. I will make concessions."

"Concessions?" Larke's glow dimmed to a less showy level. He rubbed his hands together. "Why didn't you say so, oh mighty knight? I am the master of concessions. Regale me with your offer, Lord Cadwel, and I shall take it before the council."

"I'll take it myself."

"Ah, afraid not." Larke shook his head. "They won't actually let you in. They're quite adamant. Their patience with you two has worn a bit thin, what with you showing up uninvited last winter, droves of mortals in tow, demanding entry. Set a few teeth on edge, you did."

Sir Cadwel uttered a few choice oaths, which Larke endured, shooting Ari a grin. He tried to smile back, but imagining Sir Cadwel becoming an Aluien and leaving, or getting cast out for not leaving, were both prospects too grim to allow Ari a real smile.

Eventually, the knight seemed to somewhat regained his composure. "Tell them I know I must give it all up, my place as a knight of the realm, being king's champion, and my governance of Sorga and the Northlands. I only wish to return to Sorga once. I must gather my research, and there are one or two books there, belonging too much to the keep to be removed, that I wish to finish reading. That is all," he grated out.

Larke crossed his arms, eyes narrowing. Ari felt his hopes die. That was Sir Cadwel's plan, to come back long enough to pack his papers and read something? Ari wanted Sir Cadwel to stay in Sorga for years more.

"Well?" Sir Cadwel demanded.

"Your desire to return to Sorga strikes me as infinitely reasonable." Larke continued to scrutinize the knight. "I've heard you have quite the collection of work amassed. It would be foolish not to bring it." Still, he stared. "But why, pray tell, can you not return to gather your research first and then come to us? Why must it be now?"

Sir Cadwel let out a heavy sigh. His eyes locked on Larke's, the knight raised his hand before him, as he had to Ari. The trembling was terrifyingly obvious. "Tell your council that if they don't make up their minds soon, their vaunted repository of military skill and knowledge may be lost to them forever." He let his hand fall.

Larke stepped closer, his face suffused with compassion. "I didn't know." He reached tentatively toward Sir Cadwel. "May I?"

The knight scowled, but nodded. Ari watched with wide eyes, wondering what Larke was going to do. The bard placed long fingers on Sir Cadwel's forehead. His lids closing, Larke's face took on a look of concentration.

"It is there, winding through your mind." He opened his eyes, dropping his arm. "It isn't far along, the sickness."

"Can you fix it?" Ari asked in a surge of hope.

Larke shook his head. "Our powers speed healing, often to miraculous affect, but they do not create it." Sadness tugged at the bard's features. "There's no healing to speed. Lord Cadwel's body progresses, rather, in the opposite direction. I'd

41

heard, but passed off as rumor, that such an illness lurked in your line."

"So you agree, then," Sir Cadwel said. "It must be now."

Ari didn't know if the knight's scowl was aimed at Larke or fortune, but it was daunting.

"Such an illness usually progresses quite slowly," Larke said.

"Usually, but not always, and even this slight diminishment in my skills weakens my value."

"True."

Ari scrutinized the bard's face, trying to glean his thoughts. The blue glow emanating from him made him harder to read than usual.

"That's all there is to this, Cadwel? You'll renounce it all? You simply want to finish your reading in Sorga and return with your research? You swear it?"

"You accuse me of artifice?" Sir Cadwel awarded Larke his most severe look.

"Not I." Larke took a step back from the knight's glare. "Not I, old friend." The bard gave Sir Cadwel another piercing look, which the knight returned calmly. "Well then, I shall bring this before the others. Trust me to plead your case, most glorious of knights. I shall not fail you. In this, I shall be your champion." Larke bowed low, pivoting to disappear back up the trail.

Sir Cadwel scowled at the retreating bard until he was lost from view.

Chapter 4

Once they were alone, Ari turned to the knight. "That's your plan?" Ari couldn't keep anger and despair from his voice. "You'll come home long enough to pack and read a tome? You may as well have read it before we left." He clenched his fists at his sides. Never before had he felt such fiery disappointment. Sir Cadwel's earlier reassurance meant nothing. The knight's actions verged on betrayal.

"Aye." A smile formed on Sir Cadwel's face. "Long enough to read a tome." The knight shook his head. "Old warrior like me, no way of knowing how many years that could take."

Ari's anger dissipated with such speed, it left him weak.

Sir Cadwel clasped him on the shoulder. "I won't abandon you, lad." He gave Ari's shoulder a squeeze before heading back around to his side of the fire.

Wobbly, Ari sank down to await the bard's return. He gazed into the fire, his thoughts too turbulent to grasp. He didn't realize he'd fallen asleep until the sound of Sir Cadwel standing woke him.

"My lady," the knight said, bowing.

Ari struggled to his feet, shaking off sleep, as he realized the diminutive figure of the Lady followed Larke down the trail. The Lady, the ancient Aluien who'd wrenched Ari back from death over a year and a half ago, when a vile Empty One had tried to take his life. Ari's sleep-addled mind stumbled over the idea that it had been so long since he'd disobeyed his adopted uncle and snuck out into the woods, simultaneously the most foolish and wonderful act of rebellion he'd ever undertaken.

Ari bowed as well, one hand reaching almost unconsciously to touch his tunic where the strange amulet he wore rested underneath. The Lady had made it for him. So long as he wore it no Empty One, the evil race that was the mirror opposite of Aluiens, could use dark magic to search Ari out or control his mind. "My lady," Ari said, adding his greeting to Sir Cadwel's.

"Cadwel, Aridian." The Lady's voice was musical with the magic of the Aluiens and an ancient Wheylian lilt. "Larkesong has told me why you have come. We have argued your case before the council." She smiled at them, her warm regard a balm to Ari's worn nerves. "They bid me list you their terms, all of which must be sworn to or they deny your request."

Sir Cadwel nodded. To Ari's surprise, the knight looked attentive, not angry at having his initial request denied. Ari knew it was because the Lady spoke to him. No one could be angry with the Lady. Her very presence seemed to ease the coldness of the night and blanket Ari in a peaceful somnolence. Taking in Larke's smug expression, Ari wondered if the bard had asked the Lady to deliver the council's demands for that very reason.

"First, you must swear to relinquish all of your worldly titles and ambitions," the Lady said. "You shall no longer make decisions affecting the outcome of the fates of men, even and especially those which center on Sorga."

"When you leave here, it will be for the purpose of returning to Sorga only. You must swear to journey to no additional places. You will make every effort to minimize your contact with mankind as you travel both to and from Sorga." The Lady's voice was soothing, her words diminishing the strain built up in Ari's chest. "Also, before you may return to gather your research, you shall dwell here with us for the turning of one moon, that you may learn how to properly conceal your magical nature from the eyes of men, among other things. Lastly, once you return from Sorga, you will adhere to tradition and absent yourself from the mortal realm for at least three generations."

Ari let out a sigh of relief. The Aluiens were going to allow Sir. Cadwel to become one of them and still go home. He wasn't quite certain how they'd work out Sir Cadwel not telling anyone what to do anymore, but they would find a way.

"It's your sterling reputation that swayed them, oh mighty one," Larke said. "Your standing as a man of your word and a pillar of honor."

Sir Cadwel's face was grave, showing none of the relief Ari felt. The knight nodded slowly. "I fear some of the council's imperatives may be more difficult to achieve than others, my lady."

"You need not agree, Lord Cadwel," the Lady said. "You may turn and leave this place. You are marked. When the time is come for death to find you, I will be by your side."

Sir Cadwel glanced at Ari before shaking his head. "No. It shall be now. I am ready. I swear to uphold the conditions set out by the council. I swear on my honor to do this, or my life be given in pursuit of it."

Silence stretched out into the night, heavy with Sir Cadwel's vow. Ari looked between the knight and the Lady.

"Then there is but one more thing you must do," the Lady said, her lyrical voice returning sound to their world.

"What now?" Sir Cadwel looked startled. "I gave my vow."

"Yes, you gave it, and the council accepts. Now, if you wish to become one of us, the time has come, Lord Cadwel, for you to die."

Ari shuddered. The Lady's face was serene as always, but Larke looked worried.

Sir Cadwel cleared his throat, his mouth pulling down in a perplexed frown. He turned to Larke. "How did you do it, when you took your life?" he asked in a quiet voice.

"How did I?" Larke blinked, surprise showing on his face. "Why do you think I did? I could easily have died at the hand of another, not my own. You know my abhorrence for fighting, my ineptitude in defending myself."

"I had you followed, that night."

Ari turned incredulous eyes on the bard. Larke had killed himself? Even more distressing, he must have meant it. It was very unusual for someone to know they were going to become an Aluien. Ari longed to ask Larke what had made him do such a thing, but he knew it was an unacceptable question. Maybe he could get Sir Cadwel to tell him later.

"You what? Why?" Larke asked.

"For the good of the realm," Sir Cadwel said. "I always wondered why the man I sent was so vague on the details of your death, yet so certain of the fact. Now I know." He nodded toward the Lady.

"And if I had made a different choice that night?" Larke asked, his eyes narrowing.

"He was under orders not to let you make that choice."

Larke frowned at Sir Cadwel. Anger darkened his features. "For the good of the realm," he reiterated, his tone hard.

Sir Cadwel nodded, not looking away.

After a long moment, during which Ari had to remind himself to breathe as the two glared at one another, Larke shrugged. "If you must know, it was a knife through the heart." His tone was almost even.

"Ari, fetch a knife," Sir Cadwel said.

Ari wanted to say no, but he nodded instead, going to rummage in the packs he'd tossed inside Sir Cadwel's tent. He came back with a short sharp blade they used for a variety of tasks. He held it out to Sir Cadwel, working hard to keep from shaking.

Sir Cadwel took it, the blade looking small in his hands. He held the knife awkwardly in front of himself, his eyes going from it to each of them and back to the blade. Muttering something to himself, he turned his back to them. A moment later, he knelt, holding the hilt in both hands now, out above his chest. The tableau of him thus, his face turned up toward the stars, seemed to last forever.

Finally, Sir Cadwel lowered his arm. "Ari?" He turned, holding out the knife. "I don't think I can do it. You'll have to, lad."

Ari took a step backward, too flabbergasted by the request to voice his absolute rejection of it. He shook his head vigorously.

"You can't ask it of the lad," Larke said, stepping forward. He held out his hand for the blade. "You're sure you wish this, old friend?" He locked eyes with the knight.

"Get on with it." Sir Cadwel slapped the weapon into Larke's palm. The knight pulled his shoulders back and raised his chin.

Ari gasped as the bard, with the lightning speed of an Aluien, plunged the blade toward Sir Cadwel's chest. Equally fast, Sir Cadwel's arm came up, knocking the knife away.

Larke yelped, rubbing his wrist. He glared down at Sir Cadwel.

"Sorry," the knight muttered, reaching over to retrieve the knife where it quivered, blade first, in the ground. "Instinct. Try again."

"Are you sure you want to do this?" Larke said again, gingerly taking the knife back.

"I am. Do it."

"We're doing it my way this time." Larke raised his free hand. He started to weave symbols, drawing them in glowing runes of Orlenia, each one dripping from the air before him as it reached completion. In moments, Sir Cadwel's eyes glazed over. The face he raised to Larke was dull and expressionless. Larke looked to the Lady.

She nodded.

It was all Ari could do not to lunge forward and stop him as Larke plunged the blade into Sir Cadwel's heart. When the knife struck, conscious thought returned to the knight's eyes, only to be instantly quenched. He toppled backward, Larke pulling out the blade as he fell. Ari watched in horror as Sir Cadwel's heart's blood poured from him.

Ari rushed to his side, falling to his knees by the knight's head, but Larke was already there, and the Lady. Larke placed a hand over the hole in Sir Cadwel's chest, casting the knife aside. His lips framing incantations, he drew his hand back. A guttural choking sound forced its way out of Ari's throat as more blood followed the bard's gesture, bubbling out. Sir Cadwel's body seemed almost to flatten, deflating into the red-soaked earth beneath him. Ari's breath came in ragged gasps.

On the knight's other side, the Lady's delicate fingers wove symbols in the air, murmured words of magic falling from her lips to scatter on the night wind. Reaching out, her delicate fingers closing on nothing, she plucked glowing strands into being, laying them on Sir Cadwel's still form. Each strand flickered once, glowing bright blue, before sinking into the knight, right through his clothes.

As he watched, Ari realized the pattern the Lady followed was that of a man's veins. As the blue of the Orlenia fused with Sir Cadwel's body, the knight lost his deflated look. His eyelids twitched. A building glow emanated from his flesh, the deep wound in his chest closing.

Ari rocked back on his heels. Realizing his face was wet with tears, he wiped it on his sleeve, sucking in a ragged breath.

Sir Cadwel's Orlenia-infused eyes flew open. He sprang from the earth, barreling Larke over, his hands around the bard's throat. Growling, the knight bashed Larke's head into the rocky ground. The bard tore frantically at Sir Cadwel's arms.

"Cadwel," the Lady snapped, her usually peaceful voice filled with as much command as Ari had ever heard Sir Cadwel bring to bear. "Stop."

The knight hesitated. He looked at her, blinking, then down at Larke. Appearing as if it took a supreme effort of will, his fingers peeled back from Larke's throat, one at a time. He rolled to the side, freeing the bard. Larke gasped, rubbing his throat.

Ari struggled to his feet from where he'd knelt by Sir Cadwel's head, his movements clumsy with confusion and shock. Looking down, he made sure not to step in the large puddle of blood saturating the ground in front of him.

Sir Cadwel raised a glowing hand, holding it out and turning it from side to side.

"What in the name of all the gods were you doing, Cadwel?" Larke demanded, his voice ragged. Ari could see dark welts on the bard's throat.

"I . . ." Sir Cadwel looked at Larke, his eyes wide. "You stabbed me."

"You told me to."

The Lady sighed, shaking her head.

Ari slumped back to the ground, exhausted.

"But, you . . . you killed me."

"You told me to," Larke repeated, getting up and brushing dirt from his white garments.

Sir Cadwel stood as well, glaring at him. As the knight opened his mouth to speak again, the Lady caught Ari's eyes. She gave him an amused smile. Ari realized this was the beginning of an argument that could go on, literally, for ages.

Chapter 5

Ari stepped out into the cold morning, shivering. Even for his enhanced body, the winter air was frigid. It was especially cold in the Aluiens' practice yard, as it was hemmed in on all sides by tall peaks and the winter sun could only touch it at its zenith. That wouldn't be for hours yet, but there really wasn't much else for Ari to do with his time, other than practice.

He glanced back at the glowing corridor behind him, considering returning to the warmth and beauty there. There was nothing cave-like about the Aluiens' home, though it was carved within the peaks of the mountains. The walls of the corridors and rooms were smooth and decorated in glimmering blue runes. Ari didn't know if they were designs or some arcane writing, but they were rounded and flowed along the walls, ceilings and floors.

His favorite space, though, was the massive central cavern, where Aluiens congregated. It alone retained the unevenness of a natural formation, though the floor had been smoothed. The roof of the vast central cave swept upward, revealing veins of sparkling minerals, each one enhanced by more glowing runes.

Yet, as beautiful as it was, there were only so many hours each day Ari could spend gawking at it. He made his way to the center of the practice yard, leaving the door ajar. Only an Aluien could open it from the outside. It was a precaution Ari found a little silly, since no one could possibly know the peak-enwrapped yard was there, even if anyone had the fortitude to climb over the tall mountains to reach it.

The Aluiens were an overcautious race, though, to Ari's thinking. Even when it came to him. Not for the first time, he wished they hadn't taken away his memory of the brief time he'd spent with them, leaving him with only hazy recollections and general knowledge. Ari could overcome spells suppressing his memories, but he couldn't regain memories that had been completely removed.

Shrugging, Ari tried to shake off his growing irritability. It wasn't as if the Aluiens weren't kind to him. Quite the opposite, though he knew his ability to unravel their magic frightened some of them. The Lady said his extra-human abilities, like his speed, strength and endurance, stemmed from them changing him into an Aluien and then back into a human. It was something that had never been done before. None of them had known what the end result would be. In view of their dissatisfaction with much of his behavior and their continued inability to agree on how Ari fit into the rules governing their world, he didn't think it was an experiment they would ever try again.

Ari drew his sword and leaned it against the practice dummy, executing a series of stretches to warm his chilled muscles. Not that he had as much to worry about as most people. Since he healed so quickly, a muscle pulled this morning would be fit as ever by afternoon.

Retrieving his sword, Ari saluted the dummy. He smiled a little before he launched into his attack, running through his daily drills. The good thing about practicing there was that the Aluiens had kindly bespelled the dummy, wrapping it in charms so even Ari could hit it as hard as he wanted without it being chopped to pieces. He had to admit, it was a relief to be able to swing to his fullest instead of always holding back his enhanced strength for fear of hurting someone or chopping practice dummies in half at every swing.

So, that's one good thing, he told himself, and their kindness is another. Of course, those two things didn't exactly balance out being stuck in the Aluien caves where no one really wanted to talk to him. Not after all the trouble Larke had gotten himself into by befriending Ari. Or that Sir Cadwel had to spend all day every day in his own training with Larke and the Lady, and Ari wasn't allowed to watch. Or that it was starting to seem like he'd never get home to ask Ispiria to marry him. He'd planned to ask her up on the battlements, where they'd first kissed. Since they hadn't gone home right after the tourney, it would be so cold and snowy out there by the time they got back that he didn't know if that was still a good idea. In fact, by the time Sir Cadwel's month of training was up and they could depart, the deep drifts would make it take them twice as long to get home.

With an inarticulate yell he was surprised to realize came from his own throat, Ari jammed the point of his sword into the supposedly unbreakable dummy. The wood to split up the center with a resounding crack. The noise echoed off the rock walls around him. Ari released the hilt of his sword, the blade quavering with the force of the blow. He wiped his hands on his thighs, only then realizing he was covered in sweat from his exertions.

"Well, that won't do," Larke's voice said behind him.

Ari turned to see the bard watching him from within the shelter of the doorway. Uncrossing his arms, Larke stepped out, closing the thick wooden door behind him. Carvings twisted across the dark surface.

"Morning," Ari said. He swallowed, hoping Larke didn't hear the sullen note in his voice.

Larke pulled his cloak more tightly about him, walking over to examine the dummy. "Those who still deem you an aberration can't be allowed wind of this. That wood should be well nigh indestructible." Larke raised fine-fingered hands, but his eyes glanced at Ari. "Would you be so kind as to remove the sword, lad? No sense mending it with your blade still in there."

"Sorry." Ari had to use both hands to wrench the weapon back out. A glance at the tip told him it was going to take hours to sharpen out the damage. In truth, he was surprised it hadn't broken since it was a sword he'd selected at random from the king's armory. The soldiers of Lggothland went well-armed, it seemed. Then again, King Ennentine had been the chief supply officer in Sir Cadwel's army before becoming king, so he probably cared more about such details than many leaders would. Ari had read about their campaigns as part of his studies.

Ari watched in fascination, and a little bit of envy, as Larke wove patterns of magic in the air. The wood of the dummy mended back together, the great splintered crack disappearing as if it had never been. Ari remembered how the Aluiens had fixed the castle gates, the stable and other damage that spring, when they'd come to clean up the memory of the evil Empty

One who'd attacked Sorga. He hadn't witnessed the process then, only the results.

Ari couldn't help but look at Larke in awe. "That's amazing." Sheathing his sword, Ari reached out and touched the dummy. It felt as solid as it looked.

"It is also, truth be told, apropos."

"Huh?" Ari wasn't sure that last part was even a real word.

"There's a warning I've long meant to give you, lad, and I've wheedled permission out of the others to reveal it." The bard looked smug.

"What warning? Why wouldn't they want me to have it?"

Larke grimaced. "You know how they are. Secret this, secret that, but it's something you need to know."

"What is it?" Ari asked, realizing he was in danger of allowing Larke to digress to another topic. The bard's mind had a way of wandering, and sometimes jumping, here and there.

"It's about the way we, and therefore presumably you, heal. You've seen plenty of examples of it, yes? On yourself and Empty Ones you've fought."

Ari nodded.

"What I worry on is you getting over-confident. There are still ways you can die, to be sure, and still ways you can be, shall we say, maimed." Larke twisted his mouth, revealing his dislike of the idea.

"I know I can die."

Larke raised an eyebrow.

"What I mean is, I assume I can die, because I can kill Empty Ones," Ari clarified.

"Exactly." Larke sounded pleased. "A fatal blow shall always be fatal, to Aluien, Empty One or, we may assume, you."

"That's not much of a secret." Ari was a little disappointed.

"For a race which prefers to think of itself as immortal, it is." Larke grinned. "I take your meaning, though. Not much of a secret from you, who have slain many Empty Ones, both man and beast."

"So what about the . . . the maiming part?"

"It's only this." Larke's face turning serious. "Once a piece of us is removed from, shall we say, the whole, it doesn't grow back. Nor, may I add, can you reattach it."

"Removed from the whole?" Ari repeated, glancing inadvertently at his hands. He had the immediate vision of his fingers being cleaved off. "Like, my fingers?"

"Fingers, hands, arms, noses, ears, legs." Larke nodded as he listed them. "Anything, really. Anything you can get away with cutting off without killing. You can heal, but you won't regenerate."

Ari turned that over in his mind. He wasn't familiar with the word regenerate, but he could construe its meaning. He looked at his hands again. "Uh, thank you for telling me."

"My pleasure. Or, rather, not really so much of a pleasure, talking about missing digits and all. A duty, maybe?" He shook his head. "Less of one, more of the other, all of neither. I wanted you to know, lad, so you wouldn't grow too bold. You aren't invincible."

"Thank you," Ari said with sincerity. He hadn't really intended to ever let anyone cut off any parts of himself to begin with, not if he could help it, but he appreciated Larke's concern.

"So, this is where you've been spending your days?" Larke glanced around the barren practice yard.

"Yes." Ari nodded. He shivered, his sweat having quickly dried his tunic to his back in the cold air. A splash of sunlight filled a third of the yard now, but they weren't standing in it.

"I've an idea," Larke said. "How about a lesson or two in Wheylian? Ancient Wheylian? Your choice."

Ari grinned, nodding. "I'll get cleaned up and meet you in the central chamber?" A month ago, he would have done most anything to shirk studying languages but now, bored as he was, it seemed like the kindest offer anyone had ever made him.

"And, later, I'll play you my new ballad about your momentous victory this spring," Larke said, crossing to open the door.

Ari's face heated. Fortunately, Larke's back was to him as they entered the passageway. Ari had no love of hearing ballads about his own deeds. Still, it was an honor to have the most renowned bard in Lggothland's history write about him. He knew it frustrated Larke that he couldn't distribute his new music to the populace, bound as he was by the Aluien code not to influence the mortal realm. The least Ari could do was listen.

Ari's days passed more agreeably after that, with practice in the mornings and Larke's lessons in the afternoons. For, it turned out, Larke was now forbidden attendance at the lessons with Sir Cadwel. The bard seemed to bring out the worst in the knight, who wasn't proving as successful at the intricate movements and strange utterances required to manipulate the Orlenia as he'd been with every other undertaking in his life. Ari supposed it didn't help that Larke and Sir Cadwel used to travel together during the long war, when Sir Cadwel was young and Larke a mortal. Back then, when death was a constant presence in every life, Sir Cadwel's skills had been much more meritorious than those of the flighty bard.

Ari sympathized with his mentor, for he struggled with what he was learning as well, although he found Larke an excellent teacher. The bard had far more patience with Ari's inability to quickly master Wheylian than his best friend, Peine, ever did. Plus, Larke would make up ridiculous fake ballads to help Ari remember lists of new words. They were the sort of silly tunes that were almost impossible to get out of your head, and Ari found himself chanting them long after his understanding of the languages moved to a higher level of mastery.

When the day finally came for them to leave, Ari had to admit he did so with a touch of sorrow. He wouldn't want the past twenty-eight days to go on forever, but there was such peace in the Aluien caves, such a soft rhythm to the life the Aluiens led, that Ari could see how someone might want to stay. Not him, because he had to get back to Ispiria, Sorga and his obligations to the crown, but someone else. Someone who, he realized, everyone thought was dead. That sort of someone could be quite happy there.

Ari was eager to see Stew who, Larke assured him, would be waiting for him. The Aluiens were elusive when pressed to know where the magical race of horses they rode went. That there were no horses in the caves, Ari was reasonably sure, because he'd searched for Stew. It wasn't that he didn't believe Larke when the bard told him the horses were safe and happy, but he missed Stew. Ari shoved his spare tunic into his bag, ready to be packed and away.

"Ari," Larke called from outside the little stone room Ari slept in.

"Come in." Ari tucked the last of his things, including a small book on Ancient Wheylian Larke had given him, into his saddlebags.

The bard entered, quietly swinging the door shut and turning to Ari with a worried expression.

"Is something wrong?"

"What?" Larke looked surprised by the question. "No, nothing's wrong."

"Well, that's good," Ari said after Larke was silent for a moment.

"Get to Hawkers much these days, lad?" Larke asked, referring to the mountain village north of Sorga's keep. The Hawkers' village was where the Sorga hawks, the little brown hawks who were the symbol of Sorga, lived. That spring, as part of the disaster that had ended in Larke's three-year confinement, an Empty One had attacked the village.

"I haven't gotten to much of anywhere." Ari looked around the small room meaningfully but put no rancor in his tone.

"Ah, right." Larke reached into his tunic, pulling out a thick sheaf of parchment, bound and sealed. "May I ask a favor?"

"Yes." Ari eyed the parchment, wondering why Larke seemed so nervous.

"Could you, when you've the chance, get this to Mirimel?"

"Of course."

Larke held the parchment out with something approaching reluctance. Ari took it and carefully tucked it into his bag before buckling it closed. He could understand the bard's worry now, and guilt. Larke had hid Mirimel when the rest of the Aluiens came to erase everyone's memories of the Empty One who'd burned the Hawkers' village. Although Ari had no idea why Larke would write to Hawk Guardian Mirimel, the bard was undoubtedly breaking the rules by corresponding with someone who wasn't supposed to remember he even existed. It wasn't Ari's concern, though. No one had told him not to take letters from Larke, Mirimel already knew of the Aluiens, and the bard was Ari's friend.

"Ready, Ari?" Sir Cadwel's voice came in conjunction with a loud knock on Ari's door.

Ari hoisted his saddlebags to his shoulder, calling, "Ready, sir." He marched from the room, Larke following.

Ari trailed Sir Cadwel down the hallway, pleased to see no trace of a nebulous glow surrounding the knight. It had taken the knight nearly a score of days to master the skills that allowed him to hide his glow from mortal eyes. Ari hadn't mentioned it, had barely dared to think about it, but if Sir Cadwel hadn't been able to master that, Ari was sure the knight would not have been allowed to leave.

Only Larke and the Lady walked with them, but other Aluiens looked up from their work to smile or wave. Ari smiled and waved back. As they crossed to the entrance, he worked to take in the beauty of the central chamber one more time. The roof of the cavern soared so high overhead, it would be cloaked in darkness if the cave were lit by torches. The Aluiens needed no torches, however, their glowing designs of light filling the space with beauty and wonder.

They reached the blank wall of the hidden entrance and the Lady gestured. In a swirl of vanishing runes, the stone drew back, revealing a mundane and snow-choked cave beyond. Though it was morning outside, the glimpse of sky Ari caught through the cave entrance was gray and drab. The world beyond the Aluiens' layer seemed frozen, colorless and devoid of life.

"Safe journey to you Cadwel, Aridian," the Lady said.

"Thank you, my lady," Ari answered with a bow, speaking in Ancient Wheylian.

60

The Lady smiled. "Why, what a fine accent you're developing."

Larke chuckled.

Ari was disconcerted, unsure now if he got it right or not.

Sir Cadwel raised his eyebrows, but added his own bow. "Thank you for your patience with a slow-thinking fumble-fingered old knight."

"Nonsense." The Lady patted him on the arm. "You're a very apt pupil."

Larke snorted. Sir Cadwel glowered at the bard, which only broadened Larke's smile.

Ari decided he'd better intervene before the two fell to bickering. "Where are Stew and Goldwin?"

"At the base of the trail, waiting, as is your packhorse," Larke said. "Retrieved to help our mighty friend uphold his vow."

"I promised the stableboy a silver," Sir Cadwel said. "And my armor best not have a scratch on it."

"It's pristine, I assure you, but the silver will have to wait for another day. I'm sure the honor of helping so vaulted a knight is all the payment the boy needs."

Sir Cadwel favored Larke with another scowl. He bowed to the Lady again, turning to stride out into the cave.

Ari gave a hasty wave and followed. "Bye, Larke, goodbye, my lady." He stepped back into the mortal world.

"Safe journey, Ari." Larke's voice drifted after him.

Ari turned, meaning to give them one last smile, but the cave wall had already solidified behind him. Larke, the Lady and the glowing home of the Aluiens were gone. There was nothing but hard stone and the bitter cold of the mountains. Ari sighed, following Sir Cadwel's footprints out of the cave.

Chapter 6

Ari was right about the possibility of the snow slowing their journey, especially on the small back roads Sir Cadwel insisted they travel. Heavy drifts weighed down the horses' legs. Stew and Goldwin took turns going first, the deep snow taxing even to them. The old packhorse was better off, never having to break the trail, but in the evenings Ari had to spend a considerable amount of time rubbing all three down to remove the hard clumps of snow from their legs.

He was a little sad they wouldn't be stopping at his uncle's inn on the way back. Even though he now knew he wasn't truly their nephew, they still felt like family to him and the inn felt like home. When they'd visited on the way south, Ari's older cousin's wife had been near term with their first baby. Ari had thought he'd be able to meet the infant on the way back. Not to mention, he wouldn't have minded letting them all congratulate him on winning the fall tourney.

Sir Cadwel had vowed to spend as little time with other people as possible, however, and the knight took vows very seriously. So they traveled bleak back roads that wouldn't be used again until spring. At least they didn't have to stop early each day due to the light. As Sir Cadwel was an Aluien and Ari was enhanced by them, both could see in the dark.

In the evenings, Ari always retired before Sir Cadwel, able to see or not. One of the Aluien abilities that didn't seem to extend to Ari was their complete lack of the need for sleep. Ari would climb into his tent, the knight sitting in his, his eyes scouring the pages of a small book of incantations the Lady had given him. Even though Ari could see in the dark, it still struck him as wrong for someone to read in it. Although, if he were allowed to see the wonders contained in the little blue volume, he wouldn't be able to put it down either. The one time he'd caught a glimpse, he could see it wasn't written in any language he knew.

One such night, as Ari lay inside his tent, eyes drifting closed, he was shocked out of somnolence by an explosive curse. A second followed, and a third, though Sir Cadwel's voice modulated from startled to angry. Tangling himself in his blankets in haste, Ari scuttled out of his tent into the snow.

Jumping to his feet, he found Sir Cadwel in the process of overturning the tent he used, which was on fire. The stakes holding it in place popped free with a heave of the knight's muscles. Ari rushed to help as Sir Cadwel took one corner, twisting the burning side into the snow.

Glancing at the knight, who nodded, Ari helped him flip the tent back over. He could hear Sir Cadwel's possessions sliding around inside as they righted it, revealing a hole burned through the roof. As soon as it was upright, the knight ducked in, pulling out the Lady's book. He examined it carefully, but it appeared undamaged to Ari.

"What--" Ari started to ask.

"Not a word," Sir Cadwel growled.

"But--"

The knight shot him a stifling scowl. "It's not a point of discussion."

Ari took in the hard line of Sir Cadwel's mouth, downturned under his drooping gray mustache. He also noticed the way the knight was grinding his teeth, although he held the small book carefully, his hands unclenched. "So, I'll go back to sleep?"

"You will," Sir Cadwel said.

Ari stared at him, willing the knight to tell him why his tent had caught on fire. Their campfire was a barely glowing smudge in the snow. It didn't look like it could have shot a big enough ember at the knight's tent to ignite it. Sir Cadwel met Ari's gaze with a look of pure obstinacy. Ari shrugged, turning to enter his tent.

"And not a word about this to that bard," Sir Cadwel said, going inside his own tent.

Ari mastered the urge to snap back that he couldn't well say anything since he had no idea what had happened and crawled into his blankets.

He wasn't very surprised, early the next morning, to be awakened by another string of curses. Climbing out of his tent with more decorum this time, he sleepily noted the hole in Sir Cadwel's tent was impressively well-mended. There was still a blackened ring, but the missing material had somehow reformed.

Rubbing his eyes, Ari also noticed that the tent was sunk in a slushy pit, revealing the hard-packed snow on which they camped to be knee high. Shaking his head, Ari turned to rekindle the fire. Aluien imperviousness aside, they would need to dry Sir Cadwel's things before they moved on. Plus, it was probably better not to gawk at the knight in his moment of misfortune. It would only make him angrier.

"I thought Aluiens didn't really get cold," Ari said once the cursing behind him stopped. Warmth was Ari's best guess at Sir Cadwel's goal in his recent experiments.

"Cold is cold," the knight muttered.

Ari nodded, pleased he'd guessed correctly, and they set about putting Sir Cadwel's possessions right.

The remainder of their journey was uneventful, and it was with relief and joy that Ari crawled from his tent the morning of the day they were to reach Sorga. He found Sir Cadwel already up, the horses saddled and everything stowed but the tent Ari had slept in. The knight was wearing his heavy fur cloak, the hood turned up, and pulling on thick winter gloves. Ari worried something might be wrong with Sir Cadwel if he needed to get warm so badly, until he recalled the similar way Larke had dressed the few times he snuck into the capital.

"The cloak helps?" Ari asked, having always wondered at Larke's choice of a heavy cloak inside the city, knowing it had something to do with hiding his magic, but not exactly what. While he waited hopefully for an answer, Ari took down his tent.

"Less skin, less glow," Sir Cadwel said, tugging his second glove on.

"You mean, it's an easier incantation?" Ari asked, thinking perhaps Sir Cadwel would be less rigid in his secrets than the average Aluien. During the silence that followed, Ari finished packing up. Then, with nothing left to do, he turned to face Sir Cadwel, upset the knight hadn't even bothered to answer.

Standing there in the snow, it seemed to Ari there was a great space between them. It hurt him that Sir Cadwel was learning so many new things in preparation for taking up a life Ari couldn't know. The knight was his teacher and mentor, yet he wouldn't instruct Ari in this. He didn't even seem to want to talk about it, or let Ari see his precious book. Emptiness loomed in the silence between them, a gap Ari wasn't allowed to cross.

Sir Cadwel regarded him with narrowed eyes and shook his head. Ari felt a stab of betrayal, but the knight opened his mouth to speak.

"No, lad, the same incantation, just easier." He frowned. "I have to press the magic outward, at everyone around me."

Ari could tell by the deep lines creasing Sir Cadwel's forehead that the knight struggled to find the right words.

"It's the difference between having to press something narrow into your opponent's gut, like a dueling blade, and trying to force the head of a mace in there. Just as it takes a lot more force to press something as wide as a mace into someone's innards, the larger the image I must press into people's minds to cover the reality of me glowing, the more power it takes to get it there."

Ari nodded, trying to hide his surprise, his disquiet diminished. He'd despaired of any answer, let alone so elaborate a one. He could hardly recall another time Sir Cadwel had said so much at once.

"Perhaps we should indeed have stopped to see your family," the knight continued. He smoothed his mustache. "I could have practiced on them. Fewer people at the inn than the keep."

Sir Cadwel ran his fingers over his mustache again and tugged down the hood of his cloak. He turned to Goldwin, adjusting the girth on the destrier's saddle. Goldwin shook himself, pawing at the snow, and Ari realized what was going on. Sir Cadwel, the mightiest knight in the realm, was nervous.

"I haven't seen a flicker of a glow this whole trip," Ari said, uncertain how to reassure his mentor.

"I appreciate that, lad," Sir Cadwel said. He pulled himself up into Goldwin's saddle. "Hand me the packhorse's reins."

"You?" Ari asked, surprised. Sir Cadwel was returning home. He always rode in looking triumphant. His hounds, Canid and Raven, would run out to greet him, the people of the keep cheering for their master. Ari was the one who led the packhorse.

"Me," Sir Cadwel said firmly.

Ari knew it wasn't wise to argue with that tone, so he did as he was told. He mounted Stew, twisting to look at the knight.

"Lead the way, lad."

Feeing decidedly odd about it, Ari did as he was told. He pulled out some hard travel bread to eat as he rode, but it did little to settle his stomach. Sir Cadwel wasn't the only one who was nervous.

They sighted Sorga before the winter sun reached its daily zenith. From out on the plain, the soaring towers looked small against the backdrop of the mighty northern range. The blue and white banners of Sorga fluttered in the breeze, but it was much too far to really discern the colors or see the brown hawk adorning them. In fact, Ari could barely make out the outer wall where it spanned the narrow gap between two outstretched arms of the mountain.

The tall peaks behind and the mountainous arms surrounding it made Sorga nearly impenetrable. The only way to the keep was through a pass between the mountain ridges, and that pass was blocked by an outer and inner wall. The keep was built half outside the mountain and half in, the deeper rooms carved from the range itself.

Not long Ari sighted the keep, the longsighted guards atop the outer wall must have seen them, for they waved the signal flags, alerting those atop the inner wall that someone approached. As they drew closer, Ari could tell the moment when the guards recognized who they were, for they raised a second flag, signaling the return of the lords of the keep. Ari smiled, picturing the excitement inside.

The wide gate in the outer wall was open, as the realm was at peace. Ari and Sir Cadwel rode under the thick fortification, coming out into the broad empty space between the outer and inner battlements. The killing zone, meant to trap enemies while they were annihilated. The inner gate was shut, a sign of Sir Cadwel's increased vigilance after the attack on Sorga that spring. It swung open as they neared. Through it, Ari could see people gathering on the keep's steps.

If anyone thought it odd that Ari rode in first, it didn't show. Stew, always one to show off, pranced up to the steps, his head held high. Stew loved Ari being the center of attention much more than Ari did.

Ari's eyes roamed over the people on the steps. Chief Steward Natan was there, resplendent in black. Ari's best friend and valet, Peine, was there, almost seeming to bounce on his toes in excitement. Ispiria's great grandmother, Lady Enra, stood glowering on the wide top step. Ari turned his head this way and that, keeping a smile firmly in place. Where was Ispiria?

"Ari," he heard her cry. She burst from the maw of the keep's doublewide doors in a flurry of creamy skin and red hair. A distraught maid chased after her, waving a brush. Ispiria

69

flung herself down the steps, dodging around the assembled castle folk. Ari barely dismounted in time to catch her as she launched herself from the bottom step and into his arms, covering his face with kisses.

"You're finally home," she said, squeezing herself against him.

He buried his face in her bright red curls, hugging her as hard as he dared, happy to finally have her in his arms again. His throat closed, cutting into his ability to breathe properly. He squeezed his eyes shut and kissed her hair.

"Ispiria," Lady Enra snapped. Her voice was worn and thin, but it rasped down the steps well enough, piercing Ari's joy.

The people of the keep murmured. Ari was sure he heard more than one chuckle. Against his chest, he felt Ispiria wrinkle her face into a grimace. She pulled back and he forced himself to open his arms.

As soon as she stepped back, Ari was assailed by her outfit. No longer did she wear the high-waisted high-cut dress of a girl. This dress, while still in her favorite shade of green, was a dress like Princess Siara always wore. One that squeezed her middle and placed certain other parts of her anatomy prominently in his view. Ari fought against the heat crawling up his neck. He hadn't comprehended that, once she was sixteen, Ispiria would start dressing like that, even though he knew it was one of the differences between being a woman and a girl.

"What I meant was, well met, Lord Aridian," she said, composing her face into a look of mild boredom, though her eyes still danced. "It is both my duty and honor to welcome you home."

Ari raised his eyebrows, trying not to gape at her. Beside him, Sir Cadwel dismounted. Pages stepped up to lead the horses away. Distractedly, Ari gave Stew a pat, murmuring a thank you for the smooth journey.

Flashing Ari a smile, Ispiria whirled away, skipping across the space separating her from Sir Cadwel. A glance toward the castle showed most people looking amused. Natan, who usually had the honor of greeting them first when they returned from a journey, was smiling indulgently, but Peine looked a bit affronted. Peine, though two years younger than Ari, was a stickler for manners and protocol.

"Well met, Great Uncle Cadwel," Ispiria said, curtsying. She whirled back. "Ari, I forgot to curtsy to you."

Ispiria curtsying in that dress was almost more than he could take, so Ari was very glad Canid and Raven chose that moment to come shambling down the steps from the keep. People pressed against each other, moving to make room for the old dogs to pass. The giant shaggy gray hounds skidded in the slippery courtyard, their balance almost as worn as their hearing. When they neared Sir Cadwel, instead of running in circles about him and Goldwin as usual, they stopped. Canid raised his muzzle, sniffing. Raven cocked his head to one side, looking confused. Ari held his breath, suddenly more worried about Sir Cadwel's secret than Ispiria's new attire.

"Canid, Raven," Sir Cadwel said, holding out his hands.

As if the sound of his voice released them, they shuffled forward, more eager than ever. Butting up against Sir Cadwel's outstretched palms, they angled their heads to be scratched. A smile pulled at the corners of the knight's mouth.

"For a moment, I thought something was terribly wrong with the world," Natan said, coming down the steps. Peine followed him like a shadow and Ari recalled his friend was supposed to be learning to do Natan's job. "Lord Aridian rode

71

in first, Ispiria almost acted as a proper lady, and those great beasts of yours didn't seem to know you."

Sir Cadwel chuckled.

Ari hoped Natan and Peine didn't hear the strain in the sound.

"They didn't come out when the gate opened," Sir Cadwel said, looking down at them in worry. Canid sank to the cobblestones at his feet, Raven sitting by his side.

"Their hearing's gotten worse while you were away." Natan's happy expression became forced. "Truth be told, old friend, I wasn't sure they would last until your return. It frets them more and more to have you gone, the older they get."

Sir Cadwel grunted in reply.

Ari looked away, not wanting to think about Sir Cadwel losing the hounds. It seemed like the knight's entire life was littered by the funeral pyres of those he loved. Ispiria slipped up beside Ari, sliding her warm hand into his cold one, her eyes on the dogs, too. A glance at Peine's pale Wheylian face, framed in neatly trimmed black hair, told Ari that Ispiria wasn't doing a very good job of acting like a lady, not that Ari cared.

"So you have returned to us, my lords." Natan's loud voice cut through the murmuring of the castle folk, who were starting to fidget in the damp cold. "And, as word from the king precedes you, we already know you return triumphant."

A cheer erupted from the people. It took Ari a moment to realize it was for him. Ispiria popped up on her tiptoes, kissing him on the cheek.

"I've taken the liberty of ordering a feast, my lords," Natan continued, bowing almost as elaborately as Larke would. "A feast to honor Lord Aridian, winner of the king's fall tourney two years in a row."

The cheering amplified.

"Any announcements?" Natan said to Sir Cadwel, lowering his voice.

The knight shook his head, glancing at Ari. Natan revealed a slight moment of surprise that Sir Cadwel would consult with anyone before he turned his gaze on Ari as well.

"Lord Aridian?" Natan asked.

"Uh, no, no announcements, thank you," Ari said. He saw Peine roll his eyes and knew he was in for another lecture on how to sound lordly. Ari had been raised a commoner. As his valet, Peine felt it was his special obligation to turn Ari into a proper heir to a dukedom.

"Let us all see to our duties," Natan said, raising his voice to the assemblage. "The masters of Sorga are returned. Lord Aridian is victorious. We shall feast at dusk."

There was more cheering, becoming ragged as people turned and went into the keep, breaking off into smaller groups. There was jostling and happy chatter, and Ari smiled. It was good to be back in the relaxed atmosphere of Sorga. It was more comfortable than the stuffy ways of the capital or the ethereal hidden realm of the Aluiens. Sorga was a place where he could feel at home.

"To the study?" Natan asked Sir Cadwel and Ari. The knight nodded. He nudged Canid with his foot. The old dog woke from his doze, looking around as if confused, but he got up and trotted after Sir Cadwel and Natan, Raven falling in step beside him.

Before Ari and Peine could excuse themselves from Ispiria, two maids came trundling toward them, blocking their way. Moving to stand beside Ari, Peine's comely face formed a scowl. The younger maid, the one clutching Ispiria's silver hairbrush, dimpled at Peine and blushed.

"Lady Ispiria." It was the older who spoke. Ari recognized her as Lady Enra's personal handmaiden. She bore a very determined look. "Your great grandmother bids you return to your suite at once to finish readying for the feast."

Ispiria scrunched up her nose, but she nodded. "I know." She turned to Ari. A mischievous look flittered across her face and she stood up straighter, tossing her head to throw her hair back. "Do you like my new dress, Lord Aridian?"

"Ah," Ari stammered. He tried to force himself to keep his eyes on her face.

"Good," she said, grinning. "I'm glad to hear it, because now that I'm all grown up, I have a whole wardrobe full of them. In my own rooms."

Ari had no idea what to say to that. He knew, in addition to new dresses, Ispiria got her own suite once she turned sixteen, no longer having to stay with her great grandmother. He also knew that new suite was the afore unoccupied set of rooms next to his. He couldn't think of anything to say about it, though. At least, not in front of everyone.

Ispiria laughed, turning and gesturing to the glowering maid to lead the way. The stout woman shot Ari an extra scowl. He had no doubt the whole conversation, brief though it was, would be immediately repeated to Ispiria's great grandmother.

"We're going to have to do something about that," Peine said, sighing.

Ari didn't know if he meant Ispiria's behavior, or her new dress, or the maid's evil look, and he wasn't sure he wanted to ask.

"Congratulations on winning the tourney, Ari," Peine continued. "I wish I could have seen it. We all knew you would win. You wouldn't believe how boring it's been around here. Natan may complain that Sir Cadwel always leaves him to take

74

care of everything, but really, the place pretty much runs itself. We should go in. It doesn't do to keep Sir Cadwel waiting."

Ari nodded, wondering if he should check on Stew. The chestnut destrier was nowhere to be seen, but Ari was sure he was getting a well-deserved rub down and some warm oats. Maybe even some dried apples. Ari would have to go out later to make sure of the apple part. Bringing his gaze back from roaming the snowy courtyard, Ari trotted up the steps, which were swept relatively clear, Peine half a step behind him.

Chapter 7

Ari and Peine entered the vaulted foyer, two guards inside swinging the double doors closed, shutting out the cold. The keep was well-lit with flickering torches, spreading a warm glow over the gray stone. Ari smiled, pleased to be home. He was looking forward to a brief update from Natan on the recent doings of the keep, then a hot bath, clean clothes and a feast with the people of Sorga, the place he now called home.

Ari led the way into Sir Cadwel's study, where the knight and Natan waited, Peine closing the door behind them. Natan had already poured thick straw-colored liquor into delicate cordial glasses. Sir Cadwel held one where he stood beside the crackling fireplace, Canid and Raven sprawled at his feet. Reclining on one of the heavy leather couches with a glass of his own, Natan gestured to a tray on the table. Appropriating their drinks, Ari and Peine sat opposite the chief steward.

"A toast to Lord Aridian's success," Natan said, raising his glass.

They all followed suit, although Ari wasn't sure if he should raise his glass and drink, or stay still while everyone else toasted him. He would have to ask Peine later. Taking a sip, Ari was pleased at the warmth that coursed from his throat downward. Less pervious to extreme temperatures or not, he had to agree with Sir Cadwel. Cold was still cold, and being warmer was comforting.

"So." Natan set his empty glass down on the table. "What news from the south? When you said you would be slow to return, I hadn't imagined you meant quite this slow. Why, may I ask, did it take you three times as long as usual to return from the capital?"

"Snow," Sir Cadwel said.

Natan's mouth pulled into a frown, marring his overly handsome face. "Snow?" he said, annoyance in his tone. "That's your answer? I suppose you were off on some secret mission for the king, like last winter. You've undoubtedly been sworn to secrecy to keep unworthy and irresponsible lesser men like myself from knowledge beyond our ken. I was a knight in the king's service, you will recall. Nor was it my loyalty to the crown that was ever questioned."

"Knowledge of your former standing is well-ingrained in my mind," Sir Cadwel said. "But a vow is sacrosanct."

"Yes, so you always say." Natan shrugged, clearly trying to set aside his pique.

Ari wondered how much of it was really for Sir Cadwel. It wasn't Sir Cadwel's fault Natan had been stripped of his knighthood for overindulging in his more licentious appetites. It seemed to continually chafe Natan to be stuck in their remote northern corner of the kingdom, but Ari rather thought the ousted knight was lucky anyone would take him in. Ari took another sip of his drink, noticing Peine's was already gone.

"So, the sum of your news is that Lord Aridian is once again victorious?" Natan said with forced cheer. "If that's all, we had a b--"

"It isn't all."

The strain in the knight's tone caused Natan to raise his eyebrows. Ari gulped the rest of his drink, his eyes watering as it burned down his throat.

"As of Midwinter's Day, I'm abdicating Sorga to Lord Aridian. I'll be making the announcement at the feast on Midwinter's Eve."

Peine gasped.

"You're what?" Natan said. "I know you've always done everything you could not to be the Duke of Sorga, but this is taking guilt too far, Cadwel."

"I was never meant to be duke." Sir Cadwel slammed the little cordial glass down on the mantel, liquid sloshing out. Ari was surprised the stem didn't break. "It was my brother's right, his honor and his responsibility."

"But you've been duke in all but name for twenty-five years," Natan said. "Why do you work so hard to avoid the title? No one thinks you let your family die on purpose so that you could rule Sorga, if that's what you're worried about."

Sir Cadwel leveled a scowl on Natan that made Ari flinch. Beside him, Peine huddled back into the sofa. Ari hoped the rest of the keep wouldn't be this upset by Sir Cadwel's decision, because it couldn't be unmade. The knight swore an oath. Ari hadn't expected it to happen so soon, though. He wasn't even seventeen yet, the age at which a man could become a knight, or become a lord without a regent.

"I'm not old enough," Ari said into the strained silence.

"Ennentine and I discussed it." Sir Cadwel's scowl lightened as he turned to Ari. "As you're a foundling, we have no accurate information about the time of your birth. We know only that you were born before the day you were left at the inn, the day you celebrate as your birthday. Therefore, he's declared you to have reached your majority when the new year begins on Midwinter's Day, as it is your seventeenth year."

"You think of everything," Natan muttered.

"I do, and I have a document declaring it, should any take exception, sealed by the king. It serves Ennentine's goals as well, for he wishes a new king's champion at the conclusion of the spring tourney, which also takes place before the day Ari celebrates as that of his birth."

Ari suspected, based on a dream he'd had in the spring, that the Lady would know the real day of his birth. If he'd known Sir Cadwel's plans, he might have mustered up the courage to confront her about it before they left the caves. He wondered if Sir Cadwel had known as much and factored it into his decision not to warn Ari, for Ari was sure he really hadn't been born until the beginning of the summer, as his uncle and aunt always said.

"You're resigning as king's champion as well?" Natan's voice was high with disbelief. "Is the boy even ready yet? He's won two tourneys, but the competition will be fierce in the tourney held to replace you. It isn't like you to leave something this important to chance. What aren't you saying, Cadwel?"

Ari winced at the honest worry in Natan's tone. The well suppressed inkling of self-doubt Ari kept hidden deep in his gut sprang to life as a fully formed fear at the chief steward's words. What if, indeed, Ari didn't win the tourney held to replace Sir Cadwel as king's champion? True, Ennentine could hold a new tourney for the spot the following fall, but Ari would lose the faith he'd built with both the monarchy and the people.

"I have every confidence in Ari's ability to win the spring tourney, no matter if every knight in the realm rides in to compete for my place. I'm giving up fighting to dedicate myself to my studies." Sir Cadwel made a sweeping gesture, taking in the room. All around them, where once stuffed trophies and battered weapons had decorated the walls, stood shelves full of books and scrolls of all shapes and sizes. "The choice is already made. I'm concerned with a different legacy now."

"Be that as it may, this really isn't the time for it," Natan said. "As I tried to tell you, we've had a bird from the capital. Not only the one announcing Lord Aridian's feats, but another, with much more dire news."

He gestured to Peine, who rose, pulling a small tightly rolled bit of parchment from his doublet. He held it out to Sir Cadwel.

"Give it to Ari," Sir Cadwel said.

Natan sighed, nodding to Peine. The chief steward poured himself another drink, swallowing it in one gulp. Peine gave Ari the scroll and sat back down. It was of the miniscule type that was strapped to messenger pigeons. It took Ari a moment to decipher the cramped writing.

"Siara's older cousins are dead," Ari gasped out, looking up. "She is now the next in line for the throne." Siara's warning filled his mind. Her grandfather, her aunt and now her two cousins. She was right. That was too many people for them all to be accidents.

"How?" Sir Cadwel said, his scowl returning in full force.

"It doesn't say," Natan said while Ari reread the brief lines, seeking any additional information. "They'd already sent the hawk we lent them with news of Ari's victory. This came via one of the king's pigeons. You know they can only carry short notes. I'm sure a more involved report will arrive by courier, eventually. Of course, we all know the snow is very thick out there, so it could be ages. Probably take him three times as long to get here as usual."

"Why don't we give the king some Sorga Hawks?" Peine asked.

Sir Cadwel ignored the question, his face thoughtful as he tapped one finger on the mantel. When Peine glanced at Ari, he shook his head. Few knew it, but the Sorga Hawks were actually a sentient race, though Ari didn't know how to speak to them. They served the lord of Sorga willingly. One might volunteer to spend some time in the capital, waiting to bring back an important message, but you couldn't order them to leave their home and live there.

"Siara can't leave Parrentine and the people of Wheylia will never take a foreign raised princess as their queen," Sir Cadwel said. "Queen Reudi's lack of an heir won't affect Lggothland."

"And what if whoever takes the throne after Queen Reudi isn't as amiable to us as she is?" Natan asked. "I'm telling you, Cadwel, now is not the time for you to step down."

"Queen Reudi is known to be in good health," Sir Cadwel said. "I'm sure Wheylia will work out its succession troubles long before she expires, giving us plenty of time to build ties with the future queen." Sir Cadwel pulled on his mustache. "In fact, the only way Lggothland could be pulled into this is if Princess Siara has a daughter before Queen Reudi is forced to select a new heir from one of the other houses. The prince and princess have only recently begun speaking to each other with cordiality. It will be ages before Siara is with child."

"Uh," Ari said, unsure if there was any way to impart his news without revealing something Siara obviously wanted kept secret. Of course, for all he knew, it wasn't a secret anymore and word hadn't reached Sorga yet. How long, after all, could

Siara hope to hide something like that? "Princess Siara is with child. She expects her baby in the spring."

"What?" Sir Cadwel's voice was loud enough to wake Canid and Raven.

Ari flinched. "She didn't want anyone to know."

"I am not anyone," Sir Cadwel roared. "Did it occur to you such important news might figure highly into my plans?"

"Now who doesn't like to have secrets kept from him?" Natan muttered.

Sir Cadwel either didn't hear Natan or, Ari suspected, chose to pretend he didn't. The knight's eyes stayed locked on Ari. "You best hope it isn't a female babe, boy, because I renounced my place as king's champion. You'll be the one forced to take Princess Siara's daughter away come spring, or Lggothland and Wheylia will surely go to war."

Ari nodded, glumly certain now that Siara's premonition would come true, though he saw no point in antagonizing Sir Cadwel by mentioning it, given the knight's dislike of mysterious premonitions. Sir Cadwel glared at him from where he stood by the fire, absently patting Canid on the head. Raven rolled over and went back to sleep.

"Well," Natan drawled, standing. "If we really are done exchanging news, there are some things I should see to, and you two, if you don't mind me saying, could both use a bath." He turned to face Ari. "Lord Aridian, let me be the first to congratulate you on you upcoming ascension, and may I say, it is not any lack of faith in you that spurred my incredulousness. I was merely taken by surprise."

"Ah, thank you," Ari said, wondering why they all had to use words he didn't know when they were saying important things.

"Speaking of which," Sir Cadwel said, his voice less heavy with anger. "I'd appreciate it if, in the few days between now and Midwinter's Day, you act as though Ari is already duke. Any decisions you would bring to me, take to Ari instead. He needs the practice."

"Yes, my lord," Natan said, bowing. "Lord Aridian." He bowed to Ari as well before strolling from the room.

"Canid, Raven," Sir Cadwel said, nudging Raven with one foot. The knight left, giving Ari a parting glare. Shaking out their limbs, the two giant hounds followed.

"Well," Peine said. Ari didn't know if his friend was imitating Natan on purpose or if Peine was picking up the chief steward's habits after shadowing him for months. "I guess you're going to be duke now."

"I guess so." Ari scrubbed his hands over his face. He realized his head was pounding. He wondered how long Sir Cadwel would stay angry with him. His tenure as duke didn't seem to be starting very well.

"You'll need new clothes," Peine said, a thoughtful look on his face.

Ari sighed.

Peine turned to him. "Well, you will. You'll want to wear something special when Sir Cadwel makes you duke. I don't even know if there's enough time left to get anything ready. It's an embarrassment to me if you don't look good, you know. I haven't even figured out what to have you wear when you propose to Ispiria. Are you going to do that before or after Sir Cadwel makes you duke?" Peine seemed unaware every word he uttered was tying Ari's guts into a tighter knot of worry. "I thought you would ask her Midwinter's Eve, but now that Sir Cadwel's making his announcement, maybe you should wait until after you take over on Midwinter's Day. At least you don't have to worry about her saying no, if the way she acted outside today is any indication. You're really going to have to talk to her about that, Ari. She does not act like a proper duchess."

Ari leaned back into the worn leather and closed his eyes, letting Peine's chatter wash over him. Was it only an hour ago he'd thought his life would return to happy normalcy once he was home? Well, that idea had flown away on hawk's wings. He suppressed a second sigh.

Chapter 8

The hawk Ari sent with Larke's message to Mirimel returned with nothing more than a thank you and standard seasonal pleasantries, to Ari's mild annoyance. As much as he knew it was none of his concern, he had to admit a certain curiosity as to the nature of the correspondence between bard and hawk guardian. He was tempted to write back, offering to take a message in return, but his conscience wouldn't permit him to suggest he had a sure way of contacting Larke. Thwarted, Ari was forced to put his suppositions aside, losing them in the bustle of readying for the midwinter celebration.

Midwinter's Eve, when it finally arrived, was a blur to Ari. Sir Cadwel made his announcement to a hall stunned into silence. Then the cheering began, and the toasts, which Peine said Ari was to drink to. After the first seven or so, Ari wasn't really sure what much else happened that evening.

He didn't wake until nearly noon the following day, his first day as duke of Sorga. He felt fine, much to Peine's astonishment. Waving away his friend's assistance, Ari dressed, entering the sitting room to find a table full of food waiting for him.

"Is there porridge?" Ari asked, seating himself. He was rather hungry.

"It's already lunchtime," Peine said, sitting across from him.

Ari always insisted that Peine eat with him, not stand along the wall like a servant at the king's castle. Ari selected some fresh bread, sharp white cheese and several pieces of dried fruit.

"You eat like a girl," Peine said. "If you don't eat enough meat, you'll lose your strength."

Ari raised an eyebrow at this and, as usual, ignored Peine's mothering. He broke open the still warm loaf of bread, slicing off a large slab of cheese to fold into it.

"Have you thought about how you'll make things up to Ispiria?" Peine piled three slices of last night's roast onto his plate, almost defiantly.

"Make up to Ispiria?" Ari frowned, searching back through his foggy memory.

"You don't remember?"

Ari shook his head, the amused glint in Peine's eyes making him uneasy.

"Right before we carried you up here, you got up on the head table and yelled across the room that you were the duke now and you were going to marry her, no matter what anyone said. It was an order, you said, and everyone had to obey. Then you toppled over. You broke one of the chairs. You really don't remember? I'm going to have to keep better track of how much you drink."

"I did what?" Ari set his food down, suddenly not at all hungry. "What did she do?"

"She ran out of the room. I didn't get a good look at her face. I was busy making sure you hadn't broken anything. Aside from furniture."

Ari jumped up. He had to make things right. He ran to his desk drawer, fumbling with the secret compartment where he kept Ispiria's betrothal gift. He pulled it out, still wrapped in the soft cloth Larke had given it to him in. Ari raced from the room, ignoring Peine as his friend called after him.

Ispiria's rooms were right next to his, across from Sir Cadwel's, so Ari didn't have any time to think of what he was going to say before he found himself pounding on her door, calling her name. Fragments of all of the different speeches he'd rehearsed swam around in his mind, colliding with broken memories of what Peine described him doing the evening before.

The door swung open. Ari was surprised to see Ispiria there, not a maid. She was wearing one of her new dresses, and a scowl. "What do you want, Ari? Have you come to carry out your order that I marry you?"

"No, I'm sorry," he said, so distraught he wasn't even tempted to look anywhere but in her eyes. "I meant your great grandmother, not you," he clarified, recalling his befuddled notion of ordering her great grandmother to approve of their marriage now that he was duke.

"You want to marry my great grandmother? Well, you can go right ahead."

She moved to slam the door. Ari put out a hand, stopping her. He winced when her eyes went wide at how easily he accomplished it. She pushed harder, but he didn't let the door move. "You know that's not what I mean. May I please come in? I have something for you."

She glared at him for a moment. He made his face as pleading as he knew how. She had to let him in. They'd waited too long for this.

"Oh, alright." She backed into the room. "But my ladies are staying. After last night, I don't know how trustworthy you are."

She turned, moving to sit primly in one of the chairs, obviously not wanting to share the couch with him. Ari sat on the corner of it, as close to her as he could get, their knees almost touching. He held out the wrapped bundle.

"I have something for you," he repeated. He willed her to relent enough to take it. He was sure one look at the pendant Larke had carved for her, secretly imbued with spells to protect her mind from evil Empty Ones' magic, would thaw her heart. It was a delicate wildflower, carved from luminous green stone. Larke had made it for Ari that spring, in preparation for this very moment.

"What is it?" she asked.

He could see she wanted to take it. Ispiria loved presents. "It's a betrothal gift," he said, his voice a little shaky.

"Oh really?"

Ari winced at how much anger she managed to put into that question. He slid from the chair onto his knees, aware that her maids glanced nervously at each other as he did so. He was improperly close to Ispiria now, he knew, but he hoped they wouldn't ruin things by demanding he return to his seat. Reaching out, he took Ispiria's hand, placing the bundle into it and wrapping her fingers closed around it, holding them there, her hand cupped in both of his. She stared at him with wide green eyes.

"Ispiria." He kept his voice low and intense, so it wouldn't come out as shaky as he felt. "You must be aware that I've loved you from the very first moment I saw you. From before I knew your name or who you were. From the first glimpse I had of your face. When you look at me, when you smile at me or . . . or kiss me, those are the only moments when I am ever really and truly happy." Squeezing her hand, he willed her to acknowledge his sincerity, to not be too angry with him to say yes. "Please, please forgive me and say you will be my wife. Please make my whole existence that happy, and I promise I'll work every day to make last night up to you and to make you as happy as you make me."

She stared at him, her luminous eyes round, and burst into tears.

"I'm sorry," he said, anguished. "I didn't mean to do it wrong. I'm sorry."

Wrenching her hand from his, she flung herself into his arms, knocking him backward against the couch. He realized she was laughing, even though she was crying, and then her lips were on his and her hands, one still clenched around the pendant, were tangled in his hair and Ari's whole world was complete.

Her maids rushed forward, their indignant exclamations made less effective by happy overtones. Not happy enough to let him keep kissing her, he resentfully realized as they all but picked Ispiria up and put her back in her chair. Her face was covered with tears but she was smiling wider than he'd ever seen her smile before.

"Is that a yes?" he asked, retaking his seat on the corner of the couch.

"Oh Ari. All that reading Uncle Cadwel makes you do must be paying off. I never thought you could say anything so wonderful."

"Uh, but is your answer yes?" he repeated, starting to feel a tinge of concern at her lack of clarification.

"Of course it's a yes. How could it not be a yes?" Looking down, she seemed to realize she still held his gift. She pulled back the cloth, one of the ones Larke used to clean his lute, revealing a delicate green flower on a silver chain. "It's beautiful. Put it on me." She held it up.

Ari would have been happy to, but her maids rushed forward to do it.

"I love it," Ispiria said, touching the pendant. "I'll never take it off."

Ari didn't stop smiling, but her words cast a shadow over his happiness, bringing back thoughts of how Larke had told him to save the necklace to be a betrothal gift for that very reason, so Ispiria would never take it off. As long as there were Empty Ones, as long as Ari was the guardian of the strange little stone the Empty Ones had tried so hard to procure that spring, Ispiria would always be in danger. Ari had no idea what to do about that.

Pressing that thought away, he reached out for her hand. "I really am sorry about last night. I promise I'll never drink again."

"You don't have to promise that." She laughed. "Just don't turn into such a great big oaf next time."

"Is everyone very angry with me?"

"Angry? I shouldn't think so. I can't say they won't laugh at you, though, and tease you." She tilted her chin up at a prim angle. "And I can't say I don't think it's what you deserve." Her smile returned, driving away the haughty look she'd affected. "But I can say I love you, Lord Aridian of Sorga. Forever and always, with all my heart."

Chapter 9

It took Ari the rest of the season to live down his Midwinter's Eve antics, even though he didn't drink again. For a while, he thought he would be teased every evening, duke or no, but when spring started to stir the land, the minds of the castle folk moved to new thoughts. For one thing, a pigeon arrived from the capital announcing Princess Siara's pregnancy, earning Ari a dark glare from Sir Cadwel at the reminder of his secrecy. The rest of Sorga, and probably the kingdom, was ecstatic over the news of the princess's condition. Speculation on the sex of the babe was rampant, but Ari was glumly sure it would be a girl.

Most exciting to those in Sorga, however, were the preparations for Ispiria's trip to the capital. As she was sixteen now, her great grandmother deemed it time for Ispiria to be introduced into society. Usually, this would be when she met a man to take her as his wife, but Ari had rather strategically rendered that function of the journey irrelevant. He was a little smug about that.

He was also a little worried. He knew Ispiria loved him very much. She said so quite often. There were lots of people in the capital, though. Lots of men. Looking around Sorga, it wasn't as if Ispiria had much to choose from. What if she only liked him because she didn't realize how many other men there were? Men who weren't going to be king's champion and travel all of the time and leave her alone. Ones she could marry without being in constant danger from Empty Ones, although he knew she didn't realize that part.

Ispiria and her great grandmother were traveling south much earlier than Ari and Peine were. She said her great grandmother wanted her to have as much time in the capital as the season allowed, which increased Ari's worry twofold. Not only would it give Ispiria more time to be wooed by other men, it also planted in Ari the suspicion that Lady Enra was hoping Ispiria would fall in love with someone else.

Whatever her aspirations might be, Lady Enra insisted they depart Sorga as soon as the snow melted enough for a carriage to pass. Ari, along with the rest of the keep, said goodbye on the castle steps. Under the hard scrutiny of Lady Enra, he resigned himself to bowing over Ispiria's hand. He hoped she would defy her great grandmother and kiss him, as she always did when he returned from a journey, but she didn't.

Even worse, though she squeezed his hand with her beautiful green eyes locked on his, when she turned away it was with an eager step. Her face as she waved from her carriage was smiling. Ari worked hard not to frown, watching the carriages, guards and packhorses lumber away.

Suppressing a sigh, he followed Sir Cadwel back inside the keep and into the study. He knew this was Ispiria's first trip outside the dukedom of Sorga and she was very excited to travel the land, see the capital and meet the royal family. He wished she'd acted a little sadder about leaving him, though. Not that she hadn't, over the past few weeks, told him many times how much she would miss him.

Shown him too, he thought, recalling their clandestine kisses. The delight such thoughts usually brought him was dampened by the hollow pain spreading from his gut as she rode farther from Sorga. Ari already felt like the keep was empty. He wondered if this was what it was like for her each time he left.

He sat down on one of the leather couches, picking up a book in Ancient Wheylian. After reading the caption under a drawing of a Wheylian trebuchet five times without actually getting himself to understand it, he sighed and put the book down. Gloomy, he turned his gaze to the fire dancing in the hearth.

"You seem troubled," Sir Cadwel said, setting down the book he was reading. Canid and Raven sat on either side of his chair. Canid rested his chin on the leather arm, begging for attention with his eyes.

Ari shrugged, picking his book back up. Sir Cadwel probably didn't want to hear about how much Ari missed Ispiria, especially when she'd only just left.

"I have something for you," the knight said, standing.

His old hounds immediately stood too, walking on either side of him as he crossed to the back of the room, where a large table covered in books and scrolls stood. Watching from his seat, Ari didn't notice the sturdy wooden chest tucked under the table until Sir Cadwel reached for it. He pulled it out smoothly, in spite of its size. Ari wondered if he should remind

Sir Cadwel not to let others see his Aluien strength, but then, they were alone and the knight had always been strong.

"Come, open it," Sir Cadwel said, grinning.

"What is it?" Ari asked as he set his book aside and got up.

"A Midwinter's gift."

"But that was ages ago."

"I'd planned to give it to you Midwinter's Eve." Sir Cadwel's smile took on a suspiciously smirk-like cast. "But you seemed to have enough to occupy your mind that night, so I decided to save it for a better moment."

"Thank you," Ari said, ignoring the jab and remembering his manners. There was no lock so, with a last glance at Sir Cadwel for permission, Ari lifted the heavy lid.

Inside was a lush blue cloth, fine enough to be one of Siara's dresses. Ari tugged back the top layer of fabric to reveal two gauntlets and two vambraces. A thrill went through him, for he realized what must fill this chest.

"My own set of armor?" he said, his voice coming out in a whisper.

"Crafted by the son of the man who made mine." Sir Cadwel hooked his thumbs through his belt. "Their family has been making armor for the lords of Sorga for generations."

"My own set of armor," Ari repeated, dropping to his knees in front of the chest. He carefully lifted out the left gauntlet to examine it.

"Of course, you'll have to have it resized as the years turn," Sir Cadwel said. "Mostly the straps, unless you grow too much more. Hopefully it will last. You're tall, but I don't see you becoming a giant of a man. Not that we can't get a new set made if needed, and this one put aside for your son."

Ari placed the left gauntlet on the floor beside him, taking up the other. "Thank you," he said again. He could hardly believe it. Putting the second gauntlet down, he lifted out a vambrace. The armor was unadorned, like Sir Cadwel's, but quality was evident in every curve, every edge.

"You can take back the set you borrowed from Ennentine when you go south for the spring tourney."

Ari cleared his throat, his fear of losing the spring tourney, letting down Sir Cadwel, the king and everyone else, returning. "Sir, what if I don't win? What if someone else becomes king's champion?"

Sir Cadwel regarded Ari with serious eyes. Canid and Raven nosed at the chest. Raven tilted his head as if to say, why is this interesting, then nudged Sir Cadwel for attention. The knight patted him on the head. "Impossible."

Ari sighed, not reassured.

"You're the best warrior I've ever trained." Sir Cadwel's firm countenance added force to the statement.

"You still beat me last fall."

"But I wouldn't again. That was my last trick. I was saving it for a special occasion."

"Thank you for the armor," Ari repeated, trying to feel reassured. "I'll make sure to keep it perfect."

"I'm glad you like it, lad." Sir Cadwel patted Ari on the shoulder before he turned away, muttering something about returning to his reading.

Ari looked down at the armor, deliberately putting aside his fear of losing the tourney for the joy of the moment. Taking out the second vambrace, he lifted the next layer of cloth to reveal pauldrons. Reverently, he reached for one of the gleaming shoulder guards, part of his own set of armor.

Ari's armor didn't stay pristine for long. He didn't want to practice in it, hoping to keep it perfect for the spring tourney, but Sir Cadwel insisted.

"It isn't like a new pair of boots, lad," the old knight said. "You don't wear in your armor. It wears in you. Put it on."

The first time they headed out into the snow to practice, Sir Cadwel suddenly whirled, landing a vicious swing across Ari's gut. Taken off guard, his sword not even drawn, Ari took the full impact of the blow. It felt like being run into by a horse. He doubled over, his hands clutched against the long indentation Sir Cadwel's sword left. The shock of the blow and the damage to his new armor almost brought him to tears.

"Good to get that over with," Sir Cadwel said.

Ari gasped, still not quite able to breathe.

By the time they were done sparring, the snow under their feet was trampled to slush. Sir Cadwel insisted on helping Ari repair the dents and scratches their bout left, a task Ari normally did himself. Ari knew it was Sir Cadwel's way of apologizing for marring his new armor, but he was still grumpy about it. He tried to hide his annoyance, though, knowing Sir Cadwel only wanted to make sure he would concentrate on his fighting during the king's tourney, not on keeping his armor perfect.

The days passed quickly for Ari after that, as Sir Cadwel insisted they spend the greater part of each morning sparring and that Ari practice nearly all of the hours it was light out, curtailing his studies to a brief time in the evenings. Canid and Raven seemed to find new life in watching them battle in the snow. The old hounds would lie outside all morning, not seeming to mind the cold, eyes alert, while the two men fought.

In spite of the distraction of getting to spar in his new armor and the change in his schedule to mostly martial training, Ari's evenings still dragged. He was glad the days were getting longer, for once the sun fell and he had to go inside to read, his mind would inevitably turn to Ispiria and wondering what she was doing with her evening. Then he couldn't focus on the pages before him and usually ended up staring into the fire.

While indulging in that one evening, he noticed Canid and Raven were, as had become their custom of late, sitting on either side of Sir Cadwel's chair, instead of sprawling before the fire asleep. They looked around the room. They butted his hands to coax attention from him, making it so he continually switched which hand held his book to pet each one. Ari searched back through his mind, trying to figure out when the old hounds went from sleeping nearly all day to being so alert. Midwinter's Eve?

"What's wrong with Canid and Raven?" he asked, closing his book.

Sir Cadwel lifted his own higher, almost burying his face in it.

"Canid," Ari called in a low voice. The hound didn't turn. "Canid," he said more loudly. The dog's head swiveled toward him. "They still don't hear very well, do they?"

"Haven't for a while," Sir Cadwel said, not looking up from his reading.

"But they seem so alert." The knight's aggressive silence made Ari even more suspicious. "What did you do?" he asked.

"Do?" Sir Cadwel finally looked up, his visage one of impossibly perfect innocence. "Me?"

Ari frowned. He pulled the amulet the Lady had given him out of his doublet. Larke always said Ari could to see through illusions, if he would only concentrate. He wrapped his hand around the amulet. He wasn't sure if that would help, but the amulet kept magic away, so maybe it would. He imagined he could feel the strangely ephemeral designs engraved into it writhing against his palm. Narrowing his eyes, he stared at Sir Cadwel, willing himself to penetrate the illusion of normalcy the knight projected into the mind of anyone near enough to see him.

"What are you doing?" Sir Cadwel asked.

Ari ignored him, pressing at the illusion Sir Cadwel put in his head until he pushed it out. Suddenly, the knight began to glow, the light of the Orlenia suffusing him. Ari took a deep breath, his heart pounding as if he'd been wielding a sword.

"Go back to your studies, lad." Sir Cadwel tugged at his mustache. "They're more important than playing about with magic."

Ari continued to ignore the knight, sure Sir Cadwel was only trying to distract him. Now that he had a feel for it, he turned his gaze on Canid, concentrating. He thought there was something insubstantial about the vision of the hound sitting calmly beside Sir Cadwel. Ari pressed at it with his mind, focusing his will. He felt a bead of sweat trickle down the side of his face. Distantly, he was aware of Sir Cadwel talking to him, but he didn't let the knight's words break into his concentration.

"Ari," Sir Cadwel said, placing a hand on his shoulder as Canid began to glow.

Ari looked up, startled. He hadn't realized the knight had moved from his chair. Canid padded over, resting his glowing head on Ari's knee. "You changed them." Ari reached out to pet the dog. "Like the Lady's bird, the one I told you takes messages between her and Larke. You made them into Aluien dogs."

Sir Cadwel sat back down in his chair, scowling.

"Is that allowed?" Ari asked, recalling that Larke told him it was discouraged and immortality was lost on animals, as they were unaware of the change.

"I didn't ask."

"Because you didn't want the answer," Ari said. He blinked, relaxing his will until nothing glowed anymore. He didn't like seeing Sir Cadwel that way and it was outright strange to see Canid glowing. "They're going to be angry with you."

"Then they will be angry." Sir Cadwel picked back up his book. "Do your reading."

"Yes, sir," Ari said, his mood lightening. He was sure Sir Cadwel had planned this from the start. Canid and Raven had obviously been a factor in the knight's plan to become and an Aluien before returning to Sorga. Though his opinion would not be sought by the Aluien council, Ari was glad. It comforted him to know that Sir Cadwel would have Canid and Raven forever.

***

When the time came to head south for the spring tourney, Ari set out from Sorga in high spirits, a message from Sir Cadwel to the king tucked into his doublet alongside the stone. Ari knew it was a formal declaration by the knight, saying Sir Cadwel was renouncing his position as king's champion. Even though Ennentine already knew Sir Cadwel's plan, Ari still felt the weight of the message.

If Ari was a bit awed by the change to the kingdom implicit in the words he carried and the responsibility they placed on him to do well in the tourney, Stew was not. The destrier pranced the whole first day of their journey, happy to be out of the keep and, Ari suspected, looking forward to jousting and winning.

Peine wasn't as happy to leave. He was in love again. Ari could hardly keep track of with whom. Since Peine had turned fifteen that winter, he'd been in love at least four times. Ari hadn't realized there were so many young women in the keep.

After all the times Peine was in love the year before, it seemed like he should have broken the heart of every girl in Sorga by now, for it was always Peine who broke off the affairs. Well, except for the previous spring with Kimmer, but that was a special case.

They traveled companionably, riding till near dark each day, until they reached the village of Sallsburry, where Ari had grown up. He'd made sure to leave enough time to stop to visit his family this trip, not having seen them since journeying south in the fall. He was looking forward to visiting with his aunt and uncle and meeting his cousin Mactus' new baby, but he had another motive, too. Now that the king had declared him to have reached his majority, Ari was free to pursue his own interests. At least, he was when they didn't interfere with his duties. The first thing Ari wanted to do, now that he could, was try to find out more about his parents.

Chapter 10

They entered the village from the east and made their way to the only inn, owned by Ari's adopted uncle. Stew started prancing again as they drew near, making a spectacle of himself, though no one was around to see. Peine's horse Charger, an old and non-magical beast, plodded along at his usual steady pace until they halted inside the inn yard and dismounted.

"I'll let them know we've arrived," Ari said, handing Peine Stew's reins. A formality, since Stew would go to the stable on his own.

"You'll send someone to tend the horses?" Peine asked. He had Charger's reins in his other hand. Their packhorse was tied to Charger's saddle.

As a valet, Peine's duties didn't include tending horses, an activity he didn't care for and often shirked if it was placed on him. Pages tended horses, but valets had a more domestic role, and Peine didn't show any inclination to mix the two. Although he was a duke, Ari had tended Stew, Charger and the packhorse thus far during their journey, not wanting the horses to suffer from Peine's lack of enthusiasm for the task. He also did it to keep Stew from biting Peine. Not realizing Stew was considerably smarter than a normal horse and perfectly capable of holding a grudge, Peine didn't know how much harm his lackluster handling did to his relationship with the destrier.

"Depends on who's around," Ari said.

Peine frowned, but led the horses away. Ari's gaze lingered on the stable. It used to be his job to take care of the guests' horses. It was a job he loved, though he'd dreamed of greater things, like becoming a coachman for a lord. He grinned, thinking of how much bigger his dreams were now. Shaking his head, Ari turned toward the inn, hurrying across the yard when his uncle came out. The innkeep's face broke into a grin as he espied who his newest guests were.

"Ari," his uncle cried, throwing his arms wide before hesitating, obviously caught between a hug and a bow.

Ari laughed, embracing his uncle. He had long ago decided it didn't matter that they weren't related. The people he called his aunt and uncle had raised him with all the care they gave their own sons. "Uncle Jocep."

"Come right into the kitchen, lad." His uncle steered him by the arm as he spoke. "We'll see if your aunt has any sweets left. She's been saving some out each day, knowing you'd arrive soon."

The kitchen was as Ari remembered, with well-scrubbed copper pots dangling from its low ceiling. The air was warm from the oven and bright with afternoon sunlight. It smelled even better than he recalled, baking bread and spices permeating the air. Ari smiled to see his Aunt May, her hair up in a neat bun, fussing over a large pot.

"Ari," his aunt exclaimed, much as her husband had. She pulled off her apron and raced to the kitchen door, standing on tiptoe to hug him. "Look how you've grown since fall. Our little Ari, a man now. Almost seventeen." Tears sprang to her eyes, but she was smiling. "You got my letter about Jare leaving last fall to join the king's guard? Oh, all my boys grown up and leaving me." Jare was the younger of Ari's two cousins, and they'd enjoyed a good-natured dislike growing up, owing mostly to Jare's endless laziness and his greater size, which he used to get Ari to do both of their work.

"Don't worry, Ma," Mactus said. Ari turned to see his older cousin Mactus and his wife Amma come through the inn yard door behind him. "Amma and I are busy making a whole new lot of them for you to care for. Ari, well met."

"Mac." Ari clasped hands with his cousin. "Amma," he said. He nodded to her, but his eyes were on the little bundle she carried. "This is your son?"

"Yes, a fine strong boy," Ari's aunt said, holding out her arms for the baby. "That's all I need, more boys to look after," she said, as if she hadn't lamented their growing up only moments before. Taking the child, she tickled him. He made happy gurgling noises.

Amma gave Ari a timid smile before crossing to put on an apron and look inside the bubbling pot.

"You must have made good time south," Mactus said. "I'd stay and chat, but I've horses to tend." He raised a hand when Ari opened his mouth, seeming to know what he was about to offer. "No, you stay here and visit. I've more to care for than yours. We'll catch up over supper. You are staying the night?"

At Mactus' question, four pairs of hopeful eyes fixed on Ari. He laughed. "Of course we are. Peine's watering our horses right now. Keep an eye on his work for me, and don't tell him I said to."

"Bit like Jare, is he?" Mactus asked, grinning. He turned back out the door, not waiting for an answer.

"Any chance of some sweets, May?" Ari's uncle asked, pulling out a chair at the table and gesturing for Ari to seat himself.

"Sweets?" she cried, looking up from the baby. "Oh, you work me to the bone, you do. How glad I am to have Amma. At least one woman on my side in this inn full of hungry men."

She handed the baby back to Amma, donning her apron.

Ari sat, eyeing the pot they kept checking. He and Peine hadn't stopped for a noonday meal, wanting to reach the inn before supper. His uncle leaned across the table toward him, conspiratorial. "Have you heard anything about where the king plans to build the second way? Rumor has it he might put it right through town. Maybe as you travel, you're surveying possible locations for him, ah?"

Ari shook his head, chuckling. "I'm no surveyor. I know the road through Sallsburry is one they're considering, but I'd not presume to give advice to my king."

"Why not?" his uncle asked, leaning back. "You're to be king's champion soon. The whole of Lggothland is abuzz with it. I've met Sir Cadwel. I daresay he presumed to give out any advice he felt was warranted."

Ari shook his head, keeping his smile in place even though he didn't like being reminded that everyone anticipated he would win the tourney. He knew it wasn't his uncle's intention to heap expectation on him. Not that trying to influence the king through Ari was a very honorable intention itself. "We'll see," he said, shrugging.

"Would be fine for business, it would," his uncle said, unabashed.

"And surely Jare would be close to home, then," his aunt called across the kitchen from where she was transferring some pastries from under a dishcloth to a baking sheet. "The king would station him right here, like they do on the King's Way. No closer he could get to his home. Is it true the new road will be called the Queen's Way?"

"I've heard that rumor," Ari said. "But I don't know if there's truth in it."

"Silly name. Queen's Way," his uncle said.

"Well, I like it," Aunt May said, sliding the pastries into the oven.

"Uncle," Ari said, drawing back the innkeep's attention. He lowered his voice. "I was wondering, I'm seventeen this summer and, well, I was hoping now I might try to learn about my past. It worries at me, sometimes, not knowing."

"Such a fine lad you've grown into." His uncle shook his head. "What difference does it make with all you've earned for yourself?"

"Still, I'm curious," Ari said. "Do you recall much about my parents? What they looked like, any clue as to from whence they came?"

"I'm afraid I saw them only once, lad, across the town." His uncle's eyes took on a distant look. "Your ma was a delicate thing, for all she was already showing. They rode in on as magnificent a horse as you ever did see. A big chestnut stallion. Traded it to the mayor for money to secure their farmstead and animals. He rode it all year, too, till it ran off."

"Ran off?"

"After your parents' farm burned. Mayor searched for that horse for days. Said it was the best horse he ever bestrode."

"You never went to the farm?" Ari recalled this from the only other time he and his uncle had spoken of the events. "How do you know it was burned?"

"Oh, people went out, lad, and people talk." His uncle leaned close, his eyes scanning the room to make sure the two women were busy. "They said other things, mind. I suppose you're old enough to hear. Rumor all, of course. They said 'twas all burned, right down to the outhouse and sheds. Your folks and all the animals dead, and those that escaped the fires, they weren't natural dead, but all ripped up like some great beasts was at them. Of course, was probably wolves, but those what went out there were sure it was something more sinister."

"You mean--" Ari struggled to keep his voice low, images of the burning farmstead from his dream the spring before vivid in his mind. "You mean, the haunted farm everyone tells stories of? That was my parents' farm?"

"Well." The innkeep shrugged, obviously now wishing he'd kept his tale telling to himself. "Rumor grows like black ivy, son. I wouldn't put much stock in it."

"Of course not." Ari mustered a smile. "But you never saw for yourself?"

"No, lad." His uncle shook his head. "The lady what brought you said not to go out, and not to tell any that's where you were found, and she was the sort one listened to."

"Not to tell anyone I was from there?" Ari frowned. That seemed an odd precaution. In his dream last spring, the Lady had carried a baby from the burning farmstead. If she'd given such orders, there was sure to be a reason. "Did you ask her why?"

"Well now, we never thought to. As I said, that lady wasn't the type you asked questions of. Wasn't even inclined to. We put out that you were the son of one of May's cousins what

108

died birthing you, so no one would think anything of you appearin'."

"What did she look like?" Ari asked, even though he suspected he already knew. A half-remembered vision of the Lady holding up the baby she'd saved from the fire came to him, along with her words, 'It is you, Thrice Born.' When he'd dreamed it last spring, he wasn't sure if it was premonition or memory. He wasn't sure now either, but he was feeling more and more certain that, whatever it was, it was true.

"I can't rightly recall, lad." The innkeep shifted in his chair, his eyes wandering around the room as if seeking something to distract his mind. Ari knew what kind of magic had such a slippery purpose, forcing a man's mind from the thoughts he wished to pursue. Aluien magic. "She was noble, I can assure you of that, and old, but not one ounce of frailty in her. Her face . . . I can't recall, lad. I'm sorry. It must have been night, and dark, and she in a shawl. Maybe the sweets are ready. May," he called.

"They're comin'," his aunt hollered back with a good-natured pretense of annoyance.

"Then we're in time," Mactus said as he and Peine came through the inn yard door.

There was a happy bustle. Everyone crammed around the little table, May complaining that her kitchen was full to bursting with men, the baby gurgling, not minding new people. Ari kept a smile on his face as the warm fruity sweets were devoured, truly happy to be with his family, but his mind churned.

Was it indeed the Lady who'd brought him to the inn? Why save him and not his parents? If he was important enough to save, why abandon him here? Or had she? When his life had all but ended in the woods two years ago, the Lady was there to save him. Had he ever truly been alone?

Chapter 11

Once their impromptu late lunch of pastries was finished, everyone excused themselves back to work. Ari knew his family would be busy with guests until fairly late in the evening. Those who kept the inn didn't usually sit down to eat until the guests were done. Then, they'd leave the barmaids to mind the taproom while the family had dinner.

Ari decided to go out to the farmstead his uncle spoke of, as there was plenty of time to ride there and back before supper. He helped Peine carry their things up to their room and resaddle Stew and Charger, and they rode west out of Sallsburry. Ari knew the way. When he was young, the older boys would dare each other to go there at night, though Ari had never been.

When they reached it, memories of whispered tales were heavy on Ari's thoughts. The sight of the tree-choked path, a dark tunnel of greenery little sunlight penetrated, made him shiver. Turning resolutely off the main road, Ari led the way to the place he'd always thought of as the haunted farm, finding it noticeably cooler among the trees.

They weren't long in the shadows before it grew brighter ahead. Soon, Ari glimpsed light glinting off spring wildflowers. He urged Stew forward, but the brown slowed, ignoring him. When they reached the edge of the clearing, Stew halted, unwilling to leave the concealing shade of the massive oaks. Ari was surprised, for the open expanse of sunlight ahead seemed to beckon to him. He reached up to touch his amulet, but it was the same temperature as his skin, not the almost searing cold he'd learned was a signal for danger. He nudged Stew's flanks with his heels, but the destrier tossed his head, not moving. Not one to press his horse, Ari dismounted, gesturing for Peine to do the same.

Entering the clearing, Ari could see that after seventeen years, not much was left of the burned-down farm. Trees encroached on the once cleared lands and vines engulfed the few scorched planks poking upward. The ground they trod was lumpy under the tall grass and swaying flowers. Ari feared what scraping back the thin layer of earth would reveal.

He stopped in what he assumed was once the front yard, looking about without much hope. He could already see there was nothing. No mementoes to uncover. No memories stirring from deep inside him. Only the screech of a nearby grackle and the bright afternoon sun. Seventeen years of weather and scavengers, both man and beast, had scoured the place clean.

"There's nothing here," Peine said, looking around. "Do you think this was your parents' home?"

"I do," Ari said. He turned in a slow circle, taking in unidentifiable mounds and the barest hints of the house and large barn.

"Should we try to dig?" Peine asked, his expression showing he found the idea distasteful. Ari did as well, though he expected Peine's reluctance sprang from his dislike of digging, whereas Ari wasn't sure he wanted to unshroud those long buried. "What are we looking for?"

"No digging," Ari said. He ignored the second question. He didn't know what he was looking for. He'd hoped being there would give him some certainty as to what had happened. Of course, if his dream was true, he was only a newborn babe when the farm was burned down by an Empty One. Even if he'd been there, how could he recall anything?

Hearing Peine sigh, Ari turned to look at him, but his friend's brown eyes were pointed north, toward their home. "Are you well?" Ari asked, dreading the answer. He could tell from the look on Peine's face that he was lovesick. Ari would have thought his best friend could put aside mooning over women for one afternoon, especially when they were likely standing where Ari's parents' had died. It wasn't as if Peine was ever really in love. In Ari's opinion, real love only happened once, but Peine was never in love with the same girl for more than a score of days.

"Sorry," Peine said. "I was missing Vidia's adorable smile."

Ari frowned. "I thought it was Delini when we left."

"Delini?" Peine pulled a face. "That woolhead? She couldn't read the alphabet if you spelled it for her. I need a woman with a mind. Someone I can talk to. Like Vidia." Peine let out another sigh, his comely face folding into lines that mirrored his languishing heart. That face, coupled with the fact that his Wheylian dark hair and eyes were a rarity in their northern home, was helping him leave a trail of broken hearts through the young ladies of Sorga.

Ari shook his head, fighting against his growing annoyance. For all of his endless lectures to Ari on proper behavior, every time Peine was infatuated, he shirked his duties and moped about. It was one thing not to want to tend horses, not really part of a valet's job, but they were on Ari's parents' farm and –

Behind them, Stew let out a snort. Ari whirled, reaching for his sword. A dark shape moved at the edge of the forest.

"What's yer business here?" a voice barked.

Peine let out a startled squeak, stumbling in his hurry to turn toward the sound.

"I don't take to people riffling through here," the man at the edge of the clearing said in a half snarl, moving into the light to reveal a gnarled frame.

"My pardon." Ari bowed, though the man brandished a pitchfork. "We didn't realize these lands were occupied."

"They're my lands, alright, and my lads'll be along to help you off'em if you don't heed me."

"Have they been your lands for long?" Ari took a step forward.

The man's glower deepened.

"We were seeking to learn of the man and woman who used to live on this farm. I--" Ari hesitated. The Lady's warning to his uncle not to say Ari was from the farmstead made him leery, but the man didn't look to be anything more than a normal farmer. "I think they were my parents."

He scrutinized Ari for a long moment. "You have the look of your father about you, boy," he finally said, lowering his makeshift weapon. He came forward and offered his hand, hard and knotted. "I'm Tenvar."

"I'm Ari, and this is Peine."

114

Peine inclined his head to the farmer. Ari shot his friend a look that said, 'let it be,' knowing Peine wanted to correct him. To Peine, it was always Lord Aridian, Duke of Sorga and Protector of the Northlands, protégé to Sir Cadwel.

"So this truly was their farm?" Ari asked, turning his gaze back to the desolation. A small part of him had hoped his uncle was wrong and the haunted farm wasn't his parents'. Or, though he knew it was unlikely, that the entire idea was foolish and his parents were somehow still alive, somewhere.

"I sold the land to 'em," Tenvar said. "After what happened, the mayor said as I could have it back."

"But you don't farm it?" Peine asked, earning squinted scrutiny of his own.

"Wouldn't be proper. They were right fine people and this is where they rest."

He gestured to two low mounds. They were as grown over as the rest of the farm. Ari wouldn't have noticed them if the farmer hadn't pointed them out.

Hesitantly, Ari walked to the mounds. He stopped next to them, slight elevations in the grassy glade all that marked where his parents rested. His mother and father. This was all he would ever have of them. His throat constricted. He cleared it, trying to swallow his sorrow.

"I never knew what happed to the babe," Tenvar said, having worked his way through the tall grass to stand beside Ari. "I searched for it, for you could see it'd been born. I always feared them what did this spirited it away."

Ari nodded, not knowing what to say, assuming he could get words out. He felt Peine come to stand on his other side.

"They were decent folks," the farmer continued in a quiet voice. "The woman, she was right good to my boys and me. My sweet Ebbie passed, and I don't know we would have made it through those times without a woman's care. Then someone did this." His hand flicked out, the gesture encompassing the burned down farm.

Ari cleared his throat again, harder. "Who?" he asked, though he was almost certain of the answer. It had been a vile Empty One. "Who did this?" His voice cracked.

"I don't rightly know." Tenvar shook his gray head. "We came runnin' when we saw the fire, but by the time we got here . . ." His voice trailed off. "I'd've marked it for a beast, the way all was torn and tossed, but for the fire. No beast I ever known sets blazes."

"And there was nothing left?" Ari said. "Nothing of the people who lived here? Who they were, from whence?"

"We buried their things with 'em," the farmer said. "But one day, me and my boys came across some rotscum robbin' the graves. We chased 'em. Got some of 'em good, we did, though I'm 'fraid they made off with most everything. That's when we started taking walks round here more often, and I guess it's just my habit now. Haven't seen no one here for years."

"So there's nothing?" Ari repeated. "Did they ever say where they were from? Who they were?"

"They were right closed about that, and I'm not one to pry."

"Are their names known to you, at least? No one has ever been able to tell me their names."

"Your father's name was Ardan and your mother's was Cyanna," the farmer said. "That, I can tell you."

Ardan and Cyanna. Ari wished the names would stir something in him, but found them to be only names. Though he could see his name fit with his father's, it did little to fill the void inside him. They were just the names of two people he'd never met. His eyes fell to the gravemounds again, melancholy filling him.

"There is one thing." Tenvar reached under his shirt, pulling out a small medallion on a silver chain. "Your pa, he used to wear it, even when he worked the fields."

Ari blinked in surprise. The pendant was a near match to the one the Lady had given him. Its swirling silver lines twined about, sometimes resembling spreading branches, other times, for no reason Ari could discern, bringing to mind a mass of serpents twisting in upon themselves.

"I only kept it to remind me of them," Tenvar said. "By rights, it should be yours."

The farmer pulled the chain over his head, dropping the pendant into Ari's hand. It rested there, heavier than it looked. Ari traced the pattern with his eyes but, as with his own medallion, the lines eluded his attempts to sort them. Here was something of his father's and almost certain proof of the Lady's involvement. Ari closed his hand around his father's amulet.

"I guess it's time I let of go their memory," Tenvar said, looking down at the graves.

"Please, take mine in trade." Ari pulled his own amulet over his head. He didn't want this farmer, the one man who seemed to know his parents, to let go of any memories of them. As soon as it was off, he regretted his impulse. The Lady gave it to him to wear always.

"Now, lad." Tenvar shook his head. "I can't take that. Seems to me it must be a family sort of thing."

"You must take something for all you've done." Ari dropped his amulet back over his head, hoping he hid his relief. "Some coin?" He gestured to Peine, who carried their small purse.

"It wouldn't be proper. Me and my boys only did what's right."

"Still, I insist you take some coin for your years of vigilance, and as I know you'll bear them company henceforth." Ari considered digging up the bones to properly burn them to ash, but thought the old gods would be satisfied with the joint cleansings of fire and time they'd already endured.

Peine handed Ari their purse. Ari removed one of their few gold coins. He pressed it into the farmer's palm, not giving Tenvar another chance to decline.

"My thanks," the old farmer said, his hand clenched around the coin.

"It's only a fraction of my debt to you," Ari said. "If you're ever in need, send a message to Sorga for me and I'll do my best for you and your boys."

"We only did what's right," Tenvar repeated, seeming embarrassed.

Ari took one last look about the clearing and the low graves of his parents, pondering the jumbled emotions it invoked, this empty clearing that held so much. "We best head back. Thank you, Tenvar."

"Keep yourselves well," Tenvar said.

Ari led the way into the trees toward Stew and Charger, tucking his father's amulet into the pocket inside his doublet, with the stone the hawks had given him. Waving once to Tenvar, who stood looking bent and timeless as an ancient willow, Ari turned Stew down the path toward the inn and an evening with the family he did remember. He tried to shake loose his melancholy, reminding himself that he planned to announce his engagement to Ispiria at dinner.

***

The following morning dawned clear and cool. It was, by Ari's thinking, a perfect day for travel. They made their farewells with many promises to return soon from Ari and wishes for his success in the tourney from his family, and set out toward the King's Way. Ari tried not to rush his farewells, knowing they had plenty of time for their journey, but they weren't departing as early as he would have liked. Peine, it seemed, wasn't feeling his usual lively self.

At dinner, Ari had announced his engagement, which resulted in his uncle fetching a bottle of the inn's famous three-berry brandy for a round of toasts. Mindful of his last experience with toasts, Ari drank only one small glass, but Peine took a fancy to the stuff. Although Peine didn't indulge in anything more theatrical than talking endlessly about love, Ari was uncharitably pleased he wasn't the only one foolish enough to make the mistake of drinking too much.

Unfortunately, Ari was now paying for his friend's suffering, though not anywhere near as much as Peine. As he didn't seem to share Ari's ability to shrug off the after effects of overindulgence, Peine was a terrible travel companion. Ari was sure his groans could be heard all the way back in Sorga, and their pace was abysmal.

"My head," Peine groaned for the twenty-third time that morning.

"I warned you not to drink too much of my aunt's three-berry brandy." Ari had little sympathy for his friend. He'd tried to get Peine to stop drinking after three glasses, but he hadn't listened. Ari considered Peine's current condition a good learning experience. Sometimes life lessons were hard.

"How can something so sweet make you feel so terrible?" Peine said, wincing with every step Charger took.

"But that's the way of spirits, me lad," a lyrical voice lamented from behind them. "And love, truth to tell, but you've well learned that lesson, I'm thinking."

"Larke." Ari ignored Peine's grimace at his exclamation. The tall figure of Larkesong rode up the lane behind them, his bright tunic and hose startling against the backdrop of spring green. Happiness at seeing his friend warred with worry. Larke wouldn't make the Lady go into the deep sleep for anything unimportant. "Is all well? What are you doing here?"

"Why, looking for you, lad." Larke nudged his horse to a faster pace, coming abreast of them. "And I met a fascinating farmer. Threatened to put a pitchfork in me arse, but by the time I took my leave, we were fast friends."

"Tenvar?" Ari asked. His eyes narrowed. "What did you do to him?"

"Me?" Larke's face folded into lines of sorrow. "Why must I be the villain? 'Twas the farmer began it, I say." Receiving nothing but a skeptical stare in reply, Larke grinned sheepishly. "I may have accused him of trying to steal yer amulet. A tad."

"How do you accuse someone a tad?" Peine asked, rubbing his head.

"How was I to suspect you willingly took it off?" Larke said, ignoring the question. "I seem to recall we told you to always be keeping it on. You gave us quite a scare. The Lady had me out the door and down the mountain before I could grab my hat."

Ari wondered if that was true, for indeed the bard's blond head was without his usual bright broad-brimmed hat with its outrageous clashing plumage.

"I only took it off for a moment," Ari said, adding by way of an apology, "I can buy you a new hat at the next town, if you like. The farmer gave me this amulet." He pulled out his father's amulet, watching Larke for a reaction.

The bard's eyes widened before he raised them to meet Ari's.

"Well?" Ari prodded, seeing Larke squeeze his lips into a thin line.

"It's a fine day, is it not?" Larke smiled at the two of them, pulling his lute around from where it hung on his back.

"Larke." Ari's voice held a note of command, stopping Larke before he could begin to sing.

"Ye know it 'twas your father's?" the bard asked. Ari nodded. "Well, lad, that be most all there is to know. It's the Lady's work, and must protect the wearer from being sought, as your own does, but as to why she gave your father one? I am not so deep in her counsel. None are. Recall, I am young to the fold. My years number like to Sir Cadwel's and I've been Aluien a mere half of them."

Ari scrutinized the bard for a long moment. Unfortunately, Larke appeared to be telling the truth. Ari sighed. He would have to take his questions to the Lady herself, it seemed, but first, he had to win the spring tourney. Ari frowned, one hand going to check the carefully folded missive from Sir Cadwel to the king where he kept it tucked into his doublet. He slid his father's amulet back into his pocket alongside the stone. "I just want to know what happened, Larke."

"Aye, and someday I'm sure you shall."

"Can't you two be any quieter?" Peine groaned from where he'd fallen slightly behind.

With a grin at Ari, Larke poised his fingers over the strings of his lute, took a deep breath, and launched into a somewhat bawdy tavern song. Behind them, Peine whimpered as if about to cry.

Chapter 12

Larke continued to travel with them, obviously reveling in his freedom. Occasional hints that the bard might be abusing the Lady's willingness to enter the deep sleep while he checked on Ari only elicited guilty shrugs. Since it wasn't really his business, Ari dropped the matter in favor of enjoying traveling with his friends. When they finally crested the hill overlooking the gleaming white city of Poromont, Larke reined in his gray.

"You won't go into the city?" Ari asked.

"The city is not for me, lad. Too many eyes to hide this from." So saying, the bard let out a sigh, seeming to relax without having looked tense. The blue-white glow of the Orlenia radiated forth, turning him into a miniature moon.

"Ohh," Peine breathed, his eyes going round. While Peine knew about the Aluiens, Ari realized his friend had never seen Larke unveiled before.

"But you keep the illusion up all the time, anyhow." Ari was aware he sounded petulant. He was also aware of the deep longing that sprang up in him at the sight of Larke's glow. He saw the bard's eyes narrow, as if he had some inkling of what went on in Ari's mind.

"You don't understand the nature of the thing," Larke said, his glow dimming until he appeared normal once more. "The magic of the Aluiens works only in the minds of men. The Orlenia does not cease to glow. It is you who cease to see it. There are simply too many people down there for me to keep track of and bespell."

"You did it once before," Ari said, turning over Larke's explanation in his head, comparing it to the halting one Sir Cadwel had given him during their travels the previous fall. Both pulled at his thoughts, mixing with how he focused his will to break the barrier Sir Cadwel had put in his mind to keep him from seeing that Canid and Raven were glowing. "If my amulet protects me from being bespelled, shouldn't I see you glow all the time?"

Larke opened his mouth. His face flushed. He shut his mouth without saying anything.

"Larke?" Ari said, anger mounting in him. "You said my amulet keeps me from being found or bespelled. The Caller ripped it from my neck when we fought so that he could enchant me. Why can't I see you glow all the time?"

"I think, lad, if you recall the exact conversation, the Lady told you it would keep you from being found," Larke said, his voice at its most placating. "It also has some spells worked in to guard against malevolent magic, but their value will be determined by the strength of the magic. It isn't a certain thing."

"Malevolent magic? As in, Empty One magic, but not Aluien magic." Ari scowled. His voice rose. "You said--"

"Not I." Larke held out his hands in front of himself in protest. "'Twas a conclusion you came to, lad."

"And you let me."

Larke looked down, his shoulders lowering in dejection. "Aye. I let you."

Ari gritted his teeth over the first few retorts that came into his mind. He couldn't believe that after two years, Larke was still lying to him. Had Larke been bespelling him again? Doing secret Aluien things to him? Why was the bard really there, even though he was supposed to be serving out his punishment? Peine watched them with wide eyes.

"I'm sorry, lad," Larke said, not looking up.

"You always are." Ari was aware his tone was biting, but he wasn't feeling very charitable toward Larke at that moment. "Why are you here? Have you come to stop me from winning the tourney for some reason?"

"No, on my honor," Larke said, looking up. "We knew you removed your amulet, and we knew you put it back on. We were worried you were tricked into taking it off so that spells could be placed on you before the tourney. That's all."

"Were there?"

"No." Larke shook his head. "I could find none when I arrived, and nothing has manifested itself. I'm sure your friend the farmer was all he claimed to be."

"Good." Ari unclenched his hands. "Larke, I would prefer if, aside from hiding the glow, you did not work any more magic on me in the future. Not without asking."

Larke stared at him for a long moment. He sighed. "I'll do my best, lad."

Ari frowned, but nodded. "Thank you." There was a painfully drawn out silence. "You really won't come to the capital with us?" Ari struggled to remove the anger from his tone.

"No, lad. Even with that great mass of a cloak covering all but my face last time, I could barely hide the glow and walk straight. No, the city is not for me."

"Farewell, then." Ari's tone didn't reflect the graciousness of his words. He forced himself to smile, raising one hand in salute.

Larke made as if to sweep his hat off and bow, but he still didn't have one, not having allowed Ari to purchase one for him. "You as well, lads," he said, waving.

"We may see you soon," Ari said as the bard turned away. "After the tourney, I will seek counsel with the Lady."

"Truly?" Larke looked back. "Then soon it may be. Good luck with the jousting."

"Thank you, Larke."

"Bye, Larke," Peine blurted, waving at the bard's back.

Hearing the strain in his friend's voice, Ari turned to look at Peine. He was quite pale. "Are you well?"

"I've never seen him do that before." Peine stared at the increasingly diminishing form of Larke as the bard headed up the King's Way. "It was creepy." Peine shuddered.

"But you knew. You're one of the few who does. He's still Larke."

"Yes," Peine said, but he looked uneasy.

With a shrug, Ari turned Stew toward Poromont, leading the way down the hill to the sprawling costal city. He was as impressed as ever by the uniform whiteness of the structures, the long paved avenues and red-shingled roofs. His eyes traveled over the city, alighting on the gleaming white castle in the center with its soaring towers and fluttering banners, before being pulled out to sea. The ocean looked smooth and bluer than any sapphire dug from the ground, but Ari knew it rolled with waves. He could already smell the tang of salt and feel the invitingly soft air. The ocean in the south differed greatly from the brutal gray waves that broke along the coast near Sorga. Still too far off to read their colors, graceful ships rolled in the harbor. Also down there, somewhere in the king's castle, Ispiria was waiting.

Ari had assumed that without Sir Cadwel they would ride quietly to the castle, but soon the streets were lined with admirers. He would never understand how rumor could travel so much faster than he could ride, although the crowd did slow their progress to a crawl. The people of Poromont spilled from their homes and businesses to cheer him. So many young women ran up to press flowers on him, he had to keep turning to give them to Peine, who struggled to hold them. Ari waved to the cheering people, his impatience to see Ispiria sublimated by the overwhelming realization that their adulation was all for him.

It seemed like hours before they made their way through the gates of the castle at the heart of the city and left the cheering throng behind. Their horses' hooves clattering on the cobblestones as they crossed the courtyard, Ari surveyed the gathered nobles. In their center stood the royal family, the queen's brother and his offspring to their left.

The lines on King Ennentine's face curved in a welcoming smile above his gray beard. In spite of his advanced years, the king's shoulders held only the slightest stoop of age, his height undiminished. Queen Parrella was tall and lovely as ever, the silver strands in her gold tresses sparkling in the afternoon sun. Prince Parrentine was whip-like and dashing in dark gray, his blond hair and even features making him appear everything a prince should be, his relaxed demeanor a welcome sight. Beside him, Princess Siara looked as perfect as always, her black hair piled elaborately on top of her head.

Ari took them in with the quickness of familiarity, his gaze roaming past them to search the throng of nobles, seeking blazing red curls. It didn't take him long to spot Ispiria, although at first he wasn't sure what he was seeing. She was standing beside her great grandmother, near the back of the crowd as befitted their low rank. She was easy to find because she was bouncing up and down on her toes like an excited woodland creature. Her exuberance was a stark contrast to the affectedly disinterested ladies around her, as was her smile. It was her hair that confused him, though. It was sleek, flat and as straight as could be. Ari was horrified.

He wrenched his eyes off her when Stew, his neck curved to heighten the effect of his overblown prancing, came to a halt at the bottom of the castle steps. Ari made sure to smile as he slid from his saddle, halfway to the ground before he saw that Princess Siara was holding a small wiggling bundle. He realized he and Peine must have departed Sorga before word of the baby's arrival could reach it. The babe was wrapped in the royal blue of Ennentine's house. Ari hoped that meant it was a boy.

"Welcome and well met, Lord Aridian," King Ennentine said.

Ari bowed low. Peine dismounted as well, pressing his armload of flowers on a groom before coming to stand at Ari's shoulder. Behind them, servants were leading the horses away. Ari resisted the urge to call after them to take extra care, aware that this was the king's court in the capital, not Sorga with its less formal ways.

"Your majesties, your highnesses," Ari said, rising from his bow. "We are honored by so vaulted a reception." He could see Peine nod slightly, approving of his attempts at courtly speech.

Maybe there really was something of value in being made to read so much, he thought, for the dry history tomes he studied were the guidelines for his wording.

"Lord Aridian," Princess Siara said, stepping forward. She held the baby out for him to look at. It squirmed, starting to whimper. "May I present Princess Tiana, heir to the throne of Wheylia." Siara's tone was expressionless. She brought the little princess back to her chest, cradling her and stroking her cheek.

Ari bowed low, but Siara's proclamation rang in his mind. It was as she'd foretold. She had a baby girl and her other female relatives were dead. All but her grandmother, the current queen and high priestess of Wheylia. Did that mean the last part was true as well? Would Ari have to take her baby away from her to keep the two lands from going to war? Rising from his bow, he looked back and forth between his friends, seeing the tension behind their polite smiles.

"She's beautiful, your highness," Peine said. He bowed, poking Ari in the ribs.

"Congratulations," Ari said, reminded of his manners. In the background, he could still see Ispiria fidgeting. He searched his brain, trying to remember what was supposed to happen next. Usually, Sir Cadwel was there and in no mood for extended courtesies, so the official greeting on the steps was brief.

"It's a long journey from the north," the king said. "Shall we adjourn to the study?" Not waiting for an answer, he offered Queen Parrella his arm. The two turned to enter the castle. Siara didn't look up from her baby as she followed them. Parrentine gave Ari a smile, but hurried after his wife, putting an arm about her slender shoulders. Ari bowed at their retreating backs.

The nobles on the steps began to disperse as he straightened. He could see Ispiria indecorously weaving her way between them. She was holding up her skirts in one hand, higher than Ari felt was appropriate, but dropped them when she reached the cobbles, dipping in a deep curtsy. She didn't lower her eyes demurely, however, but instead peered up at Ari through her lashes, grinning.

"Lord Aridian," she said. He could tell from her tone that she found her own attempts at proper behavior amusing. "Well met. I trust you and Valet Peine had a safe journey?"

"Ah, yes," he said, fighting down the urge to sweep her up and kiss her.

"Lady Ispiria," Peine said, bowing. "Have you been enjoying the capital? How goes the season? I hope your engagement hasn't left your dance card empty."

"No," she said, wrinkling her nose. "But almost. Everyone is so afraid of Ari. If they knew him like I do, they wouldn't mind dancing with me, but all the young men here have it in their silly minds that if they even look at me too long, he's going to chop their heads right off."

Ari grinned, pleased. He hadn't realized he had such a fierce reputation. Undoubtedly, people assumed he would be like Sir Cadwel, well known for his touchy temper and harsh retributions. As happy as he was to hear that Ispiria hadn't been dancing with anyone, one thing was troubling him. "What happened to your hair?"

"This," she said, lifting a limp lock. "Siara's ladies worked on it all day. They usually do more things to it, so it will look like Siara's, but I could hear all the commotion. I knew you were here."

"It looks, uh, nice," he said, not wanting to hurt her feelings. As the crowd on the steps thinned, he became acutely aware of Ispiria's great grandmother, dressed in black, glaring down at them from the top step.

"It looks silly." She tossed her head. "And even if it didn't, it takes a ridiculous amount of time. As if I have nothing better to do than sit and have people play with my hair. I'm sure they have better things to do, too."

"My lord, my lady," Peine said, his eyes on Lady Enra. "I believe the king awaits us in his study." He bowed formally, indicating Ari and Ispiria should precede him up the steps.

Ispiria smiled at him. Ari offered her his arm. It was nice of Peine, Ari thought, to include Ispiria so he could see her for longer. In truth, the king hadn't made any mention of her coming to his study.

Ari placed his free hand over the one she rested on his arm, squeezing it as they crossed the marble-floored foyer to King Ennentine's private meeting room. She looked up and he met her eyes, trying to convey how happy he was to see her and how much he wanted to hold her, if only it were allowed. Briefly, she leaned her head against his shoulder as they walked, straightening when they neared the study door.

"I don't really like your hair that way," he whispered.

"You may have to get used to it, for now," she whispered back. "Apparently, curly hair is not acceptable here in the capital. Even my hair isn't well enough behaved."

She said it lightly, but Ari heard a tinge of duress in her tone. He wondered who was telling Ispiria she wasn't well enough behaved. He didn't approve of that. He knew people had to behave properly while at court, but he liked Ispiria the way she was.

The king's study was cozy as ever, with its green walls, dark wood and heavy leather furnishings. Ari was partial to the weapons displayed about the room, though he could have done without the dead animal heads that hung alongside them. The chief steward, Kamers, was circling the room with a tray, offering glasses of wine. Noticing only Ennentine took one, Ari declined as well.

Siara and the queen were seated close together, fussing over the new princess. Ari didn't miss the shadow of sorrow in the queen's eyes as she reached out to tickle the baby's plump cheek. A little leery of the tiny wrapped form, Ari crossed to stand before the unlit fireplace with the king and Parrentine. Ispiria pulled away from him, going to sit with Siara and the queen. He was a little hurt that she left his side so soon after his arrival. Peine settled himself on a footstool in front of the ladies.

"Cadwel mentioned he most likely wouldn't attend this spring," King Ennentine said, drawing Ari's attention back to the men he stood with. The king's gaze followed the chief steward as he departed, quietly closing the thick wooden door behind him. "Had a bit of a time convincing Kamers you should keep your usual rooms without Cadwel. He's of the mind those rooms are for the king's champion and letting you stay in them shows a certain bias."

"I can take any room, your majesty." Ari wasn't sure he'd even feel comfortable in Sir Cadwel's rooms without the knight along. He wondered if there were any empty rooms near Ispiria's and if he'd be allowed to take them.

"Nonsense," Parrentine said. "We are biased, after all. I have every expectation and hope you'll win the tourney. We don't want any to fill the post but you, Ari."

Ari felt his neck heat at the praise. "Oh, yes." He reached in his doublet, retrieving Sir Cadwel's letter and handing it to the king. "I have a correspondence from Sir Cadwel for you, your majesty."

"A correspondence?" Siara said with a laugh, though Ari was sure he'd used the word properly. He glared at her, but she was looking at the baby.

"It is as anticipated," Ennentine said, looking up from the parchment he was skimming, his eyes gazing across the room at nothing. "A formal declaration of what he told me in the fall."

"The end of an era, Father," Parrentine said.

The king nodded. "I guess none of us can stay as we are forever."

"Sir Cadwel is as he always was," Ari said, a little perturbed by King Ennentine's melancholy, although he, too, was sad to see his mentor step down. Ari wondered if the king was aware Sir Cadwel would in fact never grow old and die. King Ennentine knew about the Aluiens, but Ari had no idea what details Sir Cadwel had shared with his oldest friend.

"He still practices with Ari all the time," Ispiria said.

"I'm sure he does," the king said. He took a sip of his wine, placing the glass on the mantel before turning to Ari. "There will be a banquet in two days' time to launch the tourney. You will sit in your usual seat and we'll leave the one to my right empty. We really don't want to appear too biased, now, do we?"

"Of course, your majesty." Ari was pleased he wouldn't yet be forced to take Sir Cadwel's chair.

"Where will I sit?" Ispiria asked.

Ennentine looked at her, frowning slightly.

"It's just that I'd like to sit with Ari," Ispiria said. She reached to wrap a curl around her finger, a habit of hers, but her straightened hair slithered away.

"I'm afraid protocol doesn't allow it, my dear," the queen said. "Until you and Aridian marry, you must sit near the end of the table with your great grandmother as suits your station."

"Oh." Ispiria looked down at her hands where they rested in her lap.

"And you should say your majesty, Ispiria," Siara said, but her tone was kind.

"I'm sorry, your majesty." She looked up at the king with wide green eyes.

Ari knew, were those eyes turned his way, he would forgive her much more than a dropped honorific.

"Don't let it trouble you, child," the king said. "I was merely confounded by your question. Seating is, for the most part, not an area where I boast much expertise."

Ari felt tension drain from him at the king's reply. He had a deep respect for his monarchs and, for a brief moment, he'd feared they wouldn't live up to his image of them as the sort of people who wouldn't be self-important enough to take offense at some of Ispiria's slightly unpolished edges. Ari was sure they understood she grew up in Sorga with Sir Cadwel as her guardian, and Sir Cadwel did not keep a formal hall.

"May I read the letter, Father?" Parrentine asked.

Ennentine handed the parchment to his son.

"Ari, come see the baby," Ispiria said, waving him over.

With a bow to his king, whose gaze had lost its focus once more as he stared across the room in thought, and another to Parrentine, Ari crossed the room to where the women and Peine sat. Peine's eyes were locked on the baby, an oddly possessive look in them. Ari realized that as a Whey, Peine was looking at a member not only of Lggothland's royal family, but his kinsmen's as well.

"Isn't she precious?" Ispiria said.

Ari nodded, but he wasn't really looking at the baby. For some reason, he found it disconcerting to see Siara and Ispiria, black-haired and red, leaning close together over the wriggling little bundle.

"The ladies of the castle are planning a picnic tomorrow," Ispiria said, looking up at him. "Princess Tiana is coming too."

"We will require an escort," Siara said. "A prominent lord, I should think. Someone fitting to head up the queen's private guard on this jaunt."

Distracted as he was, Ari could still discern the strain hidden behind Siara's light tone. "Yes," he said, watching the baby wave her little arm about and tangle it in Ispiria's hair. "Although it's pretty safe around here."

Siara sighed and Peine nudged him in the ribs. Ispiria giggled.

"What?" Ari asked, feeling as if he were the butt of a joke.

"You're supposed to volunteer, dear," the queen said. "It's an honor for Princess Siara to give you the opportunity to offer to serve us in this capacity."

"Oh." Ari marshaled his thoughts. "If you are in need of an escort, your highness, and find my lowly self suitable, it is my honor to offer my services."

"What did you think?" Siara turned to Ispiria and the queen, acting as if Ari wasn't standing right there.

"There is potential," Queen Parrella said. "But it needed a bit more polish."

"A bit?" Siara shook her head. "Your majesty is being kind. The disastrous form of the offer changes my afore held inclination to accept it."

"But you must also consider how gallant he'll look riding out with us." Ispiria smiled up at him. "And how hopeful he looks now."

"That's a look of hope?" Siara looked Ari up and down.

135

Normally, he would have scowled at her, but he could see the sorrow lurking in her eyes. Tormenting him was an attempt at normalcy, a moment's distraction from thinking about giving up her daughter. He marshaled his expression.

"I'm glad you have practice interpreting his face," Siara continued. "To me, it looks more as if he ate something unpleasant."

"No." Ispiria shook her head. The baby gurgled as her hair moved. "He tends to look that way. I'm sure he very much wants to go."

"There is also our duty to the realm to consider," the queen said. "We must take him under our wings and mold him."

"I suppose you're right, your majesty," Siara said.

Ari was torn between chagrin at their teasing and pity for Siara. He smiled, hoping to hide both emotions. Siara despised pity.

"We shall, between us, mold him into a fine champion for the realm. Someone we can all be proud of." Siara looked up at him, taking her most formal tone. "We would be most pleased for you to head our escort on this outing, Lord Aridian."

"It will be my great honor to do so, your highness," Ari said, bowing.

"But for now, I think you and Peine should go get cleaned up. You smell of horses."

"Yes, your highness," Ari said, not giving her the satisfaction of reacting to her jab. "If we may be excused?"

Ispiria bounced up off the couch, her hair slipping from the baby's grasping fingers.

"And where is it you intend to go to, Lady Ispiria?" Siara asked.

"With Ari."

136

"Ispiria." Siara's tone held a certain amount of resignation.

"It would be entirely inappropriate for you to accompany Lord Aridian to his rooms," the queen said, though she sounded amused.

"But we aren't going to do anything. It's Ari. He doesn't even stop thinking about chivalry when he's asleep."

"Be that as it may, it is not acceptable." Siara's tone was firm. "You shall have to wait to see him after dinner tonight. You know the prince and I are hosting a ball this evening. Perhaps you may permit Ari to accompany you in a dance or two."

Ari frowned. It was one thing to keep Ispiria at the end of the table at the king's formal dinner two days hence, but at the ball tonight, Siara could ask any lady she liked to sit at the head table with them. She knew he hadn't seen Ispiria in ages.

Ispiria flopped back down on the couch, looking up at Ari with a shrug. Her eyes glinting, she leaned close to Siara. "I'm going to permit him to escort me in all the dances, and then, I'm going to kiss him," she whispered loudly. She flashed Ari a grin.

Ari looked down at his feet, his frown gone.

"Ispiria," Siara exclaimed.

Ari brought a hand up to rub at his chin, hiding his smile.

"I think you should go freshen up now, Lord Aridian," the queen said.

"Yes, your majesty." Ari bowed. "Your highness," he said to Siara, bowing to her as well.

She caught his eye. There was a contemplative glint there he didn't trust, but her wry expression let him know she wasn't as shocked as she pretended. He hoped not, because he fully intended to take his fiancée up on her offer to kiss him, and not even Princess Siara was going to stand in his way.

Chapter 13

When they reached the chambers Ari normally shared with Sir Cadwel, Peine disappeared to arrange things to his liking with the castle servants. Ari stood at one of the tall windows and peered down into the courtyard, bright with spring sunlight. He worried briefly over what heading up the queen's guard on a picnic entailed before turning his thoughts to Ispiria. It was obvious Siara was trying to make a courtly lady out of her. Ari didn't think the princess would have much luck. He certainly hoped not. It wasn't as if Ispiria needed any pretension to live with him in Sorga.

Footsteps behind him signaled Peine's return, his chatter about castle gossip starting so immediately that Ari wondered if his friend had ever left off talking. Turning from the window, Ari followed Peine into the adjacent chamber where Peine started unpacking, laying Ari's things out on the massive bed.

"I'm not sleeping in there," Ari said, having already decided to sleep on the sofa, like usual. Peine kept unpacking.

"That's Sir Cadwel's bed, and the king's champion's bed. I'm not even one of those things."

"Have you seen the line-up of knights?" Peine asked, his voice full of excitement.

Ari realized, as Peine gestured him toward the bathing room, that his valet wasn't ignoring him in disagreement, but rather out of excitement over his news.

"They have a copy of the roster in the servants' hall." Peine's face, as animated as his voice, was alive with enthusiasm. "There's a Whey on the list. Sir Keite. I don't know if the king has ever let a Wheylian knight compete in one of his tourneys before. They say Sir Keite had a special meeting with the king for dispensation, since only those loyal to Lggothland's crown may compete. He has a missive from Queen Reudi requesting he be allowed to participate on this special occasion."

"Now seems an odd time for that." Ari paused in the doorway to the bathing room. "I mean, what if he wins? A Whey can't be king's champion of Lggothland. I didn't even think they had a knighthood."

"Well, we don't, but Queen Reudi knighted him especially for the event, so Wheylia can contribute to this momentous occasion. There hasn't been a new king's champion chosen in twenty-five years, after all."

Ari didn't miss the use of the word we. Peine, born of mixed heritage on the western border of Lggothland, was one of the king's subjects, but he always thought of himself as a Whey. He looked like a Whey, and he spoke Wheylian, and everyone treated him like a Whey, so Ari could see where his friend might find it difficult to embrace the Lggothian portion of his heritage.

"It seems odd," Ari said. Why would Queen Reudi send a knight to compete for a prominent position in Lggothland? Especially when her own government was teetering precariously close to turmoil now that her sole heir was a swaddling babe? Did she worry that Lggothland wouldn't give the baby up? Maybe she thought Keite would win and therefore insure that the baby was brought to Wheylia without a war.

"It's not like there's anything to worry about," Peine said. "We all know you're going to win. Now take a bath. We don't have much time to get ready before dinner. I'll save your best outfit for the banquet tomorrow, but you still have to look presentable tonight for Prince Parrentine's ball."

Ari nodded, shutting the door firmly in Peine's face. Ari doubted he would ever accustom himself to the habit many nobles had of having someone help them bathe, and he didn't feel getting used to it was a goal to strive for. Even alone, he shucked his travel clothes quickly and hopped into the warm water as if someone might see. He still couldn't bathe in peace in that room. Not since the time King Ennentine had appeared, without warning, through a hidden door in the wall. Glancing at the location of the secret door to make sure it was closed, Ari picked up the scrub brush.

"They say Sir Keite is amazing," Peine said from without. "Some people say he might even be good enough to beat you. Of course, they don't know the truth of it. It's not like anyone can actually beat you."

There was silence on the other side of the door, but Ari was not immune to the strain in his friend's voice.

"Ari, do you ever wonder, well, that is, if it isn't like you're cheating, a little?" Peine asked, breaking the silence.

Ari dropped the hard-bristled brush he was applying to his left foot with a splash. "Cheating?"

"Well." Peine's voice was muffled. "It's only, you're stronger and faster than anyone else, even Sir Cadwel, and you wouldn't be, would you, if it weren't for the Aluiens and what they did to you."

Ari stared at the floating wooden brush, frowning. He hadn't thought of it like that. It wasn't as if he'd asked them to save him, or to change him. The Lady made all those decisions for him. He couldn't very well pretend to be a worse swordsman than he was, could he? Should he? And now that Peine mentioned it, what about Stew? Stew wasn't a normal horse. He was a magical Questri, smarter, faster and stronger than a regular horse. Before Ari could think of an answer, he heard feet shuffle as Peine walked away.

Ari's clothes waited for him on the bed, but Peine was nowhere to be seen. As he dressed in a favorite outfit of unassuming brown, Ari couldn't get Peine's question out of his mind. He decided to ask Siara what she thought, when next he was able to speak to her in private. He wished he could ask Ispiria, but she knew nothing of the Aluiens, Empty Ones, or any of the secret mystical side of Ari's life, and he'd sworn an oath to keep it that way.

Peine felt Ari should break that vow, since Ispiria was to be Ari's wife, but he took vows very seriously. He wasn't even sure he wanted to tell her. Her world was innocent and uncomplicated by the evil he knew existed. Why take that from her?

Trying to shove his worries to the back of his mind, Ari made his way to the ballroom. He didn't care for the idea of dinner in the ballroom. For one thing, at a less formal dinner like this, Peine and the other lesser nobles who acted as servants to the greater lords wouldn't be in attendance. They would be seated at the lower tables themselves, or off attending other parties. It wasn't that Ari wanted Peine there to serve him, only to make sure he didn't embarrass himself. On top of that, there was also his memory of standing in the ballroom, watching the distressing scene of a possessed Princess Clorra dancing with Parrentine. It wasn't a memory Ari relished spending the evening with.

Arriving, he nodded to two guards in fancy dress and entered, stopping just inside the doorway. The familiar sight of the soaring narrow windows and candle-bedecked walls greeted him, along with a barrage of sound. He had a perfect view of the room, as he stood on a raised dais, which was mirrored on the opposite wall.

Musicians played to one side of the door, filling the room with soothing noise as people arrived to be seated below. On the other platform, across the room, a small table replaced the thrones that adorned it on more formal occasions. Already seated there were Siara, Prince Parrentine and three others Ari recognized as Parrentine's cousins, the son and daughters of the queen's only brother. The king and queen, Ari guessed, were not attending, snippets of Peine's gossip finding their way to the top of his mind. Ari seemed to recall something in Peine's stream of chatter about the queen having a private dinner with her brother and his wife.

Ari descended the steps into the center of the room, where dancing would take place later, taking in the single seat left at the head table. He kept a smile on his face as his earlier annoyance returned. Why wasn't Siara letting Ispiria sit with them? Was it some misguided attempt to rein in her spirit?

Ari gave a mental shake of his head. He was being ridiculous. Siara probably hadn't even done the seating. With a new baby, she would have a lot to keep track of. Thinking of Tiana, he looked around, but the little princess was nowhere to be seen. Yet another way Poromont differed from Sorga or his aunt's kitchen.

Ari spotted Ispiria at one of the smaller tables near the wall and smiled at her. She half-stood, waving. The young man next to her said something and she glanced his way, laughing. Someone across from her gestured and Ari realized it was Peine. He didn't turn, probably more concerned with his manners than Ispiria was, but whatever he said made her sit back down. She gave Ari a little shrug. Ari kept smiling at her for as long as he could before he had to turn his head or walk into something.

"Ari," Parrentine said as Ari climbed the steps onto the dais. "You remember my cousins, Lord Janvis, Lady Meylona and Lady Sandora?"

"Yes, your highness." Ari bowed to each in turn. "My lord, my ladies."

He'd met them the previous year when he was in Poromont for the fall tourney. He liked them well enough, although it was always hard to know people well within the stiff formality of court. Lord Janvis, heir to the largest dukedom in the west, looked in many ways similar to Parrentine. Both had the queen's heavy blonde hair, but Janvis' face was rougher, speaking of many hours out of doors, and he seemed more boisterous and relaxed than Parrentine.

Meylona was slightly older than Ari. Sandora, who he took his seat beside, was slightly younger. Ari remembered thinking before that Meylona, who was across from him, was the prettier of the two with her long blonde hair and cool aloofness, but Sandora seemed to have changed a lot. Even seated, he could see she was taller now, and instead of a smock, she wore a gown similar to the low cut ones most of the ladies of the court wore. Her deep brown hair wasn't in a single braid, but carefully arranged with half of it piled on top her head and half over one shoulder, the way Siara always wore hers.

Ari risked a glance over his shoulder at Ispiria, missing her fiery locks, but she was laughing and talking to a young man seated near her. For the first time, he noticed there was only one other girl at her table, a limp mousy little thing, and the five men aside from Peine seemed to be hanging on Ispiria's every word. Turning back, he caught Siara scrutinizing him, although she quickly dropped her eyes.

"I hear you're to be Parrentine's new champion, Lord Aridian," Meylona said. Her tone conveyed what an honor it was she spoke to him. Ari had heard rumors her father was having trouble marrying her off, in spite of her family name and ties to the crown.

"We can only hope, cousin," Parrentine said.

"Who were you looking at, Ari?" Sandora asked, sounding as young as he remembered, in spite of how dressed up she was. "Is that the girl you're promised to?" She craned her neck to see past him. "She's awful pretty."

"She's Lady Ispiria, my fiancée," Ari said. Servants began to arrive with plates of food, having likely been waiting on Ari's arrival.

"She must be one of the luckiest girls in Lggothland," Sandora said. "Maybe even luckier than whoever my brother finally settles on."

"Yes," Meylona said. "She is luckier. Sorga and the Northlands combined are the largest and most influential dukedom, which you would know if you paid any attention to your lessons. What house is she from, Lord Aridian? I don't recognize her name."

"House?" Ari repeated, realizing Meylona was referring to lineage. "She's Sir Cadwel's grand-niece on his wife's side. The daughter of his wife's sister's daughter."

"I see," Meylona said, her tone dismissive.

Ari tensed. He turned his attention to the dainty piece of smoked fish before him, hoping his expression didn't inform Parrentine's cousin what he thought of her and her tone.

"Any woman who doesn't have to live with Janvis is lucky," Sandora said, giggling. "She has such pretty hair," she added, sounding a little wistful.

"So, Aridian," Lord Janvis said, neatly folding his fish into one bite on his fork. "They tell me challengers come from far and wide, in total disregard of your reputation. From what we saw last year, they could have saved themselves a trip. I certainly wouldn't go against you."

"You're too lazy to go against anyone who isn't obligated to let you win," Meylona said with a sniff.

Next to Ari, Sandora rolled her eyes. Meylona didn't appear to notice, absorbed as she was with cutting her food into increasingly smaller and smaller pieces. Everyone else was almost done with their first course, light as it was, but she had yet to place any in her mouth.

"Sandora," Siara said. "Weren't you saying before dinner how you loved dancing with Lord Aridian last year and were hoping he would escort you again?"

Ari recalled dancing with Sandora in the fall. He enjoyed dancing with her because it freed him from partnering the endless line of young, and not so young, women who would never accept he was in love with Ispiria. Plus, dancing wasn't one of Ari's strong suits, but that didn't matter when he was dancing with Parrentine's cheerful little cousin.

"Oh yes," she said, turning to Ari. "Especially when you spun me around. Could we dance again?"

"Of course, my lady," Ari said, surprised by how excited she sounded about the idea. He was sure Ispiria would give up one dance for Sandora.

"And, certainly, you must partner me in a dance as well, my lord," Meylona said, looking up from her tiny fish bits.

"I would be honored, my lady," Ari said. He could feel Siara's eyes on him again. Was she worried his manners weren't up to the task of dining with the royal cousins? Well, he hoped she would get over it. They had a whole evening to spend together, after all.

Chapter 14

Although dinner dragged a bit for Ari, it proceeded amicably enough. Janvis and Parrentine carried the bulk of the conversation, speaking of hunting and riding, and nothing of consequence. At some point, Siara too asked Ari to dance with her, to which he readily agreed. He always danced best with Siara as his partner. She subtly corrected him, reminding him of the steps as they went, and he knew he actually looked as if he was good at it when he danced with her. It wasn't the same as dancing with Ispiria, who made everything more enjoyable and didn't care how he danced, but he liked to dance with Siara.

When the apparently much anticipated time for dancing arrived and all of the tables were moved from the center of the room, Ari stood to take his leave. Sitting half a room away from Ispiria all evening and not being able to speak to her was very much wearing on him.

"Lord Aridian." Siara's voice cut him off before the pleasantries of excusing himself could leave his mouth. "I'm sure you intend to dance with Sandora and Meylona first, as they are your tablemates."

"Yes, of course," he said, trying to hide his annoyance. He could see Ispiria watching him from across the room, waiting for him. He gave her a little shake of his head and turned to offer his hand to Sandora.

As the dancing proceeded, Ari became increasingly suspicious that Siara didn't want him to dance with Ispiria. Every time he tried to get to her, Siara would appear with a different young lady, introducing her and immediately turning the conversation to his dancing with her. Unless he wished to be terribly rude, he couldn't seem to find a way to decline. By the time he escorted Siara into the center of the room, he was starting to get quite annoyed.

"What are you doing, Siara?" he said in a low voice as they walked together through a tunnel of upraised arms.

"Whatever do you mean?" she asked, her face a caricature of innocence. They stepped apart, adding themselves to the end of the tunnel as more couples came through.

"I'm not stupid," he said when they clasped arms and swung close, before the steps of the dance drew them apart again. Ari kept a smile on his face, aware people would be watching them, but he didn't hide the anger in his tone.

The dance didn't offer any more opportunities for private conversation, but by the end, Ari had a new plan. He didn't care what Siara was doing. He would find out where Ispiria's rooms were and leave a note for her, asking her to send word on where they should meet. He bowed to Siara as the music ended, offering his arm to lead her back to their table.

Parrentine and Janvis were still seated, talking in low tones about religion. They broke off as Ari and Siara drew near.

"I think I shall retire for the evening," Ari said.

"So early, Lord Aridian?" Janvis asked, although the night was no longer young.

"Sir Cadwel always says, if you get a head start on the day, it can't sneak up and surprise you, and I'm sure I'll have a lot to do, what with the ladies picnicking tomorrow."

"I heard they roped you into being their showpiece," Janvis said, chuckling. "Better you than me. Parry and I are off for a hunt. Nothing like the thrill of a hunt."

"Yes, my lord," Ari said, although he hated hunting, himself. "Please bid your lovely sisters good evening for me, my lord, as I see they are well occupied on the dance floor."

"Good night, Ari," Siara said.

He wasn't sure, but he thought she might sound repentant. He gave another round of bows and smiles, to be on the safe side, and made his way from the room. On his way past, he tried to catch Ispiria's eye where she danced, but it was a quicker dance and he wasn't sure if she saw him.

The guards had no idea where the room Ispiria shared with her grandmother was but, eventually, Ari found a maid who told him. It was in the royal wing, which surprised him, but he didn't know much about what went into organizing such things. He went to his own room first and scrawled a hasty note, letting it dry while he walked, before folding it. Reaching her door, he paused, hearing Lady Enra's voice inside. Would he be able to convince their maid to give Ispiria his note without telling her great grandmother about it? He'd assumed Lady Enra would already be asleep.

"How nice to see you again so soon, Lord Aridian."

Siara's voice came from the direction of the stairwell. Ari winced. He turned to see her and two of her ladies in waiting gliding down the hall toward him, the smug look on her face instantly annoying.

"Your highness," he said, bowing. "Would you be so gracious as to allow me a moment of private conversation?"

"Oh?" she said. "Is that why you're in this hallway? Looking for me?" Her eyes came to rest on the parchment in his hand.

He tucked the note into his doublet, not answering her. She gestured to her attendants to wait, coming ahead alone.

"What are you doing, Siara?" he said once she drew near. "Why are you keeping Ispiria and me apart?"

She looked away, pursing her lips, before turning serious blue eyes back to him. "I only want you to think about it for a little while. There are so many young women of station in the kingdom. Ispiria is the first girl you met. You don't have to stay with the first girl you fall in love with. You may choose anyone you wish. You should at least make an effort to recognize your options."

Ari blinked, reorganizing his thoughts. This wasn't about him and Ispiria, he realized. It was about Siara and the Curse of Whey. Many people didn't believe in the curse, but Ari had seen its effects on Siara firsthand. He knew it was true what they said, a Wheylian woman could love once, and once only. If she couldn't be with the man she chose, she would wither and die.

But that wasn't what made the situation so delicate. All Wheylian women suffered the curse. What made Siara different was that her family had left her to be raised in Lggothland, where no one believed in the curse and no one had warned her about it. Ari remembered how angry Siara had been when she found out she had to make Parrentine love her or she would die.

"Siara," he said, irritation flowing from him, leaving his tone gentle. "I know I may choose, and I have. I love Ispiria.

She's the most beautiful and exuberant person in the world. She is perfect in every way. I love her."

"But how can you know? All you've done is hide in Sorga for two years."

"I just do," he said, managing not to ask her how she'd known she loved Parrentine when she first met him. Especially since Parrentine had hated her then. That was the type of stupid comment sure to bring out Siara's temper.

"It isn't only that," she said, looking nervous. "The woman you marry will be second only to the queen and myself in standing. A great amount of responsibility accompanies that. She will be scrutinized, and gossiped about. She'll dictate the bounds of acceptable behavior for generations of young women. I don't know if Ispiria is ready for that." She put a hand on his arm. "I like Ispiria, I really do, but do you want the free spirit you love so much put under that pressure? Do you want her to have to become the type of woman she'll need to be as your wife?"

"That's ridiculous." He was aware he'd spoken too loudly, for the women at the end of the hall looked startled. He modulated his tone. "Ispiria is perfect the way she is. She isn't going to corrupt your precious young noblewomen with her free spirit any more than you are corrupting them by being a Whey."

He regretted it as soon as he said it. Siara couldn't help but be aware of the sentiment that ran against her in the kingdom, of people whispering the word witch behind her back. People Ari always corrected, forcibly if need be. His position on the matter didn't make it any more acceptable to bring it up, though.

"Just think on what I've said." Her face and voice were suffused with anger. "And go to your own room, Lord

Aridian." Slipping her hand into his doublet, Siara pulled out the note, crumpling it. "I believe it's that way." She pointed down the hall.

"I'm sorry, Siara." He lowered his voice again. "I will think on it, I promise, but I won't change my mind."

She gave him a curt nod. He bowed, sad he'd let the conversation end on such a sour note.

Ari did think about their conversation on the way back to his room to write a new note, but most of his thoughts were on how he could have avoided angering Siara and how, by angering her, he'd squandered an opportunity to ask her about Peine's accusation he was cheating. There was no point thinking about the rest of it, because the things Siara said about Ispiria were completely nonsensical.

The sitting room was dark, save for lingering coals in the fireplace. Ari could tell Peine wasn't back yet, as he would have stirred up the fire. Ari didn't bother, since he could see clearly in almost any amount of light. He crossed to the sleeping chamber, frowning at finding the door ajar. He was sure he'd closed it. Apprehension heightening his senses, he realized he could hear someone breathing inside. Reaching out, he flung the door wide.

"Ispiria." She was sitting on the end of the giant bed in her green ball gown, kicking her feet and grinning at him.

"That was dramatic," she said. "You should always enter a room that way."

In two long strides, he was in front of her, lifting her off the bed and into his arms for her promised kiss. Ari felt all the tension of the evening drain from him. This was how he needed to end every day, holding Ispiria in his arms.

"Your hair smells awful," he said, finally setting her back down. He sat next to her, catching up her hand. "It won't stay straight, will it?"

"Oh no. As soon as they let me wash it, it will be right back the way it's supposed to be."

"They won't let you wash your hair?" Ari was starting to wonder what was wrong with the people in the capital.

"Well, they worked so hard for hours to do this to it. They mix old ale with the clear part from eggs, which is a terrible waste of food, don't you think? I'd be horrified if I found anyone in Sorga wasting food like that. How silly. Anyhow, then they stir it very fast, which is funny because the women Siara sends to do it are both so fat. They have to take turns and they start sweating all over. So, once it's foamy, they comb it into my hair. They use a metal comb they warm near the fire and it combs away all my curls."

"Why don't you say no?"

"They work so hard at it, and it makes Siara so happy, and I know she pretends to be normal, but she's very sad about Princess Tiana. I can't say no. It does stay out of my mouth when I'm eating this way, so that's nice."

"Well, so long as you don't intend to keep it this way." He reached out to touch it. It was very shiny and bright red, but so boring, and it smelled like a dirty tavern someone had sprayed perfume in. "How did you manage to get here? I tried to go to your rooms to leave a note, but Siara caught me."

"I saw you leave, but I couldn't get away then because I was dancing with some boar Peine introduced me to." She made a face. "When Siara left, everyone was watching her, so I slipped away from the ladies great grandmother has following me around. It wasn't hard. I was a little worried when I didn't find you here. You were dancing with a lot of pretty girls."

She sounded forlorn about it, so he kissed her again. That always cheered them both up. She leaned toward him, her lips soft and yielding. Ari let it go on as long as he dared, acutely aware they were sitting in the dark on the end of a bed. He pulled back and she followed, forcing him to place his hands on her shoulders to hold her away.

The nearly off the shoulder style of her dress left her skin bare where he held her. It was warm and soft under his calloused palms. He drew in a deep breath. She knew he'd promised Sir Cadwel he would respect her virtue. Why did she do this to him?

"Ispiria." He cleared his throat, aware his tone had a ragged edge to it. "I should escort you back to your room."

"And have someone see us together so late in the evening?" she said. "The whole city would be mortified. Anyhow, I don't have to go yet."

"Yes, you do," he said, trying to compose himself.

She rolled her eyes at him. "Fine, I'll go." She stood up, smoothing her gown. "But you'll miss me."

She crossed to the door, shooting him one last mischievous grin before slipping away. Ari collapsed backward onto the bed. He missed her already.

Chapter 15

Feeling like he might belong after sitting there with Ispiria, Ari decided to sleep in the massive bed, but it was as miserable as he'd suspected it would be. He tossed and turned, worrying about the picnic in the morning, about Princess Tiana, but most of all, about Peine's question. Was he cheating?

He woke groggy and later than normal. Peine was nowhere to be seen, but Ari's clothes were laid out and a bath drawn. Ari was a bit perturbed to know he'd slept through so much activity. Dressing quickly, he forwent breakfast and hurried to the courtyard, hoping Peine had asked someone to ready Stew and Charger.

When Ari arrived in the courtyard, most of the ladies were already assembled. He could see Ispiria standing with a group of young women near her age. He noticed several of them wore ribbons tying their hair back, the way Ispiria often did. Was Siara right? Were they copying Ispiria? Or did girls wear ribbons like that all the time? Looking about, he realized many of the women mimicked the way Siara and the queen wore their hair as well.

Ispiria saw him and started across the courtyard, but before she reached him, the captain in charge of the guards accompanying the ladies on their picnic strolled over.

"I hear Princess Siara put you in charge of this jaunt, Lord Aridian," the captain said. "Nominally."

Ari knew he'd met the man before, but he couldn't recall his name. "Yes, Captain, and as I have never been even nominally in charge of a ladies' picnic before, I hope I may follow your lead?"

"It was my hope that would be your hope. I should have known you'd have the sense you were born with, what with being Sir Cadwel's heir. Smile at the ladies and I'll take care of the rest, my lord."

"Thank you, Captain" Ari bowed slightly. "If you'll excuse me, I see one lady in particular I'd like to smile at right now."

"Certainly, my lord," the captain said with a bow, backing away so Ispiria could take his place before Ari.

"Did you miss me?" she asked, bouncing up on her tiptoes, her green eyes bright.

If they were alone, he would have kissed her, but it seemed like everyone in the courtyard was watching them. "Very much." He wondered if taking her hands would be too improper. "Will you ride alongside me, my lady?"

"I can't, my lord. Princess Siara asked me to ride in the coach with her, Tiana and the queen."

Ari shot a glare at Siara, but the princess was climbing into the coach.

Ispiria followed his gaze. "I best go. Everyone else is almost ready."

She gave him a little curtsy and walked away. He watched her entering the coach, grinding his teeth. Siara was nothing if not tenacious.

Pages were almost finished assisting the other ladies up a set of stone steps and onto their mounts, so Ari crossed to the stable to look for Stew. As he'd hoped, the horses were ready, Peine standing between them, apparently about to lead them out.

"Good morning, Ari. I was starting to worry I'd have to go wake you."

"You almost had to," Ari said, taking Stew's reins and mounting.

Ari let Stew set their course, Peine's presence bringing back his worry about cheating, overshadowing his annoyance with Siara. Was he really a cheater? Certainly, he had an unfair advantage. If he was cheating, he must withdraw from the tourney. He didn't want to withdraw, though. His thoughts whirled, getting him nowhere. He needed someone who would tell him the truth, even if it was harsh. He resolved to ask Siara about it before the picnic was over.

The assembled ladies meandered through the city, Ari leading on a prancing Stew, and up the long slow hill until they reached the tall forests lining the King's Way. Following a trail Ari had never paid much attention to, they arrived at a clearing where pavilions and food were already prepared. A low table was set on thick rugs, with a throne of cushions on one end. Under another tent, a group of musicians strummed peaceful music. With such elaborate preparations, Ari wasn't sure it should qualify as a picnic at all.

When the meal was finished, eaten with the hands but in very delicate fashion, the ladies rose and began wandering about the clearing in small groups, chattering. Ispiria and some of the others took up a game of croquet. Ari would have liked to play, but his turbulent mind wouldn't allow him such simple distractions. He sought out Siara, seeing her walking alone with Princess Tiana in her arms. "Your highness." He bowed as he spoke.

"Good afternoon, Lord Aridian." She gently rocked the little princess in her arms. Tiana stared at her with huge blue eyes, Siara looking back with sorrow in her gaze.

"Siara, I have a --" He stopped, not wanting to use the word problem.

"A what?" She raised her gaze to frown at him. "What is it?"

"Do you think I'm cheating when I compete in the king's tourneys?" He squared his shoulders, trying to quell his nerves.

"Cheating?" Her tone conveyed complete surprise. "In what way?"

"I'm not normal. You know that. The Aluiens changed me."

"That's the most ridiculous thing I've ever heard you say, and I've heard some silly things come out of your mouth. Where on earth did you get that idea?"

"Well, it's just --" He floundered, not wanting Peine to suffer Siara's wrath. "There are people who may deserve to win, you know, and I'm making it impossible for them. Did you know there's a Wheylian knight favored to do well?"

Her eyes narrowed. "Peine. I'll have a word--"

"Siara." He put a hand on her arm, trying to recapture the attention of her gaze, which was scanning the clearing for his valet. "Please don't tell Peine I said anything. I asked to find out what you think, not to censure him."

"I told you what I think. It's the most idiotic thing I've ever heard."

"So you said."

"Where is the queen?" Siara asked, still searching the gaggle of women.

"She was right there, by that path." Ari turned to point, but the queen was gone.

"She shouldn't wander unattended." Siara pursed her lips.

"I'll follow her. Please don't say a thing to Peine. I mean it, Siara."

"You mean, I mean it, your highness," she corrected, but she smiled, nodding that he should go after the queen.

"Your highness." He bowed, rising to headed across the clearing.

Ari followed the narrow path for several turns. Tall trees and dense bushes leaned in, all of them bright with spring's new leaves. He saw no one, and he quickened his pace, his mind warring between doubt the queen had come that way and a nagging certainty she had. Why would she walk so fast? He'd seen her only moments ago, standing in the clearing with the rest of the court ladies, watching the croquet game. He strained his ears from some sound, some clue she was near.

A familiar voice trailed down the path and he froze.

"Your majesty," Larke said, out of sight ahead of Ari. "Your beauty outshines even the glory of so perfect a spring day."

"This is remarkable," Ari heard the queen answer. "You look so like your father. If it hadn't been twenty-five years, I would say you were one and the same."

"I came to beg forgiveness of you, my lady," Larke said. "I meant not to startle you so these two years past at the tourney. Had I known the great distress my visage would cause, I should have had my nose cut off and grown whiskers."

The queen laughed. Ari had never heard her laugh like that before. It was a young sound. It was musical. "You speak as your father did."

"I can but take that as a compliment."

Ari could picture the extravagant bow Larke must give to accompany those words.

"Sir, you look of an age with my son. Mayhap a bit older."

"I've had the pleasure of meeting the prince, and I would give myself more than a year on him," Larke said.

"Just so." Queen Parrella's voice was sad.

"I have distressed you, your majesty?"

"No, it is nothing. Surely, I was one of many young women possessed of the romantic notion that when your father sang, he sang only to her. I suppose it was much of what made him so great a bard."

"I suppose it was." The bard's tone was even but knowing him as well as he did, Ari could hear the pain hidden in his friend's voice. "And my age puts an end to such illusions."

"Did he ever speak of me? At all?" Queen Parrella's voice was so low, Ari's enhanced hearing could barely discern her words, but even a deaf man would have recognized the sorrow in her tone.

"I entered this world at much the same time Larkesong left it," Larke replied.

"We never knew what happened to him. He simply disappeared."

In the forest, beyond Ari's sight, there was silence.

"Well, it is of no moment." The queen's voice was almost a sigh. "I thank you for your apology, and for laying to rest the lost fancies of a young heart."

"I live but to serve, your majesty."

This last must have been accompanied by a bow, because Ari could hear the light footsteps of the queen coming his way. He cast his gaze left and right before melting into the trees beside the path. She passed him unawares, and Ari was certain he saw her brush tears from her eyes. He stayed where he was, waiting to be sure she was well away.

"Skulking?" a musical voice whispered in his ear.

Ari jumped, twisting, and banged his head on a low branch.

"Eavesdropping is unbecoming, lad. Have I taught you no better manners?"

"I wasn't, that is . . ." Ari stuttered, rubbing his head. "I didn't mean to. I was coming to see if the queen was well."

"And?" Larke raised an eyebrow at him.

"Uh, she seems fine."

"And she seems to have headed down that path." Larke pointed.

"Was it safe to let her see you?" Ari asked, ignoring the dismissal. "How did she know to come? Did you call her? With magic?" He wasn't sure how he felt about the idea of Larke enspelling the queen.

"I may have put the gentlest of suggestions into her head," Larke said. "I know it wasn't noble of me, lad. I wanted but to speak to her this final time. 'Twas an opportunity too good to let pass by."

"But you made her think you never loved her." Ari was stung at the injustice his friend did himself. Larke looked away. "And I know you did."

"Who knows what Larkesong did or did not do in life, lad? 'Tis hard to say, now he's gone." The bard shook his head, still hatless. "She made the right choice, those years ago. There is no reason to leave her doubting it."

"But she didn't really choose. You disappeared."

"She has ever had a fierce heart. She could have come searching, or refused the love of another. It's a braver thing than most realize to do your duty."

"And you wrote that song about her," Ari said, recalling the tragic melody he'd heard the bard play only once.

"Larkesong wrote it, lad. The last act of the greatest bard of his day."

"I don't know why you do that. I know you and Larkesong are the same person."

"But do I know it?" The bard chuckled, but it was a melancholy sound. "Larkesong died that night and, by the Lady's hand, I was born. It was best the master bard left these lands, and I wouldn't do ought to bring him back."

"You're a confusing person, Larke," Ari said. "Do you think I'm a cheater?" he added, his own anxiety springing from him.

"You are what you are, lad. You can be no more. Why should you be any less?"

Ari pondered this for a moment, but found another thought growing in his mind. "Larke, you can summon people into the woods." He fixed the bard with a hard look. "When I was younger, my uncle forbid me to go into the woods at night, but I did, and somehow the Aluiens were right there--"

"I believe Princess Siara is seeking you," Larke interrupted.

Ari tuned, hearing footfalls approaching down the path. When he looked back, Larke was gone.

"Where have you been?" Siara demanded as Ari stepped back out onto the path. Princess Tiana was nestled in her arms and two ladies in waiting and a guard were in tow. "The queen has called the picnic. They're about to send a search for you.

164

You're supposed to be here watching over us, not the other way around."

"I was, um, thinking. I'm sorry, your highness. I was on my way back."

"Well, come on." She turned to usher her entourage back down the path.

With one last look around for Larke, Ari hurried after her, feeling like he would never be able to sort out all of the thoughts in his head. What he really needed was a little time practicing. Swinging a sword always cleared his mind.

Chapter 16

It wasn't until Ari caught Peine's glare as they entered Sir Cadwel's rooms that he had any idea his friend was angry with him.

"I can't believe you went running to the princess on me," Peine said as soon as he closed the door. "We aren't children, Ari."

"I wanted her opinion," Ari said, but he knew that wasn't a good excuse. "I didn't tell her it was your idea. She guessed. I told her not to talk to you about it."

"It's difficult enough to be a Whey in this kingdom without having the princess think badly of you." Peine paced the sitting room. "How will I ever advance myself if I'm not in her good graces?"

"Advance yourself?"

"Ari, you're my friend, but do you think I want to stay your servant forever?"

"I don't think of you that way."

"Then what do you think? That I'm going to follow you around my entire life, living off you?" The anger in Peine's voice startled Ari. "I need a living of my own, and I don't have your good fortune. No one came along and made me an unvanquishable swordsman, and no one will swoop down and dub me heir to their dukedom. I may be a younger son, but I'm of noble blood, and a Whey. My people have been landholders since before your people even landed on our shores."

"Won't your father give you some land?" Ari asked, his tone contrite, even though it wasn't his fault his ancestors had sailed to Lggothland. Somehow, the conversation felt like it was spinning out of control.

Peine shook his head. "There's no more land to give, no more ways to divide what he has."

"Can't I give you land?" Ari hadn't realized Peine wanted his own lands. He probably wanted a wife and a baby, too, like Parrentine and Siara.

"You would do that?" Peine asked, his expression lightening.

"Of course I would. You're my closest friend."

"I'm sorry, Ari." Peine plunked down on the stiff sofa with a sigh. "It's just, I always hoped to be a great knight, like Sir Cadwel. Like you will be. Only, I've realized I have to make a different life. Maybe as a courtier, or I could try being a landholder, if I had land. A lady like Chinella will never marry me if I can't offer her something."

"Who's Chinella?"

"That's not the point," Peine muttered, his chin in his palms. "It doesn't have to be her. Just someone like her."

"When you find a girl who really loves you, she won't care."

"Of course she'll care. You really think Ispiria would give up her life in Sorga to go live in a dirt hovel with you? And even if she would, if you really love her, would you want her to?"

Ari pondered that, sitting down on an ornate chair. "What about Natan's job? He's been training you to be chief steward of Sorga."

"Sure, once he dies. That won't be for years." Peine shook his head. "And chief stewards don't marry. They run their lord's household instead of having one of their own. I thought at first I would want to do that, but not anymore. Of course, there's not much point in having children without any legacy to leave them."

"The king will knight me this spring, unless I disgrace myself in the tourney," Ari said, hitting upon a plan. "You could be my page. I could train you. I'm sure Sir Cadwel would help."

"Ari, look at me." Peine threw his arms wide. "I'll never be strong enough to wear a suit of armor, let alone fight in one. Yes, I could learn to fence, but that's not the same as being one of the king's knights."

Ari didn't know what to say. Peine was right. He wasn't cut out to be a knight, and Ari couldn't think of anything to do about it. You couldn't grow someone, after all. Even the Aluiens didn't have powers like that. Ari didn't like to think of Peine not being around. He hadn't really considered how Peine must feel about it, though. He leaned back in his chair, this new worry settling in with the rest of his anxieties.

There was a knock at the door, which Peine jumped up to answer, returning with a note for Ari. Taking it, he recognized Ispiria's hand immediately. With mingled happiness and relief, he read her request he join her in the castle library.

"Ispiria wants to meet in the library," he said, handing Peine the parchment. Ari felt guilty about cutting their conversation short, though he didn't know what else to say. "Look, we'll figure something out. Don't worry. You can come to the library too, if you like."

Peine shook his head. Ari hurried out the door.

Ispiria wasn't in the library when he arrived, but she appeared moments later. The two ladies who followed her in were kind enough to sit unobtrusively in the back of the room, stitching intricate designs onto costly silk. Ari wondered if they'd tried to make Ispiria participate. She hated embroidering.

After a time, Peine did join them, his good temper apparently restored. They scoured the library, dragging out books about weapons and breeds of horses and faraway lands across the ocean. They'd spent many hours thus in Sir Cadwel's library in Sorga, and Ari's cares fell from him as he lost himself in the company of his two closest friends.

Dinner that night was also a pleasant affair. The entire royal family was dining in seclusion with the queen's relatives. Freed of anyone else of sufficient rank to warrant a head table, Ari sat with Peine and Ispiria, and danced with Ispiria as much as he could without being blatantly rude to anyone. Peine, he noticed, danced with as many young ladies as there were songs played.

They didn't retire until the musicians stopped performing, and Ari contented himself with a bow and a kiss on one of Ispiria's hands before her ladies escorted her away. Ari retuned alone to his room with its giant uncomfortable bed. Peine disappeared somewhere. Ari hoped Chinella, or whoever it was tonight, didn't fall too in love with his friend.

He decided not to worry about that, though, or anything else. Pushing thoughts of cheating, usurping Sir Cadwel, Siara's heart breaking over her baby, crafty Aluiens, Peine's future and trouble in Wheylia out of his mind, Ari summoned up an image of Ispiria, with her hair properly curly. His fiancée's pretty face smiling at him in his mind's eye, Ari drifted off to sleep.

He rose early the next morning and went down to the practice field, only to find Prince Parrentine already there. To the delight of those few other early risers, the prince and Ari crossed swords, each testing the other until Ari finally lowered his, signaling they should take a break. He didn't need one, but Parrentine looked to be on his last leg. Ari rather thought the prince should put more time into his swordwork, but he supposed rulers had a lot of other concerns, which was why they needed king's champions.

They crossed the raked dirt of the practice yard to the well, where a page drew up a bucket of water for them. Ari waited while his monarch drank deeply, splashing water on his face to cool it. After Ari drank, Parrentine gestured they should take a walk around the field.

It was different for Ari than the first time he'd practiced for a tourney. Back then, Sir Cadwel was with him, and took him to practice in hiding in the woods so others wouldn't guess at Ari's skill. Now he practiced on the castle's own field, inside the walls, where the tournament would take place. Another difference was the constant audience. There seemed to be people who came to the field in the early hours of the day and stayed there, waiting to watch him practice. Not a small number of them were ladies of the court, who commandeered a section of the nobles' boxes. They were a mildly nerve racking collection of soft colors, flowery scents and frilly parasols lurking at the edge of his vision.

"I hear your resolve to be our champion has wavered," Parrentine said once they were down the field, away from prying ears.

Ari cast the prince a surprised look.

"If you do not wish me to know things, avoid telling them to my wife," Parrentine said with a chuckle. "But surely it's not true?"

"I want to be champion more than anything, my lord." Ari worked to squelch any anger that might surface in his tone. Next time he spoke privately to Siara about something, he would have to be more insistent about the private aspect of it. Although, he supposed it was only natural she would tell Parrentine. "But to be a knight takes more than skill. It's a post of honor, and one where the ways of honor must be upheld. My worry is I fail in that. I'm not what I am by nature, but by enchantment. Is this truly fair?"

"You are faster and stronger than you've a right, but I think not so much as you believe. You stand fingers taller than I." Ari got the impression Parrentine, probably with the help of his meddling wife, had been practicing his argument. "Surely you would be fast and strong regardless of the tampering of the Aluiens. And you needn't hone those skills so well. The choice of that great work is your own. How many hours of the day do you work with the sword?"

"Only two, usually, my lord." Seeing the surprise in Parrentine's eyes, Ari felt obligated to elaborate. "I don't have time for more, since there is jousting to practice, and foils, flails, maces, archery, and more other weapons than I ever realized. And since I learned to read, Sir Cadwel insists I study books of tactic, and now he has me translating them from other languages. He advises this will help me be a greater leader of men as well as learn to understand those from other lands. I find it tedious."

Parrentine stared at him. The prince shook his head, looking bemused. "Let me rephrase. I don't mean the sword specifically. How many hours of the day do you devote to learning the ways of war, both practical and theoretical?"

"Well." Ari paused to consider. "All of them, I guess, and some of the night too. I do eat, of course."

"Yes, well." Parrentine cleared his throat. "I think that more than illustrates my point. Never has a young man been so dedicated. For that alone, you are deserving."

"But it still remains that I am different."

"I could argue the fallacy of your thinking with you the day long, but the truth of the matter is this." Parrentine stopped walking, turning to face Ari squarely. "The king's champion is the protector of the royal family. That's why we hold a tourney. To find the strongest and the best. I do not believe you violate the laws of honor, but to my discredit, even did I, I would still want you to be champion. When the lives of my family are in the balance, you are the one I want protecting them. And what of the Empty Ones? At least some of them aspire to control our lands. If they try to take the throne again, do you ask me to send a man other than you against them? I say you are but evening the score."

"Against an Empty One, yes, but what of when I face mortal men?"

"But you must vanquish all of the mortal men to win the post. If it makes you feel better, I order you, as your prince, to win the tourney."

It did make Ari feel better, but he still wasn't sure it made it right. They walked on in silence. Ari wondered if he dared ask his prince what he thought of Ispiria. They were friends, but there was still the distance of rank between them. After they made the turn around the far end of the field, Parrentine spoke again.

"Ari, what gods do you believe in?"

"I was raised to the old gods," Ari said, wondering why Parrentine asked.

"In Sorga, do many worship the Overgod?"

"Sir Cadwel doesn't turn away the priests and nuns of the Overgod." Ari didn't elaborate on Sir Cadwel's low opinion of those priests and nuns, especially the nuns, one of whom Sir Cadwel had sentenced to beheading a few years past. "But in Sorga, the people seem content with the old gods."

Ari was thankful for this, for the old gods were the gods of the peasantry, and he'd grown up a peasant. As far as Ari knew, his people had no real gods before arriving on the shores of what was now called Lggothland. The Wheys had taught them to worship the gods around them, and most religious practices were quite simple.

The village his aunt and uncle lived in, where he'd lived most of his years, had a large standing stone of unknown origin in the middle of one of the fields. Most of the time, it was ignored, and crops were planted around it, but at the changing of the seasons, it was decorated and celebrations held there. He knew, as well, that many would leave offerings at its base, asking the god that dwelled inside to help them win the heart of another, or to bring them a good harvest, or any number of wishes.

The old gods were the gods of the people. They lived in every glen and hollow. They were familiar and comfortable, not like the constant levies, mysterious ramblings and arcane teachings that went with worshiping the Overgod.

Ari knew little of what those teachings were, or why the Overgod needed money. He did know its priests and nuns were becoming more prevalent as they strove to make headway in Lggothland and that the Overgod had more of a following among the nobility, especially in the south. He also knew, and it worried him, that the wars which once plagued Hapland and other nearby kingdoms were the result of a feud between the followers of the Overgod and other religions. For this reason, if no other, Ari was distrustful.

"Why do you ask?" Ari said into the silence surrounding them.

"Some of the nobles worry about Siara's heritage. She wishes to accompany you to her homeland when you take the princess and that wish has become known. It's agitating them. They seem to think she's going to come back a witch who worships trees and river stones, or similar nonsense. They want me to hold a ceremony and have her dedicate herself to the Overgod."

"Will you?"

"Surely you realize I've recovered my sanity enough not to do that. I have no intention of asking Siara to do any such thing. I only wondered where northern heads stood on the issue, should anything ever come of it."

"You know you have my support and the support of all Sorga in whatever you do, your highness."

"And where Sorga leads, others will follow," Parrentine said, but his smile still looked worried to Ari. They finished their walk in silence.

Later, after another enjoyable day in the library with Ispiria, Ari and Peine returned to Sir Cadwel's suite to ready for the king's banquet. Ari would prefer a restful evening the night before the tourney was to begin, but there was no help for it.

He was obliged to attend and he wouldn't insult his king or embarrass Sir Cadwel by shirking his duty, so he arrived in the great hall promptly and well-dressed in Sorga blue and brown. The evening progressed better than he'd expected, with one short speech from the king proclaiming the start of the tourney with the dawn. Ari could glimpse Ispiria from where he sat, and Peine was attending him so he wouldn't make any unseemly mistakes.

Ari was starting to relax, his mind wandering to the dancing which would commence soon, when a man dressed in dark blue rose from the far end of the table and headed up the length of it.

Peine bent close under the guise of serving Ari more wine, although Ari hadn't actually consumed any yet. "That's Sir Keite," he whispered, excitement coloring his tone.

Conversation stilled as all eyes followed the Wheylian knight's progress toward the king. Keite stopped behind Sir Cadwel's empty chair where it stood to Ennentine's right and bowed.

"The vaulted chair," Sir Keite said as he straightened, placing both hands easily on the back. "Your majesties."

"Sir Keite," the king acknowledged with a nod. "You honor us with your participation in our tourney."

"It is I who am honored, my lord." Sir Keite raised his voice to carry through the hall. "Both to compete on your fine field, and by the prestige of the prize, for all hold it to be true it is this very seat for which we contend."

"Yet it is rumor still," the king said. "One that will surely be put to rest on the morrow."

The knight chuckled, and murmurs filled the room. "As his majesty wishes," Sir Keite said with another bow.

The king nodded his dismissal, turning his attention to his wife.

Ari watched Sir Keite with a nervous prickle along his spine. Keite had the pale skin and dark hair and eyes of all Wheys, but something about him tugged at Ari's awareness. As if sensing the scrutiny, Sir Keite turned to Ari with a slight inclination of his head. Their eyes met, the Wheylian knight's flickering with fear before he composed himself.

"Lord Aridian, I hear as well that all in the land hope to see you ascend to knighthood this tourney. May I add my wishes."

"Thank you, sir." Ari nodded, barely aware of his words. There was something about the man, something that reminded Ari of . . . Sir Keite's skin was overly pale for one who must practice for long hours in the out of doors. His dark eyes seemed to hide a strange wideness of pupil. His light frame did not look the type to be clad in mail, let alone plate.

Sir Keite pulled back his lips in a thin smile, revealing even teeth. "That's a remarkable piece of decoration you wear." his eyes narrowed on Ari's amulet.

Ari reached up and tucked the silver pendant back into his doublet, trying not to wince at how deadly cold it was.

"One wonders from whence it came?" Keite continued.

"It's a family heirloom," Ari said, meeting the man's gaze.

"I see." Sir Keite gave Ari a bow. "Until the morrow."

Ari nodded, keeping his visage carefully calm. He watched Sir Keite as the knight returned to his seat at the far end of the table. Ari's appetite was spoiled. What was it the prince had said earlier about Ari being the one to protect the kingdom from the grasping claws of Empty Ones? That one of the foul flesh-eating villains should stand fearlessly before the king seemed nearly impossible to Ari, but everything about Sir Keite told him it was so.

Ari danced several dances with Ispiria, Siara and Parrentine's cousins, but much as he wanted to enjoy himself, his worries wouldn't let him. He excused himself early, on the pretext he wanted a long rest before the start of the tourney in the morning, and returned with Peine to their rooms. Once there, Ari gave voice to his newest concern. He was almost positive Sir Keite was an Empty One, member of the evil magical race who had tried to secure Lggothland's throne, invaded Sorga and burned the Hawker's village. Worse, by all reports, Queen Reudi had sent him.

"You can't know for sure he's an Empty One," Peine said. "I was there, too, and he seemed perfectly normal to me, and it is an interesting amulet you have. There's no harm in someone observing that."

Ari sighed. He should have realized how determined Peine was to idolize Sir Keite and kept his concerns private. Ari knew he could make arguments for his case, but after their conversation the day of the picnic, he didn't have the heart to point out things like how Sir Keite was a typical Whey and had not the stature for the role he was playing. Something was amiss.

Ari was amazed an Empty Ones would walk so brazenly amongst them, yet his first great foe, Lord Ferringul, had. The average Lggothian seemed unable to sense the pall of evil that clung to them. Ari wondered what mischief Sir Keite was working and if it really was at Queen Reudi's order or if the High Priestess of Whey was herself under the Empty One's spell. Becoming king's champion of Lggothland couldn't be the whole of the plot.

He considered going to the king to voice his suspicions about Sir Keite, but in truth he had no proof. Just his feeling of unease and the icy chill of his amulet when Keite was near. Even though Ari felt in his bones that Sir Keite was evil, was that enough to accuse a man on, when Lggothland's peaceful relationship with Wheylia hung in the balance?

He climbed into the giant bed with his mind even less settled than the evening before. Holding his amulet in his palm, he thought of the Lady. Someday soon, when the tourney was over, he needed to find her. He had, he feared, more questions in his life than answers. Some of them needed to be laid to rest.

Chapter 17

The first morning of the tourney dawned bright and hot. Ari stood in his blue and white striped pavilion beside the tourney field, looking down at the pile of metal he was about to encase himself in. He could already see a disadvantage over the fall competition. It was going to get very sticky in his armor before the day was out. Even the shade of his tourney tent did little to help.

Hot or no, Ari loved his armor. Lifting the breastplate, he ran his hand over the long mark where the dent Sir Cadwel had put in it had been hammered out. As sharp as his dismay was at the making of it, it was almost a good luck charm to him now. It was a part of his armor.

He started getting ready, not sure where Peine was. Ari could fasten all of the buckles on his armor himself, although with varying degrees of difficulty. He was almost done when his valet arrived.

"Sir Keite's armor is dark blue," Peine exclaimed, hurrying to take the last buckle from Ari's fumbling fingers and fasten it deftly. He grabbed Ari's surcoat from the rough wooden table. "We really should get you something fancier to wear."

"I like my armor. It was made by the son of the man who made Sir Cadwel's. He's the best smith in Sorga."

Peine stood back and looked Ari over critically. "It's boring. It doesn't have any scroll work or dyes or anything. Once you have your helmet on, no one will even know it's you."

"That's what that is for." Ari pointed at the bundle in Peine's arms, holding his own out so Peine could drape the surcoat over his head and lace up the sides. "None of those things help keep you alive any better. Besides, people haven't seemed to have any trouble keeping track of me the past two tourneys."

Ari smoothed down his surcoat. He was very proud to call the blue and white field and brown hawk of Sorga his own. None other had the right, save Sir Cadwel himself.

Trumpets blared without and Peine grabbed up Ari's broadsword and helmet. "We should go. The king's speech is about to begin."

Ari trailed Peine out of the tent. Looking up, he searched the boxes for Ispiria, finding her sitting at Siara's side. Ari smiled, waving to them. He was pleased Siara had asked Ispiria to sit with her, hoping it meant the princess was relenting in her judgment and happy that, if he won, Ispiria would be in the royal box, at hand to see him made champion.

Spying him, Ispiria jumped up and waved back, leaning out over the railing. Ari could see Siara's lips move as the princess reached out, drawing Ispiria back to her seat. She gave Ari a grimace and sat down, her back straight. Ari tried to keep amusement off his face, worried Siara would glance over and see him laughing at her attempts to change the woman he loved, who was as unchangeable as the sun.

The king stood. The crowd settled into hushed silence. Everyone waited to hear if Ennentine would confirm Sir Cadwel's resignation.

"Rumor runs like spring rain across the land." The king's strong voice carried across the tourney field. "I know all must have heard ere now that our dear friend, our unconquerable champion, Sir Cadwel, Duke of Sorga and Lord of the Northlands, abdicated his titles to Lord Aridian this winter."

Ari was surprised by the cheering this evoked.

The king raised his hand for silence. "Furthermore, Sir Cadwel has, as of the opening of this tourney, relinquished his post as champion of our realm."

The crowd murmured. Around them, the heavy banners of the nobility snapped in the spring wind.

"Heavy is our heart at the news, for while Sir Cadwel stood beside the crown, we knew Lggothland would know peace unbroken and prosperity for all. Lucky we have been, my people, to have a knight of such uncompromising valor and might to watch over us for these many years."

Ari looked about, unsurprised to see tears fall. Sir Cadwel had been king's champion for twenty-five years, and his ascension to that position came on the heels of generations of war. Ari knew the tales of those times, when Lggothland was in constant turmoil and the people suffered harsh levies and lived and died under the burdens of famine and terror.

"But we need not fear," the king said, raising his voice, his tone lifting with hope. "For this tourney shall choose a new champion. One of might and honor. One who will hold back

183

turmoil and strife, defend the weak, and keep out borders safe. Let the tourney begin."

Trumpets blared, nearly drowned out by the roar of the crowd. The chaos of voices melded into a cadence, and Ari realized they were chanting his name. He hesitated, unsure of how to conduct himself before so much adulation, before going to stand beside Peine to watch the day's bouts be drawn.

The competitors divided into two groups, the older knights who had already proven themselves worthy of the joust standing to one side, observing the drawing. The unproven knights and pages clustered around the tourney master, who began to pull wooden markers from a hammered gold vessel. All new knights had to prove themselves before they could be exempted from the opening rounds. Ari had proved himself, but since he wasn't a knight when he did it, he could not claim his exemption.

Not that he minded. He looked forward to testing himself against new opponents, and there were many gathered that day. Anyone who could wield a sword and piece together a suit of armor had come, as rumor spread far and wide that this tourney would choose a new king's champion.

Ari felt sorry for his first opponent and so ended it quickly with three light blows to the chest, before the other even realized the bout had begun. He was an unintelligent fellow, but large, and it was obvious his two brothers had brought him there in the hope he might somehow make a name for himself.

Ari was sure the man was quite strong, but he was also sure his helmet was a hammered-out cooking vessel. None of the three seemed to mind the man's loss, appearing more interested in meeting Ari in person. Ari gave them a few coins and told them to have a drink on him at the day's end. He wasn't sure, two more competitors or no, that they would wait that long.

Both of his other two opponents that day were better equipped, but fared the same. Ari dispatched them easily, working hard to be gracious. He really would have preferred a bit more of a challenge.

Between bouts, he was able to observe two of Sir Keite's matches. The Whey fought well, dealing with his opponents easily. Ari saw no evidence of sorcery at work. Skill seemed to be the main determinant in both wins. He started to concede to himself that there was a chance he was wrong. Sir Keite could be a normal knight, and Ari a worrier, seeing danger lurking where none truly hid.

The following dawn brought out flails, which Ari enjoyed. It was a weapon requiring greater skill, challenging to wield and avoid even if your opponent was incompetent. Drawing early matches, he ended his day quickly, although he drew each out more than was his wont, playing to the crowd. Not concerned with adoration, he did it more for their enjoyment, ignoring Peine when he rolled his eyes. When Ari's matches were concluded, he and Peine went to lean against the rails to watch Sir Keite's second match.

The Wheylian knight seemed at ease and it was with obvious surprise that he allowed the young man facing him to score a hit on his left arm. Face suffusing with anger, Sir Keite swung his flail in a high arch, smashing the top of his opponent's wooden shield, sending splinters flying into the lad's eyes. Pressing his advantage, as debris and blood now compromised his opponent's vision, Sir Keite wound the flail around the other way, taking the same swing from the opposite direction.

Ari cried out, realizing before anyone else what must result. The young man with the broken shield could not yet see and made no move to duck or raise the remains of his shattered protection. The flail took him full in the side of the head. There was a dull thunk as it crushed his skull. A woman screamed, the tourney master and sawbones hurrying forward.

Ari clamped his mouth closed as Sir Keite raised his visor, peering down at the lifeless form with no emotion. Turning away from the body, Sir Keite crossed to stand before Ari and Peine, loosening the buckles on his shield as he approached. Around them, the crowd rumbled with hisses and boos.

"As this was a friendly bout, I'll not demand you satisfy my honor for the way you attempted to warn my opponent of his fate." Sir Keite's tone was low and cold.

"Since this was a friendly bout, it was an unworthy fate you led him to," Ari growled.

"He knew the dangers in it." Sir Keite watched seemingly without care as they shut the lad's eyes and bore him away.

"Then you should know the danger awaiting you, should you face me," said Ari, barely master of his emotions.

"I see little danger in it, boy." Sir Keite turned away.

The crowd booed as the Whey returned to the center of the field and his final opponent of the day.

"You were threatening him," Peine said.

"He killed that man." Ari's voice betrayed his surprise at his friend's tone.

"He probably didn't mean to. It's hard to stop a flail once you set it moving."

"I could have stopped it." Ari winced at the look Peine gave him. It clearly said, 'Because you cheat.'

"Maybe a normal man couldn't." Peine walked away.

Ari frowned after him. He knew Peine wanted Sir Keite to do well. He wasn't unaware of the prejudices in Lggothland against their Wheylian neighbors. Peine wanted a hero. A Wheylian hero. Ari could understand, but he didn't like it.

Ari was disappointed not to draw Sir Keite for any of his duels the following day, but knew it to be for the best. It forced him to surrender his secret notion of teaching the Whey a lesson. Dueling was the last one-on-one competition before the final jousts, making it increasingly likely Ari would never face Sir Keite at all. The crowd now booed Keite, but the knight made no more life-ending attacks, seeming content to win with light touches to the chest.

Archery, the event of the fourth day, was once Ari's greatest weakness but now yielded him three of three possible points. He had Hawk Guardian Mirimel to thank for that, he knew, for the training she'd given him the spring before. He was pleased to see Sir Keite did not fare as well, though the Wheylian knight still had enough points to qualify for the pre-jousts to be held over the following two days.

During those two days, Ari excelled, skewering colored rings and dummies alike, much to the joy of the crowd. Blue flags adorned by a gray hawk, the conglomeration of Ennentine's and Sir Cadwel's heralds that thus far served as the king's champion's symbol, waved all around him as the people of the realm cheered.

Evenings at the head of the table where filled with stories of the great campaigns of the past. Tales of when the flag of Sorga stood against innumerable odds, and tourneys long gone where blue and gray material were scarce to be found for seasons following, due to all the flags sewn in Sir Cadwel's honor.

No one seemed to care that Sorga's colors were blue, white and brown. Sir Cadwel had worn the conglomeration of the two houses, his blue with the king's silver, for so many years, people could picture the hawk of Sorga in no other color. There was even a tale of a young woman who sewed a shining hawk of silver thread across the bosom of her gown, its talons reaching up to pull at the top as if about to reveal her.

Ari was glad Ispiria wasn't at the head of the table to hear that, his imagination immediately picturing her in such a dress. He worked hard to press the image from his mind, knowing concentration was paramount. He had a tourney to win, after all. Everyone was counting on him.

Chapter 18

When the day of the final joust dawned, Ari was the only page still in contention, the others unable to prevail against the steep competition of so many seasoned knights. Fought every spring and fall, the tourneys were both displays of skill and a proving ground for aspiring young men, or unknown knights from the edges of the realm. Most veteran warriors, names already known about the land, did not feel the need to participate. This spring carried a greater weight, however, as all had suspected Sir Cadwel's decision to forgo his role as champion. Many had come, young and old, tried and untried, to vie for the honor.

If ever displeased with his champion, the king could dismiss him before the next tourney, but none could recall a time when this had been done. In days faded almost to myth, before Sir Cadwel held the honor, the champion generally died on the field of battle, defending his king, and thus at the next tourney, a new champion arose. In more recent times, the realm was quiet.

Sir Cadwel had reigned as champion for an unprecedented number of years. Therefore, many an accomplished knight had waited long for this chance. The younger men, new to the craft and never tested in true battle, fell like a fall harvest before them.

The first veteran Ari faced was a man he'd fought many a casual bout with on the practice field. It pained Ari to have to dash a friend's hopes, but he unhorsed the other knight three successive times, allowing no hits to himself, and was proclaimed the victor. Far from angry, the older knight congratulated Ari with good grace, saying there was none to which he would rather fall.

Thus proceeded the bouts, it becoming clear early on that Ari and Sir Keite were fated to meet in the finale. Both showed no inclinations toward defeat. Ari watched each of the Wheylian knight's matches intently, studying his opponent's weaknesses, his strengths, and with the lingering doubt as to his good intentions.

It wasn't until Sir Keite met with Sir Bran, the knight who'd unhorsed Parrentine in Ari's first tourney, that the Whey faltered. It was the match to determine who would meet Ari in the final, and on the first pass, Sir Bran, an old and wily knight if ever there was one, scored a roaring hit on the Whey. The crowd came to their feet, stomping and cheering. Ari could see the cold anger in Sir Keite's eyes as the knight rode toward him before turning his horse for another pass.

On the second pass, Sir Keite's back was to Ari. At the last moment, Sir Bran twitched, his lance angling to meet his opponent's shield full on, his own defense dropping to yield a clear target. Ari gasped along with the crowd as Sir Bran took

Keite's lance to the chest, barely managing to stay ahorse. Ari saw the king lean forward, his eyes wide in surprise.

The two men sighted up again. This time, Sir Keite faced Ari, giving him a clear view of the Whey's gauntleted hand and the arcane movement he made with it before the two met. Sir Bran flew from his saddle, landing hard.

Ari felt a sharp twinge of anger as Sir Keite's use of magic confirmed his fears. Sir Keite was indeed an Empty One, Ari's sworn enemy and an unquestionable danger to the crown. Ari glanced up to see the king whisper to his son. Parrentine rose, making his way down from the royal dais.

Sir Keite pulled his horse around. Jumping down, he moved to stand over his opponent, placing the jagged end of his shattered lance against Sir Bran's chest.

"Do you yield, sir?" The Whey's voice was a cold echo under his visor. Around them, the crowd gasped. It was customary to settle the joust with passes. Sir Bran had been hit but twice. He was allowed a fourth pass to even the match, and, if successful, a fifth to settle it. Weapons were drawn only in the case of an unclear victor.

But Sir Bran only raised his head, giving a weak nod before letting it fall back to the earth. His page and the sawbones hurried onto the field. Four stout men lifted a litter to follow.

"Ari." Parrentine's voice was low, but Ari started, so focused on the scene before him, he hadn't noticed his prince's approach. "I think this Wheylian knight fights without honor."

The prince's eyes darted about. It was obvious he wished to say more, but in the crowd, there was no space for privacy. Peine arrived with Stew, flushed from running to fetch him after watching Sir Keite win.

"Did you see?" Peine's eyes were bright. "Sir Keite beat Sir Bran like he was a page. He must be the greatest Wheylian knight to ever live."

"Perhaps," Parrentine said, turning to assist Ari in mounting.

Observing this favoritism sent a cheer through the crowd. They were unforgiving of Sir Keite's wanton killing of that local lad in the flail match, and lustily roared out what they thought Ari should do to him. A scowl formed on Peine's face.

Taking up Stew's reins, Ari rode past the royal box. He lifted a hand to wave to Ispiria. The crowd cheered. Ari hoped Siara took note of how much the people approved of his fiancée.

Ari circled around until he was on the opposite end of the list. Across from him, Sir Keite already had his visor down, an insult. Ari sighed. He liked a challenge, but he preferred amicable bouts to this. In a frenzy, the crown stood already, feet stomping an incoherent rhythm on the bleachers and the soft spring earth.

With a bow from his saddle to the royal box, and a polite nod to his opponent, Ari closed his visor. He took the lance Peine offered him. All around him, blue and gray flags filled the air, making a bizarre churning sea out of the stands.

Their first pass was a draw, both men shattering their lances against the shield of the other. Ari swayed at the impact, as did his opponent. The crowd gasped, sucking in a brief thrill of fear for their champion, before bursting into wild applause as Ari went into the turn. He reached down, plucking up one of the lances Peine had stocked for him at that end of the field.

They sighted up again. This time, Sir Keite made the same slicing gesture he'd used on Sir Bran. Against his chest, Ari felt his amulet burn with cold. Much as Sir Bran had, Ari lowered his guard and turned his lance, but unlike Sir Bran, Ari's will remained his own.

At the last moment, he jerked shield and lance back into place, blocking the Whey's blow while taking his opponent full in the chest. His muscles coiled with suppressed anger and loathing for this Empty One who came there so brazenly, Ari didn't restrain his enhanced strength. Sir Keite flew from his steed at the impact, sailing through the air to land in the hoof-churned dirt with a loud clank and an audible cracking sound.

Ari was off Stew and at his opponent's side before the crowd seemed to comprehend what had come to pass. He wrenched Sir Keite's visor open, issuing a silent prayer the other wasn't dead. That the Empty One must die was a certainty, but Ari knew he'd let his anger best him. It should be the king's choice when the villain died, and there were still too many questions. Ari didn't even know if Queen Reudi knew her envoy to Lggothland was evil.

Ari watched in sick fascination as the flesh of Sir Keite's cheeks sank and the skin retreated from the cartilage of his nostrils, his lips shriveling to reveal his gums and teeth. Keite's eyes stared up at Ari in silent surprise for a moment before collapsing in on themselves, folding into wet looking gray globules. The skin of his face thinned, becoming patchy and molten and revealing the bones of his skull beneath, but the decay stopped there. He did not turn to dust as Lord Ferringul had. Ari knew that meant Sir Keite was a newly made Empty One.

Ari heard footsteps, a quick glance revealing Parrentine arriving before the others Ari could see hurrying onto the field. Ari nodded to the face in the visor. Parrentine's mouth thinned as he took in the expedited decay. He gestured for Ari to shut the helm.

"We don't need anyone to see that," the prince said. "I will decree that he be burned in state, his armor still about him." With a nod, Ari clamped the visor shut. Exerting his strength to bend the joints slightly, he rendering it unable to be opened by hand. Sighing, he pulled off his own helm, tucking it under one arm.

"Is he dead?" Peine asked, sliding to a halt at their side as the two rose. The look on Ari's face must have answered him. "You didn't have to kill him," Peine cried, his voice ringing out in a crowd gone momentarily quiet as they strained to hear what transpired on the field.

To Ari's dismay, cheers resounded as the crowd realized their chosen enemy was dead. The stretcher arrived. Rabid cries of joy swelled as the body was lifted.

Ari removed his gauntlets, shoving them into his helm. He put a hand on Peine's shoulder but, with an angry scowl, his friend pulled away. Turning his back on Ari, Peine took up Stew's reins, leading the destrier from the field. Watching them, Ari saw Peine cock his head to the side, momentarily resting it against Stews warm neck.

"I'll tell him of Sir Keite's villainy," Parrentine said in a low voice, for they once more stood alone.

"I'm not sure he'll believe you."

"He will. It's time for you to present yourself to the king."

Ari followed Parrentine across the field to the royal family's raised platform. Ennentine, the queen, Siara and Ispiria rose as the prince ascended the steps. Ispiria had her mouth squeezed shut, looking as though she was so happy she had to work to keep her words in. An olive-complected page Ari didn't know handed Parrentine a wrapped sword.

Ennentine gestured Ari to the top of the platform, calling his page over to take Ari's helm and gauntlets, as Peine was nowhere about. The king turned to the crowd, Ari at his side. Ari wasn't sure if the crowd would stop celebrating long enough to hear what their monarch wished to say. Eventually, Ennentine raised his hand, calling the people to order.

"This tournament began with uncertainty, for our hero and champion, Sir Cadwel, relinquished his post. Yet even in his departure, he watched over us, making us a grand parting gift. The sun sets on an era, but our champion fails us not, for he has sent to us his replacement, plucked from obscurity, but imbued with a talent and strength that is surely noble. I give you Lord Aridian, Duke of Sorga and Protector of the Northlands, winner of the tourney."

Again, the cheering swelled. Flags and banners were raised high. The roar of sound, the undulating mass of churning cloth and flesh as far as the eye could see, was overwhelming. It was with something near relief that Ari turned from it and fell to his knees before his king.

King Ennentine extended his hand. Parrentine drew a long gleaming blade from the bundle he held, placing the leather-wrapped hilt in his father's palm. Although in his sixth decade, Ennentine was a strong man still, and Ari was surprised to see the king needed to exert effort as he clasped the hilt in both hands and lowered it to Ari's left shoulder. The blade was straight and showed not even a trace mark of the smith's hammer. Its edge, resting near Ari's ear, looked sharp enough to cleave a feather drifting down to rest on it.

"Lord Aridian, Duke of Sorga and Protector of the Northlands," Ennentine said. "I proclaim you, by trial of arms, winner of this year's spring tourney, champion of the field."

Here, the king was forced to pause as the crowd drowned him out. Ari, his head bowed, swallowed hard in anticipation of what was to come next.

"As this year marks your majority, and as Sir Cadwel advises me that you have been a good and honest page, excelling in all knightly arts, in his name, I release you from your service to him, and in the name of the crown, I dub you Sir Aridian, knight of the realm." This last, Ennentine roared, his voice barely audible over the cries of the people.

The sword lifted from his left shoulder, moving to his right. Silence fell with a suddenness that was almost startling. The crowed seemed to hold its breath in anticipation. Ari found he did as well. He dared a glance up, taking in Siara's look of pride, the queen's smile, Parrentine's satisfaction, Ispiria's glowing countenance and the king's serious face.

"Furthermore," Ennentine said into the waiting silence. "It is with pride in your valor and joy in our certainty of the rightness of it, that I proclaim you, Sir Aridian, to be King's Champion, protector of the crown and paramount knight of our realm."

This time, there was no stopping the cheering. It exploded manically across the tourney field. It swelled and spilled out of the castle grounds and into the city beyond. Ari didn't realize he was still kneeling until Parrentine stepped forward to pull him to his feet. The king reversed the huge blade he held, laying it hilt first across his arm to offer it to Ari.

"Our champion can't go about wielding a sword he found lying around the castle armory," Ennentine said, smiling.

Ari clasped the leather-wrapped hilt, aware of the three empty encasements set into it, where three stones must once have stood. Aside from their absence, it was obviously a well cared for weapon. The hilt was smooth but not too slick. The blade shone in the sunlight, clear and true, with a line of arcane rune work down the center. It was heavier even than Ari expected, but he would be able to wield it with one hand when the need arose.

"Hold it up for the crowd to see, Ari," Parrentine said. "Wave to them. You're their hero."

Ari did as he was told, aware of the king and prince standing on either side of him, waving as well. Ispiria, Siara and the queen followed suit farther down the platform. Ari waved with one hand, looking up in awe at the blade he held aloft in the other.

It was true. It had finally come to pass. Everything he'd always wanted. He, Aridian, was a real and true knight, and champion to his king.

Chapter 19

Ari walked to his quarters alone. He'd lost track of Peine after he left the tourney field with Stew. Ari didn't mind this moment of silence, though. He took a deep breath, trying to sort out the blur of images after Ennentine had declared him the winner. At least there'd been no shortage of hands to help him out of his armor.

He stepped into his sitting room and closed the door, looking around. He felt as if it was days ago that he'd left, not that morning. He crossed behind the stiff couch to the sleeping chamber, stopping mid-stride when he saw Ispiria within, sitting on the end of his bed. Although it was something she'd done before, the look on her face this time made Ari's heart stutter.

"Peine isn't with you?" she asked.

"No." He made no move to enter the room.

"Good."

She rose from the bed and crossed to him, reaching up to pull his face down to hers. Ispiria was tall, but the top of her head only came up to Ari's nose. She seemed quite serious about the kissing, her hands running over his body until he forced himself to pull away.

"Ispiria," he said, surprised at how little voice he had to say it. He turned away, moving to stand at one of the lead-glass windows in the sitting room, trying to catch his breath.

"Sir Aridian, you come back here this instant."

He didn't dare look at her. "Why do you do this to me? You know I gave my word. You know I promised."

"I gave my word, too, but I don't care. You were so magnificent today. You're a man now, Ari, and it's time you enjoyed a man's privileges in life."

"You gave your word, too?" He turned. "You never told me."

"Yes." She looked down. "I did. I promised Great Uncle Cadwel I wouldn't make you break your vow."

"He made you promise that?" Ari was indignant. Didn't Sir Cadwel trust him? Ari had given his word and he'd meant it.

"He told me when he asked you not to sully my honor, you agreed without hesitation." She glared at him. "How could you, Ari? Think of all the sullying we could have been up to." She paused, as if she actually expected him to answer that.

He stared at her in bewilderment.

"Anyhow, he said I had to promise not to make you break your vow, because you're the noblest man he's ever known, and if you broke your vow, a little bit of you would die." This last, she muttered at the floor, sounding sullen.

"But then--" he stammered. "And you -- and you're always – Ispiria." He glared at her. "Why?"

200

"It's so fun, teasing you." She gave him a sheepish smile. "And I knew I wouldn't have to break my vow, because I knew you wouldn't break yours."

"And just now?" he asked, his tone stern. He was a trifle put out with her.

"I meant it." She pulled back her shoulders, standing tall. "I don't care that we promised. Watching you in the tourney was so exciting. What difference does half a year make? Why do we have to wait until autumn?"

"Because you won't be seventeen until autumn and we won't be married until you are," Ari said, although he was sure she knew the answer. "Does this mean you're giving up on the idea of a spring wedding?" he asked hopefully.

She was so beautiful, with determination flushing her cheeks. Waiting until next spring really did seem ridiculous. Looking at her, he found himself giving serious thought as to what actually constituted breaking his vow. They could probably come up with something to do that wouldn't compromise their honor.

"Yes, I want a fall wedding, with fall leaves and evergreen boughs." A smile flittered across her face, as if she could see his determination wavering. She took a step closer.

"The king wants to see you before the banquet," Peine said, entering the room.

Ispiria whirled to face him.

"Ispiria?" Peine frowned. "What are you doing here?"

"Absolutely nothing," she said with an exasperated sound, almost a growl, and stormed from the room.

Peine looked after her with confusion on his face.

"Where have you been?" Ari tried to tell himself he was relieved at the interruption.

"I followed Sir Keite's body, to see it laid to rest, and guess who was there?"

Peine was obviously excited. Ari was confused by the excitement, but happy his friend didn't sound upset about Keite's demise anymore.

"My brother," Peine hurried on. "My next older brother, Gauli. He was Keite's page. I don't know why he hasn't been to see us. I didn't ask, because he was pretty upset about Sir Keite."

"I really didn't mean to kill him, but you should know, he was an Empty One. He used his magic to unhorse Sir Bran."

Peine's face betrayed a war between disbelief and surprise. "You're sure? How can you be sure? They look no different from us."

"I saw him do it, and after, when I looked inside his helm, he was turning into dust, like Lord Ferringul did."

"Is Gauli in danger?" Peine looked worried.

"I don't know. Did he seem odd? I mean, was he beguiled, do you think, or did he believe he was serving a normal knight?"

"I don't know. I'll check on him later. I guess I can't ask him, since the Aluiens made you promise to keep them and the Empty Ones a secret. It does explain how a Whey was strong enough to ever be a knight." Peine let out a sigh. "You best get into the bathing room. You need to go see the king, and you smell."

"It isn't my fault. It gets hot inside my armor, especially in the sun."

"I don't care why you smell, Ari, just that you do. You're not embarrassing me by going to see the king smelling like sweat, metal and horses."

Peine made a stern gesture and Ari headed toward the bathing room. He could hear Peine open the discreet servants' door beside the fireplace. Soon a parade of castle pages appeared, bearing buckets of steaming water. After they left, as Ari bathed, he listened to the sound of Peine readying his things in the adjoining room. Tension drained out of him. He was relieved Peine believed him about Sir Keite.

Later, on their way to the king, Ari could feel the scrutiny of everyone they passed, from rigid guards to noble women who giggled behind delicate fans, their sparking eyes peeking over the tops and making him nervous. When they reached the door to Ennentine's study, a guard opened it. Ari crossed to stand near the sputtering fireplace before his king, bowing.

The royal family was in attendance, except baby Tiana, and Ispiria was there. Everyone stood at Ari's entrance and as he rose from his bow before Ennentine, they clustered around him. Their attention seemed to be focused on a parchment-wrapped bundle Princess Siara held. She smiled, handing it to him. Ari held it gingerly, unsure what was transpiring.

"Unwrap it, dear," the queen said.

Carefully, Ari unfolded the parchment to reveal a knight's tabard in deep blue with the hawk of Sorga carefully stitched in gleaming silver. Awe filled him as he tentatively traced one perfectly wrought wing with his finger.

"Well, unbuckle your sword so we can put it on you," Siara said, taking the garment from him. "Peine, help me."

Ari removed his sword belt, unsure what to do with it until Parrentine took it from him. Relieved of the weapon, he ducked down, and Peine and Siara dropped the heavy tabard over his head, deftly lacing up the sides. When they finished, Parrentine buckled Ari's sword in place and they stepped back, smiling and scrutinizing. Ari stood still, feeling awkward under their inspection.

"You look terribly handsome," Ispiria said, giving Ari a quick grin.

"Here." Siara took him by the arm.

She dragged him to the far corner of the room, where he belatedly noticed something tall and draped. With a flourish, she removed the cloth to reveal a standing mirror. For a moment, Ari was too stunned by the obvious value of so large and clear a looking glass, set in a heavy silver frame, to peer into it. Such a piece must belong to the queen herself. Then his gaze shifted to what was reflected there, awe melding into wonder.

It was a man who stood before him in the glass, not a boy. A man who towered over Siara's diminutive form. Ari topped six feet now, which he knew, but never before had occasion to really take in. His shoulders were broad and square under the tabard, his well-muscled chest the perfect scaffold for the proud silver hawk, so long a symbol of the union between the ancient house of Sorga in the north and the newer throne of Lggothland in the south.

Ari took in the face looking back at him, surprised at how much his hours practicing in the sun had streaked his thick brown hair. He conceded to himself that it wasn't a bad face. Certainly, his even features would never be called ugly. It was his eyes that truly spoke to him, though, and the set of his mouth. That slight thinning of the lips, the bright glint of alert tension in his hazel gaze. It was an expression he'd seen many times before, and must have adopted in unconscious imitation. Though no blood bound them, he looked amazingly like Sir Cadwel.

"It's perfect," Siara said, turning him back around to face the room.

"Yes, it is." Ispiria bounced up on her tip-toes and back down again.

The king nodded to Parrentine, who went to the door to beckon in a servant. Effervescent wine was passed around in delicate glasses.

"To Sir Aridian, King's Champion," Ennentine proclaimed, raising his glass.

The others followed suit and they all drank, a new round of congratulations pouring forth. Ari had never been so happy.

The morning after the banquet, Ari rose early, slipping out without rousing Peine to head to the practice field. He felt the keen need for the clear openness of space and to give in to the tension in his muscles. The ball held in his honor had been vibrant and sparkled in his mind like a bouquet of jewels but the press of so many people, and the continued need to keep his movements slow and contained, wore on him.

Stepping up to the practice dummy, he lifted his new greatsword in one hand, testing the weight of it. To wield it thus, instead of gripping it in both hands as was custom, was a challenge even to him, and he was pleased. Taking his stance, he started with slow swings, his muscles warming.

With controlled speed, Ari touched the target lightly over what would be a man's left ribcage, the small vulnerable area under each arm, the throat. He relaxed into the rhythm of it, swinging faster and faster. Wielding a knight's sword with the precision of a rapier soothed him, melting his worries away. In those moments where only sword and muscle mattered, Ari could find true piece. It was almost with anger that he broke off when someone cleared their throat.

"I can see now how much you're toying with me when we fence." Parrentine's tone was light.

Years ago, Ari had been forced to beat his liege senseless, an act he'd regretted and feared would forever hinder their friendship, but the prince was a different man now and it stood not between them.

"I've never seen a blade move so fast, let alone a greatsword," Parrentine said.

Ari rolled his shoulders back, sheathing his sword. "You wish to speak with me, your highness?"

"Yes." The prince's eyes still reflecting awe at Ari's swordwork. He shook his head. "I'm afraid I've come to speak to you about your first mission as our champion. I sought you in your rooms, but Peine drank so much last night that I don't think he even remembers who you are." Parrentine's tone was thin with forced lightness. "Come, Father and Siara await us in the study."

"I should change."

Parrentine waved his concern away. "You're fine."

They traversed the halls of the castle in strained silence. Ari tried to contain his dismay at the summons. Was he to take Princess Tiana to Wheylia so very soon? He knew the Wheys wanted to raise her, but she was less than a month old. Parrentine would scarcely know her.

The chill inside the king's study erased all memory of the warm spring sun in the practice yard. Siara sat on one of the leather couches, rocking Princess Tiana in her arms. Her blue eyes were dark when she looked up at him. The king, as was his wont, stood by the fireplace, which held no blaze. Ari wished it did, the tension in the room leaving him cold.

"Your majesty." Ari crossed to bow to the king.

Parrentine closed the door, waving away a servant, and sat with his wife and daughter. Siara leaned against him, his arm going around her. Greif etched deep lines in their faces.

"I'm sorry we cannot give you more of a respite to enjoy what you accomplished yesterday, Sir Aridian," King Ennentine said.

Ari stood straighter at the sound of his newly earned honorific, trying to hold his sorrow for Siara and Parrentine at bay.

"Respite?" Parrentine's tone was forcedly light. "I found him in the yard, hard at practice."

"Truly?" The king looked surprised. "Even Cadwel knew how to take his repose, before he became the portrait of gloom he is now."

"Rumor has it Sir Cadwel worked as fiercely at his repose as he did at war," Parrentine said.

King Ennentine's lips twitched, almost becoming a smile, and Ari recalled the king and Sir Cadwel were comrades in arms in their youths. The king sighed, seriousness returning, even the hint of a smile fading. "You are aware of the situation in Wheylia, Sir Aridian?"

"I am, sire." Ari glanced at Siara, but she was looking at her baby. "Someone has murdered every heir to the throne. Only Queen Reudi and Princess Tiana stand between the strife of an unknown succession."

"Well put, although we have no proof of murder."

"It can be little else," Siara said, her voice bitter.

"More disturbing news came to us shortly before the tourney, though we have kept it secret," the king said. "Queen Reudi is laid low by sudden illness. The queen's son, Lord Reido, has written on her behalf, beseeching us to send Princess Tiana now. Not only must she be raised among them to be acceptable as their ruler, Queen Reudi feels she will be a beacon of hope to the nation, which trembles with unrest under the weight of so many ill happenings."

"I feel she'll become the next victim of whoever is behind this evil." Siara spat the words out, the face she raised to them twisted with anger.

"Ari won't let that happen," Parrentine said, though his countenance betrayed his misery.

"Queen Reudi's illness forces us to send Tiana now," King Ennentine said. "Princess Tiana must arrive in Wheylia and be proclaimed Reudi's heir before the queen succumbs. It is the only way to prevent a war."

"If they war among themselves, what is it to us?" Siara said.

Parrentine rubbed his eyes, sighing. Ari got the impression this was not a new argument between them. "We cannot have a war along our western border. We need the security of peace with Wheylia. And you know our daughter would become a prize. Whatever factions arose, they would seek to claim her, for she would give them legitimacy. They would make her a puppet with a regent of their choosing."

"They will do that now, as soon as my grandmother is dead." Siara glared at him.

"No, your Uncle Reido will be regent. To insure the continuation of so ancient a line, Wheylia will accept a male regent. You know the oracles say Wheylia will prosper so long as your line sits upon the throne." The eyes Parrentine turned on her were beseeching.

"The high priestesses of my line are the readers of the oracles. Of course they say that."

"Enough," King Ennentine barked, his voice that of a leader of men. "We have weighed the options, considered the arguments. You always knew your children would be placed to the advantage of the crown. It is the role of the nobly born. Though I lament it must happen so soon, I cannot allow a mother's sentiment to overshadow the good of the kingdom. Even though I love you, dear." This last he said in softer tones.

Ari met the prince's eyes. Over his wife's head, Parrentine nodded. A heavy weight of responsibility settled on Ari. Not only must he keep the new princess safe, in a land he didn't know and had never seen, but Siara too. He, who'd already failed to save Parrentine's first bride.

He wondered how long Siara could be away from Parrentine, suffering from the curse of the Wheys. That ancient pact, established in days obscured by the passing of time to end the strife of their people, hadn't seemed so harsh to Ari until he'd learned its true nature. Wish it or no, Siara could not stay in Wheylia to raise her daughter or she would wither and die like a flower without rain.

"My heart knows fear at sending Siara and our daughter there," Parrentine said. "Especially after your discovery of Sir Keite's true nature, though I now mistrust his claim that Queen Reudi sent him. I place my faith in you, Ari."

"I will not fail you, your highness." Ari hoped fervently that his words would prove true.

"I know you won't." Untangling his arm from Siara, Parrentine stood, crossing to stand before Ari. "But there will be no surety until the perpetrator of these deaths is removed. I charge you to find what evil lurks among the Wheys and destroy it, will they or not. Our daughter cannot be safe, our boarder secure, with such villainy in their midst."

"Yes, your highness." Ari bowed, but his mind churned. How could he do this? He had no power to exert in Wheylia, no influence. If he couldn't find a wrongdoer, did he bring

Siara home and leave Tiana there, or did he stay and keep looking? He wished Sir Cadwel was there. This was too great a responsibility, too vast a charge to lay on him alone. He drew in a deep breath.

"Ari." Parrentine placed a hand on his shoulder. "Remember what I said. There is no other I would entrust the life of my family to."

Ari nodded, standing tall under his prince's gaze. "When do we leave?"

Chapter 20

The first thing Ari did once he, Parrentine and the king were done discussing travel plans was compose a message to Sir Cadwel. He hadn't had time to do so the day before, so the hawk sent to take news of the tourney was still waiting in the king's dove cote. Ari's letter was brief and carefully devoid of anything resembling bragging. It stated that he, Aridian, had won the tourney, was knighted, was named king's champion, was awarded a fine new blade, and now must depart immediately on a mission. About the mission he said little, constrained by space and apprehension, though Sorga hawks almost never lost their way. He suspected Sir Cadwel could extrapolate most of what Ari might write anyhow, as the knight knew what was transpiring in the kingdom.

Watching the Sorga hawk fly away, he wondered how Sir Cadwel was doing with his vow not to give orders while in Sorga. Shrugging, Ari decided he had a lot of other things to worry about and went looking for Ispiria. He'd considered asking Siara to take Ispiria with them as one of her ladies, but discarded the notion almost immediately. Ispiria must accompany her grandmother back to Sorga.

Ari knew she wouldn't be happy about it, but he'd made his decision. Where he was going, there was danger. He wouldn't even take Siara there if he didn't have to. Not to mention, taking Ispiria would set a precedent he didn't wish her to become accustomed to. He would spend the rest of his life riding into danger, and he couldn't take her with him each time. Not only would it put her in peril, he would be lying to himself if he didn't admit she would be a distraction.

He found her in the library, apparently engrossed in a book documenting the wild flowers of Lggothland, with her chaperones nearby, sewing. She looked up, smiling, as he approached. "Sir Aridian, the very person I was hoping to see. There's an exceedingly heavy book, high up on a shelf over there." She pointed to a dim corner of the library. "I thought you could help me with it."

Ari was tempted by her offer, worried she would rescind it once she knew he wasn't returning to Sorga with her and that he might be gone for quite some time. "I need to tell you something." He sat in the chair across from her. "The king has ordered me to Wheylia. I'll be away for quite some time. With the carriages, it will take three months to go and three to return, and I'm not sure yet how long we'll stay. I estimate I won't be home before midwinter, at the earliest."

"Midwinter." She closed her book with a thump. "But that's almost a year."

"I know," he said, looking down. His throat constricted. "But when I return, we can be married. You can plan the wedding, and--"

"Go," she said, pointing at the library door.

"Don't be angry."

"I'm not." Her voice was choked. "We'll talk more later. Just go."

Ari stood, unsure what to do. She started to cry. He walked around the table and pulled her up from her chair, taking her in his arms. "I'm sorry, Ispiria."

She buried her face against his chest, sobbing.

***

Ari spent the next several days carefully planning the journey to Wheylia. He shirked no detail, but often found himself wishing he had more time to spend with Ispiria. When they were together, he could see she tried to be herself, cheerful and loving, but he knew she was upset.

As part of his preparations, he handpicked every guard, page, lady in waiting and horse to accompany them. The humans found his methods more disconcerting than the horses did. Ari would stand before each candidate, look them square in the eye until he was certain he knew if he could trust them, and then issue a curt yes or no.

While his instruction under Sir Cadwel hadn't contained anything about ladies' picnics, it did include extensive information on armed escorts. Ari found himself making the arrangements with ease. He also found himself sounding more and more like his mentor. It was easy to put on a grim face and bark orders at people. They seemed to respond more promptly than when he asked them to do something in his usual polite manner. In three days, they were ready to leave.

Saying goodbye to Ispiria was one of the most unpleasant things Ari had ever had to do. They did it in private, to spare themselves from prying eyes and to help Ari maintain his dignity, for even though he was a knight and king's champion, he wasn't quite seventeen yet and almost every man he commanded had years of experience over him. Privacy also provided a splendid opportunity for goodbye kisses, which Ari couldn't enjoy as much as usual because they were both so sad.

There were short goodbyes on the castle steps, with well wishes from the king, queen, Parrentine and the royal cousins, and then they were making their slow way through the city. People came out to wave or cheer, seeming happy to treat the procession as a parade. Ari smiled and waved back, but he couldn't relax until they reached the open road. While he didn't expect trouble so early in their journey, he found it nerve racking to lead his charges past the many hiding places the city provided.

The new princess necessitated a carriage, and Ari was resigned to it. There were two, to accommodate Siara, Tiana, Tiana's nursemaid, Siara's ladies in waiting and her maids. Day after day, he watched their tortoise-like progress and tried not to grit his teeth, reminding himself the carriages were necessary and he didn't begrudge Siara the time. Every moment longer it took for them to reach Wheylia was another moment for her with her daughter.

Their days took on a smooth rhythm, with Ari and the men rising before the sun to eat and strike camp so that, as soon as the ladies appeared and filed into their carriages, they could begin to move. A small contingency was left behind to pack up the ladies' pavilion, as the wagon it was stowed on moved twice as quickly as Siara would allow the carriages to be driven. A few hours before lunch time, Ari would send a different wagon ahead to set up an open-sided tent and make ready for lunch. As in the morning, this group of men was left behind to pack up and catch up, so the carriages could stay moving as much as possible.

There was no point in sending anyone ahead to prepare dinner, as dinner time marked the end of travel for the day, even though Ari felt there was plenty of light left. Squandering light annoyed him, especially as the days grew in length with the nearing of summer, but it did allow Ari time to practice his swordwork after dinner, which he took with Peine, Siara, Tiana, Tiana's nursemaid, Camva, and the two ladies in waiting. Once they finished dining each night, Ari would inspect the camp, asking for volunteers as he went, and then he and the men would engage in friendly bouts. Ari thought this a good way to spend the evenings, especially since most of the places they camped offered no other entertainment.

Summer reached them as the border of Wheylia did, and Siara requested they halt early that night. Ari chaffed at the delay, wondering if she was reluctant to cross out of Lggothland, until he reached her pavilion that evening and found a celebration waiting. Half the camp was assembled about a long table weighed down with food. Ari stopped just inside the tent, it dawning on him even as they raised their glasses that it was his seventeenth birthday.

"You forgot, didn't you?" Siara asked later as they danced. The music was terrible, played as it was by servants and soldiers, but she was wearing Ari's favorite of her gowns. The blue brocade perfectly matched her eyes. "Peine said you hadn't any idea but I hardly believed him."

"I guess I wasn't paying attention to the days, so much as our progress," he said, smiling down at her. He forwent bringing up that no one really knew the true date of his birth, or that the king had already declared him to have reached his majority. This was the first time he'd seen Siara at all happy thus far on their journey and he didn't want to spoil it.

"Happy birthday, Ari," Siara said, curtsying to him as the music stopped.

"Thank you, Siara." He bowed, watching her return to her seat to take Tiana from Camva. One of her ladies in waiting, Annell, appeared in the vacant spot before him.

Once full dark settled and the camp fell silent for the night, Ari crept past the perimeter guards. He was pleased with how alert they seemed, even if they didn't manage to spot him. He made his way to the base of a narrow road that left the great Wheylian Highway and wound its way into the mountains of the Wheylia-Lggothland boarder. It was the same trail he'd followed the previous fall with Sir Cadwel. It passed by the hidden path leading to the secret cave of the Aluiens.

Ari stood in the moonlight, staring up the road in longing. Up that road lay Larke and the Lady. Up that road lay answers about his parents. He looked back over his shoulder at the camp, fires burned low. Certainly, they weren't in any danger yet. He and Stew were fast. He could leave someone else in command, returning to them before they reached the Wheylian capital.

Ari sighed, turning away. He knew he couldn't go. He was charged to watch over Siara and Tiana. It was his duty to stay with them and protect them.

He snuck back into camp as unseen as when he'd left.

***

"Ari," Peine said the following evening as he was organizing Ari's small pavilion. "I've been thinking. I know I grew up in Lggothland and I've never been to the City of Whey, but I am a Whey, and we're traveling awful slow. Maybe I should go ahead and have a look around. You said the prince is worried there may be something amiss there."

216

Ari pursed his lips, thinking. The idea had merit. More and more, he found himself wishing he could ride ahead and do what Peine suggested. Peine would blend in well. Better than anyone else they had with them.

"That is, if you think you can manage on your own," Peine added.

"Manage on my own indeed. You're just tired of plodding along with these carriages and you mean to abandon me to it."

"It's a good idea," Peine said.

"I think it may be. We can use all the information we can get."

"But you must promise me you'll make yourself presentable before you ride into the city." Peine's tone was one of long-suffering. "You're Sir Aridian, Duke of Sorga and Protector of the Northlands. Not to mention, King's Champion and commander of this venture. You must look the part."

"I'll wear my new tabard."

"And keep your boots clean?"

"And keep my boots clean."

"I'll need some money," Peine said.

"Take some of ours."

"I was planning to."

Ari smiled. He rarely used money, anyhow. Peine liked to keep it and count it. Ari probably wouldn't notice if his friend took it all.

"It'll be good to see my brother, too," Peine said, excitement lifting his tone. "He was chosen to return Sir Keite's sword and shield to his family. I want to check on him, to make sure he's well. You know, because."

Ari nodded, the smile falling from his face. He wished he hadn't agreed so quickly. He didn't like the idea of Peine near anything that had to do with Sir Keite. He wouldn't retract his permission, though. It would speak too strongly of a lack of faith, and he did trust Peine. They were best friends, after all. He was sure Peine would be fine.

Peine set off early the next morning, Ari's worry following after him. Trying to set it aside, he concentrated on their journey. They were in lands Ari hadn't before seen, having only traversed Wheylia's mountainous border. The caravan route they took, the slow southern road, was the only way carriages could enter Wheylia. It wound toward the coast and through gentle hills formed of the barest inclination to be mountains, where the tip of the range stretched out to meet the sea.

His first report from Peine arrived as they were stopping for the evening, about three weeks out from the City of Whey. The messenger Peine hired to carry it was very polite and very curious. Ari took the packet of parchment and sent him off to the cook fire, amused at how intently he peered around. Ari was sure the young man was not only in the employ of his valet but also someone else in the capital of Wheylia, and charged with reporting as much about Ari's camp as possible. Ari didn't mind. This wasn't a military venture. They had nothing to hide.

He retired to his tent and opened the packet, skimming over the list of his titles, wishing Peine wouldn't waste paper on them.

The city is amazing. It climbs the mountain in four massive tiers. Soldiers and workers live on the bottom one. Shopkeepers, tavern owners, minor nobles, officers and the like on the second, along with reputable businesses. The third tier is full of parks because that's where the wealthy live, and where the university is. On the fourth tier, there's only the castle.

Ari frowned. He knew from his readings that the city stepped up the mountain. He'd always thought it embodied an ingenious technique for defense, but had never before realized there was such a strict division of the populace. He was struck by the hard practicality of it. If the city were besieged, the poor would fight with great vigor, for it would be their homes destroyed first. If the lowest tier fell, Ari was sure renewed fervor could be drawn from that same fighting force, for they would stand atop the wall of the next tier and watch the attackers pillage their homes below.

The rest of Peine's letter was concerned with details about the markets, what a fine array of goods Wheylia had to offer and a brief mention of how pretty the girls were. Ari read it twice, not finding much of strategic interest, but gleaning some insights into the female-dominated Wheylian society. He also came away with the unsettling feeling Peine would prefer he lived in the City of Whey. Ari looked up at a sky still full of light and wished they could travel faster.

Chapter 21

Even bolstered as he was by reports sent from Peine and numerous descriptions he'd read in books, Ari was still unprepared for his first sight of the City of Whey. Poromont, the only other great city he'd seen, appeared to have been dropped onto the seacoast the day before when compared to the eternal solidity of the capital of Wheylia. The city was carved out of the mountainside, its four tiers rising in harmony with nature. Walls of gray stone grew from the valley floor, so weathered as to appear almost natural in spite of their rigid linearity. The buildings, ranging from small cramped structures on the bottom tier to the soaring towers of the castle at the top, were of the same gray stone, dark slate roofs topping all but the wealthiest.

From where he halted his cavalcade, Ari could see the main road slicing diagonally through each tier, going from ground level to a raised walkway by the time it reached the next level. Each gate was offset from the one above, and Ari deduced this was to impede advancing forces. Furthermore, the ramps were not built of solid earth at their highest points, right before reaching each gate, but of arched stone. They would be easily knocked down, allowing an attacking army no ready means of attaining the gate above.

Ari took all of that in as his eyes traveled to the top tier, on which stood the castle. Its outer wall and corner towers were lined with battlements, but the pinnacled inner towers were clad in copper shingles. They looked like overlapping teardrops, calling to Ari's mind a drawing, from one of Sir Cadwel's books, depicting the scalemail armor they wore across the sea in the southern kingdoms. The ancient copper was as weathered as the stone, green and pitted with age, and it wept down the slender towers in dark rivulets. On some of the inner towers, thick vines reached up to meet the copper streaks. In a smattering of places, the roof glowed as if on fire, and Ari realized here and there new shingles glinted in the afternoon sun.

Ari knew the guards, gray tabards blending with the stone on which they stood, could see his command at the end of the valley. He halted his troop, ordering them to make themselves presentable. He sent a page to ask if Siara and her ladies needed anything before heading to his own tent, which two soldiers had set up for him.

Ari was not much for show, but he knew he ought to put on the accoutrements of king's champion for this visit. It was the first official visit of Lggothland nobility to Wheylia in over ten years, and he wanted to make a good impression. He was working on buckling his armor, wondering if he should call in a page, when Peine arrived. His friend took one look at him, rolled his eyes, and came forward to help, batting Ari's hands away.

"There are scores of men in this camp who would be honored to help you with this," Peine said. "I knew I better come make sure you managed to look the part."

"I was managing," Ari said, but he smiled, happy to have Peine back and looking well. "How fares the city?"

"Ari, you should have had this out before now," Peine said, scrutinizing Ari's surcoat as he lifted it from a small trunk. "There's a crease right through the hawk." Peine shook out the heavy material. "Do you see what I mean by how splendid the third tier is? You can see it from here, all the green. Wait until we ride past the estates. Each one is more extravagant than the last. Wouldn't it be grand to make third tier?"

"I guess I didn't realize the Wheys were so warlike." Ari held out his arms, ducking so Peine could drop his surcoat over his head.

"Warlike?" Peine looked up from the laces. "We aren't. Not anymore. The tiers are a holdover, I guess. They do work nicely to keep everyone sorted."

Ari didn't know what to say to that. He knew Peine put great stock in rank and titles, but he hadn't realized his friend thought people ought to be sorted.

"There were wars, long ago, of course," Peine said. "We've seen two civil wars, in days long past."

Ari nodded, having read about them in the course of his studies, although they were but briefly mentioned in the Lggothland texts. He'd had to translate more detailed tales from Old Wheylian, but those still left much out. Accounts were broken and hard to find, as Wheylia's civil wars were already ancient history long before Ari's ancestors came to the peninsula.

"And there were often attempts to take our lands before your people came to our shores," Peine said. "Your people

223

were cunning, though. They approached in peace, asking to farm lands we used little, and they married with my people, and in the end they got half of our peninsula with no wars at all."

"My people?" Ari asked.

Peine stepped back to scrutinize him, then turned to retrieve his helm.

"Your father is a noble of Lggothland," Ari said.

"He's a minor noble and always will be, because he's a Whey" Peine frowned. "It isn't fair his land is on the wrong side of an arbitrary line the high priestess and the nobles of Lggothland drew long ago."

"Did you learn any more about the university?" Ari asked to change the subject, perturbed at Peine's concerned with borders and tiers.

"It's where people go to learn things."

"I know that." Ari belted his sword on over his surcoat and armor, reflecting that if a knight wore all his garb every day, there was no way he could ever lose his strength. He felt as though he was carrying the weight of his own personal castle. "I've read about it. I know Wheylia has one, and there are two of great renown across the southern seas."

"Well, it has four buildings, spread out along the third tier," Peine said. "One is home to things such as music and sculpture, the arts. A second houses the studies they call the philosophies of the living world, and a third the histories and works of culture. The fourth--"

"I forgot to ask anyone to ready Stew," Ari said, breaking into Peine's narrative as he realized he'd missed a key step in his preparations.

"I already tasked one of the pages to do it. I knew you would forget. The fourth building is the girl's school."

"Girl's school? They aren't allowed in the other schools?"

"No, it's the other way around," Peine said, a look of disgruntlement on his face. "They're allowed in every school. It's men who aren't."

"Then why do they need their own school?" In Ari's readings, the format of the university had been little addresses.

"Every girl in Wheylia, no matter her station, must attend the women's school for a year when she comes of age," Peine said. "That's when they come into their power. Most of them don't have much ability with magic, but the school is to teach them how to use what they have, and to find those who are skilled and press them into the priesteshood."

"Every girl?" Siara had been abandoned by her Wheylian grandmother and Lggothian father to linger untutored and unknown in a convent. She didn't have any training at all.

"My sister went, even though our lands aren't actually in Wheylia." Peine handed Ari his helm.

"She did? Did she have any skill with magic?"

"No, and was happy not to. Most women don't," Peine said. "I mean real magic, not the ability to sense changes in weather or soothe animals. Things like that are common enough, but real magic is rare. She said it was fun, though, to spend a year here and learn so many different things at the university."

"She didn't want to have magic?"

"She wanted to marry the younger son of the dukedom east of ours, and she did. If they'd found power in her, they would have tried to make her stay."

"Could they really make her stay if she didn't want to?"

"I don't know. Put your helmet on, Ari. The city is waiting for you."

Ari nodded, pushing his plumed helm down on his head. There would be time for talk later. Right now, he had to go present himself to the Wheys.

He rode out first, Stew festooned in blue and silver. Behind him came Siara's coach, the dirt scrubbed off to reveal deep blue paint and silver gilt. The heavy blue curtains were tied back, so all could look upon Siara's perfect face, on which Ari saw her most rigid smile. In her lap she held Princess Tiana, the baby almost indiscernible among a plethora of lace.

It was not unlike riding into Poromont. People lined the streets and the overall mood was celebratory, although curiosity replaced jubilation. In Wheylia, ladies apparently didn't bestow flowers on a knight, or else none of the ladies of Wheylia favored him, but children tossed a multitude of white petals onto the path before them. Their sweet fragrance mingled with those of horses, sweat and dust.

Ari led his party through the narrow streets and tightly packed buildings of the first tier, and the cobbled streets and larger, but still tightly packed, buildings of the second. At intervals, the roadway would widen into a circle, and such businesses as the area supported would form a ring, often with a well in the center.

The third tier boasted streets paved in stone with large houses set back behind sweeping lawns. Here, when the road was interrupted by a circle, there were no shops or stalls but, instead, miniature parks. The wells were gone, replaced by fountains or statues, shrouded in shade by the outstretched limbs of ancient trees. The statues were of tall, serious looking women, often holding swords. They would have been grim, were not great age apparent in the pitted granite and their feet and shoulders cloaked in lichens.

While none of the mansions surrounding them stood over two stories in height, not including the occasional tower and their sweeping copper roofs, four massive rectangular buildings rose above the other structures, two to each side of the central roadway. They took the form of battlement bedecked boxes, scored at regular intervals with leaded glass windows. At their corners soared thin towers, each pointed roof thrusting a waving banner into the cloudless sky.

Like the others, the gate to the fourth tier stood open, and was made of thick wood, whole trunks of trees in truth, bound together with iron. Unlike the others, this gate bore intricate copper scrollwork inside and out. The curving metal reminded Ari of the wandering lines of his amulet. For some reason, the similarity didn't bring him comfort.

They passed under the tunnel created by the thick outer wall, twice as wide as the walls surmounting the previous tiers, and into the sunlight of the cobblestone courtyard in front of the ancient castle of the Wheys. Guards lined either side, corralling Ari and his troop toward the broad steps on which the nobility of Wheylia stood. Here, the guards' gray uniforms were exchanged for red and the stylized black dragon of Queen Reudi's house adorned their chests. Flags of similar design flapped from each of the soaring pinnacled towers above.

Ari drew his horse to a halt at the foot of the steps, dismounting as a groom came forward to take Stew's reins. Others approached the coaches rolling to a halt behind him. He was pleased to see Queen Reudi waiting, hoping it meant word of her illness was exaggerated. Casting a quick glance around the courtyard to make sure nothing seemed amiss, he removed his helm and tucked it under his arm, bending on one knee before the Wheylian queen. Behind him, he could hear his troop follow suit. Head bowed, Ari contemplated how Queen

227

Reudi was surrounded by women, with two small groups of men standing off to the sides. In Poromont, the men of each noble family would grace the steps with the king and queen, their wives gathered to the sides to watch.

The only man near the queen was a well-dressed gentleman of about forty, who Ari guessed was Lord Reido, Siara's uncle and Queen Reudi's only surviving child, assuming the prolonged absence of Siara's younger aunt could be construed as death. Lord Reido looked dashing in deep red, his dark hair slicked back and his face adorned by a thin mustache.

Ari heard the women descend the carriage steps and saw the hem of Siara's blue gown pass him before billowing out around her as she curtsied.

"Lavarina," Siara greeted in a formal tone, using the Wheylian word for the combined position of high priestess and queen. "I bring greetings from their royal majesties, King Ennentine and Queen Parrella of Lggothland. All rejoice in the peace and unity shared by our kingdoms."

"Rise, all," Queen Reudi said.

Ari was shocked at the quavering note in her voice. When he'd met her not two years past, she'd seemed old, but strong and filled with power. Standing, he took in the stoop of her shoulders. He realized there was a cane in her left hand, held close among her gray robes to make it barely visible.

"It is with great happiness we see you returned to your homeland, my granddaughter, and joy fills our heart that you have come to present to us our heir, the newest princess of our house," Queen Reudi intoned.

Siara gestured. One of her ladies came forward to hand Princess Tiana to her. She held the wide-eyed infant up for all to see, the assemblage murmured in approval at the lace clad bundle topped with a tuft of dark hair. Beside his mother, Lord

Reido pressed thin lips together in a smile. Siara lowered her daughter, cradling Tiana in her arms as she ascended the steps.

"May I present to you Princess Tiana, of the ruling houses of both Lggothland and Wheylia, Grandmother." Siara spoke in a quieter voice now.

A smile brought some life to Queen Reudi's face as she touched Tiana's cheek with one wrinkled finger. The baby gurgled.

Siara looked toward Ari. "May I also introduce Sir Aridian of Sorga, newly anointed champion of King Ennentine and the Lggothian realm."

At this cue, Ari bowed again.

"Lord Aridian is known to us." Queen Reudi leveled her dark fathomless eyes on him. "Welcome to our home, Thrice Born. We await with curiosity and trepidation the reshaping of our fates."

Ari knew he was supposed to thank the queen no matter what she said, but he found her words a bit ominous. He wasn't sure if a thank you applied. Almost able to feel Siara's and Peine's joint consternation as he paused, he decided to say it anyhow. "Thank you, High Priestess."

Her lips curled in an enigmatic smile and Ari was sure she understood his hesitation.

"My granddaughter," Queen Reudi said, turning toward Siara. "May I introduce you to your Uncle Reido."

"Uncle," Siara said with a small curtsy and a tentative smile. "I rejoice to finally meet you."

"And I you, your highness." Lord Reido bowed. "For your fair visage is so like that of your mother, it is as if my sister has finally come home."

"Kindly put, my lord," Siara said. "I hope we three may come to know each other, that we may reform some semblance of family to sustain us in this turbulent world."

"A worthy goal," Queen Reudi said. "Preparations have been made for the housing of your men, Lord Aridian, and rooms prepared for you. Granddaughter, it would brighten our hearts if you would consent to stay in your mother's rooms, for the royal wing of the castle grows silent and dark in these days."

"Thank you, Lavarina," Siara said, but Ari knew her well enough to hear the unease behind her controlled tones. "It would be my honor."

"Then you may repair to your quarters that you may refresh yourselves," Queen Reudi said. "We have a great feast prepared for this night, after the thanking of the wellspring for your safe arrival."

"Yes, Grandmother." With a last curtsy, Siara and her ladies flowed up the steps and into the castle.

Ari bowed as well, turning to see stewards approaching his men. He nodded to his sergeant to proceed, watching as the Lggothland soldiers were led into one of the low buildings flanking the courtyard, while their mounts were escorted the opposite way. When the groom holding Stew's reins attempted to lead the brown away, Ari gave his horse a slight nod as well, hoping no one noticed. Peine appeared at his side, followed by Wheylian pages carrying Ari's possessions. Ari was aware of the nobles dispersing behind him, and the castle guard standing down. When he turned back, only Queen Reudi and her son Reido still stood before the castle.

"The gods have sent you here for a reason, Thrice Born." Queen Reudi's voice was so quiet he ascended a step to hear. "Perhaps, at this late hour, they relent to an old woman's prayers. Disquiet hangs as thick miasma over my house and my powers desert me. Whether by the will of the gods or malicious intent, without them I cannot ascertain. I would see this malediction lifted err I die."

Ari stared at her, doubly sure this time that a thank you was not the correct response.

"Mother." Lord Reido took her arm, supporting her. "Don't upset yourself so. Come, I shall ask Ciada to administer your medicine early today, before the banquet. Already you grow weary."

"I do grow weary." She seemed to shrink in on herself even more with his words.

Lord Reido relieved his mother of her cane, tucking it under his arm as he steadied her. "Please forgive us, but my mother needs rest. There is much she must do this eve."

"Yes my lord, your majesty." Ari bowed to both of them. He rose, staying where he was until they disappeared inside the vast maw of the castle, Lord Reido carefully supporting his mother. Ari turned to the Wheylian pages. "Please, lead the way."

He and Peine followed the castle pages inside. Unlike Ennentine's castle, here there was no soaring foyer, but instead a long vaulted corridor, more akin to the castle Ari and Sir Cadwel had entered two years ago to question Lord Mrakenson. As with that castle, no marble clad the floor, nor tapestries the walls. All was bare gray stone.

Unlike that ill-fated place, however, clean beeswax candles glowed along the walls, bathing the passage in light, their regularly spaced absence underscoring the several corridors branching off to each side. Far down the hall, Ari could see into the throne room, which was filled with the natural light of the sun. A multitude of colors dappled the floor, and he realized it must be vaulted and incised with numerous stained glass windows. On a dais set into the far wall, he could see the high-backed stone throne of Wheylia, looking stern, empty and alone. In Poromont, there were two thrones, for the king and queen ruled side by side.

Their guides took the first left they came to, which led them up a set of steps and into a long corridor that bisected what Ari assumed was the guest wing of the castle. He felt an odd strain as they walked along it, knowing he was being led farther and farther from Siara and her baby. He wished they could be in the guest wing with him, but he could think of no graceful way to rectify the situation.

They didn't stop until they reached the end of the corridor, entering a room that took up the entire corner of that level. It was an odd shape, for the large square of the outer tower was cut from it, but Ari was pleased to see windows in two walls. One set displayed the western side of the mountain range, where it reached along the castle to cradle it. The other faced the front courtyard and offered a spectacular view of the city dropping away to meet the plains to the south.

The young men carrying Ari's possessions set them to the side of the door, bowing their way out. Peine immediately began rummaging in their packs. Ari went through the only other door in the room, finding a sleeping chamber boasting a canopied bed as large as the one in the king's champion's chambers in Poromont. More searching revealed a second room beyond, with a smaller bed, presumably for Peine, but nowhere to clean the dust of travel from him.

"Peine," Ari called. "Where is the bathing room? We've been forever on the road. I think I've enough dust in my hair to sprout a tree."

"I'm glad to hear you know it. I was worried you were indifferent." Peine looked up from the doublet he was shaking out. "You won't like this, but I hear they have giant bathing chambers in the bowels of the castle. There's one for the women and one for the men, and they are filled by hot springs that well up from the ground. They say --" Peine broke off, staring at Ari's face. "That is, I'll send for a tub."

"No," Ari said, though highly tempted. "If that's what they do here, that's what I'll do. You did say no women are allowed in the men's bathing chamber, right?"

"Right." Peine nodded emphatically. "Everyone uses them. It's not as if you'll stand out. No one will even notice you."

The bath, Ari soon found, was a large underground pool deep beneath the castle. It seemed natural, although there was evidence of work done to enhance and smooth the shape nature had first carved. Steaming water welled up from unseen springs, trickling away in constant music through a myriad of miniscule holes in the stone. Massive columns upheld the ceiling and the castle above. They too looked natural, formed over millennia by dripping water, but each was smooth near the base, whether by design or the constant wear of moving bodies, Ari didn't know. Vapor filled the cavern, obscuring the ceiling above and the far edges of the space.

Standing at the side of the pool, Ari clenched a rough bar of soap and contemplated removing the rather small towel Peine had found for him before they'd left the dressing room. Everyone was staring at him. There were quite a few Wheylian men in the water, probably bathing in preparation for the night's festivities, as Ari wished to. He could see that were Peine there alone, no one would look at him twice.

But Ari was king's champion, a stranger and, at slightly over six feet tall, he topped any other man there by half a head.

He wished he'd taken Peine up on his offer to have a tub brought, but there was no help for it. Ari dropped his towel and got in, heading for the deeper side of the pool and its obscuring steam as fast as possible.

Chapter 22

By the time he got back to his room, his modesty thoroughly pillaged, Ari only had time to don a clean set of blue and gray clothes and his tabard before he was to join Siara in the throne room.

"You can't be late, Ari," Peine said. "You have to be there when Princess Siara presents Tiana to the court, then the two of you will be taken to the wellspring."

Ari wondered how Peine always knew where he was supposed to go, though he suspected any good valet would seek out that knowledge. "You aren't coming?" he asked Peine, who was standing back to scrutinize him.

Peine shook his head. "Men are almost never allowed near the wellspring. It's a great honor they bestow upon you. Remember, after that you'll be going to the banquet hall, so don't do anything to your clothes between now and then. I want you to show up to dinner looking pristine."

"What would I do to them?" Ari smiled at Peine's fussiness. "And why don't men get to go to the wellspring?"

"Because this is Wheylia. Only those of very high rank get to go, and that's almost always women. You're going to be late. Do you remember how to get to the throne room?"

"Of course I do." Ari spared a glance for his sword, resting sheathed against the far wall. As in Poromont, it was not acceptable to wear it about the castle. He wished himself as brash as Sir Cadwel, sure his mentor would ignore such courtesy.

The throne room did indeed have vaulted ceilings, arching high above him into interlocking panicles, each supported in its center by a slender column. Along the tops of the walls were rows of windows, colored glass forming the coats of arms of all the Wheylian noble houses, and below those hung corresponding banners. On a raised dais across from the entrance stood the large stone throne, its pointed back mimicking the formation of the ceiling. Behind it was the red banner of the ruling house, a stylized black dragon centered on it. The columns created a walkway to the throne, with nobles gathered to either side. Ari strode between them, coming to a halt before the queen with a low bow.

Queen Reudi looked no better than before she excused herself to rest. She seemed small and frail on the massive throne. Lord Reido stood protectively by her side. As Ari bowed, Reido leaned down to whisper in his mother's ear. She straightened slightly, nodding regally to Ari, and whispered to her son.

"It brings us honor to have the greatest knight in two realms grace our halls," Lord Reido said.

The dark eyes Queen Reudi leveled on Ari were unreadable.

"It is I who am honored, your majesty, to be here at the center of the legendary Kingdom of Wheylia." Ari bowed again and stepped aside to await Siara. He had to work hard not to fidget, unable to dispel his unease at having her so immediately removed from his presence upon their arrival.

When she arrived, Siara looked as pretty as the first time he'd seen her, though her blue eyes, so startling in a Wheylian face, held more sorrow than on that day. She had the dark hair of her people and wore it coiled and interlaced with pearls in a design too intricate for him to follow. He checked a sigh, unsure why the sight of her prompted one.

Behind the princess walked a girl in an unassuming gray gown. She carried a pile of lace Ari knew was Princess Tiana in her formal attire. Coming to a stop before the dais, Siara executed a graceful curtsy.

"Lavarina," she said as she rose. "I have come to present to you and the court of Wheylia my daughter, Princess Tiana, heir of your line. Thus, I perform my duty to my heritage, and fulfill my mother's obligation to the throne." She turned and took her daughter, once again holding her up for all to see. Princess Tiana started to cry.

Siara received her grandmother's nod and curtsied again, no less elegant for holding a crying baby. Ari had worried Siara would cry, but he should have known better. As she turned to hand her daughter back to the waiting maid, he saw anger flash in her eyes. He knew from experience, except when it came to Parrentine, Siara always met adversity with her temper.

"Let all assembled know the will of Lavarina," Lord Reido proclaimed as the nursemaid tried to hush Tiana. "This child is a Princess of Whey. She shall live among us and be raised in our ways, that she may be a true Lavarina when the time comes

237

upon her. All shall acknowledge this child as their princess on this day or their titles and lands be forfeit."

There was applause from the assembled, although Ari heard low murmurs as well. Queen Reudi came to her feet with effort. The room fell silent.

"As Lavarina," she said, her voice stronger than any she had used thus far. "I declare this child my true heir." She gestured.

A loud note echoed through the hall, sounding like a giant bell directly above their heads. Many of the nobles flinched, some even cowering. Ari saw acceptance bloom in their eyes, a bit daunted by the power behind Queen Reudi's words. Under his surcoat, his amulet grew hot.

The queen sank back into her throne, a look of exhaustion stealing over her, and tension eased from the hall. The assembled nobles began to talk among themselves, or leave in small groups. Siara turned to the maid and the two of them fussed over the baby, who was crying loudly. With a nod to Siara and a curtsy in the general direction of the throne, the girl took Tiana and hurried from the room. Ari saw two guards fall in behind her and sighed. Tiana belonged to the Wheys now.

Lord Reido leaned over his mother, whether to receive words or impart them, Ari couldn't tell. When the Wheylian lord straightened, he descended the dais and moved to stand before Siara. At a gesture from her, Ari joined them.

"Where's Peine?" Siara asked. "He didn't attend the ceremony?"

"I didn't realize he was invited," Ari said. "I thought this was a formal presentation of Princess Tiana to the Wheylian court."

"He could have come," Siara said, glancing at her uncle.

Lord Reido nodded. "And now he shall miss visiting the wellspring.

"We didn't realize he could do that, either." Ari could tell from the look on Siara's face he was embarrassing her. "We didn't think he was of sufficient rank."

"How's this?" Lord Reido asked. "If that was the impression given to you, it was surely in error. All in Wheylia have a right to worship at the wellspring, for it is our most sacred place."

"We should send for him," Siara said. "His father may be a noble of Lggothland, but this is his heritage. I'm sure he would be sad to miss it."

Lord Reido waved over a page. "The princess wishes you to seek out the young man, Lord Peine, Lord Aridian's valet," he told the boy. "Make haste and bring him at once to us."

The boy bowed and hurried away.

"Thank you, Uncle," Siara said.

Lord Reido smiled, but it was a sad expression. "If you'll permit me to say so, your highness, you look so like your mother. You're even a similar age to her, the last time I saw her."

"Why did my mother leave here?" Siara asked. Her voice was low, as if she worried the subject was taboo, a concern Ari shared.

"It was mother's vision," Lord Reido said. Ari marked deep bitterness lurking in his tone. "The Lavarina is always blessed with vision. It helps her rule with foresight. Mother never shared with me what the vision was, but one morning she called my two younger sisters to her and told them they must leave. Where they chose to go she cared not, but go they must. Mother seemed to think the fate of the kingdom rested on it."

"You sound unconvinced," Siara said.

239

Ari looked down at his boots, thinking this was a conversation better suited to a private dinner than the queen's throne room, although most of the nobles had departed after seeing Tiana.

Reido must have agreed, for he looked about as if gauging the nearness of those around them. "The vision is not a precise thing. I'm told it comes in the form of a waking dream, filled with nebulous allegory. It's not that I doubt my mother's powers, but in the years since, I've seen only sorrow come from her decision that day."

"Why was I left in Lggothland when my mother died birthing me?" Siara asked in a hushed tone. "And when my father grew tired of the reminder of her and sent me to live in a convent, why not retrieve me then? Why leave me exiled and unacquainted with my heritage?" Tension emanated from Siara.

Reido frowned. "Believe me, I argued for your return. I beseeched them to retrieve you, but mother wouldn't allow it. She said you were the result of my sister's choices, so the path you took must be the path of destiny, and your aunt agreed with her. Of what worth was my voice, compared to that of Lavarina and her heir?"

Ari blinked, surprised to hear the queen's son complain of his station. As if realizing he'd admitted too much, Lord Reido clamped his mouth shut. Siara, however, opened hers. Ari knew her well enough to know Reido's answers wouldn't satisfy her. Siara was not one to let something lie. Much to his relief, the page Lord Reido had sent came hurrying toward them.

"I couldn't find him, my lords, your highness," the page said, bowing. "I asked, and the guards say he left the castle."

"How unfortunate," Lord Reido said, though there was no surprise in his tone.

240

Ari was surprised, but Peine had every right to go where he chose.

"Left the castle?" Siara repeated, frowning. "Why?"

"I don't know, your highness."

"Whatever could he be thinking?"

Ari could see she was still angry, as she always became when discussing her estrangement from her family. He hoped she wouldn't turn any of that anger on Peine.

"You show him too much leniency, Ari," Siara snapped.

"He isn't a servant," Ari said.

"Yes, he is. Just as much as you were to Sir Cadwel. His father gave him into the service of the king until his seventeenth year, and the king gave him to you. Honor bids him fulfill his obligation. I should remind him of that."

"I'll speak to him." Ari didn't need Siara going behind his back and reprimanding Peine again.

Lord Reido cleared his throat. "Shall we? The wellspring is eternal, but the banquet is not, and we must go if we're to return."

"Yes, Uncle." Siara cast Ari a look that clearly said Peine had best conform to her expectations.

Instead of departing through the wide doors of the throne room, Lord Reido led them out a smaller one to the left of the dais. Queen Reudi watched them go, but looking into her eyes, Ari saw a disturbing lack of understanding, as if she went through the motions of observing them but her mind was uncomprehending. Whatever magic she had worked to seal Tiana to Wheylia, it seemed to have exhausted her. He wondered again at how different this old woman was from the Queen of Wheylia he'd met in the mountains two years ago.

From the throne room, they entered a narrow corridor that seemed to lead into the very mountain itself. The two guards inside the corridor fell in behind them, and Ari felt a slight chill run up his spine at having armed men following him when he wasn't carrying a sword.

The passage became roughhewn, winding its way upward. To Ari's surprise, they passed through a doorway and out of the peak behind the castle, into the open air. They crossed a narrow stone bridge spanning a valley he would never have guessed was there. The bridge led them to a cave set into the peak beyond. Looking down as they crossed, Ari found the valley was deep enough to hold full grown trees, even their tall tops a disturbing distance below.

Reaching the other side, they stepped into the cool, small cave. It housed a large granite boulder which, at some time in the past, had been cleaved in two. The path from the bridge to the stone was worn by countless feet. Ari could see two smooth patches where it looked as if hands were often placed against the hewn boulder, allowing whoever stood there to peer into the fissure and what lay beneath.

Low stone benches ringed the outer walls of the cave, smokeless sconces burning above. An old woman in flowing gray robes greeted them with a bow. Lord Reido led the way around the stone to sit along the wall opposite the entrance. As Ari walked past the rock, he thought he saw something flicker within the gap, but before he could be sure, it was gone. The castle guards took up positions to either side of the entrance almost, but not quite, as if blocking them in.

The old woman moved between them and the boulder, silhouetted against the backdrop of afternoon light outside the cave. She bowed her head, appearing deep in thought. When she at last raised her face, Ari saw she was blind.

"The Lavarina asks that the wellspring be praised for delivering the granddaughter and great granddaughter safely to us," the old woman said in a voice that surprised Ari with its clarity and strength, for she was thin and stooped with age. "And in her wisdom, bids me tell you of the old times. It is not a story often shared with outsiders but her decision is wise, for it is wrong to give praise without understanding. What good is praise, when the voices giving it know not what they give it to? You sit politely before the wellspring, but with no knowledge in your hearts."

Ari glanced to either side of him. Siara watched the old priestess with great concentration, while Lord Reido's face took on a resigned look, tinged with boredom. He leaned back against the wall.

"Long ago, when man was new to this world and magical creatures flourished, all women of Whey wielded great power. All people carry the spark of the wellspring inside them, for the wellspring is the source of life, but women carry it more strongly, for women are the creators.

"In those days long past, it shames me to say, the women of Whey allowed corruption to taint the great power they wielded. They were grown wicked and wanton with it. They enslaved the men of Wheylia and their reign was cruel."

Ari blinked in surprise. This was not the story he was expecting to hear.

"Even so, the people of Whey flourished, as did people elsewhere, and so the race of man grew. As it grew, the wellspring was ever more divided, and the great Witches of Whey, as they were known, found their abilities diminishing. It became more and more difficult to harness enough power for great works of magic, as the spark of the wellspring was dispersed throughout the creatures of the world.

"Unwilling to accept this constraint, the Witches of Whey hunted down those creatures of magic they could find and slew them, releasing their portion of the wellspring back into the world. This worked for a time, but even as the magical creatures declined, the races of men increased, and the wellspring divided further still. In this late hour of their reign, and in unfathomable wickedness, the witches made a pact. Henceforth, all but a chosen few male children must die. Thus, they hoped more of the wellspring would be free to serve their purposes."

Ari stared at her in horror. Did she mean they were killing all the boy babies? No wonder the texts he was able to find on ancient Wheylia were so obscure about the causes of the old wars. It wasn't exactly a sterling history she was reciting.

"But the men of Wheylia learned of this pact and could bear no more. Rising up against the witches, even as their powers were deserting them, the men overthrew their rule. A large boulder, imbued with spells, was brought here to the mountains and placed over the wellspring, that no more power could escape it. The magic of the witches was gone.

"Even though the wellspring was capped, a law was made. As each girl reached womanhood, she was examined for traces of power. Those suspected of possessing any skill were banished across the sea. Thus, the men thought to keep peace and never again be slaves.

"What they did not comprehend was the wellspring, thus capped, could not receive back its power. Whenever more death overtook the land than life, the power of the wellspring would once again build. So it was, after many years, women again knew strength. The testing of them had by then grown lax, and one was able to hide her magic and make herself queen.

"This queen sought out what magical creatures still remained, hidden and scarce, and slew them, subverting nature and drawing the spark of the wellspring directly from the dying and into herself. In her evil, she would have returned the world to its former state.

"And thus it was the stone capping the wellspring was cracked, for to defeat this evil, a young man and woman banned together on a quest to free the wellspring, that all women of Wheylia would once again know power and could rise up against the queen. With the sundering of the stone they made a pact, these two valiant heroes. Each woman of Wheylia could love once, and but once only. Never again could they use their power as tyranny over their men, for each man held a greater power, the power of a woman's life. She may never be long away from him, never betray him, and never make him her slave."

The priestess bowed her head. Ari struggled to digest the tale. Looking over, he saw something close to anger on Siara's face, and was surprised to see a similar emotion on Lord Reido's. It must run in the family, he thought, and turned his attention back to the priestess as she raised her head.

"Now you may each approach the stone and give thanks to the wellspring, the heart of our people, that its power brought you safely here to our lands."

Siara stood abruptly, taking the few steps to the stone. It seemed to Ari as if the princess had to pry her fingers open, her fists were clenched so tight. She laid shaking hands upon the two halves of the stone and closed her eyes. Ari had no idea what thoughts went through her mind, but he had his doubts over whether they were thankful.

Once she stepped away, Lord Reido stood. He bowed to the stone, almost mockingly, and stepped to Siara's side. Whispering low in her ear, he offered his arm, and the two circled to the exit. Siara's stiff spine bespoke volumes on her way out. The guards followed them.

"Lord Aridian," the old woman said, her sightless eyes on him. "The wellspring awaits you."

Ari stood, but hesitated. He wasn't sure if he wanted anything to do with a magic that drove people to such madness as he'd just heard. Still, nothing the old woman had said bespoke of inherent evil in the wellspring, only in those who wielded its power. Carefully, he stepped up to the stone, putting his palms against it as Siara had. Unlike her, he did not close his eyes.

"Thank you," he whispered, as the old priestess seemed to be waiting for him to speak. Deep within the fissure, something flickered, catching his gaze. The harder he looked, the more he seemed to see a swirling bluish-white glow, akin to the Orlenia, spiraling far below.

He leaned closer, letting go of thoughts of the old woman and why he was there. He could sense power in the swirling mist below. He felt like he could almost touch it. His amulet slid from his shirt, dangling toward the light deep in the well as if called. If he could reach that glow, he knew it would fill the void left in him by the Orlenia. Sliding his hands down the boulder, he braced himself to push it out of the way. It was a large stone, over waist high, but he had the strength.

"There are not many who can taste such power unscathed," the old woman said.

Ari stepped back, aghast. What had he almost done? Moved the most sacred object in Wheylia, so he might do what? Plunge himself into a bottomless pit? All for a power that once drove women to kill their own babies? Shaking his head, he hurried from the cave and across the bridge, feeling the sightless eyes of the old woman on his back as he went.

Chapter 23

The banquet hall ran half the length of the castle. Four tall windows were cut into the thick stone at the far end, two on each side of another raised dais with a throne, on which Queen Reudi sat. Aside from the main door across from her, there were four archways from which servants continually spilled, and an equal number opposite them, opening into the grand ballroom.

The queen sat alone, beyond the long table, and Ari realized she would watch them eat, but not dine herself. He wondered if she was even awake. Lord Reido graced the head of the table in her stead, with Siara on his right and Ari his left. Peine, who reappeared as Ari was entering the banquet hall, sat next to Ari, for in Wheylia they didn't have the apprentice system of noble servitude they did in Lggothland. Here, only the lowborn ever served. Ari would have preferred it the other way because if Peine was allowed to act as a servant, he would have access to parts of the castle and gossip a noble didn't.

Ari wanted to ask Peine were he'd gone that afternoon, but no one else was chatting as people entered the room. The table was of such length, and so many nobles attended, that announcing titles and seating went on for over an hour. Although he was surprised to see the queen wouldn't eat with them, Ari started to think that were she indeed asleep, she had the right idea. Finally, the last noble was seated and a crystal bell sounded. Released, everyone began to talk with their neighbors as soup was served.

"What's in this?" Ari whispered to Peine, suspicious of the dark meat floating in his bowl. It looked terribly oily.

"It's water fowl," Peine whispered back. "Just eat it, Ari."

Ari did, but he didn't like it. As dinner progressed, he decided he preferred the way it was done in Lggothland, where diners were offered trays of food and could accept or decline. Here, every few minutes the servants carried in a new plate of food for each person. If Ari didn't eat at least half of each, Peine glared at him.

"Does the queen not dine with us?" Siara asked her uncle, pausing in cutting her food. "We would not find it rude if she chose to retire."

Lord Reido shook his head. "Lavarina, being both queen and high priestess, does not eat in the company of others," he said. "To us, she is nearly a goddess, and she must always uphold her image as being above the frailties of normal people. The Lavarina knows not hunger, nor exhaustion, nor illness or fear, for she has her magic to sustain her."

Siara shot a worried look at her grandmother. Ari had to agree with her concern. Even weren't evidence of her frailty before their eyes, Queen Reudi had intimated to Ari earlier that her power faltered. He realized this woman, as both high priestess and queen, had even more restrictions placed on her

248

than a princess. Did every ascension in rank dictate less and less freedom?

"Sir Aridian," Lord Reido said as a plate holding something looking suspiciously like a whole pigeon was placed in front of Ari. "A goodly number of people have asked me if you would consent to a test of arms, and I myself have become quite taken with the idea. Of course, we would ask you to forgo your knight's plate when sparring with our weapons masters, for the unfair advantage it would give, though certainly you must wear your metal shell when you demonstrate the joust. Jousting is not customary here, but we can make up some of those dummies they impale in Lggothland."

"I'm unsure, my lord," Ari said, his mind groping for a polite no. He couldn't think of any good that would come of it. If he defeated the Wheylian weapons masters, Peine would say he cheated and the Wheys would have a better gauge of his skills. If he lost, the respect he inspired would diminish. "I don't believe there's room in the courtyard before the castle for jousting lists."

"But this is easily solved," Lord Reido said in his cultured voice. "We shall hold the competition outside the city. That way, even the lowborn shall have the opportunity to witness the prowess of Lggothland's champion."

"I think it's a splendid idea," Siara said. "I rejoice at this opportunity to spread the repute and glory of the champion of my house. Once your people see the glorious might of Sir Aridian, bolts of silver and blue shall become scarce as an adoring populace scrambles to bedeck themselves in his colors."

Ari groaned inwardly.

"Excellent," Lord Reido said. "I believe we can have the field ready in three days' time." Lord Reido stood, the room falling silent. "Nobles of Wheylia, I have a joyous announcement. In three days' time, Sir Aridian shall grant us a demonstration of Lggothland's fine art of jousting." He paused here, letting the assemblage murmur their pleasure. "Furthermore, he has agreed to participate in a tourney with our own fine men of arms and, as a man of great honor, he will forgo his heavy metal cage and meet them as equals."

This generated applause. Glasses were raised in salute. Ari raised his as well, though a prickling of warning scaled his spine, turning the small sip of wine he took bitter in his mouth. Siara, at least, looked pleased.

***

"Lord Reido said you could have come to that ceremony," Ari said to Peine later, once they were back in their guest chambers. "We sent someone to find you, but apparently you were down in the city."

"I went to see my brother." Peine turned his back on Ari as he fussed with tomorrow's tunic.

"You two must have gotten to spend a lot of time together after you left me behind with the carriages," Ari said, not quite willing to voice his concern that Peine's brother Gauli might have known about Sir Keite.

"Some." Peine rummaged in their packs. "I explored the city a lot, for you, and Gauli has his new duties to attend to."

"New duties?"

"Well, he did serve Keite, but you know how that ended, and it's not like he can be page to someone else. We don't have a knighthood in Wheylia, after all, or knight's pages. Or lord's valets."

"All the lords here have valets," Ari protested, his mind straying from their discussion to other worries. He'd hoped to speak to Queen Reudi alone, to ask her if she'd sent Sir Keite,

250

but that was seeming increasingly unlikely. Should he ask Lord Reido? "When we went down to the bathing pool, it looked like there was a valet for every noble there."

"But those are real servants, Ari. Peasants."

"If they don't apprentice, how do Wheylian men learn skills? What do all the younger sons do?"

"Whatever they want," Peine said. "Some become scholars, or officers. A lot live with their wives and help manage their estates. We don't have a problem with women over birthing in Wheylia, because that's one of the easiest things to do with magic, they say. It's rare for a Wheylian woman to have more than two children. Not like in Lggothland, where your women are like broodmares, spreading your people to all corners of the realm." Peine glared at him.

Ari stared back, surprised at the vehemence in Peine's tone. "So, we have too many people in Lggothland?" he finally ventured.

"Yes, too many people, making it so there's not enough of anything for anyone. That's why your people fight so much, to kill themselves off, only Sir Cadwel stopped all the wars and now you'll keep them stopped, until there are so many of you, you have to invade another kingdom to get more space."

Ari shook his head, baffled by Peine's rant. He had the sinking feeling it was Gauli's influence, tainted by Keite, and had no idea what to do about it. He was sure that even a hint that he thought Gauli was a bad influence would be met with more anger.

"And now, since I grew up in Lggothland, I have to be a servant. It's embarrassing." Scowling, Peine strode past Ari, slamming the door on his way out.

Ari scrutinized the closed door, wondering if he should chase Peine down. Peine's arguments weren't even sound.

251

Surely, he could be made to see that. Queen Reudi, after all, had four children and Queen Parrella only one. Ari was more disturbed, though, by his friend's insistence on calling Lggothians Ari's people, as if Peine hadn't been born there. And why was he so worried about being a servant until he reached his majority? Peine used to take pride in being Ari's valet. In Lggothland, it was an honor, and certain to earn Peine a stewardship in any lord's castle, if ever he chose to leave Ari.

Ari rubbed at the back of his neck, trying to ease the strain there, and settled onto one of the plush sofas. He wanted to meet this brother of Peine's, who'd been page to an Empty One and who, Ari suspected, was filling Peine's mind with venom. He was worried asking would only make his friend angry, though. He had a long time to nurse his concern, for the fire burned low before Peine returned.

"Peine," Ari called, causing his friend to start.

"Why are you sitting here in the dark?" Peine muttered, crossing to stir the embers and light a candle.

Ari ignored the question. Peine knew he could see in any light. "Do you want to sleep in the big bed and I'll sleep in the servant's room? Or I could ask them to give you a room of your own. We could get you a valet, too, like all the other Wheylian lords."

"No." Peine shook his head. "I'm sorry. I didn't mean to sound so ungrateful. Being your valet is an honor. When my father sent me to Poromont, our biggest hope was that I might become chief steward to some minor noble. Getting to be your valet is the best thing that ever happened to me. It's just --" Peine hesitated, sighing. "Well, I see how the nobles here live. It isn't like in Lggothland, where younger sons have to do the best they can and older ones get everything. If my parents lived

252

on this side of the mountain, I would already have nobles' quarters and a valet."

"But if your parents lived on this side of the mountain and Wheylian women only have two children, you wouldn't have been born. You have two older brothers and a sister."

"Well," Peine said. "I guess there's that. Either way, I'm sorry. I don't know what came over me."

The room filled with a strained silence. Ari searched his mind for a safe topic.

"Everyone is talking about the tourney in three days," Peine said.

"I don't know why Siara did that to me."

"Well, everyone's looking forward to it."

Their talk moved to what sorts of weapons might be involved, and checking over Ari's suit of mail. Peine said he was worried Stew's blue and silver ribbons were getting too worn, but he knew where to buy new ones. After a while, things seemed more normal between them. Ari decided it was time to ask about Peine's brother.

"You know," he said, trying to keep his tone casual. "I'd like to meet Gauli sometime."

"Really?" Peine sounded pleased. "He's been asking to meet you, but I told him you're king's champion, not some sort of pet for me to trot out and show off."

Ari smiled. That sounded like the Peine he knew, guardian of Ari's rank and the respect that went with it. "I don't see why we couldn't go see him tomorrow, if you have to get ribbon anyhow. I'd like to go down to the city, when I'm not part of a parade, and take a look around. I don't think they have much scheduled for us aside from evening banquets."

"Well, actually, I don't know if tomorrow would be a good day. I didn't want to worry you, but I spoke with the queen's chief steward, and she apprised me of your schedule."

The amusement on Peine's face made Ari nervous. "And?"

"Tomorrow, there's a procession to show you, Princess Siara and Tiana to the people." Peine paused to give Ari time to sigh. "After that, there's a grand ball to welcome you. The next day, you have a tour of the city and the university, followed by a banquet with the scholars. Then will be the day you inspect the tourney field and give your approval of the events and the lists they're setting up, followed by a royal picnic. Of course, after that there will be the tourney, which shall take place over three days. On the first night you have a banquet with the generals, and on the second one with the merchant lords of the city. On the final day of the tourney there will be a city wide celebration and, of course, another ball."

Ari stared at Peine. "You're making all that up to torment me."

"I'm sorry." Peine was grinning now. "I guess it's the price you pay for being king's champion."

"I'm going to bed," Ari said, not bothering to hide his chagrin.

***

Stew, prancing fit to throw Ari off, enjoyed himself immensely during the procession the following day, but poor baby Tiana did not. She was fine at first, quiet as they wound themselves back and forth across each tier of the city. By the bottom tier, though, she was fussing and it seemed all Siara and Camva could do to keep her from screaming when they held her up to the crowd. Siara and the baby rode in an open carriage, so while Ari did get to keep a close watch on them, he couldn't easily speak to Siara. He felt oddly removed from her, and nurtured a vague sense of worry.

At the grand ball, a sea of dark haired girls enveloping him, Ari found the pain of missing Ispiria nearly debilitating. He longed for her unaffected grace and her ready smile, her red curls that never stayed where they were supposed to, and the way she didn't care that they wouldn't. For the first time in his life, he questioned if being king's champion was worth spending so much time away from her. That night, he fell asleep with a vision of Ispiria's laughing green eyes filling his mind with longing.

Ari found their tour of the university buildings much more interesting than the ball or the parade. Inside the buildings were wonders of a like he hadn't seen beyond the Aluien caves. They first visited the building where the Wheys studied the philosophies of the living world. There was a section filled with the skulls and bones of long disappeared creatures, including what the scholars insisted was the tail of a dragon. Looking at the size of the bones, Ari wondered how any man had ever defeated such a beast.

The second building was the school of history and culture. It housed a vast library. Although many of the books appeared to be in ancient Wheylian, many were in the modern tongue common to both kingdoms, and other languages still. Ari vowed, should he have any free time during his stay, he would return there.

After leaving the histories of the real world behind, they made their way to the building where the Wheys studied the arcane, also known as the women's school. Ari and Peine, along with all the other men in their convoy, took their ease in a sun dappled courtyard while Siara and Princess Tiana continued their tour. Servants arrived with a midday meal of hearty brown ale, sharp white cheese and warm bread.

Ari devoted most of the meal to a pleasant conversation with Lord Reido on the topic of how much more defensible the City of Whey was by comparison to Poromont, although Ari added that Sorga had a very sound design. Peine said little, and Ari often saw him looking up at the building of the arcane with poorly veiled resentment on his face.

When Siara returned, Ari wanted to ask her what went on inside, but he didn't have the chance, for she was once again ensconced in her open carriage. They continued on to the final building of the university, the one devoted to the arts. Ari didn't know what to expect from this school, for he hadn't realized one needed such extensive training to paint things and sing.

He was caught completely off guard by the awe-inspiring works within. They were in many mediums, everything from paint to stone to the notes of a harp. There were windows of colored glass as intricate and lovely as the rigging on a sailing ship, paintings that captured the beauty of the most perfect summer day, sculptures so lifelike they made him fight not to blush, and music from enough instruments to rival Sir Cadwel's collection of weapons. Ari wondered if Larke had ever been there, because he could picture the bard wandering the halls in wonder and happiness.

After their tour, to Ari's delight, the Wheys performed a concert. Never before had he heard such an intricate combination of voice and music. There were over twenty singers, with voices of varying ranges, and Ari counted at least as many types of instruments being played. It was so complex, there was one person whose sole function was to stand before the recitalists and guide them.

Ari didn't know for how long they performed, but when it ended, he had a lump in his throat. Looking over at Siara, he saw tears on her cheeks. For the first time in months, her face held serenity. Tiana, cradled in Camva's arms, was sound asleep.

The performance was followed by the evening's banquet, which also had music, interspersed with speeches. This music, although well done, was only for background. The speeches mostly pertained to the oft repeated themes of what an honor it was to have them and how all wished for continued peace and prosperity in the two realms.

When it came time to depart, Ari followed Siara down the line of deans, thanking them for their hospitality and praising their schools. The Dean of the School of the Arcane, whom he'd met more briefly than the others, placed a hand on his sleeve after he made his pleasantries, halting him. He looked down into her inscrutable face, surprised.

"There is a particular painting I wish to show you, Sir Aridian, ere you leave," she said. "It will take but a moment. It is of your home, yet few from Sorga have ever seen it." She was a tall woman, and there was a luminescence about her dark Wheylian eyes that reminded Ari of the Aluien.

"Of course, Dean Faola." Ari turned to Siara, bowing slightly. "With your permission, your highness?"

"Certainly, Sir Aridian. We shall await your escort in our carriage, for the princess is tired."

Ari thought Siara looked tired as well. Leaving the others, he followed Dean Faola into the now dark passageways. She set a brisk pace and, though they went deep into the building, it didn't take them long to arrive at an unlit inner room. Ari peered within, the darkness thick even to his heightened perception. He could see paintings on the walls, but not with enough details to discern their content.

Dean Faola held out her hand, palm up, and spoke a word in ancient Wheylian. A ball of light appeared, floating above her skin, causing Ari to gape in awe. Holding it out before them, she walked into the room, crossing to a painting of mountains with a small cluster of buildings at the base.

"Sorga," she said.

Tearing his eyes off the globe of light she held, he leaned close to study the work. So lifelike was it, he could recognize the form of the mountains. There were a few small differences, but he suspected the cracked and aged canvas held the reality of what had once been there. The cluster of buildings was completely unfamiliar, although it stood where the keep now was. Ari began reconstructing what was there now in his mind, fitting it in place in the painting.

Dean Faola leaned her head close to his, as if scrutinizing the painting as well. "Lavarina is being poisoned," she whispered.

Ari held himself ridged, not letting his shock show. His mind tumbled with the statement, and he realized the painting was a subterfuge. She reached out, seeming to trace the detail of the small buildings with one finger, though not touching the canvas.

"I can find no other explanation for her decline," she continued, her voice barely audible. "It is a slow poison, meant to look like the ravages of age, but it works not slowly enough to ally my suspicions. It saps her will from her. It grows more and more difficult for her to draw the power to her. This is not normal. It is not right. Even a weak Lavarina has the power of the wellspring at her fingertips until the day she dies, and Reudi was never weak."

258

"Do you know who?" Ari whispered. "Do you know how?" He suppressed his inclination to squander time asking if she was sure, because he couldn't imagine her going to such lengths were she not.

"I know of only one poison which can do such a thing." She glanced at him, and he saw a smoldering anger in her eyes. "They call it the blood of the dragon. It can only be made through magic. The lifeblood of an innocent is combined with an unflawed heart stone ground into dust, but the magic renders it colorless. They say the only sign of it is the faint scent of helleborous, the winter rose."

"Is there a cure?"

"No cure is needed. It must be administered daily until the entirety of her magic is gone and death takes her, or she will regain her strength."

An awareness prickled the base of Ari's skull. Someone was watching them. He straightened. "That truly is fascinating," he said in his normal voice. "Even though it's cracked with age, you can still make out the one small flag, fluttering with a brown hawk on faded blue." He could hear quiet footsteps now, drawing near.

"I'm sure I need not tell you," she said, likewise turning from the painting, "that the hawks of Sorga are a breed apart."

"Indeed, I know it to be so," he said as someone approached the door.

"There you are." It was Lord Reido, his steps exuding no stealth as he entered the room.

Ari wondered if the faintness of footfall he'd heard earlier was an attempt to sneak, or simply the natural reaction a man might have to walking dark empty corridors alone.

"I'm sure that old pile of canvas is fascinating, but my niece and our future queen grow weary with awaiting your return," Reido continued.

"My apologies, my lord." Ari bowed. "In my absorption with the work, I lost track of the passage of time. Never would I have thought to see Sorga depicted so."

Lord Reido moved to stand beside them, frowning at the painting. "We'll have to see if you may have this. I don't believe it has much intrinsic value."

"Thank you," Ari said, unsure how to respond. "We best return before half the guard comes looking for us."

Lord Reido chuckled politely at his poor joke, and they made their way back. Dean Faola kept her light burning until they reached better-lit passages. Ari watched in fascination as she closed her palm, quenching it.

Siara seemed cross with him, but he was so accustomed to her temper, it was more a comfort than a worry. So long as Siara was angry, nothing could be too wrong with the world. They returned to the castle via the shortest route, but it was still quite late by the time they arrived and everyone retired with little preamble. Ari could find no discreet moment to impart the dean's warning to Siara and went to his room filled with frustration. Silence fell over the castle of the Wheys, and he was left alone with his thoughts of poison and deceit.

Chapter 24

Later that night, his mind restless with Dean Faola's words, Ari was roused from sleep by soft footfalls on the heavy carpet outside his room. It was Peine's stealth that made Ari suspicious, for why should his friend sneak at all? It wasn't as if Ari was some sort of tyrant, not allowing his valet to leave his quarters at night.

Peine crossed to the fireplace and Ari could hear the ashes being stirred. He realized his friend probably couldn't sleep and was sneaking out of kindness, not wishing to wake him, and felt guilty for his instant suspicion.

Then Ari saw, in the narrow gap beneath the door, a flickering and shifting of light that bespoke of someone striking a candle and walking with it across the room. As soon as the hall door swung shut, Ari was on his feet. He added a tunic to the light breeches he wore. Recalling the last time he'd crept about in the dark with suspicion so heavy on his heart, he belted on his sword before carefully following Peine.

The light Peine carried made him easy to follow. Ari kept well back, but he knew he was at an advantage. Seeing beyond candlelight was much harder than seeing what lay within it. Peine crept through the nobles' wing and down the stairs leading to the basement of the castle. At the bottom, Ari was forced to duck back into the stairwell as his friend stopped before the door leading to the changing room for the women's bath and looked about. Peine slipped inside.

Ari hurried forward, pressing his ear against the wood until he heard Peine go through the next door, into the underground cavern with its steam shrouded pool. Entering, he took in Peine's neatly folded clothes and the extinguished candle. Other clothes were folded or thrown over the narrow benches, but since the nobles often left what was dirty in favor of something clean, Ari didn't know if any of the other garb was recently vacated.

Sneaking closer to the bathing room door, Ari heard the murmur of Peine's voice. He couldn't make out what his friend said. Embarrassment overtaking him, Ari fled back to their room. If Peine wanted to meet someone in the lady's bath in the middle of the night, it was no business of Ari's. At least now he knew why his friend was worrying so much about appearing to be a servant. Obviously, Peine was in love again.

***

"You know," Ari said the next morning as Peine looked him over, making sure he was fit to inspect the tourney field. The outfit Peine had selected for him included no armor, but he wore his tabard and, for once, his sword. "You haven't said a thing about women since I got here. The whole ride south it was Vidia this, Delini that."

"Those ninnies?" Peine grimaced. "The girls in Sorga are a bunch of clucking hens. They bumble about with their blonde

262

braids and their giant chest. None of them has half the grace or poise of a Wheylian girl. Except for Ispiria, of course," Peine added hastily. "She isn't even blonde."

Ari kept his smile to himself, sure Peine was in love again. "Did you get new ribbons for Stew?" he asked, to change the subject.

"Yes, and I showed them to him when I went down to the stable this morning."

"That was nice of you. He loves it here. Every day he prances through the city in his fancy tack and whenever we stop anywhere, little girls run up and feed him apples. He's going to get fat."

"Well, he best not get too fat for his armor."

"I wouldn't worry about it. Horses' armor doesn't fit that way."

Ari made sure to smile as they rode through the city and out to the plains beyond. Directly before the gates, a field had been fenced off, with a jousting list down the center. He was impressed the Wheys had managed to erect bleachers and covered seating for the nobles in such quick time. A large red and gray striped pavilion had also been set up. Ari assumed the picnic would take place there. Farther from the city walls, looking exceedingly organized in their neat rows, ranged the tents of those traveling to the city to watch, participate or sell. There were so many tents in so short a time, Ari was suspicious the event had been planned long before Lord Reido brought it up.

Riding toward the field, his main concern was the grass. Tall grass flowed across the open plain in front of the city. In Poromont, the jousting field was dirt and the king had a joust master whose duties included maintaining the field in good condition. Ari didn't think grass would work as well.

263

He leaned forward, pretending to brush something out of Stew's fetlock, and whispered, "Will all that grass be a problem?"

Stew raised his hooves higher, turning his walk into a showy prance.

Ari had to take that as a no. "Well, at least it'll be softer to land on if I fall off," he murmured, straightening.

Stew shook his head.

Under the scrutiny of a gathering crowd, Ari made a show of inspecting the field. He rode with Peine and Lord Reido down one side of the lists, scrutinizing them. When they got to the other end, Ari gave in to the temptation to please the crowd and galloped Stew down the other side, eliciting applause. Lord Reido and Peine joined him at a more sedate pace and they proceeded to look over the straw stuffed practice dummies and ring stands. Ari tested to make sure both had the proper buoyancy, because if they broke it would ruin the show and if they were too firm they could be dangerous to him and Stew, although he wasn't too worried about that.

"So, Sir Aridian," Lord Reido said. "What do you think of our tourney field?"

"It's very well done, my lord," Ari said with a genuine smile. Though he'd been reluctant, he was looking forward to the next three days. As his time was sure to be spoken for, he preferred tourneys to endless dances and banquets. He glanced at Peine to ascertain if he should say more, but his friend half-dozed in the saddle.

"I'm pleased you like it. The people are quite excited for the event. This is as near to seeing a real joust as many will ever come."

Ari nodded, looking about at the areas marked off for dueling. "May I ask, my lord, if I'm to demonstrate the joust on the third day, what other activities have you planned? You said you wished me to engage in a display of swordsmanship, and you shall be making a show of some traditional Wheylia weapons for me?"

"Oh, I think it will be a surprise for you, Sir Aridian," Lord Reido said with a tinge of glee in his tone. "One or two of our demonstrators might even challenge you. You have enough of an advantage without knowing what the weapons will be. Give us some chance to show off the skills of our nation."

"Enough of an advantage?" he repeated. Did Reido know Ari was different? Queen Reudi knew. Would she tell her son?

"All know of your great skill, Sir Aridian."

"You praise me too highly, my lord." Ari cast an eye on the height of the sun. Having not seen Siara or Tiana yet that day was making him nervous. "When will the ladies of the court be joining us for the afternoon's festivities?"

"Within moments, it seems." Lord Reido sounded amused. He gestured northward.

Ari looked over his shoulder, catching sight of a string of coaches rolling from the city. He nudged Stew, turning to watch the long line of brightly painted vehicles meander through the grass toward the luncheon pavilion. As the ladies began arriving, he dismounted, giving Peine Stew's reins. Siara's coach came to a halt and Ari stepped forward, waving away the footman. He helped Siara down, bowing to her.

"Where's Peine?" she asked as Ari offered his arm.

"He's seeing to the horses, your highness," he said, nodding toward Peine. Ari almost groaned, for as Siara looked, Peine turned away from the grooms and opened his mouth in a huge yawn. Ari could see the princess's lips thin in disapproval.

"Ari," she began.

"He's just tired," Ari said.

"We've not even reached the hour to dine. How can he be so tired already?"

He led her toward the pavilion, her coach pulling away. The final coach, the queen's, held back.

Ari wondered if the truth would make her more or less angry with his friend. He really didn't want Siara lecturing Peine on his duties again. Plus, he had more important things he needed to discuss with her than Peine's new sweetheart. He wished he could speak to her somewhere private. They walked into the candle filled pavilion.

"Peine's in love. He's been sneaking into the women's baths at night to meet someone, but there's something I have to tell you. Is there somewhere we can meet, when we aren't being paraded in front of people, where no one will overhear us?"

"With a Wheylian girl?" Siara asked sharply, ignoring what Ari considered to be the important part of the conversation. "He does know, if she's possessed of power, even a small amount, her heart is not something to toy with. It can only be given once."

Ari hadn't considered that. He sighed. He'd definitely made things worse. "He knows that. He told me that, years ago, about you."

Her face showed Ari that was a mistake. Why did he always seem to dig himself into a hole with Siara? Of course she wouldn't want to be reminded that even the youngest son of a minor noble knew more about her heritage than she had, locked in a convent with only the teachings of the Overgod to guide her.

"We should make sure he isn't being careless with someone's heart," she said.

Servants came forward to pull back the thick wooden chairs. Siara sat to the right of Queen Reudi's throne and Lord Reido's chair was to his mother's left, with Ari's and Peine's beyond him. The long wooden table was so similar to the one in the great dining hall, they could be the same. The chairs were less ornate and squarer, their weight making them stable on the unevenness of the carpet-covered ground and pillows adding to their comfort. The dais and throne erected for the queen would put her near the table. Almost, but not quite, close enough to actually dine with them.

Ari had yet to see the queen today, and was impatient for her to appear. He wanted to look at her through eyes now colored by the idea that she was being poisoned. He needed to find some time alone with Siara so he could talk to her about what the dean had told him. With all the banquets and parades and tours, it seemed he never had a moment free except when he was sleeping.

"I'll have to find out who it is," Siara said, bringing Ari's attention back to their conversation.

"Please don't. I'll talk to him." Ari kept his voice low, as Peine was rapidly approaching.

Siara gave him a querulous look.

He shot a repressive one back. Peine was Ari's best friend. He would deal with it. He turned from her, movement outside the pavilion catching his eye. As Peine and a few other stragglers seated themselves, a herald entered through an opening in the canvas.

"All hail Lavarina Reudi," the man boomed.

Throughout the tent, chairs slid back on the soft carpet. Ari copied the others, standing and following along as everyone turned to the front of the tent and bowed. He dared to peek upward, and saw through the seam in the pavilion wall a large man lifting the queen down from her coach. Lord Reido stepped to her side, offering his arm, on which she leaned heavily.

They all remained bowed as Reido helped his mother into the tent and up the steps to her throne. Once she sat in solitude upon it, the herald spoke again. "The Lavarina bids all be seated." Ari unbent and complied.

Throughout the banquet, Ari scrutinized Queen Reudi as much as he could without feeling obvious about it. She seemed hardly aware of where she was, and Ari worried for her. Her deterioration since their arrival was noticeable. If poison it was, its hold over Queen Reudi was growing strong.

After the banquet there was dancing, and Ari escorted Siara to the best of his abilities. He dared not speak to her of anything important, for other couples were constantly near, but when Peine approached to ask the honor of a dance with his future queen, Ari reiterated in a low whisper, "I will talk to him, but we have to talk in private, later, you and I."

Siara pursed her lips, nodding. Ari didn't dance with anyone while she and Peine danced, but rather stood to the side, watching carefully to make sure their conversation seemed lighthearted. Siara must have listened to him, for once, because in their suite later, Peine seemed in perfectly good spirits.

"They have a lot planned for you, rumor has it," Peine said as he helped Ari check over his armor. "Are you sure you want to walk into these displays of skill blind? Lord Reido said some of them might challenge you. A few coins could probably gain us knowledge of what weapons they plan to use and when. Then you could think over your strategies, at least."

"Bribery?" Ari looked up from the pauldron he was inspecting in surprise. "That hardly seems chivalrous."

"It isn't as if this is a real joust, with rules, and some would argue complete chivalry has never figured into your strategy," Peine said, obviously stung by Ari's tactless rejection of the idea.

Ari sighed, Peine's words reopening his worry over whether he was a cheater. It occurred to him, sitting cleaning the armor Sir Cadwel had given him, that the great knight, who knew every secret Ari had, certainly wouldn't have made Ari duke of Sorga if he thought Ari was a cheater. Besides, what Parrentine had said was true. How could anyone but Ari hope to prevail on the side of right when faced with the evil of the Empty Ones?

"I've studied Wheylian weapons," Ari said. "Although, I would have worked harder at it if I'd known this was going to happen. I have a good idea what they might choose."

"Worked harder?" Peine shook his head, but his tone was teasing now. "You work all the time. You're the most boring lord ever."

"Not everyone likes to spend all their time chasing girls," Ari said, seeing a chance to have the conversation he'd promised Siara.

"That's only because you already have one. If I had a girl like Ispiria, I wouldn't need to keep looking."

"What about the girls here?" Ari tried to keep his tone casual. "Has anyone caught your fancy?"

"Not yet but, truly, there are some really pretty girls in Wheylia. It's a pity none of them would consent to be the wife of some minor Lggothian noble like me."

"Well, it must be harder to mingle here, since the women have to be very careful not to fall in love with someone who doesn't want them."

"Actually, I think it has an opposite effect. They seem to be quite cavalier about a certain amount of, um, experimenting. Trying out a man to see if they wish to spend any time getting to know him."

As much as Ari's curiosity pressed at him, he decided he shouldn't ask what sort of experimentation Peine was up to. Satisfied his friend wasn't breaking any hearts, he went back to cleaning his armor in silence.

Chapter 25

The summer air was still and hot the following day and Ari was glad that, for now at least, he didn't need to wear his full set of plate. His chainmail and tabard would be stifling enough. Once he was dressed, he could feel the heat building around him, even though the day was still young.

He needn't have worried about the heat, though, for he learned when he reached the tourney field that this first day was to be exhibitions by the Wheys and didn't include him as anything but an observer. He sat in the royal box with Siara, Lord Reido and Peine. The queen was too ill to attend, to Ari's disquiet. Looking at her empty throne in frustration, Ari found himself wondering how much trouble he'd get into if he tried to sneak into the queen's private chambers and find the poison. Probably a great deal.

Trumpets sounded and a group of Wheylian soldiers marched onto the field. Ari's troubles were momentarily forgotten as the demonstrations began. To his delight, the morning started with a display of formations. Responding to the loud commands of an officer, a squadron of red and gray clad foot soldiers wielding halberds marched, turned, stabbed and blocked imaginary foes. Ari was impressed by the uniformity of their movements and how the back lines of men managed not to slice the ones in front of them with the curved blades or impale them on the long points. He could picture, with grueling clarity, what such an advance would do to an oncoming force.

"You see, Sir Aridian," Lord Reido said. "Our paradigm of war differs from Lggothland's. Rarely have the houses of Whey vied amongst themselves, eliminating the need for a knighthood of the nobility to settle such disputes. Rather, when we know war, it is at the hands of those who invade our peace with conquest in their hearts. Thus, our focus has always been to meet them afield and stave off their pillaging."

"So I've read, my lord," Ari said. "The precision of your men is quite impressive. I'm honored to behold it."

"It is we who are honored, by the praise of so renowned a warrior."

Ari wasn't really sure how renowned he could be, since he was only seventeen and newly made king's champion. They paused in their conversation to join in the lavish applause for the display. After bowing to the royal box and the crowd, the soldiers quit the field.

"It does seem somewhat odd to me, my lord, that Wheylia keeps such a force. None have invaded here since my ancestors came across the sea to settle peacefully upon these shores, to live in harmony with your people," Ari said.

"This is true, but tradition lives long, and the world is ever an uncertain place. Look now, they bring the ballistae."

Ari turned, excitement filling him. He'd read extensively about the types of siege equipment used in war, but had rarely had the opportunity to see any employed, or even as relics. They didn't age well and used too much valuable timber and metal to be kept sitting about, and were therefore created only as needed.

The rest of the day, barring a break to dine when the sun was highest, was taken up with competitions of marksmanship using various siege weapons. Stones or blunt staves, brightly painted to designate teams, were repeatedly launched at far off targets. The competition was lighthearted, but Ari couldn't help picturing giant arrow-like missiles crashing into thick stone walls, drumming endlessly against them until they gave way, or the painted rocks replaced by debris coated in burning pitch, launched into a city or approaching army.

In the end, the yellow team was victorious, with yellow rocks and staves laying in undisputed profusion about each target. The grizzled veteran who commanded them came forward, his second at his side. Siara presented him with a purse of gold and kiss on the cheek. The old man grinned and bowed before the princess, and the crowd cheered. Ari enjoyed the event so thoroughly, he was considering implementing it as a summer game in Sorga.

Once the martial displays of the day were concluded, Ari's worries settled heavily onto his shoulders, but he had no time to seek out Siara as he was to attend a dinner with the officers of the queen's forces. To his chagrin, Siara wasn't even present at the dinner, for she was called to a different engagement. Ari went to bed frustrated and with a growing sense of dread building in his chest. Something was terribly wrong in Wheylia, and it seemed he was too much of a novelty to be allowed to do anything about it.

It was his tossing and turning that alerted him to the note hidden under his pillow. He cracked the seal of the royal house of Lggothland, identifying Siara's flowing script. The note requested he meet her an hour past the mid of night, a time already gone by, in a storeroom he'd never been to. He had a brief flash of annoyance. She could have left the note in the open. It wasn't as if they weren't allowed to communicate with each other and no one would have dared break the seal. He hoped she was still there. If not, she would probably blame him.

Getting up, Ari pulled on some clothes. He decided his sword would make him too suspicious, should he be seen, so he tucked a knife into his boot before creeping out of his room. He would have told Peine where he was going, but his valet had already snuck out for the night. Things with this girl, whoever she was, must be getting more serious.

As his path took him past the women's dressing chamber, Ari decided, late to meet Siara or no, it was time to put an end to Peine's sneaking before things got out of hand. Squaring his shoulders, he went in.

The dressing room was as cluttered with personal attire as always, including Peine's, but when Ari stepped into the cavern housing the hot spring, he found no one. He stood for a moment, peering into the steam. He couldn't see all the way to the back, or behind the pillars, but he couldn't imagine he wouldn't have surprised anyone in the room. They wouldn't have had time to hide.

"Peine?" he called softly. Only the steady drip of condensation from the ceiling answered. "It's me, Ari." The steam barely gave way to his voice. "I know you're with someone."

No answer came and, in truth, the space felt empty. Short of disrobing and wading in to search, Ari couldn't think of anything else to do. He waited, listening as hard as he could, but nothing stirred. Confused, Ari returned to the dressing chamber, unfolding and refolding Peine's shirt. It appeared to be his friend's, but he supposed there was no way to know for sure. Frowning, he wondered that there were so many trousers among the discarded garments. Was it some odd Wheylian custom?

A bit disgruntled his whim to confront Peine had gone awry, Ari left to find Siara. Her instructions led him down the long corridor connecting that side of the under castle to the servants' side. Warier now, he snuck through the room where the castle wash was done, carefully sliding past lines of hanging linens to enter the corridor where the storage rooms were. He turned to the first door on his left.

Ari cracked opened the door to find Siara, her blue cloak wrapped about her, sitting on a stack of grain bags. On the floor beside her was a shielded lamp. She put a finger to her lips and gestured him in. He nodded, closing the door carefully behind him. When he turned back, Siara's arms flew about his waist.

"Where have you been?" she said.

Ari stood still, his arms out to his sides. His senses reeled at having her body pressed against his. A jumble of emotions he thought he'd put aside years ago bubbled up in him. He took a steadying breath.

"Siara." He stopped, unsure what else he wanted to say.

"I was so worried when you didn't come right away."

He realized it was mingled fear and sorrow that colored her tone. The urge to protect her welled up in him. He closed his arms around her. She seemed smaller and more breakable than ever.

"I'm sorry I was late," he said, letting go of his earlier annoyance.

"They killed Annell." Her body shuddered.

Ari stared down at the top of her head in shock. "Annell, your lady in waiting?" He recalled dancing with her on his birthday. She was a pleasant, comely girl. "Who? When?"

"Last night." She stepped away from him, her face more composed now. "My note said an hour past the mid of night. Why were you not here? My mind imagined terrible things."

"I didn't find it soon enough. I don't think you needed to take such care. You could have sent it to my door. It isn't as if anyone but Peine or I would read it." He took a deep breath. Why did they always argue instead of talking about what was important? "Who killed your maid? How could I not have been informed?"

"No one knows she's dead." She retraced her steps, sitting. "I don't have any proof."

"What do you mean?" he asked, trying to stay calm out of deference to her distress, even if her answer seemed annoyingly evasive. "If she's dead, the proof is her body."

"I don't know where her body is."

"You mean, it disappeared?"

"No, I never saw it. I don't know where it is." She sounded as annoyed at his confusion as he felt.

"Are you sure she's dead?"

"Yes." She rubbed a hand over her eyes, looking weary. "Last night, I sent Annell to hide in the women's bathing room, to spy on Peine, because we couldn't find anyone who knew who he was sneaking off with."

Ari folded his arms across his chest in silent reprimand.

276

"I wasn't going to say anything to him," she said.

Siara looked up at him with such worry on her face, he crossed the space between them to kneel before her. Ari took her cold hands between his. "What happened?"

"She went down there, and she died. In violence. I could feel it." She shivered. "You know there is much I don't understand about how magic works, but I could feel it. I could feel it as it happened to her. It was awful. I think she was drowned."

Ari put aside the fact there was no body, and that Siara had never been trained in how to use magic. He'd never known her to be wrong about something like this. Any time he hadn't heeded her, it was to his dismay. "Drowning could have been an accident."

"No." She shook her head. Her hands trembled in his. "There was violence to it, and anguish."

Ari sat back on his heels, thinking. He recreated the dressing room in his mind. Both times he'd visited, the great number of articles of clothing strewn about had struck him as odd, but he'd dismissed it as the laziness of the noble class. "They aren't women's clothes. The women's changing room, outside the pool, is full of men's clothing." He started to his feet. "I have to get down there. Peine might go down there. Whatever happened to Annell might happen to him."

"Ari."

He saw it in her eyes and was immobilized by disbelief. "That's why you had someone hide the note. You think Peine . . ." His voice trailed off. He couldn't say it. "Peine doesn't have anything to do with Annell's death."

She didn't say anything. The mingled worry and sympathy on her face stirred anger inside him. Peine was his best friend.

"I should go," he said, wanting to reassure himself that Peine was well. Knowing the futility of arguing with Siara he added, "I should see if there is ought to be found of her. Some clue."

"I'm not saying Peine killed Annell," she said, halting him as he started to turn away. "I'm just worried about him. He's not himself of late. It may be he's entangled in something, or someone holds sway over him. Remember what happened to me? I could have saved Clorra the misery she suffered, but instead I set Parrentine on the path that led him to Ferringul. I stood by and could say nothing while they let that foul Empty One do as he would with her, and send you and Sir Cadwel into grave danger."

"You tried to warn me not to go on Ferringul's mission north," he said by way of apology. He knew she was right. If an Empty One had a hold on Peine, his friend wouldn't be able to fight it, and storming in on him might do more harm than good.

"You said you had something you need to speak with me about?" Siara asked into the silence stretching between them.

Ari blinked. He'd forgotten about the poison in his worry over Siara's news and Peine's danger. "Dean Faola, she told me the queen is being poisoned."

Siara gasped, coming to her feet. "How?"

"She said there's something called the blood of the dragon, and you make it with the lifeblood of an innocent and a ground up unflawed heart stone, whatever that means," he said, concentrating on remembering the dean's words as exactly as he could. "She said it's colorless, but smells like a flower, the winter rose, and it must be administered daily and will suppress the queen's magic and kill her."

"How long does she have left? She seemed so weak last night. She slept through most of dinner."

"I don't know how long she has, but Dean Faola said if that poison is what the trouble is, all we need to do is stop her from getting more and she'll recover."

Siara pressed her lips together, a faint line of concentration appearing between her brows. "I shall insist on nursing her myself. I shall be ever at her side. Nothing will pass her lips without my knowledge."

"They'll try to stop you."

"Let them." She shrugged. "Whoever protests my care the loudest, you shall challenge to a duel."

"Thanks." He was rewarded for his sarcasm with a faint smile. "I really should go look in the bathing room."

"Not tonight. It's too near dawn. It is the women's bathing room, after all. It wouldn't do for you to be found there, and everyone would hear of it, including our enemy." She crossed the room, stopping to wait for him. "In fact, we best leave here before we're discovered."

As if Siara's words were a signal, the door next to them was pulled open. Before Ari could react, Siara's arms reached up and pulled his face to hers, her lips pressing firmly against his. There was an exclamation from the hallway, and they both turned to see a startled serving girl, her eyes wide. Ari didn't need to fake a look of shock.

"You will speak of this to no one," Siara said, her voice at its most imperious. Flipping up her hood, chin high, she marched from the room.

Blushing as he hadn't in years, Ari smiled weakly at the serving girl before slipping past her into the hallway. He hoped she would listen, even if her story wouldn't be about what they were truly doing in the storage room.

He knew what Siara was trying to do. He was sure it would hurt their cause more to be found in secret council than any rumor of an affair would. He was also sure he'd never been kissed by anyone but Ispiria before, and certainly not by Siara.

As he hurried back to his room, he was assailed with guilt, and by worry their enemy would realize they were indeed plotting. Siara couldn't go behind Parrentine's back with another man even if she wanted to. Their enemy would know that. Of course, she was only half Whey, and they might not know she had any magic.

Ari stifled a groan. What should he tell Ispiria? It wasn't as if he was the one who'd done the kissing, but he hadn't done anything to stop Siara, either. She'd only kissed him for the good of their mission. There was no reason to ever tell his fiancée. There was no reason he should feel guilty about it.

Except he did, because if Ispiria was his one true love, how could kissing Siara feel so incredible?

Having gained the upper halls unseen, Ari stormed into his suite, through the sitting room, into the bedroom, and flung himself face down on the bed. He pulled his pillow over his head with a groan. People were dying, the queen was being poisoned, his best friend was in danger and, he was pretty sure, Siara was trying to make him crazy. Was being king's champion always going to be so confusing?

He was still laying that way when Peine snuck in a quarter of an hour later. Ari realized his friend couldn't see him in the dark chamber, so after he listened to Peine settle into his bed, Ari undressed and crept under his sheets so he wouldn't look suspicious in the morning.

He stared up at the ceiling in the darkness, all other worries pushed to the back of his mind as he thought about Peine. Siara was right. Something was wrong with the way

Peine was acting, and Ari didn't think it was a girl. If an Empty One really did have a hold over his friend, confronting Peine would gain nothing. He would be under a compulsion not to reveal anything.

It might even do harm, for the Empty One would have the means of making Peine tell him if Ari did anything to show he suspected. Ari would simply have to follow him, and do a better job of it this time. He would do it that night after his dinner with the merchants' guild, for Peine seemed to be sneaking out almost every evening.

Ari lay in bed, not even trying to find sleep. He was still awake at dawn.

Chapter 26

A strong breeze rose with the dawn and Ari was glad it wasn't as hot as the day before. Sending Peine to ready Stew after they broke their fast, he dressed in his chainmail. Reluctantly, he donned his tabard over his armor, thinking maybe there was something to dyeing armor after all. His tabard was an added layer of heat under an already searing sun.

He was almost ready to leave his chamber when a castle guard arrived, summoning him to the royal wing. The man looked flustered, his pace as he led Ari through the keep brisk. Ari took in the man's harried expression and walked in silence. He would know the purpose of the summons soon enough.

Upon reaching the royal wing, Ari was dismayed to see only two guards at the top of the steps and one waiting at the end of the hall by the only set of double doors, which stood open. Four guards, including the one who accompanied him, seemed hardly enough protection for Siara, Princess Tiana,

Lord Reido and the queen. He wondered if they would listen if he suggested more.

When they reached the double doors, the guard moved to one side, gesturing Ari to proceed alone. The queen's formal sitting room was stunning in its lavish elegance, gilt on nearly every wooden surface. Seeing no one within and the next set of open doors, Ari allowed the voices he could hear to lead him into the next room. It appeared to be a private, yet no less ornate, version of the first.

Dean Faola was inside, with Siara and Lord Reido. A woman Ari had never been introduced to but knew was the queen's physician, Ciada, hovered outside the sealed set of doors across the room, looking flustered. Every time a voice rose, she winced.

"I tell you," Dean Faola was saying to Lord Reido, a small crystal vial in her hand. "This is the blood of the dragon, a deadly poison."

"It can't be. That's Mother's medicine. Ciada administers it daily. It is all that's keeping Mother alive."

"Then Physician Ciada is poisoning her." Dean Faola trained her angry gaze on the woman.

All color drained from Ciada's face.

"Ciada," Lord Reido barked.

The woman flinched.

"Come forward. You're the most skilled physician in the realm. Defend yourself from this idiocy."

"Idiocy?" The dean's tone was icy. "Queen's son or no, you forget your place."

Lord Reido glared at her.

"Enough," Siara said, her imperious voice drawing their attention.

284

Ari hurried to her side as they turned on her. He had to fight down a blush, wishing he could think of something, anything, other than the way she'd kissed him only a few hours before.

Lord Reido cast him a scathing glance before turning his scowl on Siara. "Why is he here? It's forbidden."

"He is here to protect my person, as is his duty."

"Surely, we may have a disagreement without you calling a Lggothian thug to your side in violation of the sanctity of the Lavarina's chambers?"

"Consider it my ignorance if you like, the fault of my upbringing, but Sir Aridian stays where I tell him to stay until I tell him to depart."

"Yes, the whole castle is aware that Sir Aridian is here to do your service."

Dean Faola drew in a hissing breath.

Siara's chin tilted to a dangerous angle. "Are we shedding the trappings of civility, then? For I believe you insulted my champion moments ago. Shall I give him leave to exact retribution on your person?"

The anger on Lord Reido's face flickered, dimming. He glanced at Ari, clearing his throat. "I beg your pardon, Sir Aridian, for my hasty words. I consider you the noblest of men. My rage at this flaunting of tradition took too firm of a hold on me."

Ari inclined his head, hoping that was enough of an answer. He didn't trust himself to say anything nearly as regal and coherent sounding as they were. This wasn't the time to come across as an ignorant innkeeper's nephew.

Siara frowned up at her uncle for a moment more before turning to the queen's attendant. "Come here, Physician Ciada."

As the woman's jerky steps propelled her forward, Ari couldn't help but think it odd such a timorous creature could be the most skilled physician in Wheylia. She didn't behave like a Wheylian woman, certainly not a well-educated one at the top of her field.

"Where did you get this?" Siara asked, plucking the vial from Dean Faola's hand.

"I--" Ciada made a choking sound.

"Come, tell us," the dean said, reaching out to put a hand on Ciada's shoulder. "Did you make it?"

"No, Dean." She shook her head vigorously.

"Did someone give it to you?" Ari asked, eyeing her intently.

Her trembling and inability to talk pointed to the work of an Empty One. Were she under too strong a compulsion, it might be impossible for her to tell them what they wanted to know. The key was to ask questions she could answer.

Ciada nodded, looking as if it took effort to do even that.

"Who gave it to you?" Lord Reido asked.

Ciada shook her head, her eyes going wide.

"I asked you who," Reido roared. Brushing aside the dean's hand, he took Ciada by the shoulders. "Tell us who."

She turned her head away, writhing in his grasp as he shook her.

"Stop it," Siara ordered. "She can't tell you. Guards," she called, raising her voice. The two from the corridor hurried in, stopping in the formal sitting room. "Take her and lock her up, but see to all her needs. She's not a criminal."

They entered the room, looking hesitant. Reido glared at them, but the dean gestured them forward.

"Yes, your highness," one of the guards mumbled. Taking Ciada by the arms, they led the unresisting physician away.

Siara turned to face her uncle squarely. Ari stood behind her, trying to look menacing. He wasn't sure how much force his presence lent her words, but he meant to do his best. "I am taking over the care of my grandmother. Only myself and those of my choosing shall have access to her. Nothing shall pass her lips without my direct approval. Do I make myself understood?"

"Perfectly," Lord Reido said. "Hopefully I do as well when I say that if my mother dies in your care, I am not responsible for the wrath of our people. Think well on what you do, princess, for your actions could lead to war." Giving them a curt nod, he strode from the room, anger all but visible as a smoldering cloud about him.

Siara let out a deep breath, glancing at the dean. "Thank you for your support, Dean Faola." She handed back the crystal vial.

The dean took it in careful fingers. "Thank you for your fortitude, your highness." She bowed before turning to Ari. "I wish you luck on the field today, Sir Aridian. I fear your prowess may be all that stands between Wheylia and doom." With another bow, she left the room.

"Go send one of my maids, Ari," Siara said, her eyes on her grandmother's bedroom doors. "Then you best get to the tourney field. You're already late. I'd cancel the silly thing, but it might be construed as weakness and the populace, at least, must not know there is turmoil in the keep. I'll be with you as soon as I'm able."

"Yes, your highness," he said, wishing he could stay by her side. He knew she was right, though. Even those born to authority must constantly earn it. He and Siara could not be seen to falter. Besides, Peine would be in hysterics by now, if he hadn't found someone to tell him where Ari was. He bowed to

Siara, even though she wasn't looking at him, and hurried from the room.

The first demonstration of the day, with the vouge, began when Ari arrived. He hadn't been able to find Peine anywhere, or spare much time to look, so he was doubly perturbed not to find his friend already there. Trying to keep the turmoil of the morning from showing on his face, he nodded to the master of arms and watched attentively as a unit of Wheylian soldiers executed maneuvers with the long handled weapons. Even though the opponents they met were merely stuffed dummies, as straw flew, Ari pictured scores of vouge-wielding Wheys marching across a battlefield, shredding an oncoming troop.

Lord Reido, Peine at his side, reached the tourney field at the end of the vouge demonstration, smiling and waving to the crowd. Ari rose, shooting Peine a questioning look, and bowed to Reido. With so many eyes on them, none of them spoke, but Peine gave Ari a forced smile. A glance at Reido showed Ari that the queen's son was as determined as he to put on a good face.

Siara arrived halfway through the morning, sitting down beside her uncle as if nothing was amiss. Several more demonstrations commenced before their leisurely lunch, after which the mini tournaments began. Ari prepared to watch these with great attention, as he knew he would be expected to battle each victor.

For the first, eight Wheys took the field, quarter staves in hand, and proceeded to beat on each other with fierce speed. Ari amused himself by picking the winner of each bout, and he was correct all four times. Those four squared off, and then two, and soon only one man remained. He twirled his staff above him in the air and the crowd cheered. He wasn't the largest of the group, nor did he look to Ari to be the strongest, but he was fast. He came forward to stand before the royal box.

"I issue a challenge to the champion of Lggothland," he called, his tone light. He was a young man, not much older than Ari. He rested one end of the staff in the earth, his expression eager.

Ari stood. "I accept your challenge," he called down. "If you'll but loan me a weapon to answer it with."

He descended, Peine at his side, and one of the defeated men ran up to offer him a staff. Ari tested it, swinging it a few times to get a good feel for the weight. He wished it a little heavier, but it seemed stout enough. He walked with the winner to the center of the field. The tourney master followed them, leaving Peine waiting on the sidelines in case Ari needed anything.

The tourney master formally introduced Ari to his opponent, then raised his voice in a second redundancy to call out the rules. "Three blows to the trunk wins. No striking the head or below the knees. Stepping from the circle counts as a hit."

Ari and his opponent inclined their heads to the tourney master, and to each other. A bell was struck. They began circling, Ari with a slight smile on his face, his opponent wearing a look of concentration.

As they closed, striking at each other with increasing speed, Ari felt strain and tension leave him. He hadn't had any time to practice since their arrival. He sorely missed it. There was a peacefulness to wielding a weapon, a calm that came from the rhythm of it, that centered him. He needed it, like other people needed sleep or strong drink. As they sparred, he felt his worries slip away. A welcome serenity blanketing all but his weightiest cares.

His opponent increased the pace, trying to get a hit in, and Ari wielded his own weapon faster in response. He made no move to attack, for he was enjoying himself too much to want to end the bout. His opponent's eyes grew wider as Ari countered blow after blow. Ari could see surprise clear on the other man's face.

Surprise quickly faded to rueful resignation as the man realized how outmatched he was. He began to tire and, a bit sad it was over, Ari struck at him in three blindly fast blows, ending the match. The crowd was a mixture of boos and cheers, but Ari shrugged off the former. He bowed to his challenger, who returned the courtesy. The tourney master came forward and proclaimed Ari the winner. Ari returned to the royal box.

Thus they proceeded through the demonstration of maces, which Ari thought were less fun than flails, in spite of the obvious advantage of control. In common, the two weapons had the cruel result that a man scored, when the blow was not fatal, would be left crippled. Thus, he and his opponents were careful to aim only for the trunk in this friendly competition, and those were the only hits that counted. Ari didn't draw the match out, maces not being one of his favorite weapons.

The final mini tournament of the day was with the estoc. The estoc was a sword similar to a foil, but longer and with less give. Ari had watched the matches leading up to his carefully, trying to determine where his opponent might show weakness. The man Ari knew would win, named Cooro, was more than a head shorter than Ari and twice his age, but his arms were thick with muscles and he was incredibly fast.

After the formal challenge and the tourney master's introduction, they faced each other across the marked off circle, neither moving to strike. A quiet settled over the crowd. Cooro grinned and Ari felt a smile spread over his own face. As one, they charged forward, swords whipping at each other's guts, meeting with a screeching clank. Ari jumped back. Giving him no respite, Cooro attacked is a flurry of strokes and Ari had to concentrate on blocking.

Then there was an opening, Cooro's sword drawn back an inch too far, seeming to invite Ari to a thrust right at his chest. Ari felt his hand dart out, wanting to complete the move, but he yanked it back, sensing a trap. Even as he did, his opponent's blade stabbed forward in a blow that would have landed, unprotested across Ari's chest, had Ari committed to his lunge. Ari brought his blade up in a quick salute, knowing it was only Sir Cadwel's training that had saved him from the trap.

Far from angry that his trick hadn't worked, Cooro laughed, saluting back before commencing another volley of blindingly fast attacks. Parrying them took all of Ari's concentration and he felt the last of his tension leave him. Here, in this chalk circle in the trampled grass, there was nothing for Ari to do, nothing for him to think about, but defending himself from the man in front of him and scoring his three hits. For the first time in months, Ari knew peace.

By the end of the duel they were both drenched in sweat. Ari thought it would be much better to practice with this weapon in only a shirt and trousers, if you trusted your partner enough. To the crowds' great joy, Ari let in a hit over the course of the duel, but it wasn't the first hit, so Ari was pleased. As Sir Cadwel had often told him, in a real fight you didn't count to three. It was who got the first strike that mattered. Ari always tried to get the first strike.

In spite of the heat and his overall discomfort at having exerted himself so fully while encased in a suit of mail, Ari was sad to return to reality from the realm of the duel.

"That was an excellent bout, sir," Ari said, bowing to his opponent.

"Never before have I met my equal," Cooro said, amusement and challenge in his eyes.

"Equal?" Ari repeated, rising to the bait. "It seems to me I bested you."

"Only because I'm out of practice, having no opponent worthy of my great skill to bring me any challenge."

"It is a pity, then, for I would prefer to test you at the height of your skill. Perhaps if we practiced together, you might improve enough for a rematch."

Ari said it in jest, but with the sincere hope Cooro would agree. He hadn't faced anyone as good as Cooro aside from Sir Cadwel, and while the knight was proficient in many weapons, he was most skilled with the greatsword. It was with that weapon he and Ari had their best duels. Sparring with Cooro, using estocs, offered a new challenge.

"It would be my pleasure to school you in the ways of the estoc, sir," Cooro said.

"I fear tomorrow my time is spoken for, but perhaps the day following, shortly after dawn, in the yard in front of the castle?"

"I will be there." Cooro bowed slightly, coming up with another grin. "And looking forward to besting you."

Ari bowed again. The tourney master, who had been waiting politely outside the circle, came forward to proclaim Ari the victor.

The Wheys then gave him a demonstration in throwing knives, an art Ari had never practiced and at which he failed miserably. He minded not, for the crowd was pleased, seeming to find his lack of skill a source of great amusement. Ari felt it only fair they find something he wasn't good at, and insisted on a rematch so he could fail again. Looking up into the stands, he saw Siara's frown, and realized he would receive a dressing down for destroying his image of imperviousness.

Last came an impressive demonstration of crossbow marksmanship, which sent a shiver down Ari's spine. The winner again came before him, issuing a challenge, but this time, Ari declined.

"I'm afraid I embarrassed myself enough with the throwing knives," he said rising to address the assemblage. "I shall concede your victory, that we all may quit the field and find sustenance, for the day grows long." Some of the crowd grumbled over this, but Ari ignored them. The crossbow was a weapon with but one purpose, to kill those in armor from afar, in stealth, and it was repugnant to him. "Thank you, warriors all," he called out over the mild protests of the crowd. "It has been a great honor for me to learn from your expertise, and to face such an onslaught of talent."

The crowd clapped for this, but their renewed exuberance fragmented, trickling off as a commotion rose on the southern end of the field. People stumbled aside, a knight mounted on a coal black destrier riding through them. His armor was dyed a deep red, and he made no effort not to trample those who weren't quick enough to move out of his way. The destrier halted before the raised platform Ari, Peine, Siara and Lord Reido watched from.

"Sir Aridian," the red knight boomed from inside his helm, leaving his visor closed in insult. "It shames Wheylia that you trample our fair soil."

He pulled off a gauntlet and tossed it to the ground in challenge. Now the knight was closer, Ari could discern his armor was oddly mismatched, the red streaked in some places as if hastily applied. He frowned, unsure what that could mean. Keite's armor had been pristine.

Around them, the crowd shifted and murmured. Ari could see surprise clear on every face, from which he concluded this was no local man, though surely he was a Whey. Even from within his helm, Ari could hear the lilt in his voice. Although the mismatched armor was massive, Ari could discern underneath the physique of a Whey. No normal Whey would be able to bear up under such heavy armor. Not without the aid of magic.

"Peine." Ari's voice was steady as the mountains behind them. "This . . . knight?" Ari paused, locking his gaze on the two glints of iris within the visor slit until the red knight nodded. "This knight seems to have dropped his gauntlet. Would you mind retrieving it for him?"

"Are you sure?" Peine whispered, for to hand it back was to accept the challenge.

Ari felt a twinge of surprise, but didn't turn to look at his valet. Did Peine doubt his ability to win? "Very."

Peine hurried down the few steps, bending to retrieve the gauntlet. The black horse stretched out his neck to bite and the knight struck it a curt blow to the side of the head. Peine eyed it warily as he proffered the piece of armor.

"I will meet you on this field when next the sun is at its peak, Thrice Born," the knight said, taking his gauntlet from Peine. "That is, if bravery does not desert you."

Ari did his best to look bored, answering with a slight nod, but worry ran through him. There were few with the knowledge to call him by that name. Peine jumped back as the red knight wheeled his horse, wrenching the animal's head around. Blood mingled with the foam at its mouth and it

294

reared, its hooves churning the air. Ari added the knight's treatment of the beast to his offenses.

"I shall trample into the earth any who think they can brazenly flaunt their prowess among us," the red knight roared. "The Lggothians are foul usurpers of our lands. It is time we beat them from our shores."

Some among the crowd cheered. Ari had to give the red knight credit for his tactics. Somehow, instead of a visitor putting on a show for the entertainment and joy of the populace, Ari now sounded like an intruder. He kept careful unconcern on his face as the red knight turned his horse and galloped away. The crowd dissolved into murmuring groups. Scrubbing his hand through his sweat drenched hair, Ari mused that at least here was an enemy he could fight.

Chapter 27

The banquet Ari was to attend that evening with the merchant lords of the city was held in one of their vast mansions. The mansions were miniature castles of their own, though on a more symbolic scale. They had outer walls and a gate, but the walls were low enough to look over, presumably so as not to hide the ostentation of their homes, and the gates were filigreed. Ari could see they'd been left open so long, it would take several men to wrench them closed. The sweeping lawns were lined with fruit trees. Decorative parapets bordered the edges of copper-shingled roofs. The slender turrets didn't look wide enough to draw a sword in.

As they rode Stew and Charger through the third tier, following their escort, Ari heard Peine sigh. Looking over, he could see envy clear on his friend's face. Ari studied the houses again, trying to see what made them so desirable. They were pretty, yes, but huge. There was no reason for all of that space, unless a great many people lived in each. For some reason, Ari doubted that was the case.

The sun was perched on the cusp of the mountains to the west when their guide, the son of their host, turned through one of the superfluous gates. Ari saw nothing to differentiate this home from the others, save the sweeping drive of cobblestones was lined with lantern-toped poles, creating a corridor of light for them to pass through. Ari realized their host had arranged for them to arrive last, for he could see the tracks of many carriages on the stones, and two trundled, empty, down the other side of the horseshoe shaped drive.

Ari dismounted and handed Stew over to a groom, glad he had his knight's tabard to wear, for he need not worry about styles. Peine had spent hours complaining that nothing he had was suitable for the home of one of the great merchant families. Ari found it interesting that his friend was more worried about his attire tonight than when he'd dined with the queen.

They walked up the broad granite steps, Ari feeling as awkward as always not to have his sword. He didn't know what to do with his left hand if he had no hilt on which to rest it.

The foyer they entered was filled with candles. Ari could see into the vast hall beyond, where there appeared to be a room combining both dining and dance. The atmosphere sparkled with a frivolity not encountered at the university, nor during his dinner with the queen's officers, and certainly not found in the castle itself. Their guide led them across the marble-inlaid foyer, which was open all the way up to the tall roof and crowned with a window of colored glass.

In the room beyond, revelers danced in bright ensembles while others sat at small tables, drinking, eating and laughing. The light-filled room before them seemed so close to chaos that Ari had to suppress a desire not to enter. Their guide waved and a couple Ari assumed were their hosts detached themselves from a group and hurried over.

"My mother, Lady Saila, and my father, Lord Camfor," their guide said. "Mother, Father, may I present Sir Aridian, Duke of Sorga, Protector of the Northlands, and champion to the king of Lggothland. And this is Lord Peine, youngest son of Lady Voala and Lord Haoro, duchess and duke of Glenburry."

"Yes, mine isn't your usual Wheylian name," Lord Camfor said as they all exchanged bows, although Ari hadn't thought any such thing. "It's merely a tradition, you know. It isn't law. Comes from the resurgence of the magic, you know. Time was, only the top witches could use that traditional nomenclature, but they had a falling out, you see, and it was abandoned. When the magic came back, the names came back with it, but now everyone wants one. Sort of a fad. My mother felt very strongly that those names hold us back. Certainly, a Whey is often distinguished by his looks, but she felt there was no need for a merchant to further alienate those he trades with by adding crooning Wheylian vowels, her words, to the mix. But enough about names. I'm sure I bore you. Blasted strange, that red knight challenging you, I say. Don't let it reflect poorly on the lot of us. I say--"

"You'll have to pardon my husband, sir," Lady Saila said, cutting him off. "His mother raised him to be brash, that she might send him out into countries where women aren't properly respected, so that he could conduct her business. I'm afraid it's made him a bit forward."

"There's nothing to excuse, madam," Ari said, confused they should think there was. He would never become accustomed to the Wheylian culture, with its emphasis on women and obsession with social standing.

Ari was dragged about the room by his hosts and introduced to more people than he could easily count, all of them chattering about the red knight. Peine somehow managed to disappear, leaving Ari to his fate. The people filling the ornate room flittered from table to dance, drinking clear glasses of bubbly wine all the while. Each couple seemed to be vying to be the brightest clad. Laughter filled the room, and they reminded Ari of nothing so much as a collection of songbirds, bright, loud and fluttering.

It was over an hour later when his hosts finally relinquished him into the dubious care of a group of young women, who clustered around him all talking at once. Ari assumed that meant he'd been introduced to everyone present but, looking around, he already couldn't recall who any of them were, or, indeed, if he'd spoken to them. He put a polite smile on his face and tried to keep his mind on their words as the woman filled the space in front of him with talk.

"I heard your sword is as big as I am," one in yellow said. The way she looked up at him through thick eyelashes made Ari decidedly nervous. "Is it true?"

"Um." He looked her up and down, assessing her to be a little under five feet. "Well, yes, I'd say just about."

"I heard it's broken," another said.

Ari blinked in surprise.

"They say there are three stones missing from the hilt."

"Oh, yes," he said. "But that doesn't affect the sword. I mean, they're for decoration."

"But wouldn't it be nicer if they were filled?"

The others murmured in agreement.

"Why haven't you filled them?"

"Well, I just got it." Ari wasn't sure why they all needed to stand so close. He was much taller than they were. He felt very awkward looming over them, although he couldn't exactly complain about the view.

"I bet I could find some pretty jewels for you to place on the hilt," one in green suggested. "If you would come back with me to my manor this evening, I'm sure I have something lying about."

"You're the only thing he'll find lying about there," one in purple said.

They all giggled at that. Ari suddenly felt the need for a drink, and waved one of the serving men over.

"Oh, thank you," yellow-dress said.

"A splendid idea."

"I was nearly dry myself," said one in blue, holding up an almost empty glass, which she proceeded to completely empty before exchanging it for another.

With several other murmured thank you's, which Ari thought would be better directed at the man who'd brought the drinks than at him, the women appropriated everything off the tray, leaving a glass for Ari. He took the delicate crystal goblet, feeling as if his fingers were too large, and sipped its bubbling content carefully.

It didn't even taste of alcohol. It was sweet and cool, and the bubbles gave it a definite appeal. Ari remembered his aunt's three-berry brandy, though, and vowed to be careful.

"It would have to be sapphires," the woman in green said, bringing Ari's attention back to the conversation at hand. "To match your tabard." She reached out one hand and ran it across Ari's embossed hawk. Ari saw several of the other women exchange amused glances behind her back.

"Sapphires I have," said the one in blue. "It's a good thing you don't need rubies."

"Why?" Ari asked, taking another sip of his drink.

"They're terribly rare of late," she said with a shrug. "Someone is buying them all up."

"I think the queen," purple said. "They say they're all going into the castle. I wager they're making something special for the new princess."

Ari felt a chill go through him at her words. Someone in the castle was buying rubies. Could rubies be what Dean Faola meant when she said the poison used heart stones?

"Who in the castle is buying them, did you say?" he asked.

"Who knows," purple said with a shrug. "But it's someone with plenty of money, I can tell you that."

"Do you want me to find out for you?" green-dress asked. She leaned toward him, swaying slightly on her feet. One of the other women reached to steady her, but she didn't seem to notice. She peered at her empty glass and waved another serving man over. As his glass was empty, Ari took another as well.

"Do you dance, Sir Aridian?" one dressed in orange asked.

"Not very well," he said. Although, after another sip of the wine, he was starting to think he might want to try. The music was very lively, and he felt the pulse of it in his veins. In fact, now that she'd suggested it, dancing seemed an excellent plan.

The next several hours were more of a blur to Ari than the first two. He knew he danced with many of the young women at the party. He was sure he danced well. They all seemed very happy to dance with him, at least. They were such small things, these Wheylian girls. He swung them about the dance floor, their pretty faces blending before his eyes, distinguishable only by the color of their dresses.

He danced with purple several times, and with blue and yellow, and a confusing range of pinks from salmon to dusky rose. Never with green, because she soon fell asleep on a

302

delicate sofa to one side of the room and servants came to spirit her away. The other girls found this quite funny, but Ari was sad to see her go. She had the lowest cut dress of them all.

Sometime later, he found himself on the wide veranda outside the hall, overlooking a beautiful decorative pond set into the landscape behind the house. He was with the girl in the blue dress, empty wine glasses set on a table nearby. He'd lifted her to sit on the railing, since she was so short, and was proceeding to demonstrate for her everything he knew about kissing, which she seemed to be enjoying.

"Ari." Peine's exclamation caused them both to start.

Ari had to grab onto blue-dress to keep her from falling, which made them both laugh. He looked down at her, his vision slightly blurred, and tried to ignore the nagging idea in the back of his head that he was doing something wrong. Kissing her felt anything but. He loved her blue dress with her black hair. It was such a pretty combination.

"Ari," Peine said again, coming to stand beside him. "What are you doing?"

"Nothing you haven't done." Why did Peine look so angry? He'd kissed so many girls. Ari had only ever kissed two. One and a half, because he hadn't kissed Siara back. Of course, the one was Ispiria.

"What about Ispiria?" Peine asked at the same time as her name filled Ari's mind.

Ari felt his vaguely numb features twist in shock. What about Ispiria? What was he doing here with this girl in the blue dress? He didn't even remember her name. They'd been dancing, and she'd said they should go out where it was cool, and then she said she should like to kiss him, and he said no, but she kissed him anyhow, and the next thing he knew, he had her up on the railing and kissing her was all he could think about.

Ari stepped back, swaying slightly. "I'm sorry," he said to the girl. "I shouldn't be kissing you."

"I don't mind," she said, her eyes full of mischief.

"Well, he does," Peine said, scowling at her. "He's engaged."

"But to a Lggothian girl." Her tone made it clear Lggothian girls didn't count.

"Engaged is engaged," Peine said.

Ari knew his friend was right. He sank into one of the twisted iron chairs with a groan, resting his elbows on the table and putting his hands over his face. His head spun. What was he doing?

"Well." Ari could hear the girl hop down. "Since you've ruined everything anyhow, I guess I'll go back to the dancing." Her footsteps retreated across the veranda.

"Ari." Peine was beside him. "Ari, are you okay?"

"Everything is spinning," he said, not raising his head from his hands.

"How much did you drink?" Peine asked, sounding surprised.

"I don't know."

"That's never a good sign. Look, let's get you to the castle. Can you ride?"

"Of course," Ari said, offended.

To his relief, Peine didn't take him back inside but instead led him, one hand clasping Ari's upper arm, along the veranda and down some steps. They walked through the well-groomed lawn running alongside the house and into the stable. Peine saddled their mounts for them.

Peine led Stew over. Ari leaned his face against his saddle for several moments before hauling himself up. Stew seemed very tall. As he swayed atop the saddle, Ari was reminded of the first time he ever rode. He leaned forward and patted Stew on the neck affectionately. Stew shook his mane and followed Peine and Charger.

The ride back gave him time to gain control of his swaying, and to contemplate what he'd done. What had he been thinking, kissing a girl who wasn't Ispiria? He hadn't been thinking at all, he knew. The girl in the blue dress had kissed him, and then he hadn't been thinking of anything, really. Only of how nice it would be if she would let him slide her dress down off her shoulders a little farther . . . he brought his thoughts up short, ashamed. What was wrong with him? He loved Ispiria. He was sure of it.

It must be that bubbly wine, he thought, remembering how much Sir Cadwel detested the stuff. He would never ignore Sir Cadwel's inclinations again. If Sir Cadwel hated bubbly wine, then no bubbly wine. Ari never wanted to see another drop of it.

They gained their room observed only by a few guards, and Ari didn't think they saw anything amiss. He hoped they didn't, at least. Peine helped him ready for bed, his face a mixture of worry and displeasure. Ari settled his head on his pillow in relief. Never had his head felt so heavy before, or a bed so soft. With a sigh, he closed his eyes.

"You aren't going to do that again, are you?" Peine asked in a worried tone from where he stood inside the doorway to the room.

"Never."

"You really aren't a very good dancer," Peine said, a note of amusement creeping into his voice. "You probably should try harder to avoid doing it."

Ari groaned. Peine shut the door to the room with a laugh.

Chapter 28

It was sometime later that thirst woke Ari, his pulse beating dull pain in his temples. His mind was clear, but his body, when he sat up, was shaky. It seemed even his Aluien-enhanced constitution couldn't quickly undo the type of idiocy he'd engaged in that night.

He walked to his basin, pouring out cool water. He was filled with guilt over kissing the girl in blue, but for some reason it still didn't bother him as much as his one kiss with Siara. The thought of looking Ispiria in the eye and telling her about how Siara had kissed him, even though the reason for it was harmless and he was sure it meant nothing to the princess, filled him with dread. With Siara, he'd felt something, and that something worried him. It shook his knowledge that he loved Ispiria and Ispiria alone.

What he'd done with the girl in blue was different. It was only a little kissing. He would confess to Ispiria as soon as he got home, and he would never, ever do it again. She would be angry, but he would do anything she asked to make it up to her, and it would be alright, he was sure.

That decided, he dressed. Now that his head was clearer, he remembered hearing Peine leave the suite, not go into his own room. Unable to follow Peine as he'd planned, he would have to settle for searching the women's bathing rooms again. It would probably yield nothing more than the last time, but he could think of nowhere else to look.

Ari crept through the castle, glad he was feeling almost well. He was disgusted with himself for imbibing so much. He had tilting to demonstrate tomorrow and a strange knight, most likely an Empty One, coming to fight him. Siara's poor little maid was dead, Peine was probably beguiled, and it was obvious they were in danger. What kind of a fool was he?

He broke off his mental chastising as he neared the door to the women's changing area. He crept through, noting the piles of men's clothes, and slipped into the bathing room. It was empty. Stripping, he swam out into the water, keeping an eye on his clothes, nervous to leave the stone the hawks had given him sitting in his doublet beside the pool. Despite that concern, the warm steam soothed his lingering headache. As he swam, the water washed away the smells of alcohol and women's perfume, leaving him feeling cleansed.

But there was no one there. Ari searched the columns and walls, but could find no passage. Frustrated, and worried about the time, he returned to the shore and dressed, hurrying wet and disgruntled back to his suite. Almost an hour later, Peine snuck in, going to his room. Ari lay awake in the darkness, staring at the ceiling and worrying about his friend.

He woke the next morning to the sound of Peine entering the room, a worried look on his face. "How are you feeling?"

"Well enough," Ari said, sitting up. "Is there any water?" He was still quite thirsty, and tired, but he thought the latter more the effect of his nerves than alcohol.

"I have water, strong tea, and porridge. You're sure you're feeling alright?"

Ari nodded, twisting to place his feet on the stone floor, drinking in the coolness through his toes. He was going to be very hot all day and he wasn't looking forward to it. He thought the red knight's choice of hour cunning for, as far as Ari knew, Empty Ones didn't suffer from heat or cold. Ari was going to be tilting all morning, baking in his armor under the blazing summer sun.

Dressing in a tunic and hose, Ari eyed with resignation the heavy padding he wore under his armor, though he wouldn't put it on until after he broke his fast. He seated himself opposite Peine, trying not to smell the acrid odor of burnt flesh coming from his friend's plate. Their mornings were very silent of late, he realized. "Are you enjoying visiting your ancestral home?"

"What?" Peine looked up, blinking at Ari. "Sorry, I was thinking."

"Oh?"

"About the joust today. You'd better finish eating. We have to get down there. It wouldn't do at all for you to be late."

"You go see to Stew," Ari said, an awful memory of how his equipment had been sabotaged during his first joust coming to him. "I'll put on my armor."

"It goes faster with help."

"I'll be fine."

Peine looked as though he wanted to protest more, but he stood. "If you aren't down there by the time I'm done, I'll come back to help."

Ari nodded, waiting until he heard Peine's footsteps fade down the hall before jumping up. He pulled on his padding, then took up each piece of armor, inspecting it carefully before strapping it on. He felt bad doing it, but if Peine was beguiled, there was no way of knowing to what lengths he could be driven. Ari worked as fast as he could, hoping to go over it all before Peine came back. He was sliding his gauntlets on when his friend returned.

"That was fast," Peine said. He walked across the room and picked up Ari's shield. "Come on."

Ari took his sword and followed Peine through the castle. Stew, looking as pleased with himself as ever, stood waiting at the bottom of the broad steps, resplendent in his blue and silver caparison, matching ribbons woven through his mane and tail. The brown always seemed larger on jousting days. He never tired of the sport, even tacked out as he was in his heavy barding. A groom held Charger nearby.

Ari handed Peine his sword, waving him away when his friend would have assisted him. This was no time for hiding his strength. Even encased in metal as he was, he pulled himself into the saddle with ease.

As he did, he felt the straps on Stew's tack stretch near to breaking. He worked to keep his expression unchanged. It was impossible for all of Stew's equipment to wear out at once, and Ari had inspected it as recently as the day before they arrived at the city. Someone must have tampered with it, and there could be little question as to the intent of such tampering.

Peine handed him up his shield and his sword, which he sheathed. He didn't look his friend in the eye, his mind reeling. Had Peine sabotaged Stew's tack? Even if he hadn't, shouldn't he have noticed it was worn to the point of breaking?

310

Ari and Peine rode through the streets as they would in Poromont, with people coming out to cheer and wave, and Ari struggled to refocus. He could joust like this. His legs carried the strength to hold him astride Stew, and keep Stew's heavy barding in place, so long as the straps didn't actually break. Ari plastered a smile on his face and waved at the people, who formed into a sort of parade behind them. He forced his mind to the task awaiting him. Shouting crowds and skewering straw stuffed quintains were things Ari was familiar with.

In spite of the mob funneling onto the plain behind them, the crowd already waiting was immense. The nobles of Wheylia, as well as Lord Reido and Siara, were already seated in their banner-bedecked boxes. It looked to Ari as if every man, woman and child in both the city and the castle attended, and he knew it wasn't only to watch him skewer colored rings. News of the red knight's challenge filled the city.

Once they reached the practice field, Ari nodded to Peine, who would inspect the lances the Wheys had cut, and rode Stew out before the royal box. From the saddle, he bowed to Lord Reido and Siara. He glanced at the wooden throne constructed for the queen, unsurprised it still stood empty. The dean hadn't said how quickly Queen Reudi would recover, but Ari didn't expect it to be overnight.

Siara waved to get his attention, gesturing him closer, and he rode to the railing of the box. Standing, she leaned over, pulling a blue kerchief from somewhere between her breasts, completely shattering Ari's concentration. She handed it to him.

"My token, Sir Aridian," she said in the loud formal voice she used for public events. "May you carry it to victory against any foe who may challenge you today."

"Thank you, your highness," Ari answered in his own stage voice, making a show of tucking the delicate square of cloth beneath his breastplate, over his heart. "I'm sure, with your patronage, none can hope to withstand me." Bowing to her again, Ari brought Stew around until he squarely faced the raised platform once more.

"Sir Aridian," Lord Reido said, also rising. "We are honored to have a knight of your caliber demonstrate the Lggothian art of tilting, and should that villain who so brazenly challenged you be brave enough to show himself, we are sure you will be victorious and expose him for the fraudulent coward he is."

"Thank you, my lord," Ari said, a little taken aback by the harshness of Lord Reido's tone.

"As all is in readiness. Let the demonstration begin," Lord Reido declared.

The crowd cheered. Ari wheeled Stew, slacking up on the reins to let his horse know it was up to him how fast they ran. They circled the edge of the field, giving the onlookers on all sides a good view of Ari in his brightly polished plate covered by his blue and silver tabard, and Stew in his matching caparison. The ribbons in Stew's mane fluttered in the wind and Ari waved to the crowd.

Returning to his starting point, Ari snapped his visor shut and took the lance Peine proffered him. Ari was glad he'd have practice riding with Stew's compromised tack before the red knight appeared. He could see the cunning of the plan, for had he not mounted unaided, the girth would be subtly weakening as he rode, primed to snap at the first real impact of the day, his meeting with the red knight. After a look to the royal box, wishing he could tell Siara what was going on, Ari sighted up the row of stuffed quintains on the other end of the field. He nudged Stew into a gallop.

Ari spent the next several hours skewering increasingly smaller targets for the delight of the crowd. Dummies fell before him, and colored rings, and apples placed atop tall posts. Even one red rose, which he pinned on the tip of his lance and offered up to a lady in the crowd. He enjoyed himself, pleased at the chance to practice his skills in so frivolous a manner, where no one risked broken bones or death for coming before him.

So thoroughly did he win over the crowd that almost no one clapped when the red knight galloped onto the field at the appointed hour. Ari lifted his visor, nodding in greeting to the man, but the red knight ignored him. He walked his horse to the end of the lists closest to the royal box and sat waiting, lance leveled at Ari.

"I would have your name, sir," Ari called across the field.

"It matters not," came the hollow reply from inside the helmet. "For after today, I shall be known by all as your vanquisher."

The crowd booed, but Ari shrugged, having expected as much. "If that is your wish, let none say I tarried overlong in giving you the chance to fulfill it." Ari clicked his visor shut and checked that his shield was secure on his arm. He took the lance a wide-eyed Wheylian page held out to him, for Peine was at the other end of the field.

Even as Ari situated his lance, the red knight charged. Ari held Stew back for a moment, looking at his opponent in something close to sympathy. It was obvious from his overly upright posture and the awkward angle at which he held his shield the man had little experience. Ari wondered what the point was. That an Empty One lurked behind this, he had no doubt, but the strategy of the other seemed childlike. Was he simply going to create more and more knights to throw at Ari

313

in the hopes one might eventually strike him down? Was he counting so fully on Stew's compromised girths to send Ari clattering to his death?

He nudged Stew. The destrier leapt forward, Ari squeezing his legs tight to stay astride his enthusiastic mount. Stew loved to joust. He put his head down and charged flat out at their opponent. Ari felt his blood surge at their impending meeting. Mindful that the man's seeming ineptitude might be a ruse, Ari let all other thoughts leave him, concentrating on unhorsing his enemy.

They came together with a resounding crash. The crowd gasped as one, then erupted into cheers. Ari wasn't sure if they cheered him or the red knight, for neither had fallen. Though his opponent swayed in the saddle, his strength in withstanding Ari's hit was irrefutable evidence he wasn't mortal, the pass being Ari's final test. He brought Stew around for another run, taking in Siara's face, marked with triumph, worry and certain grim pleasure. Of Peine's pursed lips and troubled visage, Ari could make nothing.

On the second pass, Ari heard the sound of bone splintering when he shattered his lance on the Empty One's shield. As the red knight rode away, it became clear by the way his arm hung at his side, the shield strapped to it pulling it to an awkward angle, that it was badly broken. Most of the crowd cheered, although some booed.

Ari lined up for another pass, but raised his visor, calling, "Do you yield, sir?"

"Never," the red knight shouted back, his voice coarse with pain. He took the lance Peine was offering him, fumbling awkwardly with his working arm to fix it in place.

Ari looked down the field, wishing he could read Siara's expression from the far end of the lists. He wasn't sure if he should allow his opponent to keep going. The last thing Ari wanted was to kill a Whey in front of his people, even if he was an Empty One.

The red knight lowered his lance, though, so Ari reached for the one offered him and set it in place. He was unsurprised that his opponent once again charged before he was ready. Ari didn't expect chivalry from any Empty One.

The red knight tried to hold lance and shield in place, doing a better job of it than Ari had expected. Realizing the knight's wounded shield arm was already healing, Ari aimed for it, letting Stew run. It wouldn't be a killing blow but, if Ari kept breaking his arm, the Empty One might realize he needed to yield.

They crashed together again, the sounds of screeching metal and shattering wood overshadowed by the red knight's bellow of pain. Looking back, Ari could see how true his aim was. His lance had skewered the red knight's arm, fragments of bone and flesh littering the field. The Empty One, still howling, ripped the broken lance out. Ari hoped everyone would be too shocked to wonder why the man didn't bleed.

Swaying in his saddle, the red knight lined up for another pass. Ari looked over his shoulder at Siara, able to take in the hatred on her face now that he was on her side of the field. She didn't look like she wanted him to allow the red knight to yield. He tried to catch her eye, to beg with his gaze not to have to kill this man before his people. Lggothland needed no animosity with Wheylia.

"I ask you again, sir, do you yield?" Ari called down the field.

A page clinging to the back of a horse burst onto the field, drawing all eyes. "The queen is attacked," he yelled, his youthful voice high with fear.

Before he even told Stew to run, they were wheeling toward the entrance to the royal box. Siara hurried down the steps. Wrenching off his shield and tossing it aside, Ari swept her up as he passed, securing her before him on the saddle. Stew charged across the grassland and into the city, Ari struggling to hold the weakened gear in place, worried he'd hurt Stew if he squeezed too hard. They clattered through the streets, the zigzagging roadway making the journey to the castle drag on forever, filling Ari with anger.

He wondered how many men were left in the castle, and of what caliber. Everyone was down on the field. Any guard with seniority would have used his rank to come watch the joust, leaving someone inexperienced behind. Not normally one to curse, Ari felt a stream of expletives leave his mouth at his own stupidity.

Of course he wasn't the real target of the Empty One. Why would he be? Because he was the Thrice Born? When had he become so self-important? This was about the throne of Wheylia, anyone could see that. Ari was merely a distraction.

Stew skidded to a halt at the base of the broad steps to the castle. Ari swung Siara down, remembering at the last moment to pull up, placing her gently before clattering down behind her. He drew his sword, Siara already running up the steps. He hastened after, fear stabbing through him at the idea of letting her out of his sight.

The cold gray stone of the entrance hall was splattered with blood, dead guardsmen strewn like fall leaves. Ari slowed, torn between trying to figure out where the attackers were and following Siara. The later quickly won out as she skirted the bodies and sped up the steps to the royal wing. Ari charged after her, hoping there was no reason for stealth. He sounded like a hundred metal goblets being rolled down the stairs.

Siara raced along the hall, sliding to a halt outside a closed door. Ari could see bloodied guards slumped at the end of the corridor outside the queen's chambers and hear a woman's shrieks, but Siara pounded on the door before them.

"Camva?" she yelled, her voice catching in a sob. "Open the door." She looked over her shoulder at him, tears streaking her face. "Go check the queen," she ordered before returning to her pounding.

Ari ignored her. As much as he would like to help Queen Reudi, there was no way he was leaving Siara alone until he was sure she was safe.

"Princess Siara?" Camva's voice was muffled by thick wood.

"Yes, it's me. Is Tiana safe?"

The door was wrenched open, revealing a distraught Camva clutching a wide-eyed Princess Tiana to her bosom. Ari let out his breath in relief.

"What's happening, my lady?" Camva's voice was full of tears. She bounced the baby in her arms. "There was so much screaming."

"We're here now," Ari said, worried her agitation would upset Tiana. "Everything will be fine."

"I didn't know what to do." Camva started crying and Tiana's face crumpled as she joined in. "I'm so sorry. I knew people were dying, but I didn't know what to do."

"You did the right thing," Siara said, reaching out to stroke tears from Tiana's cheek. "Take Tiana back inside. We're going to check on my grandmother. Don't open the door again for anyone but Lord Aridian or me."

"Thank the Overgod you're safe," Camva said, hugging the crying Tiana to her. "Mommy's fine, Tia, we're fine," she

317

whispered to the little princess. She backed into the room, soothing Tiana all the while.

Ari pulled the door shut behind her.

Siara stared at the thick wood, taking deep breaths. Ari could see she was shaking. She pulled out a kerchief, wiping her eyes. "I told you to go check the queen," she said, turning to hurry down the hall.

Not bothering to answer, he followed Siara through the wide corridor and into the queen's formal sitting room. The dead guards in the corridor were echoed by more inside, crumpled amongst shards of broken furniture. Ari didn't have time to gain more than an impression of what had transpired, but they seemed to have been thrown about rather than cut down. He and Siara burst into the private sitting room, filled with more dead bodies but also with milling guards and maids.

Relief filled Ari as he realized the fighting was already over and Siara wasn't in immediate danger. A guard called out but Siara didn't stop. She hurried through the open double doors at the other side of the room and into the queen's private sleeping area, where even more still forms lay.

Crying servants stood around the queen's bed and some of the guards put hands to hilts as Ari and Siara burst into the room. Ari was aware of other guards following them. Queen Reudi lay in her bed, her breath shallow and her eyes closed, more cuts gouging her chest than Ari could tally in a glance. He realized at once the wounds must be shallow, or the queen would already be dead. Lying next to her, on her stomach, was one of Siara's ladies. There was a knife through her back, along with a multitude of holes, oozing blood. It was obvious she had thrown herself onto the queen, protecting her from the worst of the attack.

"The queen is alive," Siara said, relief in her voice. She knelt on the floor next to her grandmother's bed, casting a sad glance at her lady. "Someone bring cloths and water at once, and get a physician. Why is no one tending her wounds?" Siara raised her gaze to glare around the room.

"We're not allowed to lay hand on the queen," one of the guardsmen, as young as Ari suspected they would be, said. Nervousness rolled through the onlookers like wind before a rain. "By tradition and, your highness, your orders."

Siara scowled, standing. "You." She pointed at a man near the door. "Fetch Dean Faola. Tell her to bring her strongest healer. You." She pointed at one of the quivering maids. "Bring me dressing and boiled water. Are any of you of the queen's personal staff?"

"They're all dead, your highness," one of the girl's whispered.

"You will stay and assist me," Siara said to the girl. "You four." She gestured to four guards. "Get the bodies out of here, then start removing the others. Bring them all to the ballroom and lay them out. They will have to be cleaned and their loved ones brought. The rest of you, out. Help with the cleaning, but I don't want anyone else in this room."

Murmuring honorifics to Siara, most of the assembled dispersed, the four she'd charged to carry bodies tentatively commencing their work.

"I'm going to see if I can track the villains who did this," Ari said. "It could be I can still catch them."

Siara knelt at her grandmother's side, taking her hand. She nodded, not looking at him. Hesitating, Ari took in how vulnerable she seemed, worried to leave her. The maid she'd ordered to stay hovered at her side, looking scared and unsure.

Ari shook himself. The immediate danger was past. He would best keep Siara safe by finding the assailants.

The four men she'd tasked with moving bodies had already cleared the sleeping room, so he pulled the double doors shut behind him as he left. He grabbed a guard at random. "Don't let any in but the maid the princess sent to fetch water, Dean Faola, and whoever she brings with her," he said.

The young man blinked at him, but nodded.

"Did you see what happened?" Ari asked.

"No, sir," the young man said, eyes wide in his pale face.

"See if you can find me someone who did. A maid, a guard, anyone."

"Yes, sir."

Ari crossed the sitting room. The guards and maids were already making good progress setting it right. He pulled off his helmet as he went, feeling like he could hardly breathe inside it, and clattered back down the steps.

Chapter 29

Ari was dismayed to find the cleanup well underway in the central hall. Any tracks the attackers had left were long gone, scrubbed up by industrious maids who wept as they worked. The ones he questioned hadn't been near enough to see anything and all he could get out of them was that there was a trail of dead leading down the steps into the bowels of the castle.

Ari went down, but found nothing. He was clenching his teeth in frustration by the time he returned to the queen's chambers to report to Siara, having first stopped by his room to deposit his tabard and as much of his armor as he could quickly strip off.

The corridor to the queen's suite was wiped clean and strangely empty, no longer littered by bodies or filled with guards and servants. Ari strode past the two guards outside the queen's formal sitting room, and the two guarding her private sitting area, not giving them the chance to consider whether he should be there. The double doors between the queen's private sitting room and her sleeping chambers were open and Ari could hear Siara, Dean Faola and Lord Reido inside. Unlike the last time he'd found them together, there were no sounds of arguing.

The guard Ari had left at the doorway stood to one side, looking nervous. Ari nodded to him as he passed. Lord Reido was seated in one of the room's gilt chairs, his head in his hands. Siara stood near him, her features pinched with strain. The dean and a matronly woman Ari didn't know tended the queen, who was bandaged and surrounded by clean bedding. Her face had a gray hue to it and she wasn't awake.

"How could this happen?" Reido moaned.

Siara put a hand on his shoulder and he looked up at her. Ari was surprised to see tears streaking his face.

"Praise be for the stubbornness of Wheylian women," Reido said. "If you hadn't had your lady here, all would be lost. I'm sorry I ever argued with you."

"I'm sorry, too," Siara said. "I was heavy handed and flouting thousands of years of tradition. You had every right to be angry."

Lord Reido covered her hand with his, smiling up at her.

"And all is not lost, as you said," Dean Faola interjected. "Far from it, for the queen shall live and now we have proof foul deeds are afoot."

"The poison was proof," Siara said, nodding to acknowledge Ari's presence. She looked a question at him and he shook his head. He hadn't found their enemy. "But we still haven't apprehended those behind this. Ari, please come in and close the doors."

He complied, reaching out and pulling the double doors closed behind him.

"You found nothing, then?" Lord Reido asked Ari, letting go of Siara's hand.

"The trail is cold, my lord. I believe, though, that the villains are somewhere within the keep. The carnage led to the lower level."

"You mean, whoever did this is still in the castle?" the dean asked, exchanging a worried glance with the woman Ari didn't know.

"I believe so, Dean Faola. You said the queen will live?" Looking at her, he wondered how they could be so sure. She seemed hardly to breathe.

"Tomorrow night, Dean Faola will call a circle of priestesses to heal my grandmother. Maiva will tend her until then," Siara said, gesturing to the unknown woman.

"Her wounds are dire," Maiva said, her aged face creased with worry. "None are deep, but there are many, and the queen was already weak. True, the circle should revive her, if we can find nine skilled enough and near enough to come."

"We shall." There was no compromise in Dean Faola's tone.

"We must," Siara said, sounding less sure.

"Meanwhile, I shall seek the traitors who dared do this," Lord Reido said, his voice so harsh Ari could hardly recall his sorrowful tones of moments ago. Reido surged to his feet. "I won't rest until this is finished." Glancing around the room, he made the barest of bows. "Princess, Dean." He brushed past Ari, all but slamming the doors open as he left.

Ari cleared his throat, unsettled by the volatility of Reido's behavior. "What do you need for the messages to the healers?"

"We already sent for writing materials, and we've no shortage of guards to carry them," Siara said. She bit her lower lip, looking down at the queen. "There must be something more we can do while we wait."

"I'll see if I can find anyone who saw something useful," Ari said.

Siara nodded.

Ari hesitated, not liking how distraught she looked. He could think of no comfort to give, though, save looking for the queen's attackers. Once the villains were brought to justice, they would all be safe.

A knock at the door revealed a maid burdened by parchment, ink and quills, stirring Siara into action. Glad to see her looking a bit more herself, Ari bowed, taking his leave. Descending to the ballroom, and finding Lord Reido absent, he checked over the dead and ordered all witnesses to be gathered for questioning. Most of the bodies Ari looked at seemed to have been hurtled through the air to be shattered by whatever they met as they fell. Ari's thoughts turned to Empty Ones, for a normal man wouldn't have the strength to do such a thing.

He spoke to the five guards and three servants gathered for him, learning from them it was a lone man who stormed through the castle. A tall lean man with white skin and stringy black hair. He snarled like a beast, and his strength was enormous. It was only through sheer numbers that the guards and servants had managed to overwhelm him and drive him back. Two of the guards swore they'd cut him, but he hadn't bled. One described him as having dark eyes and a rage-twisted face.

Lord Reido, apparently having regained his composure, came to take charge of the disposition of the bodies. Ari was glad, because he felt it would comfort the populace more to retrieve their loved ones from the son of the queen than from a foreign knight. Released, Ari once again followed the glistening stones marking the scrubbed trail of the attacker down into the lower level of the castle. The trail reached the bottom of the steps and ended. Either because the attacker had vanished or because there was no one left to kill, Ari didn't know, but he searched the area thoroughly.

Finding no clues there, he stared down the long hallway. It stretched past the bathing chambers and a side corridor leading to the massive kitchen, laundry and other servant areas, before going up a flight of steps and into the guest wing of the castle. He already knew the vast bathing caverns were a dead end. He could hardly imagine the attacker was hiding among the castle servants, because surely one of the witnesses would have recognized him.

That left only the stairwell leading to the guest wing. The attacker couldn't be a noble, for that would be too conspicuous, but perhaps the villain had slipped into someone's entourage. Whoever was sheltering him may not even be aware of it. There were many nobles visiting from outlying estates in honor of Princess Tiana's arrival.

Ari shook his head. He didn't have the authority to inspect the rooms and servants of the queen's noble guests. He would have to tell Siara his theory and see if she could devise anything. He wasn't sure how far her ability to order around the nobles of Wheylia extended. Any man would likely obey her, but women of noble birth might not.

Frustrated, Ari returned to his suite and removed the rest of his armor. How could he have been so blind? The inept red knight, who Ari realized he'd let escape, was the prefect decoy to empty the castle and allow an attack on the queen.

He went to one of the large east-facing windows. Looking down, he saw Stew was no longer in the courtyard. That must be where Peine was, he realized, noticing for the first time that his valet wasn't around. Would Peine say anything about the condition of Stew's girths? If he didn't, did it mean he'd known they were compromised? Ari didn't like the idea that his best friend might be part of this plot, whatever it was, but if Peine was beguiled by an Empty One, his actions wouldn't reflect his will.

Ari wished he could send a message to Sir Cadwel for advice, but he had the terrible feeling his mentor would stick to his vow not to interfere in the affairs of men. Not that this should count, Ari felt, as Empty Ones were more akin to Aluiens than mortals. Even if he could persuade Sir Cadwel to help, they didn't use pigeons in Wheylia and Ari hadn't brought any hawks with him. The only way to reach him would be by messenger. Ari felt in his gut that they didn't have the time it would take for a man to ride to Sorga.

There was always Larke, though. Ari could remove his amulet and the Lady might send Larke, as she had that spring. Ari would risk being beguiled, but how great of a risk was it if he took it off while completely alone?

A knock at the door interrupted his thoughts. Ari went to open it, wondering what was keeping Peine. A harried looking page stood without.

"Princess Siara orders your presence, my lord," the young man said, bowing.

"Of course." Ari stepped out of the room, closing the door behind him. "Would you be able to help me with a task?"

"Yes, my lord," the page said, leading the way back toward the royal wing.

"Could you send someone to find Lord Peine?"

"Yes, my lord."

"Thank you. Ask him to check on my horse as well, please, and make sure he has my shield," Ari added, reflecting that he'd have to replace the straps on it after ripping it off his arm earlier.

"Yes, my lord."

When they reached the royal wing, extra guards lined the hallway leading to the queen's chamber, their tension palpable. The page halted halfway down the corridor, outside Siara's door, and knocked, bowing to Ari before turning away.

"Come in," Siara called.

Ari pushed the door open, stepping into a plush sitting room in blue and silver. He wondered if the room was always thus, or had been converted before their arrival as homage to Ennentine's colors.

Siara was pacing in front of a large fireplace. Ari was reminded forcibly of the last time she'd called him to her chamber, years ago and in a city far from there, to try to warn him Lord Ferringul was an Empty One. Then, she'd begged him not to go into danger, but he could hardly imagine that was what she wished to say now. Ari was a man now and, he hoped, equipped to face whatever task she placed before him.

"There you are." She halted, turning a glare on him.

Ari was also reminded that the more upset Siara was, the shorter her temper could be. Then, to his surprise, she burst into tears.

"Siara," he said, crossing the room. He halted before her, unsure of his next move, but she threw her arms around him, burying her face against his chest. Tentatively, he held her, trying to banish thoughts of her lips from his mind.

"I'm sorry," she said after a moment, pulling away. She turned from him, dabbing at her face and patting her hair, although it looked as perfect as ever.

"What's wrong?" he asked.

"What's wrong?"

Ari suppressed a smile, relieved at the anger in her tone.

"What is wrong?" She said it slower the second time, as if trying to make him better aware of the meaning of the words. "My grandmother has been poisoned and stabbed. My grandfather, aunt and cousins were obviously murdered. There are villains hiding somewhere in this very castle, almost certainly Empty Ones, and you can't seem to find them, and I have to leave my baby here, with these people, or never see Parrentine again."

"Never?" Ari repeated in response to her obvious exaggeration. He winced at the glare she leveled on him. He cleared his throat. "I think there is just one villain, actually. That's what the witnesses I questioned said. He is, though, as you surmised, almost certainly an Empty One."

"Well, one is better than many." She still sounded angry. "I have ordered you be given the rooms across the hall from mine. You are to move your things immediately. You will not be sleeping there, however, but here in my sitting room. The only way into Tiana's nursery is through this room and you shall guard it. Peine may stay in your old chambers. Tell him it was all I could do to persuade them to violate tradition in your case."

Ari looked around at the delicate couches, none even approaching the length he would require to stretch out. At least the floor had a thick carpet. "Of course, your highness. I'm surprised our hosts agreed even to let me come."

"Our hosts? Who would that be? My uncle and I are the only two members of the royal line who aren't dead, unconscious, or too young to speak, and there's an Empty One out there laying compulsions on people. Anyone could be compromised, including Uncle Reido. We have to make our

328

own decisions, Ari. As a Princess of Whey, it is my order that you move into those rooms."

"But not Peine?"

"No." Her glare softened slightly. "Not Peine. I'm sorry, Ari. I can't trust him so near Tiana and my grandmother. I simply can't."

Ari sighed, knowing she was right. He hated treating Peine like the enemy, though. "I'll see to it immediately."

"And I want you to wear your sword at all times," Siara added.

"But the custom of the palace--"

"I am convinced you are not going to attack the royal family. As that is the point of the custom, we shall ignore it."

"Yes, your highness." Ari would feel better wearing his sword, anyhow. He'd planned to mention the sabotage of Stew's accoutrements to Siara, but now he was reluctant. He didn't want to add to her worries. "Siara, do you think there's any chance I could be allowed to inspect all of the visiting servants? I think the Empty One may be hiding amongst them."

"My uncle has already suggested it."

"He must not be beguiled, then."

"Or maybe he is and knows you shall find nothing," Siara said. Anger drained from her, leaving her looking tired. "Go get your things."

Ari nodded, giving her a half-bow before leaving the room. He went first to the stable, finding Stew brushed down and munching contentedly on fresh oats.

"Did Peine take care of you?" he asked his horse.

Stew huffed out his breath.

Ari wasn't sure if that was a yes or a no. "You did a magnificent job today." He patted Stew on the nose.

The destrier's ears swiveled forward, and Ari knew he was pleased.

Leaving Stew to his oats, Ari went to inspect his barding. As he'd guessed, most of the leather was stretched almost to the point of breaking. It would be unusable until Ari had time to fit new pieces. He could ask someone to do it, but he wouldn't. He always saw to Stew's armor himself. Turning from it, he inspected his riding saddle, finding it, for now, undamaged. Realizing he was taking more time than he should, he patted Stew again and hurried from the stable, finding Peine waiting for him in their rooms.

"Was it hard to get back to the castle?" Ari asked, still perturbed by his friend's long absence.

"A bit. There was a lot going on after you galloped off. The red knight escaped."

"Oh?" Ari waited for a moment before continuing, to see if Peine would supply him with any more information. "Did you notice the wear on Stews girth?"

"Wear?" Peine looked confused.

"It was all but ruined." Ari watched Peine carefully. "Practically useless. Some of the other pieces were worn as well."

"I didn't think to check it before I readied Stew," Peine said, sounding contrite. "Or when I took it off. I was in a hurry both times. I'm sorry I didn't notice. That could have been dangerous."

"Yes," Ari said, annoyed. He could glean nothing from Peine's reply. "Siara wants me to move to the royal wing."

"The royal wing?" Peine repeated, a spark of excitement in his tone. "I've never seen any of those suites."

"I'm afraid you still won't. Siara said she bent the rules as much as she could just to allow me there." Ari hoped his face didn't reveal how near he walked to lying. "Besides, they aren't much different from this."

"I'm sure they're much nicer. That's how things are. The higher your rank, the better life you have. I suppose it only stands to reason that you would get to stay in the royal wing, not me."

"You're to stay here in this suite. It's yours now, and I don't know if a bigger bed and a larger sitting room make a life better."

"Ari, the world is divided between those who have wealth and those who don't. Of course it's better to be one of those who does. I'll fetch some servants to carry your belongings, assuming they're allowed to accompany you?"

Before Ari could stop him, Peine was gone. Ari stared at the door as it swung shut behind his friend, feeling as if he barely knew him. When had Peine gone from being excited to be Ari's best friend and valet to having so many aspirations of grandeur?

Not that he shouldn't. Ari had aspirations for himself, too, and he'd achieved most of them. He couldn't fault Peine for aspiring. It was just, there was something off in the way Peine thought about it all. Unable to define his concern, Ari turned to packing. If people were going to carry his belongings for him, it was the least he could do.

Chapter 30

That night, Ari slept on the floor just inside Siara's sitting room. As the door opened inward, it would collide with him should anyone try entering. He'd quickly realized it was the only place he'd be able to sleep in peace, knowing no one could sneak past him. The entrance to Siara's sitting room wasn't the most comfortable place he'd ever slept, but it wasn't the least.

Not until he woke the next morning did he recall his promise to duel with Cooro. For a brief moment, he considered going through with it. He wouldn't be far from Siara if he was down in the courtyard, and Cooro would be such an entertaining opponent. Ari had no proof the Empty One was interested in Siara or Tiana, after all. He also didn't think the Empty One would attack so near dawn, for the guards were well rested and new, and the bright light of day didn't lend itself to skulking.

But he knew it would be irresponsible to indulge himself in a duel. Surely word of their match would have spread, as Ari and Cooro had made no secret of their arrangement. The Empty One would know of it, and may plan to use it as an opportunity, as he had the joust with the red knight. Ari would have to go down and tell Cooro no.

He rose and went to dress. A definite advantage to the suites in the royal wing was the addition of private bathing facilities. Ari supposed it would damage the image of near divinity the rulers of Wheylia cultivated if those they ruled over saw them taking a bath each morning.

Once dressed, Ari belted on his sword and made his way through the castle to the courtyard, reassured by how little time it took to get there from outside Siara's rooms. Cooro was waiting for him at the bottom of the castle steps, a nearby groom holding a lean piebald mare. Ari descended, giving the Wheylian swordmaster a half-bow.

"I see your courage did not desert you, but I'm afraid we cannot duel today," Cooro said. "It would be an act of grave disrespect for us to make sport the morning after our city has suffered so horrifying an assault."

Ari nodded. He should have realized that. They could hardly cross swords for amusement when so many Wheys had fallen a scant day ago. "I concur, sir."

"But I have something to ask of you instead. Allow me to aid you in apprehending the villain. I would avenge my people on his body."

"I'm a guest here. I'm afraid it's not my place to decide such a thing."

Cooro's eyes narrowed. Ari realized the swordmaster wasn't sure he spoke the truth. He didn't know what the Whey wanted him to say. Ari could invite him to help guard Siara, but he didn't think the princess would approve. The silence between them was growing uncomfortable when a boy hurried across the courtyard.

"My lord?" he said, stopping in front of Ari. "I have a message for you."

"Thank you." Ari took the folded and sealed parchment the boy proffered. The seal bore no imprint and the outside of the parchment no marks. Ari cracked it open, scanning the unpracticed script.

I beg your aid. The boy knows where I dwell. Do not bring Peine. Gauli

Ari had forgotten all about his request to go into the city to meet Peine's brother. He frowned at the message, unsure what to make of it. Cooro leaned over so he could see the writing. Ari folded the paper in half.

"It could be a trap," Cooro said.

Ari gave him an annoyed look.

"I shall come with you."

Ari regarded the determined looking swordmaster for a long moment before nodding. Ari considered himself a good judge of character. He trusted Cooro, and the Whey was right. It could be a trap. Who better to have at his side than the best swordsman in the land?

"Do you know the man who gave you this?" Ari asked the boy. He appeared to be a typical first-tier Whey. His dark hair was thick and he wore loose breeches and a tunic of undyed wool.

"No, my lord. He called me from his window. He dropped the note down. He asked if I knew you and said I wasn't to give you the note until I saw you without your friend, Lord Peine."

"Do you know Lord Peine?"

"No, my lord, but I know Swordmaster Cooro, and he isn't this Peine fellow. The man gave me a silver," the boy added. "I said, for a silver, I'd go to the castle and back ten times."

Ari retrieved a silver from the small purse he wore beneath his tunic. "Today, you shall go to the castle and back but once, and get two silver for it, but as soon as we reach the place where you got this note, I want you to leave, right away." Ari waited for the boy to nod before he handed him the coin. "Would you ride with me or Cooro?"

The boy looked back and forth between them, his wide eyes conflicted. "Swordmaster Cooro," he finely said.

Cooro flashed Ari a grin.

Ari turned to the castle, conflicted. He wanted to tell Siara where he was going, but he couldn't risk running into Peine. He didn't know what any of this was about, but he had nowhere else to seek answers. Guarding Siara would never be as good as eliminating the Empty One altogether. He looked up at the windows to Siara's sitting room and found her watching him. She met his eyes and nodded. He knew she couldn't read the parchment from there, but he was sure she was giving him permission to go.

Ari saddled Stew and they headed into the city, the boy giving directions. Once they reached the bottom tier, he directed them east into a part of the city where buildings were low and narrow, squeezed together in the shadow of the looming mountains. They halted before a structure that had little to separate it from the rest, although a sign worn almost to illegibility claimed it was an inn.

"It was that window." The boy pointed to the second thin opening from the left.

The windows, barely wider than arrow slits, had no glass. A single heavy shutter hung outside each. Most were closed. Ari and Cooro dismounted, Cooro swinging the boy down.

"Time for you to go," the swordmaster said.

The boy nodded and ran off down the street. Cooro held his piebald horse's reins, looking about the less than savory neighborhood.

"Here." Ari took the reins from Cooro, tying them to Stew's saddle. "You keep an eye on Cooro's horse, and stay out of trouble."

Stew snorted.

Cooro looked at Ari as if he were mad but he turned to the building before them, drawing his estoc. Ari followed suit, his greatsword held easily in one hand.

"I didn't call you here to fight," the voice of the red knight said from above them.

Ari looked up to see a Whey who bore a distinct likeness to Peine peering down from the window the boy indicated.

"Come up." Gauli disappeared from the window.

Ari wouldn't have gone in immediately, shocked as he was to find Peine's brother speaking with the voice of the red knight, but Cooro was already moving. Ari hurried after, struggling to relax the vicelike grip he had on his sword hilt.

He followed Cooro into the dilapidated, empty-seeming inn and up the creaking steps. Cooro halted outside the door which must correspond to Gauli's window, making ready to kick it down. Ari put out a hand to stop him, trying the handle instead. The door swung inward. The swordmaster gave him a tight grin and Ari entered.

Inside, the room was as narrow as the windows suggested, with barely space for the molding straw-stuffed mattress and single stool by the window, on which sat Peine's brother, Gauli. His face was etched with pain and his shield arm hung limp and twisted at his side. The breaks, while obviously bad, looked

337

long healed. Ari raised his gaze to the soulless eyes, sorrow shooting through him. Peine's brother was an Empty One.

"So this is the red knight." Cooro's voice was tinged with contempt.

Ari ignored the swordmaster. "Gauli, what have you done?" he asked, his voice soft.

Peine's brother closed his eyes, running his good hand across his face. "What I had to. For the cause," Gauli said, but he didn't sound sure.

"What cause?" Ari asked.

"Our war against the tyranny of the Witches of Whey," Gauli said, his tone becoming more animated.

"Why did you call us here, rogue?" Cooro asked.

"I called you not at all, swordmaster," Gauli snarled, his temper rising like a spring squall. His eyes flashed as he glared up at them.

"But you did call me," Ari said. He sheathed his sword, sorrow, disgust and pity warring in him.

"Yes." Gauli's anger dwindled. "To offer you something, and ask a boon of you, Thrice Born."

"What would you ask of me?"

"I would ask you to kill me." Gauli's face was a mixture of hope and fear.

"Easily enough done," Cooro said.

Ari held up a hand. "Why?"

"The pain," Gauli said, his voice filling with it. "They said I would be invincible. They said I would heal from any wound. And I did. I did." He moaned, clutching his bad arm. "But I didn't know. I didn't collect the bits off the field. I didn't line up what was there. It healed unwhole and wrong. I broke it again, to try to fix it, but the pieces were too small, the gaps too great. I tried again. I broke it again and again and again."

338

He let out a keening wail and started to rock from side to side, digging the fingers of his good hand into his broken arm. Ari could see fragments of the shattered bone break off and shift under the pressure. Gauli's cry grew louder, tinged with madness. Crossing the narrow space, Ari slapped him.

"What if we could get it healed?" Ari asked. Could they? Would the Aluiens help? Was there a way to save Gauli? Maybe he wasn't as far gone as Clorra had been when they'd tried to save her.

For a moment, there was hope in Gauli's face, but then he squeezed his eyes shut. "No," he whispered. "No, I want to die. You don't know the things I've done." He bit down on his lips, leaving holes from which no blood came. "I asked others to kill me, and they tried, but I killed them instead. Everyone in this inn. I killed them. And then, I ate them. I feasted on their sweet flesh. Their warm blood flowed down my throat like wine." He choked on a sob, but his empty eyes let flow no tears. "Thrice Born, you must kill me."

Cooro brought his sword up. He was staring at Gauli with horror on his face. "What are you?"

"He's an Empty One," Ari said, seeing no way to hide Gauli's nature. And he's Peine's brother, he added to himself, sorrow filling him. "What will you give me if I do this for you, Gauli? What is it you offer?"

Cooro turned his look of horror on Ari. "Give you? Are you mad? We should kill him and be done with it."

"What?" Ari pressed, locking eyes with the Empty One before him.

"I know where he is," Gauli whispered. "I know what he wants. I'll tell you, if I can, but you have to save Peine. Please."

"I promise you I'll do everything in my power to save Peine, on my honor. Where is your master?"

"He lives in the castle." Gauli started to pant.

Ari could almost feel the spells of the master Empty One squeezing in around the tortured being before him. "I know, but where?"

"Under . . . under the water." Gauli fell back, gasping, his eyes closed.

"Under the water?" Ari repeated. The baths. There must be something he'd missed there. "How do I get in?"

Gauli's mouth worked, but no sound came out. His body started to writhe on the stool, his bad arm flailing.

"Gauli." Ari took Gauli by the shoulders, slamming him against the wall and holding him there. "What part does Peine play? What is Peine doing?"

"We want a revolution," Gauli roared, once again articulate. His body stopped thrashing. His face was inches from Ari's. His breath smelled of decay. "We will take Wheylia back from the witches. We will put them in their place. Cap the wellspring."

"And Peine is part of this?" Ari asked, a cold ball of fear twisting in his stomach.

"Peine wanted to be the red knight. He wanted to do it. He wanted to make sure no one killed you, but I wouldn't let him. I couldn't let them do this to Peine. I saw what happened to Keite. I'm senior. They had to take me. But the master, he wants you dead, Thrice Born." Gauli let out a gurgling laugh. "Dead dead dead."

"Gauli." Ari pressed the Empty One's shoulders into the solid planks of the wall until he felt the bone start to crumble. "How do I get to your master?"

"No," Gauli cried. He thrashed, twisting so suddenly that Ari didn't have time to let go before the Whey's spine cracked in a dozen places. Gauli's eyes widened in triumph, even as life slipped from his face, leaving his visage hardened into a gleeful grin.

Ari pulled away, feeling his hands sink into the softening flesh. As with all Empty Ones, Gauli's body took only moments to decay to the point it would have reached by now, were it not for the magic which kept it alive.

Cooro was staring at the semi-rotted corpse in revulsion. He turned to Ari, his eyes still wide. "What was that thing? What are you?"

Ari looked around for something to wipe his hands on, finally settling for the least dingy looking corner of the straw bedding. He wished he hadn't let Cooro come. Explaining what had happened without breaking his vow to the Aluiens was going to be hard. "I am Aridian, the Thrice Born, adopted son of Sir Cadwel, Duke of Sorga, Protector of the Northlands and Champion to King Ennentine, and we have to get back to the castle."

Ari locked eyes with the swordmaster. He needed Cooro on his side. He couldn't have him running into the castle yelling out accusations. They must surprise the Empty One. They couldn't allow him to escape, because until he was dead, Peine and everyone else the Empty One had enspelled would never be free. After a long moment, during which Ari never allowed his gaze to waver, Cooro nodded. Leaving the room and the corpse behind, they ran from the building.

Chapter 31

Ari let Stew choose their path as they galloped through the city, concentrating on mastering his tumbled thoughts. Having proof Peine was part of the conspiracy to murder the queen was hard to swallow. Yes, Gauli said Peine had tried to become the red knight so no one would kill Ari, but that couldn't mitigate what his friend had done.

He wondered how many people in the castle were part of the conspiracy. More importantly, how many of them would he have to fight? Was there a limit to how many people an Empty One could control at one time, and how quickly, or could he turn anyone near him against Ari, throwing innocent people in his path until he was forced to kill them or be overwhelmed? Ari's amulet protected him from being beguiled, but that didn't help anyone else. He wouldn't even be able to take any guards with him to seek their enemy, he realized. If he did, he might be forced to kill them.

He could take one person, though. He'd been keeping his father's amulet tucked away with his personal things, viewing it as a family heirloom, but it served a function. It had the same spells of protection as the one Ari wore.

For the second time in two days, Ari found himself cursing. How had he not thought to give the amulet to Siara, or Peine? Yes, it was all he had left of his father, but his father was seventeen years in the grave. He didn't need the amulet now.

They clattered into the castle courtyard, attracting the attention of the guards. Ari slid from his horse, surprised to realize it wasn't even midday yet. It seemed like the events of the morning, carrying the weight of turmoil they did, should have taken more time. He took a deep breath, turning to catch Cooro by the arm as the swordmaster dismounted.

"Wait," Ari said in a low voice. "We have to be calm. I'll explain in a moment."

Cooro looked dubious, but nodded.

They walked up the steps with the appearance of ease, both nodding to the guards as they passed. Ari saw the guards eye Cooro's blade, but didn't slow to give them the chance to question whether Ari's permission to wear a sword in the castle extended to his guest. Inside, Ari turned toward the staircase leading to the royal wing. Before doing anything else, he needed to retrieve his father's amulet and make sure Siara was safe.

"Is Princess Siara in her quarters?" he asked the guards at the base of the stairwell.

"Yes, my lord," one answered. "She and Lord Reido are discussing the care of the queen."

"Thank you," Ari said.

"Yes, my lord."

Ari headed up the steps, Cooro behind him. The hall was lined with guards, as Ari had hoped. Reaching the door to his quarters, he could hear Siara and her uncle talking inside her room, but couldn't make out the words. He left them undisturbed, entering his suite across the hall. In her rooms with her uncle, guards lining the hallway, was as safe as Siara could be outside of Ari's company, and he couldn't take her with him to confront the Empty One.

Leaving Cooro by the door, Ari retrieved his father's amulet from the sleeping chamber. "You'll need to wear this," he said, holding it out to the Whey. "The creature we go to fight, it can use magic to force you to act contrary to your will. It will surely try to make you fight me. This will stop it."

"The reason you didn't wish to alarm the guards." Some of the strain left Cooro's face. "We dare not take them with us."

He took the amulet from Ari, examining it, and Ari felt a momentary pang. His father's amulet. Not that Cooro wouldn't give it back.

"He will be a creature like Lord Peine's brother?" Cooro asked.

"Yes. I'm not sure how to get to him, but I think Gauli meant that the entrance is somewhere in the ladies bathing pool."

"Truly?" Cooro raised his eyebrows. He slid the amulet's chain over his head.

"I think so," Ari said, wishing it were the men's. "Come on."

Ari led the way down the steps to the main level, and then lower still to the long corridor outside the bathing rooms. The hallway was empty, but as they neared the door to the ladies' vestibule, Ari could hear voices inside. He stopped before it, unsure what to do. There were women in there. They could be in any state of dress, but he had to go in. There was no other way.

345

Cooro gave him an amused look and knocked on the door, calling, "Ladies, compose yourselves. I, Cooro, swordmaster extraordinaire, am about to enter your domain."

There were squeaks and squeals inside, but they sounded more laughing than fearful. Cooro put his hand to the door much sooner than Ari would have, pushing it open. Ari looked down at the stone under his feet as the air filled with giggling. He waited until it sounded like everyone was done moving before looking up.

There were six women of varying ages in the room. They had all covered themselves with something, but only two of them were actually dressed. Ari tried not to look at their long limbs sticking out from beneath the towels and robes.

"May we help you, sirs?" one of the women asked.

"I'm afraid we need to inspect the bathing pool, my ladies," Cooro said after a glance at Ari.

"Oh?" another said, with a coquettish smile. "Are they full of monsters?"

"They might be," Cooro replied, grinning.

"Enough," Ari said, exasperated with the women, and Cooro, and himself. This wasn't a game. "We're going in there. I ask that you remain here, or better still, return to the safety of your rooms."

"Yes, my lord," some of them murmured.

Ari hoped none were of sufficient rank to take umbrage with his tone. He hadn't meant for it to be quite as stern as it came out. He looked them each in the eye to drive home the seriousness of his words, before nodding and heading past them into the vaulted cavern that housed the women's bathing pool.

He was met by shrieks and splashes. Renewed giggles erupted behind him. Most of the naked women before him grabbed up towels and fled past him into the changing area, but three of the younger ones stayed, bobbing in the warm water.

"This is the ladies bathing area, Sir Aridian," one called.

"Maybe he's here for more kisses," another said, eying him.

Ari didn't think he knew them. Word of his behavior at the merchant's ball must have spread. "I'm here searching for the entrance to a secret cave beneath this pool," Ari said, deciding if they weren't embarrassed to be naked in front of him, then he wasn't embarrassed to look. Besides, he didn't have time for their games.

"You're coming in to look for a secret cave?" the first one asked before descending into a fit of laughter.

Ari ground his teeth. This was ridiculous. They were in danger. Siara, Tiana and Peine were in danger. They needed to get out of the water before he abandoned all propriety and got in with them, and not in the way they were insinuating.

"A cave?" the third one said, frowning. "I thought. . ." Her voice trailed off as she looked about.

"You thought what?" Ari recognized the look on her face. That struggle to remember something your mind has been told to forget.

"I don't know." She shook her head. "I remember, late one night, I was swimming in that corner." She pointed. "I saw a something bright at the bottom of the pool, so I dove down to look."

"And?" he said when she hesitated.

"That's all," she said, looking confused. "I don't remember anything else. I forgot all about it until now."

"That corner? How far back?" He slipped off his boots and sword belt, leaving his tunic and breeches on. He had to find that cave. He could feel time ticking away from him. This

347

evening, the priestesses Dean Faola had called would gather. He was sure the Empty One would attack the queen again before then. Their enemy would never allow the most powerful sorceress in Wheylia to regain her strength. "Cooro," he called over his shoulder. The swordmaster was still in the changing area, talking with the women.

"Excuse me, ladies," Cooro said, coming to stand beside Ari.

"That one, she may know where the cave entrance is." Ari pointed at the naked girl, who for some reason was blushing now. Ari would never understand women. The other two slithered away as Ari slipped into the water, his sword in hand.

The rest of the women huddled in an increasingly worried looking group on the shore. Cooro entered the water, stripped down to breeches and tunic as well, estoc in hand. The girl swam out before them, her body a dim ripple under the water, shrouded as it was by steam and a lack of light.

"Here," she said, coming to a halt.

Ari thought he could see something flickering below her.

She started to back away as he came forward.

"Wait," he called quietly.

She stopped, her eyes wary.

"If there's a tunnel down there, we're going in. We think the queen's attacker is inside." She gasped and he hurried on. "I need you to get the rest of the women out of here. I don't care what you have to tell them, but don't tell them the truth. I don't want any guards coming. This is something only Cooro and I can do."

He filled his words with all the intensity and sincerity he could muster. He had to convince her. He couldn't have the women stay here in danger, but he didn't want them running out into the castle calling the guards, either.

"Sir Aridian speaks the truth," Cooro said.

She gave a halting nod. "Yes, my lord."

"Once you have them away from here, please go to Princess Siara and tell her where I am and what I'm doing. Tell her to stay safe, and, well --" Ari stopped, unsure what he wanted to say. Thoughts of Ispiria and Sir Cadwel went through his mind, and his home in Sorga and all of his hopes for the future. He took a deep breath. "Tell her if I don't come back, you know where to find my body."

She looked at him with wide eyes and nodded again. Silence stretched between them for a moment before she turned and swam away. Ari watched her go, her smooth white body gliding through the water, until he realized what he was doing and looked away. How was he ever going to explain any of this to Ispiria?

He looked over at Cooro, who treaded water, watching him expectantly. The far side of the pool was deep enough even Ari couldn't touch the bottom, although if he did, the water wouldn't cover his head by more than a hand. Gripping his sword tightly, Ari dropped down, using his toe to prod the slightly shinier stone the Wheylian girl had pointed out.

His foot went right through it. He pulled back up to the surface, gasping more from surprise than lack of air. "It's some sort of illusion."

"Illusion?" Cooro repeated, looking uncertain.

"There's not really any floor there. I'll see what direction it goes."

Ari went down again, this time head first. It was very strange to deliberately stick his face against the floor but, as soon as he did, he could see the tunnel beyond. Even with his Aluien ability to see without light, he couldn't make out much in the tunnel, but it went toward the wall. He came back up.

"Your head disappeared through the floor." Cooro sounded shaken. "This is indeed the work of sorcery. One of the queen's own priestesses must be turned against her."

"I don't think so. There are more in this world who wield such powers than the women of Wheylia." He stared down through the water for a moment. "I'm going to swim through that tunnel. It's my duty, but I'm not asking you to follow. You don't have to do this."

"I doubt you could stop me." Cooro's attempt at a grin came across more as a grimace. "If we're going, let us go."

Ari nodded, took a deep breath, and dove downward through the illusion. He held his sword by his side, using his other hand to feel his way along as his feet propelled him. The tunnel took a sharp drop before arching upward again, flickering light visible as soon as Ari made the turn. It couldn't have taken him more than sixty beats of his heart to make the swim, but as he burst to the surface in the low cave, it was the sweetest breath he'd ever taken. Those moments, encased in a narrow tunnel in the complete dark under the water, Cooro blocking his exit and the unknown before him, were the most terrifying of Ari's life. He wasn't sure if his capacity for quick healing would aid him against drowning or not, and he had not the slightest desire to find out.

Cooro burst to the surface, the fear on his face reorganizing itself into calm as he took a deep breath. He and Ari pulled themselves from the water. They were in a small cave illuminated by a hissing oil-coated torch. Water dripped from the natural stone ceiling and glistened on the damp walls. Before them, a roughhewn set of steps descended, spiraling out of sight. Somewhere below, they could hear a powerful voice rising and falling unintelligibly.

Ari glanced at Cooro, receiving a nod. Greatsword held before him in one hand, Ari started down the steps. They twisted back on themselves until they were directly under the women's bathing pool, sputtering torches illuminating the way. The voice below grew louder until Ari could sort out words from the echoes around him.

"Victory is near at hand." It was a refined voice, though a bit nasal. Ari had no reason for his conclusion but, somehow, he knew it was the voice of the Empty One. "Before the sun sets, Lord Reido will slay the witch queen."

Ari's foot almost slipped from the step he was on. He stopped. Siara was with Lord Reido. Pulling himself together, he took another step. Once he slew the foul creature below, its hold on Lord Reido would break. He looked over his shoulder at Cooro, but the swordmaster was watching him, obviously waiting for Ari to decide.

"We shall be set free of the tyranny of these women once and for all, my friends," the voice continued. "Why should they have magic? Why should they have power? I offer it to you. The power to be your own masters. Who is willing? Who will be the next to undergo the transformation?"

"Me," a voice called. Pain as real as any blade could inflict pierced Ari. It was Peine's voice. "I will, master."

"Peine." The Empty One drew the name out. "I am not sure of your worth. I asked you for the amulet of the Thrice Born, yet you brought it not."

Ari inched downward, the flickering shadows and smooth floor before him telling him he was almost in sight of the room below.

"I don't see why he must die, master," Peine said. "Once the queen is dead, he will take the princess away and they will trouble us no further. This isn't Lggothland. It isn't any of his concern. I'll convince him of that."

"What if I told you your brother is dead?" the Empty One said, a note of satisfaction in his voice.

Ari crept around the curved wall, trying to see how many were in the room. As he slid round the final bit of wall separating him from the cave beyond, the Empty One turned and pointed at him.

"And that his slayer stands there."

Ari went still, anger filling him as he realized the Empty One knew he was there. Knew he went to Gauli. Probably knew the moment Gauli died and his hold on him unraveled forever.

"Ari," Peine gasped, coming to his feet where he'd knelt on the stone before the vile black-robed Empty One.

A ring of fourteen men surrounded Peine, themselves robed, even as he was. The cavern was not wide. It would take Ari only three strides to reach his enemy.

"Ari, it isn't true? My brother isn't dead?" Peine's face was white in the flickering light of the torches. Shadows bounced from the wet walls. The robed men looked to their master, as if seeking his will.

"Back away from that thing, Peine," Ari said, his eyes fixed on his enemy, his sword held low before him.

"Kill them," the Empty One ordered.

The men surged forward. Ari barely looked at them as they ran up to him with fists raised, keeping his eyes on the Empty One. Using the flat of his blade, Ari struck his attackers, knocking them back. He spared a brief hope Cooro did the same, for these men were pawns of the creature. They were likely beguiled, not willing participants in this plot against the queen.

Working to rein in his strength, Ari aimed his blows at their heads, attempting to render them unconscious. In short order, he and Cooro had reduced the mob of robed men to a moaning heap littering the cavern floor. Ari stepped over them, his sword at the ready as he faced the Empty One. Peine stood at its side, looking stunned.

"You see how he does not deny it?" the Empty One said. "The Thrice Born killed your brother."

"No," Peine yelled. He sprang forward, fists raised.

Ari watched him come with resignation. Trading his sword to his off hand, he met Peine's onslaught with a punch to the face, wincing as Peine's nose broke. His friend dropped to the floor like a sack of flour. Ari wanted to look down, to make sure Peine wasn't too badly hurt, but he dared not take his eyes from the Empty One.

"I thought you'd at least give them swords," he told it.

"Swords, no swords." The Empty One shrugged. "I knew them no match for you. There was one battle I did wish to witness, though." A look of savage triumph on his face, he gestured at Cooro. "Let us see if you can best a master swordsman without killing a friend," he snarled.

Cooro looked between the Empty One and Ari. "The amulet grows cold."

"That means it's working." Ari watched in enjoyment as the triumph on the Empty One's face flickered to fear.

Without warning, the creature lunged at Cooro, moving too fast for the swordmaster to dodge. The Empty One flung him backward, Cooro hitting the wall with a sickening crack. Ari dove after, swinging his sword in a low swipe aimed for the Empty One's unprotected flank, desperate to keep the monster from striking Cooro again. The creature whirled, wrenching

Cooro's sword from his unresisting hand to deflect Ari's blade. Cooro's limp form slid to the floor behind it.

Ari struck again, leveling a piercing blow at its right side, more to drive it back from Cooro and the other unconscious forms than out of hope his blade would land. The Empty One jumped away, two more quick stabs from Ari driving it into the center of the room.

"My master will reward me well for killing you," it said, crouching low. Its lips were twisted in a corpselike grin. It struck at Ari, aiming for his middle, but Ari flicked the blow aside.

"Your master?" he asked, intrigued. The Caller had also mentioned a master.

"You met him once, Thrice Born," the Empty One said, punctuating his words with a slash at Ari's head.

Ari ducked, gouging his blade across the creature's middle. No blood flowed, though Ari had scored it. "Who is he? What does he want with me?"

Ari found himself going back through his mind, trying to figure out who the thing's master could be. Realizing the Empty One's tactic was working, Ari forced himself to concentrate on the fight. He brought his sword up just in time to parry another blow aimed at his head, his distraction robbing him of the opportunity for a counterstrike. He would have cursed himself, but there was no time for that either. This was an Empty One before him, with speed and strength to match his own.

The glee in the Empty One's eyes showed it knew its tactic was effective. "He's offered a reward for you. Power even beyond what I already have."

"Why me?" Ari jumped back as the Empty One swung at his middle. It wasn't until he almost tripped over Peine that he

354

realized he'd let himself be maneuvered so close to his friend. Off balance, Ari could only drop to the ground to avoid a swing at his head. He was forced to roll away, springing up to parry another blow.

Reversing his blade, the Empty One swung downward, his sword aimed at Peine's unconscious form. Ari lunged forward, tackling his enemy rather than trying to block the blow. They hit the wall at the back of the cave with enough force to send both of their swords skittering away.

Ari grappled with the Empty One, pinning it to the floor. Not holding back, he aimed a punch at the creature's face. It wrenched itself away, taking only a glancing blow. Ari felt one of his fingers break as his hand hit stone.

The Empty One flailed at Ari's face, snarling. Fortunately, it lacked the strength to do more than make his head ring, because of the angle of the blows. Ari wrapped both hands around its throat and squeezed, lifting its head and smashing it back down. The creature's white face started to turn a dull purple, its struggles growing weak. Ari knew he should end it but, instead, he let up enough for it to suck in a gasping breath.

"Why me?" he repeated from between clenched teeth.

"Because of the blood in your veins. Remember this, Thrice Born." The Empty One's voice was a ruined gurgle. "When the queen is dead, remember you lingered here, questioning me, when you could have saved her."

"All I have to do to save her is squeeze. I know your kind. When you die, your hold over Lord Reido will die with you."

"My hold?" It tried to laugh, rattling the crushed bones in its neck. "Reido sought me out. He brought me here. He wants the throne for himself. He desires to see an end to men's servitude in Wheylia. My hold? You shall gain nothing from killing me."

Ari stared at it in a horror. He broke its neck, twisting its head all the way around to make sure it was dead. He sprang up as it started to disintegrate. Grabbing his sword, Ari ran from the chamber, jumping over bodies as he went.

Chapter 32

Ari took the rough cut steps four at a time. Reaching the top, he dove into the pool, almost knocking himself senseless in his haste. He erupted from the water on the other side, two powerful strokes bringing him back to where he could gain his footing. Naked blade in hand, he ran from the pool, charging through a gaggle of shrieking women that barely registered in his brain.

All he could think of was Siara. He flew up the steps and across the entry hall to the next set, guards crying out in his wake. The Empty One was right. Ari would never forget he was letting it live, questioning it, while Siara was . . .

"Where is the princess?" Ari demanded of the guards at the top of the steps.

The guards gaped at him. Ari knew he must be a sight, dripping wet, sword in hand, his face probably bruised. Indeed, he could taste blood in his mouth and one side of his lips was swollen. He grabbed one of them by the front of his mail coat and lifted him off the floor.

"Where is Siara?"

"She and Lord Reido are with the queen," the other guard said. "My lord--"

Ari didn't hear what else the man had to say. Dropping the guard he held, Ari sprinted down the corridor. The men outside Siara's suite started to draw their swords, but he smashed through them before they could. His speed barely diminished, he shouldered more aside as he ran. The pair before the queen's doors had their blades out, but two quick flips of Ari's sword sent their weapons flying. Not slowing, he smashed through the closed doors and into the queen's chambers.

The private sitting room doors were open, and those of the bedchamber beyond. Through them, Ari could see Siara and Lord Reido struggling. He charged forward even as Reido turned hate filled eyes on him.

The queen's sleeping chamber was in disarray. The sheets were torn, the unconscious form of Queen Reudi in a tangled heap on the floor. Her new physician lay sprawled beside her.

Reido held a knife poised before Siara. Ari could already see red spread across the front of her gown. A wave of nausea swept through him, the sight of her blood hitting him harder than a blow.

Siara had both hands on Reido's forearm, trying to hold his knife back. He reached out with his other arm, which showed signs of being wounded, snaking it around her body. He pulled her against him, wrenching his knife arm from her grasp to jam the point into her side. Siara tried to pull away, but he pushed the point in, the heavy brocade of her dress sucking blood from the wound to form a bright circle around it.

"Stop," Reido yelled.

Ari and Siara both went still, Ari skidding a few feet closer with his momentum. Behind him, he was aware of guards amassing.

"Ari, he tried to kill the queen," Siara yelled.

There were gasps behind Ari, and a small one from Siara as Reido dug his knife in deeper.

"I killed your pet Empty One," Ari called. He hoped Reido would realize, with so many witnesses and no Empty One to give him the magic he sought, his plot was ended.

"You have ruined my plans, Thrice Born," Reido snarled, his face giving away his intention. "I hope you are pleased, for now I have no happiness to seek, except in making you watch her die."

Before Reido was halfway through his threat, Ari drew his sword arm back. He launched his greatsword like a javelin. Letting go of Siara, Reido tried to duck, but he was too slow. Ari's sword slammed into him, point first, splitting his face in half. Reido was wrenched backward, his body slamming into the wall behind him. The hilt of Ari's sword quivered, the tip embedded in the stone.

Ari wasn't aware of conscious thought until he found himself kneeling on the floor, cradling Siara in his arms. She was crying, and her face was drained of blood. She clung to the arms he had about her. He grabbed a handful of loose bedding, clutching it to her side where blood flowed. He knew there were other people in the room, but he didn't see them, didn't hear them.

Siara had a long shallow cut on one upper arm and a bruise across her face. There was a vicious looking gash across her other forearm and blood on her hands. Ari pulled more blanket to them, trying to press them against her wounds, especially the one in her side. His broken finger wouldn't work right and he glared at it in annoyance.

"Aridian? Sir Aridian?"

The voice cut into Ari's awareness. He took his eyes from Siara's lips, quelling his obsession to watch her take every breath, and looked up to see Dean Faola standing over him.

"Sir Aridian, my healers are here. We can help her. You have to give her to us."

Ari stared at her for a moment. He took a shuddering breath, then another. He realized he was shaking. Loosening his grip on Siara, who looked up at him through pain clouded eyes, he reached over and popped his broken finger back into alignment.

"The queen," Siara whispered.

"We are tending her, your highness," Dean Faola said. "She lives still."

A woman knelt beside Ari, lightly touching him on the shoulder. "I think the princess would be more comfortable in her bed, and we could tend her better there."

Ari nodded. Gathering Siara closer, he stood, borrowed linens and all. The queen was already back in her bed, looking composed and unharmed, her eyes closed. Stepping carefully, he carried Siara from the room and to her own, laying her on her bed. The woman who'd spoken to him followed with a second. They moved forward to tend Siara as soon as he set her down.

Camva peeked out from another room, her lips trembling. "What happened?" she whispered.

Siara struggled to lift her head. "Tiana," she mumbled. "Is she safe?"

"The princess is fine, my lady. She's sleeping." Camva looked as though she might start crying.

"Good," Siara said, giving in to the two women tending her, who were pressing her to lay still.

Ari crossed the room, addressing the terrified nursemaid in a low voice. "Why don't you go sit with Tiana and make sure she stays calm?"

"Yes, my lord." Camva backed into the nursery, closing the door behind her.

"My lord." One of the healers crossed to him. "It would be best if you leave now. We must disrobe her to tend to her side."

"Yes, of course," Ari said, though his sense of propriety warred with reluctance to let Siara from his sight. "She'll be well?"

"She'll be fine, my lord. You should return to the queen's chamber and seek someone to care for your wounds."

"Ah, thank you," Ari said, having no intention of doing so.

Leaving Siara's suite, he glanced across the hall to the room where his belongings lay, but there was no point in changing. He must gather guards and return to the cave for Peine, Cooro and the other men. First, though, he needed his sword.

He strode down the hall and into the queen's chambers, nodding to the guards with what he hoped was sufficient respect to repair any damage done by his recent treatment of them. They stepped aside to let him pass, looking nervous. The door to the queen's sleeping chamber was closed. Ari knocked tentatively.

"Enter, Thrice Born," Queen Reudi called.

Weak though the queen's voice was, Ari felt relief at hearing it. He opened the door to find a room full of tired looking priestesses, the queen sitting upright in bed in the midst of them. Lord Reido's body was gone and the room put right, although blood stained the carpet and Ari's sword was still stuck in the wall. He bowed. "Your majesty."

She inclined her head. "They tell me you slew my son."

"I'm sorry," he said, taken aback. Was she angry with him?

"I believe you did me a service. Or, at the least, I will come to see it that way in time. He was the last of my children. It is a sad thing to have four children and see all of them perish."

"No one knows the fate of Lady Kiala," Dean Faola said, referring to Siara's aunt who'd traveled away across the sea.

"I hope you have come to collect your blade," the queen said, not acknowledging that the dean had spoken. "For I do not care for that sword as a decoration."

"Yes, your majesty." Ari wondered if she meant he should walk over and take it. He didn't wish to be rude, especially since he'd killed her son.

"You may take it," she said, her faint smile making him wonder if she'd followed his thoughts. "And then you may leave. I am too weary to look upon your fateless eyes."

"Yes, your majesty," Ari said again. He crossed the room, several of the priestesses stepping out of his way. Wrapping both hands about the hilt of his greatsword he yanked, pulling it free from the wall, pleased and amazed to see it looking undamaged. Holding it unobtrusively by his side, he backed toward the door, bowing. "Thank you, your majesty."

"I don't expect to see you wearing it in my castle again, and I request you remove yourself and your possessions to the guest wing."

"Of course, your majesty." Ari paused for a moment, to make sure there wasn't more, before backing out the door with a bow.

Hurrying from her suite, he jogged down the corridor, descending into the wide hallway leading past the bathing

362

rooms. The door to the women's vestibule was open, a mass of women and guards inside. Hoping he wasn't offending every Whey in the castle today, Ari pushed his way in, through the vestibule and into the large cavern with the pool.

By the side of the pool stood a number of dripping women in various states of dress. Torches lined the cavern, filling even the back corners with light. On the floor at the women's feet were the robed men, including Peine, bound hand and foot. Peine and most of the others were conscious, though Peine looked up at Ari through eyes filled with anger and pain. Blood ran from his now crooked nose, soaking into the front of his robe.

Cooro sat to one side, two pretty girls tending the wound on the back of his head. He smiled when he saw Ari, but didn't rise. Ari's father's amulet still hung about his neck. The girl who'd shown them where the cave entrance was swam up, getting out of the pool and into a robe someone handed her. Ari looked away, unable not to observe she had a singularly pleasing figure. She came to stand in front of him.

"We secured the prisoners and retrieved Swordmaster Cooro, my lord," she said, sounding very official. "All that's left in there is a decayed corpse. We thought we'd leave it."

"I think that's a good decision," Ari said. "You didn't do any of the things I asked you to do."

She smirked. "We aren't like your Lggothian girls, Sir Aridian, well behaved and good for nothing but looking at."

Ari decided there was no real point in arguing with her about Lggothian girls, although he knew Ispiria would want him to. He made a mental note never to bring her to Wheylia. He didn't see it going well.

"We heard you slew Lord Reido," the girl said. "And that the queen is safe, and the princesses as well."

363

"They'll never be safe," one of the prisoners yelled. "We'll never rest until we free Wheylia from the tyranny of the witches." Some of the others grumbled their support.

"Excuse me, my lord," the girl addressing Ari said. She walked over and struck the robed man across the face. "Hold your tongue, or this witch will have it cut from your head."

"What will you do with them?" Ari tried to catch Peine's eye, but his friend was looking down, sullen. Ari was hoping for a sign, a look of confusion on Peine's face to let Ari know his friend had been beguiled into the plot, an unwilling pawn.

"It's up to the queen." The girl looked at Peine. "I know that one is your friend. These guards were about to take them to confinement."

He crossed to Peine, who didn't look at him. Ari reached out to put a hand on his friend's shoulder, but Peine pulled away. Ari didn't like that reaction. It seemed almost like Peine was guilty. Almost as if it hadn't been the influence of the Empty One that made him a part of the group.

Or maybe Peine was angry? "I'm sorry about Gauli. He did it to himself. He asked me to kill him, but in the end, he killed himself." Ari hesitated. He wasn't sure he should go on, but it was too important a subject for dishonesty. "I would have killed him, though. He was suffering and he wanted to die."

"Did you even try to help him?" Peine asked, finally looking up. His eyes were starting to blacken from Ari's punch.

"I offered," Ari said, knowing it wasn't enough. Tears slid down Peine's face. "I'm sorry."

"How could you let Gauli die? He was my brother."

"I'm sorry." Ari wished he knew other words to say.

"Sorry isn't good enough," Peine said, looking away again. "If you'd ever had a family, you'd understand."

Stung, Ari drew back.

"If you're done talking to him, we have to take them away, my lord," the girl said, gesturing the waiting guards forward. "I'll make sure he's locked up safe and alone, and that someone fixes his nose."

"Thank you." Ari cleared his throat over the lump in it. Peine was wrong when he said Ari didn't have a family. Ari did, and Peine was part of it.

After watching guards escort the prisoners away, Ari gathered up his discarded boots and sword belt. A glance to his right told him Cooro was deeply engaged in talking to the two women who were tending him. Ari was too weary to deal with that many people, so he reluctantly decided to leave his father's amulet where it was for the time being.

He returned to his original room, calling a servant to request a tub and hot water be brought, and his things fetched from the royal wing. It wasn't Ari's custom to have anyone do his fetching for him, but he felt the keen desire for solitude. Once the servants left, he immersed himself in the warm tub, staying there until the pain in his body began to ebb, unlike the pain in his soul.

Chapter 33

Ari recovered from his physical wounds quickly, and soon his days fell into a steady routine. He went to the barracks early each morning to sit outside Peine's cell on a bench they'd brought for him. There, Ari often read aloud, as Peine wouldn't speak. They did fix Peine's nose, though his eyes stayed black for days.

After that, Ari would practice estocs with Cooro in the courtyard in front of the castle, much to the delight of many of the inhabitants. It was during those bouts Ari was happiest, his troubles subsumed by the need to bring all of his skill to bear in order to defeat Cooro, who occasionally won. Cooro returned Ari's father's amulet, though with mild reluctance.

Ari's luncheons were taken with Siara and Princess Tiana, a daily event that began well but became less and less pleasant as summer faded into fall. The little princess was a joy, always changing and growing, sometimes seemingly overnight. It was obvious Tiana was Siara's greatest happiness, but it was also obvious something was wrong with Siara. As their months in Wheylia passed, she grew thin and worn looking. Her hair lost its luster. By the time winter came and she still wouldn't let them depart, Ari was more than worried.

The queen, on the other hand, regained her health steadily, and soon the city returned to what Ari assumed was normal. There were balls in the evenings, and ridiculous displays of wealth, and even a strange night in the dead of winter when a long line of girls in gray robes walked in the moonlight from the school of the arcane, into the palace, through the throne room, and out to visit the wellspring.

To mitigate his exasperation with their extended stay in Wheylia, Ari wrote letters and studied. He made good headway through the vast library in the castle, but he found little satisfaction in it. As Siara's health worsened and listlessness overtook her, there was no one to discuss his newfound knowledge with. No Sir Cadwel to argue strategies or why an ancient battle was lost that could have been won. No Peine interrupting Ari's work with stories about sneaking off to kiss whatever girl he was in love with that day. Worst of all, no red curls twisting free of Ispiria's ribbons to fall across her cheek. Ari wrote to Sorga often, but scrawling his slow script onto dry parchment was a poor substitute for the vivacity and laughter of his fiancée.

The queen interviewed and tried each member of Lord Reido's band of malcontents, sentencing each of them to death. By the time the girls walked to the castle on the first full moon of the new year, only Peine was left. Ari tried to speak to Queen Reudi about him, but she would never allow the subject to be broached.

Still, he visited Peine every day, knowing no other comfort to give.

368

"I can't believe you still come here." Peine's voice broke into Ari's recitation from a book of Wheylian poems.

Ari didn't like poems in any language, but he had to admit they were marginally better in the musical tongue of the Wheys. He put the book down, relief filling him that Peine finally chose to speak.

"Why do you do it?" Peine didn't look at him as he spoke. "I lied to you. I betrayed you."

"You're my friend."

"I was your valet," Peine said, his voice bitter.

"No. You were, and are, my friend." Silence stretched between them while Ari racked his mind for something to say. He didn't want Peine to stop talking.

"I go before the queen soon," Peine said. "I know the fate of the others. I can't believe I'm about to die."

"I'll speak for you. I'll explain it was my fault. I sent you here. I knew I shouldn't. I had a feeling about your brother. They'll see this was my fault."

"My brother." Peine gave a bitter laugh. "My brother was so full of fire for the cause. We were going to change Wheylia. I wanted to be someone. Someone important who did things. I wanted people to look at me like they look at you."

Ari grimaced, aware of how people looked at Peine now.

"Thank you for coming every day," Peine said. "It means a lot to me. It would be worse to die alone."

Silence stretched between them. Ari stood up. "You aren't going to die."

Ari strode from the barracks and across the courtyard to the castle steps. He would go see the queen. This time, he would make her talk to him.

"Sir Aridian?" a castle page asked, stopping him inside the entrance. "The queen requests your presence."

Ari blinked in surprise. The page turned, leading him not to the throne room, but into the library.

The queen was in a small room off of the main library, the door of which had always been locked before. She was alone, which was odd. She stood tall and straight before an ornately carved table, an ancient tome open before her. She nodded to the young page, who closed the door behind Ari.

"Your majesty." Ari bowed, though he couldn't execute a full bow or he'd risk hitting his head on the table, which filled most of the small room between the book-lined walls.

"Thrice Born." Queen Reudi raised her dark eyes from the pages before her. "Come, I would show you this."

He walked around the table, careful not to touch her person as he came to stand next to her, and lowered his gaze to the book. It was a very old text, crumbling about the edges. The pages were discolored and the ink faint, but the script was in a strong hand and the letters clear. Filling one page was a drawing of a sword. Ari's sword. He leaned closer, taking in the details of the scrolled design along the blade and the three stones filling the empty holes in the hilt.

"It is Fwellian," Queen Reudi said. "Long ago, it was used to free the wellspring."

"My sword?" What did that mean? Would he have to give it back?

"Yes, your sword, though through what tangled paths it came to you, we may never know."

"Is it magical?" he asked, awed.

"No." She smiled faintly. "Not in the sense you mean. Magic merely fortifies it. It shall never fail you."

Ari frowned, trying to decipher what they meant.

"But the gems hold great power." She tapped the image before them. "The three missing gems from the hilt. They cleaved the stone which capped the wellspring."

"But they're gone."

"You have one, even now." Turning to him, she placed a long fingered hand to his chest, over the secret pocket sewn into his tunic. "Should you ever have all three, their enchantment will suffuse the blade. With it, you could slay even the mightiest foe." Her hand dropped.

Ari raised his to take its place, feeling the small white stone the Sorga hawks had given him. He was so accustomed to carrying it now, he rarely gave it thought. "Where are the other two?" he asked, though he already knew one was with the Questri, the magical race of horses Stew came from.

"No magic may seek them, yet it seems to me that perhaps you should."

"Do you know who the master is, the one who commanded the Empty One?" Ari asked, wondering if that was the mightiest foe.

"Such answers must come from your own master, Thrice Born, for even I do not cross wills with the Lady."

He frowned. He wasn't surprised Queen Reudi knew of the Lady, though he was taken aback by her reluctance. The queen's tone made it sound almost as if she feared the ancient Aluien, whom Ari knew to be the gentlest of souls.

"I will give you the life of your friend," Queen Reudi said, startling Ari from his thoughts. "But once he leaves our land, his travel protected by your honor, he is never to set foot on Wheylian soil again, on pain of death, and he shall remain caged until such time as you depart this place. This I do to right our debt. His life spared for the life you returned to me."

"Thank you, your majesty." Relief washed tension from Ari as the uncertainty of Peine's fate was laid to rest. "Thank you."

"It is I who should thank you, for allowing me to so easily settle my debt," she said with an enigmatic smile.

Ari stared at her, unsure what to say to that. She made him feel as if he'd squandered something, yet Peine's life was the only thing he wanted.

"When the weather breaks in three weeks' time, you must quit this place."

"Three weeks?" Ari repeated, his heart leaping at the thought. "But winter will last another two months, yet."

"The end of winter shall be mild and spring early. You will take advantage of this, for Siara cannot much longer survive away from her beloved. The curse of the women of Whey is taking her."

Ari nodded. He knew Siara wasn't well. He could see her slipping away. He also knew she didn't want to go. "In three weeks, it will be Princess Tiana's birthday."

"Yes. It was my hope Siara would last to see her daughter's first year, before being forced to depart."

"It's very convenient the weather will break on the princess's birthday." Ari wasn't sure if Queen Reudi had that much power, or that much compassion, but perhaps she had both.

"When you go to tell my granddaughter, remind her she may always return. I do not wish to keep her daughter from her. I know the pain of missing a child."

Ari winced, reminded that he'd taken Queen Reudi's last child from her. "I will," he said, but he knew Siara would be heartbroken. "She isn't going to take it well. She doesn't want to leave."

"She must, or she will die."

If Queen Reudi did have compassion, Ari couldn't discern it in her tone. "But you haven't died," he said, it falling into place for him that Queen Reudi's husband was dead, yet she was well enough, now that she wasn't being poisoned. "If Parrentine was dead, would Siara be free?" He didn't like the sound of the words as they left his mouth. Parrentine was his friend.

"Think you death frees one from love, Thrice Born? I never loved my husband, Aridian. I am Lavarina, Witch Queen of Wheylia. I do not have the luxury of love."

She gave him a look that couldn't be mistaken for anything but a dismissal. Ari bowed, letting himself out of the room. He crossed the central hall and ascended into the royal wing where he would lunch with Siara, Tiana and Camva. He hoped someone had excused him to Cooro while he was with the queen. Once again, only one set of guards stood in the hall. Ari nodded to them, knocking on Siara's door.

Siara was bundled into a large chair set very near the fireplace, the table pulled close before her so she wouldn't have to move to eat. She was pale and there were dark circles beneath her eyes. Ari composed his face, bowing to her. "Your highness."

"Sir Aridian." She smiled, but it only made her look more wane.

"Is he here?" Camva said, sticking her head out the door leading to the nursery. Seeing Ari, she smiled, coming out, the little princess in her arms. "Tiana's been waiting."

Tiana squealed, seeing Ari. She reached out her little hands and Camva handed her to him. Ari held her high over his head and she laughed.

"Good afternoon, your highness," he said to her. She giggled, reaching for him even though her arms weren't long enough. He knew better than to let her near his face. She would grab his nose, or stick her hands in his mouth, or try to pull his ears. He smiled up at her, turning in a circle, making her laugh more.

"Let me have her, Ari," Siara said, holding out her arms.

Ari swung Tiana down, eliciting more giggles, and gently tucked her into the chair with her mother, ignoring Siara's outstretched arms. He never handed Tiana into Siara's hands anymore. As her health waned, he was secretly afraid she would drop her baby.

Tiana snuggled against Siara. Ari smiled down at them. Even though she wasn't quite a year old, Tiana already seemed to understand a lot. She knew her mom was for cuddling, not for flailing arms and spinning, like Ari. He held out a chair for Camva and then seated himself. It was very warm so near the fire, but seeing how cold Siara looked, Ari didn't say anything.

Their midday meal was pleasant, and Ari was sad when Camva announced it was time for Tiana to nap. He could see Siara was tired, too. She used to take Tiana and put her down for her nap, but now, she didn't have the strength to carry her.

"It's Tiana's birthday in three weeks," Ari said as the door closed behind Tiana and Camva.

"I know." A smile brightened Siara's face. "Do you need help choosing a gift for her?"

Ari looked at her in surprise. He supposed he did need help, since he hadn't even thought of it. He shook his head, determined to have the talk he wanted to have. "Siara, after her birthday, we have to go home."

"It's still winter. We can't possibly travel."

"The weather will break on Tiana's birthday."

"You can't know that."

"Your grandmother told me."

She glared at him from her nest of quilts. "I see you two have my life all planned out." Bright spots of color appeared on her cheeks.

"If you don't go back to Parrentine soon, you'll die." He said it quietly. He didn't want to say it any more than she wanted to hear it.

She stared at him with eyes full of anger for a moment, but then she looked toward the door Camva and Tiana had disappeared through, a sob racking her too thin frame. Ari stood and came around the table, gathering her to him.

"I'll write to Parrentine and tell him of our plans," he said.

She nodded against his chest. Ari opened his mouth, trying to think of words to soothe her, but he shut it again. Siara had to go home, she had to leave Tiana, and there was nothing he could say.

Chapter 34

Though Ari and the men were happy to leave, Siara's sorrow and Peine's moroseness put a pall over the journey. Siara rode in her carriage, blankets and furs piled high around her, interacting little. Peine rode Charger, but he was pale, thin and silent, and often cast wary looks over his shoulder in the direction of the capital of Wheylia. Fortunately, Stew was in good spirits, and he didn't bother to hide it. As Queen Reudi had promised, the weather held clear.

The morning they rounded the tip of the Mountains of Whey, crossing Lggothland's boarder, Peine pulled Charger up alongside Stew. It had taken them two months to leave the country of Peine's ancestors, and he was looking much more himself of late. Ari nodded to show he knew Peine was there. He never tried to start a conversation with Peine anymore, but he was always happy when Peine wanted to talk to him.

"Ari, I think I'll leave you here."

Ari turned to him in surprise.

"My parents' land is due north of here," Peine said. "I think I'll go home. That is, if you'll release me from your service. I know I owe you almost a year still."

"Of course I'll release you." Ari tried to hide his annoyance that Peine still, after everything, insisted he was a servant. "I didn't know you were leaving."

"I've been thinking about it a lot. I'd really like to go home. I could be a steward for my older brother. I don't need a fancy position in the capital or Sorga. I don't need my own land."

"You mean, you're going home for good?" Ari didn't understand. He'd thought Peine was getting back to normal.

"I think I might be. I need to tell them about Gauli, anyhow." Peine looked away. "It won't be easy."

"I'll miss you," Ari said, his voice quiet.

"I'll miss you too, Ari."

"There will always be a place for you in Sorga."

"Who knows." Peine smiled a little. "Someday, I may take you up on that."

Ari stared after his friend in bewilderment as Peine turned his horse from the main road and headed north.

Ari spent the rest of the day pondering what he could have done differently, how he could have kept Peine's life from taking such a disastrous turn. It was almost a welcome distraction from his worry over Siara's health, over how much he should tell Ispiria about kissing other women and over missing her and his home. For someone who had, by most measures, successfully completed his first mission as king's champion, Ari felt annoyingly discontent.

They stopped late in the afternoon, Ari pressing the carriages as far each day as he could, for Siara's sake. As he made his way to her tent for their dinner, Ari reflected that half the reason Peine had left was probably the carriages. Even pushing their progress as he was, it would be ages before they reached Poromont. They likely wouldn't even make the spring tourney. Not that he wanted to joust in it. He wanted to go home.

At least he had plenty of time for correspondences, which enviably free and fast messengers would take away for him, bringing back replies in return. He didn't have anything to correspond about, though. There were only so many reports Sir Cadwel could want to read about their uneventful progress and only so many times he could write to Ispiria and tell her how much he missed her.

Writing to Ispiria was particularly difficult, because he longed to confess his crimes. But he couldn't. Not in writing. Not when he was so far away from her. Yet, his unfaithfulness weighed so heavily on his mind whenever he thought about her, he could hardly think of anything else to talk about.

Inside Siara's pavilion it was warm and stuffy, as it always was, though they were on the brink of spring. Siara looked wane and small in her giant bundle of blankets. Instead of feeling sympathy for her as he usually did, Ari was vaguely annoyed.

He'd seen her endure worse than this. She'd slept on the ground with only a rough cloak to keep her warm. She'd lived with Parrentine's hatred and the knowledge he was in love with another. She'd been abandoned by her father, ignored by her mother's people, teased and tormented and friendless in a convent. Why did she have to be so pathetic now?

"Your highness," he said, bowing from the waist before seating himself across from her.

"My ladies tell me Peine left today. Do you think that wise? To let him go without bringing him back to Poromont to explain himself to Parrentine and the king?"

Ari stared at her. Wise? Peine was his friend, his valet and his responsibility. Peine's offence was against Queen Reudi, not Parrentine or Ennentine, and she'd set him free. He'd already spent the entire fall and half of the winter locked in a cell. Wasn't that punishment enough?

"What I think, as I recall telling you on several occasion, your highness, is that Peine is my concern and not yours," he said, his tone bordering on uncivil.

"How dare you speak to me that way? I think you forget yourself."

"Forget myself?" He glared across the table at her. "I know exactly who I am, and I know who you are too, Siara. And it isn't this . . . this sniveling, haughty, pampered, sickly little girl you've become."

"Really?" Color brought life to her cheeks. "And how do you expect me to be? I'm cursed to never be able to leave my husband, forced to give up my only child, and my health fails me. My life is ruined and you, apparently, don't even care."

"Your life is ruined?" Ari realized he was almost shouting, but he couldn't seem to help it. "You're miserable? What about the rest of us? Forced to crawl across all of Wheylia at a snail's pace because you're too sad to ride a horse and you need too many ladies around you who have to have carriages and you need this stupid pavilion to sit in for hours every evening feeling sorry for yourself."

He didn't know when he'd stood up, but he was leaning across the table now, looming over her. "Forced to never leave your husband? You don't want to leave him, but as far as I can tell, you don't want to make it back to him alive, either. You couldn't stay in Wheylia, but we could be in Poromont by now. What happened to the girl who ran away from the convent, ready to walk across the country on her own to see Parrentine's face? If you want your health and your life back, you certainly aren't showing it."

Siara was a giant pair of blue eyes in a white face, staring up at him. He took a deep breath, all but falling back into his chair. Anxiety washed over him. What was he doing, yelling at Siara when she was so sick? He pushed a hand threw his hair.

She stood, blankets tumbling from her. "I'll have you know, Sir Aridian, I would ride out of here this very moment if I could. You have no idea what it's like to be the future queen. You think I like all these weighty trappings? I wish I were free of them. I wish Parrentine and I were just two people with no obligations or standing. Then we could live together in peace, and I would still have my baby."

Ari looked into her beautiful face, color filling it for the first time in months, anger sharpening every line from her firmly pressed lips to the tilt of her eyes. "Let's ride out of here," he said. "Let's ride out of here right now."

"What?"

"You and me. On Stew. You could be home in little more than a fortnight."

"But what would people say?" she said, surprise replacing anger. "I can't be known to ride about the countryside unattended with a man, sleeping on the ground."

"Everyone knows you suffer the curse of Whey. You can't betray Parrentine's love, and I am king's champion. I have proven my honor on the best knights in the realm. If any dare question it, or yours, I will prove it again. And I was thinking we could stay in inns, actually. It isn't as if we're poor."

"Could we really do it?" she asked, all traces of anger gone now. "Do you really think we could?"

"Look, if it makes you feel better, ask if any of your ladies ride. We don't have to go alone. You don't even have to ride Stew with me, although I'm not sure if you're up to riding on your own."

"Of course I am."

She lifted a bell from the table and rang it, bringing a nervous looking maid. Ari was certain the whole camp already knew they'd been arguing.

"I require two horses, some foodstuffs and a small tent." She looked over at Ari. "Just in case."

"Yes, my lady," the maid said, curtsying.

"Go saddle Stew and get your things in order," Siara said, turning back to Ari. "We're leaving immediately. There are still hours of daylight left."

"I know," Ari said, earning him a scathing glance. He smiled.

Life was much better after that. The lady in waiting Siara chose, Emilia, was a very pleasant girl a few years younger than Ari. She rode well. She didn't complain, even when they took the fewest breaks possible and pressed far into the evenings, sometimes passing inns in order to travel farther. When they did stay in inns, they took the facade of a noble woman with two servants, traveling to visit her sister, to stave off the unwanted attention their true titles would bring.

The only real drawback to their impulsive decision, as far as Ari was concerned, was Siara's constant nearness. As they rode, he often found himself worrying over her kiss and what it meant for his relationship with Ispiria. He wished he'd hated Siara's kiss, but he hadn't. Would Ispiria be able to accept that he didn't hate kissing Siara? Should he even tell her? He loved

Ispiria. Peine's advice not to keep things from her, not if he wanted them to be happy together, haunted him.

Even if Ispiria understood, what would the prince think? Would he dismiss Ari as king's champion? He and Parrentine hadn't started off as friends. Things could probably go back to the way they were if the prince found out Ari had kissed his wife. Worry over it gnawed at him until he could hardly look at Siara anymore. Worse, he was sure from the looks she gave him that she knew something was wrong.

On the fifth day of their ride, Siara turned to Emilia saying, "Emilia, dear, could you ride behind for a spell? Sir Aridian and I must discus something of a sensitive nature."

"Of course, my lady," the girl said, reining in her horse.

Ari shifted in his saddle, worried she had guessed the source of his unease. He risked a sideways glance at her, his eyes immediately going to her lips. He yanked his gaze away.

"All right," Siara said. "What is the matter with you?"

"With me?"

"Yes, you. You're more nervous every day and you don't even look at me anymore. Is it remorse over how you spoke to me?"

"No." He knew his voice sounded strained. "Not that I don't feel a bit bad about that. I do."

"What then?"

"It's only, well . . ." He took a deep breath. "You kissed me."

"In the storage room?" she asked with a frown.

"Yes," he said, thinking it wasn't as if there had been any other time.

"So?"

"Are you going to tell Parrentine?"

"I already have." Her voice showed no concern. "I wrote to him about everything that happened in Wheylia."

"Was he angry?" Ari's throat went dry. At least his fear of Parrentine's anger was a distraction from his larger concern. If he liked kissing Siara, did it mean he didn't love Ispiria enough? How could he know if he loved Ispiria enough, like Siara loved Parrentine? So much that, apparently, you could kiss someone else and it didn't even matter.

"Angry?" She smiled, some life coming into her wane features. She looked older than her nineteen years, and he felt younger than his nearly eighteen. "He found it amusing. Especially my description of the look on your face."

He scowled at her.

"Is that what's been troubling you?"

"It's sort of important," he said, annoyed. "Parrentine is my friend and my future king."

"Well, worry no longer for, I assure you, he's not angry."

They rode in silence, Ari working up his courage. "What should I tell Ispiria?"

"Tell her the truth. I kissed you to cover up our plotting and it meant nothing. Nothing to you. Nothing to me. It was simply a ruse."

Ari nodded, feigning agreement, but Siara's answer did little to reassure him. Trying to clear his mind, he looked about to gauge their progress. The spring air was fine and cool, the sun bringing the perfect amount of warmth. He was glad, for though she could ride, Siara was very weak. The heavy robes she wore when it was chilly weighed her down almost too much to sit in her saddle. If she deteriorated much more, Ari would be forced to have her ride with him.

Ari pressed them a bit farther into the night than he thought wise, knowing an inn was near. He hoped a night's rest in a real bed would restore Siara somewhat. She stayed in the saddle when they arrived, waiting for him to help her. It wasn't a good sign, he knew. It meant she was unsure she would be strong enough to stand. Emilia, obviously sharing Ari's concern, kept her horse beside Siara's, reaching out to steady her while Ari dismounted.

"Does my lady require assistance?" a voice asked from the shadow of the inn's porch. Ari turned to see Prince Parrentine walking down the steps.

Siara's face broke into a radiant smile as Parrentine strode to her side. He reached up and she all but fell into his arms. Ari glanced away, embarrassed, as their lips met.

"I would have ridden out to meet you, had I known you were so near," Parrentine said, his voice full of love, but also worry. "I thought you would still be days away. I was planning to press on toward Wheylia tomorrow."

Ari felt a surge of happiness, coupled with relief. Siara would be well now. His mission was truly complete. Turning back, he saw the prince still held Siara in his arms. They looked so happy together. What would it be like to have a woman love him like Siara loved the prince?

Ari didn't like that thought. Surely, Ispiria loved him that much. Just because she wouldn't die without him didn't mean she didn't love him. Would he really want a woman who had to be near him or die, especially with the life he must lead as king's champion?

Parrentine set Siara down, but kept his arm around her. She already looked more herself. "Thank you for bringing her safely back to me."

Ari nodded, bowing. "It was my honor, your highness. I'll see to the horses."

"Not tonight," Parrentine said. "I've plenty of pages with me for that. Did you leave Peine behind with the carriages?"

Ari shook his head, but didn't elaborate. Parrentine called over his shoulder and pages came running. Turning Siara toward the inn, he gestured for Ari and Emilia to follow them inside.

Chapter 35

That night, everyone did know who Ari and Siara were.
The common room was transformed into a miniature court,
with Parrentine and Siara sitting at the head of a long table. The
innkeep produced a feast of roast goose stuffed with last
season's preserved fruit, hearty stew thick with tubers, fresh
breads, a selection of cheeses and even a pastry made with
dried apples. To Ari, the dinner was reminiscent of ones his
Aunt May would make, giving him a melancholy longing for
home.

Parrentine and Siara retired early, but Ari lingered in the
common room, staring into his untouched mug of ale. He
wanted to bask in the feeling of warmth and accomplishment
that returning Siara safely to Parrentine brought him, but it was
already wearing off and his other troubles creeping back. He
stretched his legs out under the table, aware there was a ring of
silence about him in the otherwise bustling room. The music
shifted from dance to ballad, a rich lyrical voice filling the inn.

Ari raised his eyes to see Larke sitting on a table pushed out of the way for dancing. The bard's fingers picked the notes of a ballad the complexity and length of which was usually reserved for the halls of Poromont. It was the tale of how King Ennentine and Sir Cadwel had ended the hundred years of war that had ravaged the land before Ari was born. Ari's troubles fell away as the master bard's voice carried him into the past.

He saw the kingdom, torn and broken. He felt the pain of the people, starving and poor, their sons taken from them to follow their lords into battle, their shoulders stooped and wills broken by heavy taxes and levies. He saw the endless plumes of oily smoke that dotted the horizon, speaking of war growing ever nearer as farmsteads and villages were burned.

He saw Sir Cadwel rise from the obscurity of a younger son in the north, at the start of the ballad a boy younger than Ari was now. Larke's voice crafted Sir Cadwel as an almost mythical being of silver and light, riding forth on his great destrier to crush all those who stood before him. He gathered men to him, leading them to triumph after triumph as they crossed the land, peace settling in his wake.

Then came the day Sir Cadwel and Ennentine rode out with hopes of peace in their hearts, only to be betrayed by the Lord of the Northlands. Blood pounded in Ari's temple, even though he knew Sir Cadwel and Ennentine would emerge from the trap alive, Larke's voice making the events as real as if Ari were there.

Battle was joined again. The betrayal of peace was a bitter drought, but Sir Cadwel and Ennentine did not give up. Finally, the Lord of the Northlands asked to parlay once more. This time, the Lord of the Northlands wove a subtler web, endeavoring to use human nature and greed to lure Sir Cadwel into betraying his quest for peace.

Sir Cadwel's will remained strong, his vision true. Casting aside any claim to the throne, he offered it to Ennentine, a most noble and worthy man. Thus, a new dynasty was created to rule in tranquility and prosperity over Lggothland. Ennentine's rule was sealed with love's kiss, as the fairest maiden of the day was brought to him to take to wife. The kingdom rejoiced, for happiness and peace would now be forever upon them.

The last notes of the song faded away and the room erupted into applause, Ari joining in whole-heartedly. Rarely had he heard the ballad performed in its entirety before, and then usually by a host of musicians and singers, working together to create the merest trace of the magic in the performance Larke had given them. Ari knew no one else could ever top what they'd just heard, for it was Larkesong himself who'd composed the ballad, over twenty-five years ago.

Patrons came forward to speak to Larke, encircling him with chatter. He gestured to the other musicians in the room and they struck up another dance. The people about Larke melted away, forgetting him so quickly, Ari knew it wasn't natural. Looking across the room at him, Larke winked. He carefully stowed his lute, then crossed to sit before Ari.

"Enjoying your ale?" The bard removed a wide-brimmed orange hat with yellow and red feathers, setting it on the table.

Ari looked down at his untouched drink and pushed it away. "That was amazing. I wish Sir Cadwel could have heard it."

"Oh, he has, lad, worry not. In fact, he heard it the very first time it was sung, although I can't tell you I was of a mind to notice his reaction."

"How will I ever live up to him, Larke? I've only had two missions for the king so far, and neither one has worked out very well. We couldn't save Clorra, and now I've killed Queen Reudi's son and lost Peine."

"You're too hard on yourself, lad. It isn't the little things that mark how history will remember you. Had you known our vaulted Sir Cadwel back in the day, you would see."

"Maybe." Ari was dubious as to if the things he'd mentioned could be considered little. "I suppose you're here because something else is wrong? I can't picture the Lady going into the deep sleep so you can entertain." He was glad Siara had already retired. She wasn't fond of Larke.

"I came seeking you, truth be told, but the song wanted singing."

"A song can't want something," Ari said, aware he sounded grouchy. "Why do you seek me? I could have used your help last year in Wheylia, you know."

"Now lad, you know I can't be interfering in the affairs of the throne of Whey. You've gotten me in enough trouble already."

"You get yourself in trouble. Why did you say you're looking for me?"

"I didn't, though I will say the resemblance ye have to Sir Cadwel is growing. Disadvantage of the trade, mayhap?" Larke grinned, obviously enjoying himself.

Ari leaned back from the table and crossed his arms. "What do you want, Larke?"

"The resemblance is truly uncanny. I don't want anything at all. The Lady is wanting to speak with you, though, on such topics as she believes you wish to discuss with her. She sent me to fetch you."

"Really?" Ari leaned forward, his feigned indifference gone. Would he finally learn about his parents? Maybe she would tell him who the master Empty One was.

"I'm to fetch you back this very night."

"Tonight?" Ari wasn't sure he was allowed to go, and Parrentine and Siara were already asleep. "Right now?"

"Unless you have something else to occupy your time?"

Ari had brought Siara back to Parrentine. Really, what more was there for him to do? He'd best go ask, though, to make certain. If Parrentine wasn't available, at least Ari could leave a message explaining his departure.

He stood, another thought hitting him. "How long will it take, do you think?" The last time he went to the Aluien caves he was there for half a season. He wanted to hear what the Lady wished to tell him, but he hadn't seen Ispiria, Sir Cadwel or his home in a long time.

"She didn't say." Larke eyed him. "But I daresay she doesn't mean to keep you for long. I'll recommend she not." Larke must have read the consternation Ari was feeling.

Ari nodded, relieved. "I'll meet you in front of the inn. Could you ask someone to saddle Stew?"

"I suppose that won't be interfering too much in the affairs of men," Larke said, rising to make his way toward the door.

Ari hurried to his room and retrieved his meager bundle of possessions. He considered writing to Ispiria, but he couldn't reveal the existence of the Aluiens to his fiancée and, if he didn't stay in the caves long, he wouldn't even be home later than expected. He still had a long journey north to Sorga, whether he went to the capital with Parrentine or not. Slinging his saddlebags over his shoulder, he closed his inn room door and walked down the hall to the largest suite.

A servant opened the door to his knock. "Lord Aridian."

"Is the prince available?"

"I'll check, my lord," the man said, disappearing.

391

Ari fidgeted, belatedly hoping he wasn't ruining Parrentine's and Siara's reunion. The suite door opened to Parrentine, looking concerned, the servant hovering behind him.

"Ari, what is it?" the prince asked. "Please, come in."

"No thank you, your highness." Ari shot a meaningful look at the servant and the man moved to the other side of the room. "I came to ask your permission to leave. The Lady has summoned me."

"The Lady? Is something amiss?"

"I don't think so. I think she's going to tell me about my parents."

"You're to go now?" the prince asked, his eyes going to the saddlebags Ari held.

"With your permission, your highness."

Parrentine frowned. "Well, I guess there's no reason why not. I'd planned to hold a celebration for you, and you haven't made your official report, but it isn't really necessary. Unless you have something to add to the missives you've been sending?"

"Not really. Do you think, though, that you could ask your steward to arrange for my armor to be returned to Sorga? I left it with the body of the troop."

"Consider it done."

"Thank you, your highness," Ari said, relieved to have his prince's blessing, and to avoid a celebration held in his honor.

"Good luck, then." Parrentine clasped him on the arm. "I'll tell Siara in the morning. She's asleep. Report in as soon as you can, though. You are king's champion. We might need you."

"I will," Ari said, bowing.

With a nod, Parrentine closed the door.

Hurrying downstairs, Ari left the inn, finding a saddled Stew beside Larke, on his gray, waiting. Ari patted his horse on the nose before tying his saddlebags in place and mounting. Stew seemed eager to be away. Ari smiled. He was eager, too. His mission was complete, his responsibilities passed back to the prince and the royal guard. It was a beautiful star-filled night, and they were about to go riding.

The End

ABOUT THE AUTHOR

Summer Hanford grew up on a dairy farm in Upstate New York. She earned her bachelor's degree in experimental psychology and went on to do graduate and doctoral work in behavioral neurology.

Turning away from long hours spent in research, Summer returned to her childhood dream of writing fantasy novels, although she enjoys turning her pen to science fiction, Regency and adventure as well. She is now a faculty member of the AllWriters' Workplace and Workshop and has launched her first fantasy series, Thrice Born, with Martin Sisters Publishing Company. To learn more about Summer visit www.summerhanford.com.

31762104R00220

Made in the USA
Middletown, DE
10 May 2016